Cl

OF THE

GARLON T'ZEN

CHRONICLES
OF THE
GARLON T'ZEN

BOOK ONE:

Manor Town

Kyleen Valleaux

To Latrice
Happy AwesomeCon
Good luck w/ your
Book

Myles
Valleux

Chronicles of the Garlon T'zen
Book One: Manor Town

Copyright © 2016 Kyleen Valleaux

ISBN-13: 978-1-944895-00-6

www.garlontzen.com

Published by Fusion Graphics
P.O. Box 13284
Lansing, MI 48901-3284
www.fusiongraphics.org
Email: fg@fusiongraphics.org

Printed in U.S.A

To my ladies; Lynda, Robin, Carol, Kris, and Anne, for believing in me and being my best cheerleaders.

Love and Kissies.

Chapter 1

The sun was bright and hung high in the sky. The day was warm and nearly cloudless. Spring had bloomed, and bright colorful flowers lined the sidewalks of the mountain village. Truly, a glorious day.

A small knot of five made their way down the cobblestone street. It was a rest-day, and they had plenty of time before they had to arrive at the central park for a day of food and outdoor games. Kiku, High Princess of the Garlon T'zen Empire, held her youngest sister's hand as they strolled up the street. On the other side of the youngest princess was Mary's older brother, Devon Blackwood. But he was not Kiku's brother.

It was an odd arrangement, but Mary had been Celestial chosen, the same as Kiku, so they were sisters of a sort. Devon remained Mary's brother, even while Kiku was her sister. And to Kiku, Devon was . . . her friend.

Following behind the three were Marlon and Doctor Michelle Andersen. Marlon was a Garlon T'zen physician, so he and the Earth woman had much in common, including their mutual attraction. Kiku threw a glance over her shoulder with a sly smile. She loved Marlon like an uncle and it pleased her to see him happier than he'd been the entire time she knew him.

Devon held his sister's other hand as they made their way toward the open expanse of the park. Mary happily skipped between the two of them.

Kiku had asked Captain Jace to hold a shady spot for them, so there was no reason to hurry. The park would be full of Garlon T'zen, along with their other off-world allies and the locals for the festivities.

Mary was chattering with bright enthusiasm as they made their way. Kiku answered her questions in the same language. Devon looked over the top of Mary's brown curls.

"What did she say?" he asked.

"She wanted to know what games she could play," Kiku answered. "Mary-chan, you should use English when Devon is with us."

"Sorry, Devon," Mary said. A brilliant smile spanned her face. She was an intelligent and pretty child of nine years with long brown curls that fell down her back and shoulders. "I forget."

Devon shook his head. He looked very much like his younger sister, with his bright green eyes and hair the same shade as hers. Kiku had tried to explain it to him before. Because he was Mary's brother, he had a right to know. General Tamarik had been against it, but Kiku ignored his counsel. The general may be her guardian and commanding officer, but she was still the High Princess, and in the matters of her sisters, he couldn't gainsay her.

Still, her explanation had only confused Devon more, but Kiku understood. Even among the Garlon T'zen, not many truly understood the natures of their princesses.

"When did you learn Garlon T'zen?" he asked Mary. Kiku sighed and offered a half shrug with a smile.

"I always knew it," Mary answered after a moment of thought. "Just no one else could talk it."

Kiku's memories of when she was Celestial chosen were murky, most of it tied with fear and pain. Those memories brought night terrors and panic. Drawing in a deep breath, Kiku pushed them away, focusing on the moment. She was safe now. She was home.

"This place really is amazing." Devon looked around at a picturesque building they passed. "It looks like it's been here for a hundred years rather than just eight months."

~

8 months ago

"What do you mean I'm not going?" Kiku demanded angrily, looking at General Tamarik. "You can't be serious!"

"I am, Kiku-hime," he told her, with a curt nod. General Tamarik was not only the young princess's Guardian but also the commanding general of the battle group. Kiku was the High Princess of the Empire, but she was also a full lieutenant in the military. Kiku had been deployed with the general and his ship because of it. They were standing on the bridge of his dreadnaught spaceship, looking down at the Origin World. Any other time, Kiku would be entranced with its beauty: blue with its white clouds swirling above the surface. She tore her dark blue eyes away and refocused on General Tamarik.

"That's not fair!" Kiku protested. "You've never made me stay on the ship for a drop before!"

"This is different," General Tamarik told her. He was an older man, his black hair peppered with gray. He was wearing the standard black uniform of the Garlon T'zen military, the same as Kiku was. "This is not a battle. We're only trying to secure the area. If it were a straight fight, I wouldn't worry about you."

"Even more reason that it's not fair!" Kiku stomped her foot.

"Off my bridge, Lieutenant," General Tamarik ordered. Kiku scowled at him angrily. He glanced at her with irritation. "I mean it, Kiku. I don't have time for this right now."

Kiku growled under her breath and stormed off the bridge in anger. Damn him, anyway! It wasn't fair! This was supposed to be her gods-be-damned Origin World! He was only overprotective. There was no good reason not to let her drop with the rest of her unit.

She paused in the corridor and glanced back over her shoulder.

Not one good reason she could think of. A smile flashed on her features as she made up her mind.

General Tamarik would get over a minor act of disobedience. He always did. And she wanted to see the planet. Kiku needed to see it. With her resolve set, she turned and hurried back to her small quarters to change quickly into a tight black combat uniform, and yanked her honey-colored hair into a tail. Then she grabbed her helmet on the way out and set off at a light jog to the launch bay.

Captain Jace and the rest of her unit were already there, heading into the transport. She moved forward quickly and stepped into line with them. Captain Jace glanced down at her with a frown.

"What are you doing, Hime-sama?" he asked. Kiku pushed her way forward until she was standing next to the tall, well-built soldier. She looked up at him with a grin. His dark eyes watched her with suspicion. He already had his helmet on, but the chinstrap still hung loose.

"What does it look like I'm doing, Captain?" she said. "I'm going to drop."

"General Tamarik said you weren't." Captain Jace frowned again. He looked back over the top of her head toward the bay doors and then back down to her. "I don't believe he changed his mind."

"He didn't," Kiku agreed. The transport bay doors closed with a loud clang. Captain Jace shook his head with frustration.

"The general will be unhappy," he warned her.

"Like I care," Kiku retorted. "He's not being reasonable! Ji-chan has never stopped me from combat before."

"This isn't combat, Hime-sama," Captain Jace said. "Stay close to me and don't get shot."

"Gods." Kiku frowned at him. "You act like I've never done this before, Jace-kun."

"Mm." He looked at her unhappily. "Just do as you're told, Lieutenant."

"Yes, Captain," she said. Kiku briskly fastened the strap on her helmet.

They put in a low and fast landing in a sort of field in the middle of a city. There was a nearby military base controlling communications for much of the planet's offensive forces, coordinating the attacks on the Garlon T'zen. The planet had launched numerous primitive missiles at their ships until the Garlon T'zen dropped an energy net on the whole planet to stop it. The net killed all power transmission, crippling the entire world. The Garlon T'zen then traced the signaling system back to the base in this area. General Tamarik didn't wish to keep the planet's energy system's down for long, because of the potential loss of life and hardship it was creating.

The mission was preservation, not acquisition.

Captain Jace and his unit were to destroy the communication equipment. Not too difficult even if the current residents weren't so determined not to let them.

Kiku was surprised at how fiercely they were being attacked by the planet's ground forces. She knew that General Tamarik had tried to quell the panic that seemed to be rising by their appearance in the skies, but it had made no difference. They were seen as invaders, so that meant they had to act like it. At least, until they could get the planet to stop shooting at them.

The city streets they had been moving through erupted in fire and smoke, as they were attacked with rockets and small explosives hurled from the rooftops. Kiku was knocked hard to the ground. She lost track of her unit in the smoke. She could hear Captain Jace in her helmet's communicator demanding her location. She tried to answer as she took cover around a corner.

Smoke choked her lungs as she leaned against the inside wall of an ally and gasped for air. She bent over and tried to draw in a deep breath. Her ears rang from the sound of the explosion.

"Location on the princess," Captain Jace's strong voice clipped into her ear. Kiku felt a pang of guilt at the ribbon of worry she could hear in his tone.

"I'm fine, Jace-kun," she answered, but he didn't reply. "Jace-kun?"

He couldn't hear her. She pulled off her helmet and wiped her eyes. Her communicator was damaged. Gods, what a mess. Kiku shook her head in frustration.

"Go ahead and keep on with the demolition," Jace's voice ordered from the earpiece. "I'll find her."

Captain Jace would find her. He always did.

"Hey!" She heard a voice and turned to see a man looking at her. Kiku tensed. "You can't stay out here. Come on."

Kiku looked at him curiously as her mind slowly turned the language over in her mind. Yes, she knew what he was saying. But it didn't make sense to her. Kiku shook her head slightly and looked back at the alley. But the man came closer and then stared her with alarm.

"Are you with them?" he asked, pointing out at the street. Kiku glanced back into the smoke and flames. He wasn't as tall as the typical Garlon T'zen, and his eyes were bright green rather than the varieties of brown she was used to seeing. Kiku looked at him with a small smile.

"Gomen." She shook her head. Then she paused. This language, it was English. She found the words for what she wanted to say. "I don't understand."

He looked at her with confusion, but then there were shots ringing around them. Kiku ducked, grabbing the man, pulling him to the ground out of the way. But she felt a burning fire lance through the top of her arm. She cried out softly as her crimson blood spread on the arm of her uniform.

"Ugh." Kiku made a face, sitting up. Gods, that hurt. "Jace-kun will be vexed."

"What?" The man sat up as well, and then he saw she was wounded. "Oh, shit, you've been shot."

"Mm." She nodded. Kiku looked around. She thought for a moment, trying to dredge up memories of this language. But it was hard, and she was starting to hurt. It brought memories of her past slavery into sharp focus. She tightened her jaw. "I need to find shelter."

"Okay." The man looked around. He stood up and carefully helped her to her feet. Kiku held her arm as she followed him slowly. "My apartment is a few blocks away. I can take you there, I guess."

"Arigato," Kiku murmured. He looked at her with worry.

"I'm Devon," he told her over his shoulder. "Devon Blackwood."

~

Present

So Devon had been there since nearly the beginning. Jace-kun and Marlon-sensei had been very unhappy about that.

The village was named Manor Town, after the sprawling house that was at the center. Not only was it where Kiku and Mary were living, but it was the main headquarters for all the Garlon T'zen operations on the planet. The village had been modeled after the European mountain villages that could be found on the other side of the planet. For Kiku, it was home.

Devon had helped her when she had been wounded on that operation. In his small apartment in California, she had learned about his sister and Mary's kidnapping by criminals. Kiku knew something of abduction and resolved to help him find his sister. What she hadn't expected was that Mary was Celestial chosen, in the same way that Kiku was. Kiku supposed she shouldn't have been surprised. That was part of the reason they had come to the Earth in the first place.

The journey started many years ago with a promise to a young boy to save his people. And ended here, in this place with Kiku and her sisters.

Kiku knew the story. But, now that they had found the Earth, she wasn't really sure what was going to happen next.

"Hold up," Devon said, stopping them from crossing the road. Mary dutifully paused while they watched a horse and rider clip-clop by. Kiku smiled and waved at the mounted soldier in a solid black uniform with a bright smile. He returned her attention with a small, polite incline of his head and keep riding on.

Even if Kiku wasn't in uniform, there wasn't a man who didn't know her.

Mary pulled away to skip along ahead of them on the picturesque street. Devon slid his eyes to the side to watch Kiku. She was carrying part of their lunch in a basket, and he had the rest of the supplies in his backpack. Behind him, the Garlon T'zen physician Marlon was making conversation with the British doctor, Michelle Andersen. Dr. Andersen had been very helpful after they rescued Mary. Mary had been badly hurt at the hands of her abductors and had been flat terrified of men. Marlon-sensei hadn't been able to get close without Mary screaming in terrified hysterics. Thankfully, Dr. Andersen had been established here in Manor Town and had been happy to lend aid in treating the child. Kiku smiled. She was enjoying their courtship. She loved Marlon like an uncle. His happiness was apparent, and it pleased Kiku no end.

"You look great, you know," Devon said. Kiku dimpled a smile and swished the skirt of her bright yellow sundress. She didn't get to be out of uniform often, but really did enjoy wearing pretty things when she was able. Unlike most of the Garlon T'zen, Kiku was fair. Her hair was a honey blond, and it hung loose around her neck. Her eyes were bright blue. Most of the Garlon T'zen had black or brown hair, with dark eyes. Today, Kiku also wore a wide brimmed hat to keep the sun from her eyes.

"Thank you," she said. A light blush touched her cheeks.

"I only see you in your uniform," he told her.

"I am an officer." And it was true. Most of the time, she did wear the black uniform of a Garlon T'zen soldier. She shrugged. "That's what we wear."

Devon nodded. "Yeah, I know."

~

<u>8 months ago</u>

"That hurts," the young woman protested. Devon leaned back and looked at her with a hint of frustration.

"I'm sure it does," he said. "But don't you think I should clean it?"

"Hai," she answered unhappily, biting her lip. Devon wrung out the washcloth and carefully dabbed at the top of her arm again. This time she stayed quiet and looked away. Devon took the opportunity to get a good look at her. She was wearing the same tight black uniform that the other soldiers were wearing. But she was the only female he had seen. All the others were large, dangerous-looking men.

This young woman, a girl, really, didn't look dangerous at all. If anything, she was too beautiful to look dangerous. Her honey-colored blond hair had pulled loose and was hanging behind her back. Her features were smooth and unblemished, and Devon had never seen eyes that dark a blue before. He was almost caught in them when she looked at him. She had told him her name was Kiku. Just Kiku. And she stumbled around using English, but she didn't have any sort of accent. Which was the oddest thing. She spoke it like she had half forgotten the words.

When she whimpered slightly again, he stopped.

"I don't want to hurt you," he told her. "It makes me feel bad."

"I'll try not to . . ." she paused ". . . complain."

"It's all right." He sighed, getting up from the table in his small kitchen. "I'll see if I've got anything to wrap it with. I don't know if it's got anything in it or not. You should go to the hospital."

"What's that?" Kiku asked.

"Where they have doctors," he said. "You know."

Kiku nodded absently. He heard her move and turned to face her. Kiku pointed at a picture he had stuck to the fridge. "Who's that?"

Devon felt his heart stop a moment in his chest.

"That's me and my sister, Mary," he said.

Kiku smiled at it. "She's very cute," she told him. "I have four sisters. Where is she?"

"I don't know," he answered honestly. Kiku looked up at him with small frown. Devon shook his head. He didn't like to talk about it. But when he met Kiku's dark blue eyes, they held nothing but genuine concern and, maybe, understanding. Devon felt like he could tell her. That, somehow, this woman, an enemy soldier no less, would understand how it felt for him to have his sister torn from him. To not know where she was, or what sort of unspeakable things were happening to her. "Mary was kidnapped four months ago. I haven't been able to find her. The police keep telling me she's probably dead. But I know that's not true!"

"Kidnapped?" Kiku asked, paling. "Abducted?"

"Yeah." He nodded.

"I'm sorry, Devon-san," Kiku said softly, dropping her eyes. "How terrible for you both."

"She's in New York," he said impulsively. "New York City."

"Mm?" Kiku looked up with a small frown.

"I'm saving enough money for a bus ticket," he told her. "But then the attacks came. I need to go."

"You're certain she's in that place?" Kiku asked. "How?"

"The internet," Devon said bitterly. "Child porn. That's how I know she's alive. They've been selling pictures and movies. The police, they told me they can't go look for one little girl when the world is ending."

He stopped himself and turned his face away. Kiku stood up and put a hand on his arm.

"Tell me," she said softly.

"I can't." He refused to look up. "It's not the kind of thing you talk about. I can't even believe I keep the stuff. It's just my only clue to where she is."

"All right, then," Kiku said. "Show me these things, and I'll help you find your sister."

Devon smiled slightly, shaking his head.

"It's not possible," he said turning to look at her.

"You helped me," Kiku said earnestly. "And I know something about abduction. I can't let it happen to someone if I have the power to stop it."

"No one has that kind of power, Kiku." Devon felt a pain in his chest. Kiku lifted her hand and touched his cheek with a small smile.

"You might be surprised, Devon-san," she whispered. He took her hand and frowned. Her color was definitely getting worse.

"You really don't look good," he said worriedly. He poured and handed her the glass of water. Kiku drank, thirstily spilling water on herself.

"I'll be all right," she said, leaning back, closing her eyes.

"You really need a doctor," Devon said. "Please let me take you over to the hospital."

"No." Kiku shook her head. "Just find Captain Jace."

"How am I supposed to know who that is?" he asked with frustration. "More likely I'll end up shot by those guys."

"Jace-kun wouldn't shoot you," she murmured.

"Sure he wouldn't," Devon retorted. "I don't have confidence in that. Besides, how would they know I'm not lying?"

"Because you're not?" Kiku looked at him like he had lost his mind. "Gods."

The girl's color was terrible. She put her hand to her head.

"Uh, Devon-san." She got up and staggered, her eyes darting around. "I'm going to . . ."

"Ugh." He grabbed her and pulled her toward the bathroom. Kiku leaned over the toilet and retched. He held her head while she continued to empty her stomach, and then helped her lean over the sink as she rinsed her mouth. "You've got to get help, Kiku."

"Mm." Kiku nodded. But before she could say more, her eyes rolled back in her head.

Devon caught her before she could fall to the floor. Shit. He gently touched her face and she was burning up. The wound on her arm was hot to the touch. He didn't know if she was aware of it or not, but she had hardly moved the arm at all.

He easily picked her up. It was remarkable how light she actually was. She seemed almost like a small force of nature, but unconscious in his arms like this, pale and drawn, she looked so small and vulnerable. And young. Devon didn't believe she could be any more than eighteen, if that. What the hell was she doing with these strange enemy soldiers? He didn't even know what the hell country they were from. He didn't know any country used an all-black uniform that was cut like these. And their weapons? Hell, it almost looked like they were from outer space or something.

He put her on his bed and unfastened her collar, trying to make her a little more comfortable. Even the fastenings were sort of different and strange. Devon drew in a deep breath of worry. He didn't think 911 would be able to send a paramedic or ambulance while the city was under attack. And he didn't really think he could get her to a hospital by himself.

He rubbed the back of his head. If he didn't get her help, he was afraid she was going to die. She had her own people out there somewhere. Maybe if he could find some, he could bring them back here to help her.

Maybe. If they didn't shoot him. If they spoke English. Kiku did speak English though, so they might too . . . right?

He grimaced and covered her up with a light sheet. He looked around for something she had that might convince them that she was really here and needed help. On her collar there seemed to be rank insignia of some sort. He pulled it off and pocketed it with a deep breath. Hopefully this wouldn't get him killed, because if it did, then she was dead too.

And hopefully, too, it would be enough to convince anyone he was trying to get aid from that his life was worth sparing.

~

Present

While the exchange between the two younger people was going on several steps in front of them, Marlon and Dr. Andersen spoke quietly together.

"Don't you think they make a cute couple?" She hooked an arm around the Garlon T'zen physician's. Marlon frowned down at her.

"No," he said.

"You are such a pain!" Dr. Andersen pulled her arm back crossly. "They're both young, it's spring—"

"You should not encourage him," Marlon told the doctor.

"Why?" she demanded. "Don't you approve of interracial couples?"

Marlon grinned slyly and put his hands in his pockets. His dark eyes travelled Dr. Andersen's tall slender form. Like Kiku-hime, the Earth physician was wearing a sundress, her bright red hair piled up under her wide sunhat. Marlon met her eyes of s hazel for a moment before he answered. "You know that's not true."

"Then why not?" she asked. "I don't see anyone at the Manor House approaching her. In fact, the respectable distance everyone keeps is incredibly frustrating! Everyone can't be that frightened of her grandfather!"

"Grandfather?" Marlon looked at the doctor questioningly. "Whose grandfather?"

"Kiku's," she said, making hand motions in the air dramatically. "You know, General Tama-something-I-can't-pronounce."

Marlon laughed out loud. "No one is afraid of General Tamarik, and he is not Kiku-hime's grandfather."

"He's not?" she asked, blinking a couple of times. "Everyone assumed, after the New York thing."

"Yes," Marlon said. "That."

~

8 months ago

"She dropped?" Marlon-sensei demanded, eyeing General Tamarik with irritation. Not only had the High Princess deployed with her unit, but also it was reported back they had lost contact with her. Real worry bit at the physician. "I thought you weren't going to let her do that."

"I didn't let her do it, Sensei," the general growled from across the bridge. "She took it into her own damned head to do it."

Marlon drew in a deep breath and let it out slowly.

"Fine," he said. "I'll go down and join Captain Jace in the search."

"You will not," General Tamarik snapped. "That's all I need, is a damned physician in the middle of an operation!"

"I'm not waiting up here for you to bring her back to me in pieces," Marlon retorted, turning away. "You act like we haven't been through this before, General."

"Damn it, Marlon, you stay on this ship!" General Tamarik yelled after him. Marlon easily ignored him as he walked away. The general had to know that wasn't going to happen. And there was nothing he could do to make him stay either. Marlon-sensei was the highest-ranking physician in the empire. The only one who could countermand him was the Exalted Leader himself. Since it had been Leader Dessalen who had put Marlon on this duty in the first place, Marlon had confidence there was little the general could do.

Marlon stopped in the infirmary to change into a combat uniform and grab a medpack. Hopefully he wouldn't need it, but with Kiku-hime, it was hard to say. She could be fine, or she could be lying somewhere wounded and unconscious. Since Captain Jace had lost track of her, anything was possible.

The physician frowned unhappily as he made his way to the bay, ready to take the next transport down to where Hime-sama had been deployed.

Marlon had made enough drops that he easily regained his equilibrium as he stepped out of the craft into the bright sunlight. His dark eyes swept the area and came to rest on

Captain Jace, who was standing nearby, clearly waiting for him.

"Sensei," Captain Jace acknowledged when Marlon got off the transport. Marlon frowned.

"You lost her," Marlon said flatly.

"She wasn't supposed to be here at all," Captain Jace pointed out.

"Like that's stopped her before," Marlon retorted. He slung his medpack over his shoulder. "Didn't you put a transponder on her? You think you would have learned after the last time."

"It's not like the girl stands still long enough for me to put one in her pocket," Captain Jace said.

"Have the damned things sewn into her combat uniforms," Marlon fumed.

"Yes, Marlon-sensei," Captain Jace said. Marlon glared at him in annoyance.

"Any sign of her?" Marlon demanded.

"Only her helmet and a possible blood trail," Captain Jace replied.

Marlon froze. A wave of real fear swept over him. "Blood?" he asked.

"It may not be hers," Captain Jace said. "It was just near where we found her helmet."

"Who else's do you suppose it could be?" Marlon demanded.

"This is a combat zone," Captain Jace said reasonably. "It could be anyone's. Including an animal's."

"You better hope so, Captain," Marlon said coldly.

Captain Jace was taking Marlon back to the place where they had found Kiku-hime's helmet when they came upon a young man hurrying from another direction. He wasn't one of the opposing army, but Captain Jace still brought his weapon to bear on him.

"Whoa," the young man said in one of the planet's languages, putting his hands out in front of him. "Just hang on a second. Are you looking for a girl?"

Marlon flicked a glance at Captain Jace. They had both learned the various languages of the planet prior to their incursion into it. It still sounded harsh and unnatural to their ears. The young man stepped forward a little, looking nervous but determined. Marlon watched the young native critically. His skin was of a dusky brown, not so different than the Garlon T'zen. His hair was short with wide swept curls. His bright green eyes were a curiosity of color that weren't seen among the Garlon T'zen. The lad started to reach into his pocket, but Captain Jace frowned a warning.

"Stop," the Captain ordered sharply. He walked up to the dark-haired man, intimidatingly several inches taller. Marlon watched the two of them. The captain was probably near the same age. But they were clearly from two different worlds, literally. Captain Jace reached into the other man's pocket with two fingers and pulled out a Garlon T'zen lieutenant's insignia. Captain Jace's voice dropped to a dangerous tone. "Where is she?"

"She's hurt," the young native said, looking up at Captain Jace. The Garlon T'zen captain grabbed him by the shirt, and he paled further. Marlon decided it was time for him to intervene.

"Captain," he said. "The man can't tell you if you break him."

Captain Jace scowled and shoved the other man away.

"Did you come to find help?" Marlon asked the newcomer.

"Yeah." The young man pulled his shirt straight, eyeing Captain Jace with apprehension.

Marlon smiled slightly. "Good," he said. "Take us to the lieutenant."

"All right," he answered and beckoned for them to follow him. Marlon looked over at Captain Jace.

"See?" he asked. "That wasn't so hard, was it?"

"No, Sensei," Captain Jace growled, shouldering his weapon and following them.

The native took them to a large building and they walked up a few flights of stairs. Captain Jace looked apprehensive but followed along, watchful, behind Marlon.

When they got up to the fourth floor the man unlocked a door and let them in. It was a small apartment, but neat and clean. He gestured toward the back.

"She was sleeping when I left," he told them.

Marlon nodded and went back to the back room and found Kiku-hime unconscious on the bed. He dropped the medpack and leaned over to touch her forehead. It was hot. He saw her wounded arm and shook his head.

"Hime-sama," he muttered under his breath.

"I tried to clean it." The man stood in the doorway. "But she wouldn't let me take her to a hospital."

"She is a very stubborn girl," Marlon remarked. "Go wait with the captain."

"He looks like he's going to shoot me." The man glanced back over his shoulder.

"He won't," Marlon assured him. "The lieutenant would be vexed if he did."

"You think he'd care?" the man asked.

"Hm." Marlon smiled slightly as he started to unwrap the bandage. "Perhaps not at the moment. But he's unhappy with her right now. He'll get over it."

"If you say so," the young man replied as he moved off into the other room.

Kiku started to stir as Marlon looked over the wound. Marlon opened up the medpack and rummaged around in it for a handheld med-scanner. Kiku woke and looked at him with blurry eyes.

"Marlon-sensei?" she murmured.

"Yes, Hime-sama," he replied.

"What are you doing here?" she asked. He started to clean the hot, infected wound with disinfectant numbing cloths. She winced as he worked.

"What I always do, Hime-sama," he said. "Closing your wounds."

"Not always," Kiku protested with a slight whimper.

He raised an eyebrow. He dug around in the pack and found a vial and a syringe. No need for her to be in pain. He quickly dosed it and then slipped it into her other arm. Kiku glanced over, but he had it put away before she had seen what he had done.

"What did you do?" Kiku leaned up slightly.

"Lay back down, Hime-sama," he ordered.

"No," Kiku protested. "I can't think when you drug me."

Marlon paused, but he was her physician, and he had his own directives from the Exalted Leader himself about her care. There was little Kiku-hime-sama could do to countermand them. "You managed to get this infected."

"I did not," Kiku protested. "Devon-kun cleaned it."

"Devon-kun?" Marlon asked.

"Hai." Kiku smiled slightly. "He's very sweet."

"He came and found Captain Jace and me," Marlon told her. "Very brave for a native."

"Mm." Kiku started to drift off to sleep again. The sedative he gave her was taking effect. "Don't leave him, Marlon. I have to find . . ."

And then she was unconscious. Marlon smiled and stroked her cheek tenderly with a small shake of his head. Following Kiku-hime was taking years off his life. If she hadn't been so endearing he would have found an appropriate revenge on Leader Dessalen for ordering this deployment. Marlon wasn't going to complain. Caring for Kiku-hime was a far better duty that executing Leader Dessalen's enemies in the most painful, drawn-out, and creative ways he could devise. He would far better serve to keep the High Princess alive than to satisfy the Exalted Leader's dark whims.

He continued to treat her wound and injected her with the necessary antibiotic to fight the infection. Really, out of all the hurts the princess had taken, this was relatively minor.

When she was ready to be moved he stood and went to the main room of the apartment. Captain Jace had called in men, and they were crowded into the small apartment. The Earth man, named Devon, was sitting on the couch looking at them with a mixture of worry and suspicion. Marlon spoke to Captain Jace in their own language so the young man wouldn't understand.

"Kiku-hime doesn't want to leave him," Marlon told the Captain.

The young officer's eyes traveled to where Devon was sitting and looked at him for a long moment before he pulled off his helmet. "It's better we don't," he said.

Marlon immediately understood the meaning but knew that would not be acceptable to their princess. "He did save her life," Marlon pointed out in a bid to keep the young native alive. Like it or not, that would be Jace's decision, not Marlon's.

The captain hardened his features, tightening his jaw. "Then better we leave him to his life here," he said. "She's damned lucky I don't execute him outright for her being in his bed."

"You know nothing happened," Marlon said.

The captain nodded. "That's why he gets to live." He put his helmet back on. Marlon let out a small breath of relief; he hadn't been sure which way that would go. "Is the princess ready to move?" the Captain asked.

"Yes," Marlon said. Captain Jace motioned to two men and issued orders to have Kiku-hime taken back to the transport in a litter. Marlon crouched near Devon. He paused before he spoke. "Thank you for helping Kiku-hime-sama. It was a very brave thing to do. We are in your debt."

"It's okay." The young man's eyes went to Kiku's face as she was being carried out of the bedroom. "Will she be all right?"

"She'll be fine," Marlon assured him.

The young man looked at Marlon. His green eyes were earnest, and the physician could see that he was a kind soul. Marlon could see why Kiku had been drawn to him.

"She is very dear to us," Marlon told him.

The man nodded. "I'm Devon Blackwood. Tell her that I hope she's better soon."

Marlon stood up and nodded for the rest of them to leave as he shouldered his medpack.

"I'll do that, Blackwood-san," Marlon said as he left the apartment.

~

Present

"The General is her guardian," Marlon clarified. "But they are not related."

"Then what is it?" Dr. Andersen said with exasperation. "She's the only Garlon T'zen female on the planet. And I know you aren't all gay!"

"Hardly," he replied dryly. They turned the corner and entered the large open field where half the town was gathered. It was an open assembly of all of the houses and townspeople as well as a good share of the off-duty Garlon T'zen. All of the races that had delegates on planet with their embassies in Manor Town had also come out to join the festivities. Kiku and Devon each took one of Mary's hands and braved their way into the crowd, looking for the spot that Captain Jace had to staked out as theirs. Before Dr. Andersen could go on to join them, Marlon took her by the arm and looked at her earnestly.

"Listen to me," he said seriously. "Don't encourage him. It won't get his heart broken, it will get him killed."

"What?" Dr. Andersen looked at him with shock.

"Kiku-hime-sama is spoken for," he said softly.

"She's never mentioned," Dr. Andersen said with bewilderment. Then she dropped her voice to a conspiratorial whisper. "Is it an arranged marriage sort of thing? A powerful intergalactic general! Oh the heartbreak, poor girl."

Marlon laughed again at her. "Don't be so dramatic! It's nothing the girl objects to."

"Oh." Her eyes glinted. "I wonder who it is? That little snot is holding out on me!"

"You are an impossible woman," Marlon told her, wrapping his arm around her waist as they went to join the others.

~

Dr. Andersen moved close to Kiku as they sat on a blanket together. Marlon and Devon had gone off with some of the Earth men to play the Earth game of volleyball. Devon had assured Marlon that it was pretty easy, and the physician had gone alone with a bemused expression on his face. Mary was fast asleep on the blanket, too full from their picnic lunch.

"Kiku?" Dr. Andersen asked softly, nudging her.

"Yes, Andersen-Sensei?" Kiku smiled from under her wide-brimmed yellow sunhat.

"Tell me," the doctor started, "do you have a boyfriend back home?"

"A boyfriend?" Kiku repeated slowly. Kiku wasn't sure what exactly Dr. Andersen was saying. She tried to remember what that particular phrase meant. "Back home?"

"You know what a boyfriend is." She pressed. "Like Marlon and me?"

Kiku immediately turned red but shook her head in protest. Oh! That. Heat flushed through her as her mind immediately went to one person. But—

"No, no," she denied. "Not like you and Marlon-sensei."

And it was true. She did have one person, who was almost . . . that. But they hadn't. They couldn't. There was the curse.

But it didn't stop Kiku from longing for her prince.

"Come on, now," Dr. Andersen chided. "You can tell me."

Kiku looked wildly about and spotted a few of her compatriots sparring off to the side. Her eyes lit up, and she pointed. Captain Jace was among them, and it was just the distraction she needed.

"Oh look, Andersen-sensei!" Kiku smiled and hopped up. She woke her groggy charge, who protested sleepily, and dragged her up by the hand.

"Oh, Kiku," Dr. Andersen protested. "That looks rather boring."

"Maybe if you only watch," Kiku said over her shoulder with a mischievous grin. Dr. Andersen didn't immediately follow her, but that was all right. Maybe by the time Kiku had to talk to her again, she'd have forgotten all about that question Kiku didn't want to answer.

Captain Jace cocked his head to one side and set a hand on his hip, looking down at her after she approached him.

"Kiku-hime," he said. Like Kiku, he was out of uniform, wearing jeans and a plain t-shirt. Kiku had assured him earlier that it was what most of the Earth men would be wearing. Looking around, Kiku was pleased she hadn't steered him wrong with that advice.

"I want to be next," she said.

"I thought you wanted a rest day," Jace said, but didn't block her way as she went to the racks where weapons of all types were laid out. There were staffs, swords, and knives of various lengths. She started for a knife, but Jace shook his head once.

Captain Jace preferred she not use sharp weapons when training. She needed to work on those skills more, and in sparring rounds it would be too easy for her to get hurt, or wound her opponent. Kiku stuck her tongue out at him, but made her way to the short staffs. He wouldn't let her spar if she defied him.

Devon came jogging up and looked at her with concern. Kiku nodded and pointed to Mary.

"Dr. Andersen told me you were going to do something crazy," he said. Kiku glanced over his shoulder and could see the red-haired doctor dragging a smiling Marlon along by the hand. "What are you doing?"

"Sparring," she answered.

Devon eyed the men around Kiku and dropped his gaze down to meet hers. "You sure about this?" he asked. His tone was low and quiet. "Is this really safe?"

While it was true that Kiku's opponents were all men and looked fierce, there was little likelihood she would be injured.

"Baka." Kiku made a face and shoved him backward gently. "Go wait with Mary-chan and Marlon-sensei. I'll be done in a moment."

"You think so, Hime-sama?" Jace asked from behind. He nodded to where Kiku's opponent was warming up with his own staff. "The corporal won't be easy on you."

"Don't insult me, Jace-kun" she shot back. "Besides, if I don't take him, you'll have me running drills for a month."

The smirk that spread across her captain's face was all the answer she needed to know that it was true. Jace crossed his arms and stepped back as Kiku moved to square off against the larger man.

~

"What are they saying?" Andersen-sensei asked Marlon. "And why aren't you doing anything to stop this?"

"No need, it's just Kiku-hime being her charming self." Marlon smiled.

He heard a derisive snort and turned to see General Lysis leaning against a tree. Marlon frowned and pulled away, to speak to the general. Unlike most of the others gathered, Lysis was wearing his standard black uniform and stood with his arms crossed. He was a young handsome man. His curly brown hair was clipped to his head. His presence here took Marlon by surprise. Marlon approached the general and offered a slight incline of his head. "General, I didn't know you were on the Earth."

"I just made planet fall," General Lysis said, never taking his dark eyes off Kiku. His proprietary air made Marlon uncomfortable and protective. "I decided to come and watch the proceedings."

Kiku had just started her round with short staff. Marlon couldn't imagine Captain Jace would let anyone near the princess with a sharp object, even in a game such as this. There was always a chance at an assassination attempt. Marlon considered Lysis's words and realized he couldn't possibly mean Kiku-hime's small duel here. There had to be bigger things brewing.

"Tell me, Sensei, is this how our High Princess spends her time?" the general asked.

"She also invades independent nations," Marlon said with dry humor.

"I heard about that." Lysis nodded. "Tamarik can't control that girl. Leader Dessalen found it amusing."

It was Marlon's turn to smile. "Did he?"

General Lysis looked annoyed and then smiled, turning back to the action. "Ah, she's going to take him."

True enough, Kiku has disarmed her opponent, had him on the ground with the staff at his throat. He wisely yielded, and a small cheer went up from the gathering.

"That was great, Onee-sama!" Mary ran up and hugged Kiku tightly around the waist.

"Is that Mary-hime?" General Lysis asked Marlon.

"Yes." Marlon confirmed. He wasn't terribly surprised the general knew about Mary-chan's title of princess. Lysis was in Leader Dessalen's inner circle and leader of the special operatives, or spies, in the Empire. From what Marlon could gather, Leader Dessalen was trying to keep secret the fact that a sixth princess had been chosen on the Earth.

Devon smiled sheepishly and offered Kiku an awkward congratulatory hug, which she quickly accepted. Marlon could see it didn't sit well with the general, who straightened up.

"And that's the brother?" Lysis asked coldly.

"That is Mary-hime's brother." Marlon emphasized, remembering his earlier warning to Dr. Andersen all too well. "Devon Blackwood."

"Hm." Lysis narrowed his dark eyes, watching the small crowd that gathered around the princess. Marlon did not like the General's look of calculation. It could add up to Devon's doom. The physician wondered how much it would take to put the boy out of the general's reach.

"I'm sorry, General." Marlon bowed. "But I will be missed. I did attend with Hime-sama and her party."

~

Kiku waved to Marlon-sensei as he made his way back, smiling at him. She was feeling elated over her small victory. She relished playing these sorts of games.

"Did you see, Marlon-sensei?" she asked brightly.

"I did," he told her. "And you were showing off."

"You're mean!" Kiku shoved him away lightly and laughed.

"Marlon!" Dr. Andersen scolded.

"She did, Andy-chan," Marlon protested, using his pet name for the English doctor. Kiku grinned. "Kiku-hime could have unarmed him in a third the time with far less 'flourish.'"

"But I liked the way my dress flounces," Kiku protested.

"That is showing off," Marlon pointed out.

"It wasn't a time-point round." She flicked her fingers in the air.

Marlon pointed at her and raised his eyebrows at Dr. Andersen, and she nodded in agreement. Devon looked confused.

"What?" he asked. "You could have finished faster?"

"Devon-kun." Kiku smiled brightly. "Of course I . . ."

Kiku's voice trailed off as there was hush and a murmur of surprise through the crowd. Kiku instinctively moved closer to Mary and took her hand. Marlon-sensei looked uneasy. Kiku knew her first priority was to keep Mary safe. There was a hush again, and Kiku felt a chill of apprehension.

"Maybe we should head back to the Manor," she said.

A ripple fell through the crowd as they went down on one knee, particularly those closest to Kiku, her group being made up of mostly Garlon T'zen. Kiku's eye's widened as she instantly recognized the red cape on the solid black uniform of the Garlon T'zen's Exalted Leader.

But it wasn't Leader Dessalen. Rather it was his personal envoy, Ellan. When he wore this guise he carried the words and authority of the Exalted Leader.

Kiku was frozen with shock as she watched Ellan make his way straight for her. Mary clung tightly to her hand, and Devon stepped close behind her. Kiku prayed quietly that Devon wouldn't say a word. She had no idea why Ellan would be here, coming to speak to her. She didn't think it could be good news. How could it be good news? These things were never good news.

Ellan smiled at her with a wink and bowed formally to her, drawing her hand forward and her wrist to his lips. A thrill ran through her body. The kiss had come from her Ouji-sama the same if from his own lips. Then Ellan looked up at her and spoke clearly in English so everyone there could understand.

"Princess Kiku, Leader Dessalen sends greetings."

"Hai," she said shakily. That elicited a bit of laughter, and she relaxed a little.

"He also," Ellan continued smoothly, not letting go of her hand, "has been terribly remiss in paying court to you. So to make it up, he will be here tomorrow."

Kiku blinked a couple of times. Tomorrow? He's coming here? Tomorrow? Her heart began to beat fast, and her face turned hot.

"Oh, yes." Ellan paused before he turned to Mary. "He'd kill me if I forgot this: He will, of course, carry on his long tradition of bringing you a present."

"A present?" Mary piped up. She craned her head to see the new man. He bowed formally to her.

"Of course!" He smiled. "All girls need presents, don't they?"

Mary nodded shyly.

"Leader Dessalen offers you special greeting too, Princess Mary," Ellan told her. "And he is very much looking forward to meeting you in person."

"Princess?" Devon finally found his voice, and Kiku groaned. "My sister isn't a princess. Kiku?"

"Leader Dessalen's looking forward to meeting you as well, Devon Blackwood," Ellan told Devon, but Kiku could clearly see there was no friendliness there. But then Ellan turned away and wrapped his arm around Kiku's waist, and then offered his hand to Mary to lead them away. "We've got much to do to prepare for his arrival."

As they were led off, the crowd of Garlon T'zen started a cheer. "Hail, Dessalen! Hail, Kiku!"

Kiku nodded.

Yes. This was good, wasn't it? Her prince was finally coming to her. Just like he had promised. Kiku wondered if he would remember his other promises, too.

CHAPTER 2

Leader Dessalen paced in the small study chamber of the Dreadnaught-class battle cruiser after reading the last intelligence report from Earth, his golden eyes sharp with frustration. He always kept the reports regarding Kiku for last because inevitably they would either entertain him or irritate him to the point he couldn't keep his mind on the matters of running his empire.

The door to the chamber slid open, and Akane-hime came in smiling. Akane was one of the five princesses of the Garlon T'zen Empire. Six now, Dessalen added to himself, remembering the young Mary-hime. Akane was the eldest of all the girls. The princess was wearing a simple cream-colored dress. She was carrying a tray that looked suspiciously like his dinner. Dessalen stopped and frowned at her.

"Onii-san needs to eat," she scolded as she set the tray down and turned to look at him. He closed his eyes and rubbed the back of his neck. They were a family of circumstance, not by blood. And even they, as a set, looked nothing alike. Kiku's four sisters referred to him as "older brother," which he was to them. He was their guardian, but only to four. Thankfully, the same couldn't be said of the one princess that who preoccupied his mind. Kiku's guardian was Dessalen's trusted general, Tamarik.

Damn his generals. He had dismissed them with orders to be left alone. So, of course, they send in one of the only people he wouldn't ever take his anger out on.

"Akane-chan," he started, but she shook her head firmly, with her dark brown curls bouncing around her head.

"You have to eat," she said sternly. "We will be at this Earth place tomorrow. And then we'll see Kiku-chan!" Akane brightened and clasped her hands together with delight. Dessalen smiled as his anger drained away. Defeated, he bowed to the princess and offered her a chair and sat across from her.

"You miss Kiku-hime?" he asked, poking around the tray for something tasty. He pulled away a bright green piece of fruit, cut it in two, and offered half to Akane. She accepted it with a polite nod.

"Of course I do," she said. "We all do."

They sat in silence eating the fruit, and then: "You miss her too," she added.

He leaned back in the chair and feigned an innocent expression. "You think so?" he asked.

The princess wiped her lips primly. "Tell me what is bothering you, this time, Onii-san," Akane said.

Dessalen regarded Akane for a moment. No man would have the stones to ask such an impertinent question of the Exalted Leader. This, however, was one of his princesses, and he doted on them all.

"Ugh," he said finally, making a face. "I don't like the Earth man, this Devon Blackwood, around Kiku."

"Hm," Akane said noncommittally.

"What's that supposed to mean?" he retorted.

"Has Kiku-chan done something to make you think she might have feelings for this person?" Akane asked.

"How would I know that?" he muttered. Akane smiled.

"Onii-san is jealous." Akane smiled again and rested a hand on Dessalen's arm.

Dessalen grinned, leaning forward to cover her hand with his own.

"I never said I wasn't."

~

"Are you interested?"

Jimmy Davis crossed his arms and stared down at his shoes, not meeting Carl Jones's sharp eyes. He had been asked to see his guidance counselor. When the note and hall pass had come to his sixth-period English class, he had been pretty sure it was about his mom. The fact it wasn't, was refreshing; but what it was, was frightening.

"You sure about this?" Jimmy asked. "This has to be some sort of mistake."

"No mistake," Carl Jones said. He was a middle-aged Hispanic guy. Jimmy had spent a fair amount of time with him, and he knew he was a straight shooter. Which was the only reason why the young man hadn't laughed in his face. "The Garlon T'zen are working to establish diplomatic relations. This program is a way for young people, like yourself, to get to know about them. Their culture."

"Yeah, but why me?" Jimmy asked.

"Why not you? You're a good kid, you don't get into trouble, you get good grades. You ever think this could be a reward for not having screwed up your life?" Mr. Jones slid a large envelope across the desk.

"Who would take care of my mom?" Jimmy asked, not moving to touch the envelope. "I mean, how long would I be gone?"

"Your mother will be fine." Mr. Jones sighed. "It's only three months."

Three months in an "alien" village, the place they called Manor Town. Jimmy wasn't sure how much to believe about what he saw on the news about the "terrifying" Garlon T'zen. He guessed they could easily wipe out everyone on the Earth if they wanted, but they didn't. They didn't even try to take over any countries, but rather were working with them to try and establish trade treaties with other races in this Empire of theirs.

"I don't know much about them," Jimmy said. "Would I have to live somewhere they don't speak English?"

"No," Carl Jones said. "For one thing, there is an American Embassy in Manor Town, and two, the plan is to put you up with this doctor that lives there. She's from Great Britain, so her English is probably better than yours."

Mr. Jones laughed at his own joke. Jimmy rolled his dark blue eyes and moved to stand, pushing his fingers through his short blond hair.

"Listen, Jim," Mr. Jones said. Jimmy bristled. He disliked being called Jim, but it didn't seem to stop most of the staff at the school from doing it. "I know your mother is a head case, but this is a great opportunity for you! We don't know that much about the Garlon T'zen. Think about how much you could learn. You should go and then come back and tell us about them."

"I'll think about it," Jimmy said. He picked up the envelope and slid it between two books in the stack he was carrying.

"You do that." Mr. Jones's voice followed him as he left the small, cramped office.

Southfield, Michigan, didn't look much different from before the Garlon T'zen occupation. The gas stations were still open, and you could grab a big gulp at the 7-Eleven. Jimmy added two candy bars on the pile as he paid for the drink.

It was a pretty nice day. The bite of fall was in the air. School had started, they were halfway through September. He made his way up the winding street and up to the small one-story bungalow. It didn't need to be that big; it was just he and his mom.

His dad had taken off three years before. But that wasn't what had destroyed their family. That was five years ago, when his twin sister had been abducted out of a park not far from their house in Rochester Hills. That started the spiral of fights and blame. When Dad had Jennifer declared legally dead, it had been the end of it for Mom. She set his clothes on fire in the front yard, packed Jimmy up in a car, and left.

His dad was loaded, but child support had ended last month when Jimmy turned eighteen. Then came his offer to send Jimmy to the University of Michigan. Jimmy had failed every class the year Jennifer had disappeared. Now he was a straight 4.0 student.

"Mom?" he called out as he unlocked the door. There wasn't an answer. He sighed, knowing what he would find. He found her passed out on the living room couch. Empty beer cans and cigarette butts littered the floor around her. She still clutched her cell phone in her hand.

He wasn't even disappointed anymore.

Jimmy pulled a knit afghan over her and took her phone from her hand. He glanced at the history on her mobile phone. He could chronicle her day by the calls she had made.

First the police detective who had handled Jennifer's case and then list of thirty calls to out-of-state numbers; probably homeless shelters and hospitals.

She'll never stop looking, Jimmy thought. And he didn't blame her. But he didn't share the hope that Jennifer was alive.

Maybe I should go, he thought. His mother would be all right. He could call her after he'd gotten away from . . . this. It was draining. Maybe he had to put his dead sister behind him too. Maybe he had to go to this Manor Town place and make a new start, even if only for three months.

~

Leader Dessalen clenched and unclenched his hands several times waiting for the transport to open its yawning doors. His plain black uniform was perfectly cut to his form. It was the standard they all wore. Rank and insignia were worn at the collar and wrists, but his uniform was bare of rank. Leader Dessalen was also afforded the extravagance of a red cape cut just behind the knee, which none of his men were allowed. His pale blond hair made him stand out as an oddity among the mostly brown- and black-haired Garlon T'zen.

When the doors opened, he could see the row after row of uniformed Garlon T'zen come to honor his arrival. His sharp golden eyes found the small figure holding her own, as she always had, in the line of tall men around her. A smiled touched his lips, and he visibly relaxed. Worry had plagued him ever since Kiku-hime had come to this strange world that something would befall her here. But now that she was in his sight, whole, and literally surrounded by the power of his military, he finally felt at ease.

All bowed as he passed them making his way to the ranking delegation that was waiting at the foot of the large landing field. He looked around with approval. It appeared they had built their Manor Town to suit Garlon T'zen security standards but still held to the planet's local architectural style. He would reward the designers who made it possible.

Leader Dessalen gave a cursory glance to see who was in attendance. General Tamarik, of course, as he was head of the Special Earth Preservation Delegation for the Garlon T'zen. Then Dessalen's envoy Ellan and generals Rohlon, Kassius, and Jasxon, who had been assigned the task of security in this system and its outlying territory. Some minor captains, and . . . Lysis? Dessalen made a mental note to find out just what business General Lysis had made to be on Earth at this time. His first priority however, was his princess.

"Kiku-hime." He stopped in front of her and inclined his head. Dessalen took one of her hands into both of his and drew her out of the standing rank with a smile. Her honey-colored hair was pulled back away from her face. "You look well! This Earth sun must agree with you."

"Yes, Leader Dessalen," she said quietly, standing near enough he could see she was trembling. Dessalen paused for a moment at her calling him by his formal rank. But then he cast his eyes at the generals who were waiting and watching the scene unfold with keen interest. Obviously they had been browbeating her into behaving like a respectable officer. Hm.

Leader Dessalen loathed to let go of Kiku's hand but he did after a swift touch to his lips. Her face colored instantly, and she dropped her eyes to the ground. Her reaction pleased him.

"General Tamarik." He turned back to the generals, keeping Kiku firmly at his side. "During my stay, Lieutenant Kiku will be my aide and liaison to the Earth governments. Transfer her under my direct command for the time being."

Dessalen wasn't sure what amused him more, the stunned look on most of his generals faces, or the hot look of anger that Lysis shot him.

"My lord," General Tamarik protested. "You are spoiling the girl again."

Leader Dessalen smiled and returned his attention to Kiku. He leaned down to speak softly in her ear.

"Did Ellan-kun tell you I was bringing you a present?" His tone was light and teasing. The playful flicker he had missed came back to her lovely deep blue eyes.

"Yes," she said slowly. Dessalen stood up and snapped his fingers with flourish.

"Onee-sama!"

"Kiku-chan!"

"Nee-chan!"

"Kiku-nee!"

The calls came quickly as Kiku's four sisters ran out of the ship. They all squealed with joy and jumped around her, hugging her excitedly. Dessalen stepped back before he was knocked down. Good-natured laughter was heard from the ranks as the men watched the antics of their princesses.

General Lysis bowed respectfully, and Dessalen barely acknowledged him.

"Your aide?" Lysis questioned. "Really."

"She's qualified," Leader Dessalen said curtly. Then he turned to Lysis. "What are you doing here, General?"

"Why, the same as you." Lysis bowed. His brown eyes met Leader Dessalen's and never faltered. "My lord."

Dessalen felt an immediate urge to destroy something, but instead was surrounded by five laughing young ladies. Now wasn't the time to deal with Lysis, but he would if the general tried to get in his way.

"Come on, Hime-chan," he murmured, drawing Kiku away from her sisters. Escorts for the other princesses materialized.

She led him to a large, expressive animal. "We ride horses here in Manor Town."

Leader Dessalen had had experience with similar animals before. "No mechanicals in the town." He approved. It was standard practice for security. Kiku started to turn away, but he caught her wrist on an impulse. "Ride with me, Kiku-chan?"

Kiku paused, smiling shyly. He took this as consent and helped her up onto his horse. Throwing one leg over, he settled in next to the girl, feeling her slender figure against his chest. Dessalen wrapped one arm protectively around her waist, pulling her tightly against him. He saw Lysis shoot him a poisonous glare, to which he only raised an eyebrow.

The delegation began the slow trek through the winding streets of Manor Town up to the Manor House itself. There were crowds of onlookers along the way. Many were Earthers, who hadn't ever seen such an event come through the town. Others were from other worlds and were most interested in getting a glimpse of the Exalted Leader of the Garlon T'zen. And everyone had something to say about the girl he held so attentively in his arms. And that was exactly the point Leader Dessalen was demonstrating.

"I've missed you, Hime-chan," he murmured into her ear tenderly. He could feel her relax against him, and she craned her head around, her nose brushing against his chin.

"I've missed to you too, Ouji," she said softly, and Dessalen smiled. To Kiku, he was her prince. "A lot."

Dessalen closed his eyes, relishing the moment. His body ached for her. He knew she was his. He opened his golden eyes and set his resolve. He would make sure that nothing, not general or Earth man, would get between him and his princess.

~

"I don't understand why you're moving your room, Onee-sama," Mary said as she helped Kiku carry the last of her belongings down the long wood-paneled hallway.

"It's part of putting all of us in the same wing of the Manor," Kiku explained. "There weren't enough rooms for all of us on the main floor, so we're going up here."

"But why are you going in this room?" Mary said with a hushed voice as she crept in behind her. It was a sweeping, elegantly decorated room with a king-size four-poster bed in the middle. A table sat near the large window that looked out toward the back gardens. A stone fireplace place was on the other wall with a pair of wing-backed chairs beside it.

"Those doors connect back to a center suite that connects to the rest of your bedrooms." Kiku pointed to a double door on the far side of the wall. She pulled aside a curtain and revealed a small alcove room with a full-size bed and a wardrobe dresser. "And this is where I will sleep."

"Who sleeps over there?" Mary pointed.

"Ouji-sama," Kiku answered and then added to make it more clear, "Leader Dessalen. Since I'm going to be his aide, I have to be available to him all of the time. This is part of the assignment."

Mary looked back and forth between the center bed and where Kiku was putting away the rest of her things. "Isn't that sort of strange?"

"Not really." Kiku shrugged. "I am a lieutenant, Mary-chan. You just keep forgetting."

"I guess." Mary looked unconvinced.

"But now," Kiku told her, "it's time to see Andersen-sensei for your check up."

"Awww . . ."

"What's the matter?" Kiku scolded. "You like Andy-chan, don't you?"

"Yeah, but there are so many new strangers in town. It doesn't feel right." Mary turned pale at the thought of leaving the Manor House. Kiku felt a pang of worry as she looked at the eight year old. She reached out and brushed Mary's brown tangled bangs from her green eyes. There was only so much she could do to ease her fears, but Kiku swore no one would hurt the child again. Mary was one of her sisters now, and she would protect her with the same fierceness she would any of the others.

"Don't worry." Kiku pulled out a small hand-cannon and tucked it in the back of her waistband. Kiku was out of uniform, as she sometimes liked to move through the town without drawing attention to herself from those who didn't know she was the High Princess. She grabbed a black leather jacket. "That's why I'm going with you."

~

"I don't approve," General Tamarik told the Exalted Leader.

His manner was rigid and angry. Dessalen frowned, arms crossed, trying to decide who he was more annoyed with at the moment, Tamarik or the pack of cowards on his command council eagerly waiting for their leader to spill the good general's blood. Too bad that they didn't seem to remember that Tamarik was Kiku-Hime's legal guardian and that he had a right to his opinion, annoying as it was. Still . . .

"I don't care," Dessalen retorted. "It's a command decision. Live with it."

"Come now, Leader Dessalen," General Lysis put in smoothly. "It's more than that."

"You're correct, Lysis." Dessalen smiled. General Lysis was closer to his age than the others, and, while annoying at the moment, was loyal without question. "It's a good command decision."

"That's not what I meant," Lysis started, but Dessalen interrupted.

"All of you get out," he ordered. "Except for you, Tamarik."

They muttered politely, taking their leave, and Dessalen was left alone with General Tamarik.

"My lord." The general's voice sounded tired. "You shouldn't do this. You don't understand. Kiku is nothing but trouble."

"Oh, my dear general." Dessalen poured two drinks from a nearby decanter. "I know precisely how much trouble our princess is. A combat medal shall be rewarded to you for having survived the ordeal thus far."

"Don't think it's just me," Tamarik warned. "Every instructor and commander she's ever had—"

"I get the reports." Dessalen dismissed his words. "Kiku is just high spirited."

"She's reckless!" Tamarik snapped. "She needs to be put in the least dangerous place possible and maybe, just maybe, she won't end up getting herself killed!"

The two of them stood off, staring at the other. Leader Dessalen was moving beyond annoyed to angry.

"Don't you think I can't keep her safe?" Leader Dessalen's voice was dangerously soft.

Tamarik closed his eyes and sighed. "I don't think you won't try."

~

The door to the clinic opened at three o'clock just as Dr. Andersen expected, but what she didn't expect was who was with Mary.

"The two of you came alone?" she asked with surprise. After yesterday's triumphant ride through town she didn't believe Kiku would be out on her own anytime soon. The Garlon T'zen leader had looked like he had a rather proprietary hold on the young lady. His demeanor explained volumes as so why she hadn't noted any suitors among Kiku's own people.

"Sure." Kiku shrugged.

Mary hopped forward and bowed. "I'm here for my check-up!" she said. "Kiku-onee said she would bring me safe! And she did!"

"She did at that," Dr. Andersen agreed. She held out her hand to the child. "Let's go, then."

Kiku sat down and started to thumb through some of the magazines that Dr. Andersen had lying about. Dr. Andersen was curious what the alien princess would think of the last issue of Teen Fashion Smash, but while she was musing, Mary interrupted her thoughts.

"We all got moved around in the Manor House," she said. "We got new bedrooms, even Kiku-onee. She's moved in with Leader Dessalen."

"What?" Dr. Andersen fumbled the instrument she was using, and it dropped to the floor with a clang. "What did you say, Mary?"

"My room is between Dido-hime and Kaori-Hime," she continued on blithely. "And in the center is a big room you have to go through first to get to the bedrooms."

"Really." Dr. Andersen retrieved the otoscope and attached a clean ear speculum. She couldn't really figure how the floor plan Mary described would work but she was far more interested in getting the child back to the part about Kiku.

"What was that about Kiku's room?" she asked casually as she looked in Mary's ear.

"Because she's his helper or something." Mary winced from the pressure of Dr. Andersen's fingers. Dr. Andersen let go of the ear.

"Sorry, Mary," she apologized. Mary offered a lopsided smile.

Dr. Andersen continued with the exam, looking over the child's former injuries, and decided she was healing nicely. When she sent her back out to Kiku with a positive report, the evening sky was darkening.

"Maybe you should call someone at the Manor to come pick you up," she suggested. "Captain Jace, maybe?"

"Why?" Kiku asked in surprise.

"It is starting to get dark," Dr. Andersen pointed out. Kiku looked at her strangely.

"What difference does that make?" Kiku frowned.

"It's more dangerous in the dark." Dr. Andersen felt like she was speaking to a very small child. Sometimes Kiku could be so dense about certain things. But Kiku laughed outright at her.

"That is the most ridiculous thing I have ever heard. Whether it's light or not doesn't have anything to do with how 'dangerous' something is. It is or it isn't. Come along, Mary-chan."

"Okay." Mary looked back at Dr. Andersen and shrugged. Dr. Andersen silently fumed at the Garlon T'zen girl. How could she not know it was more dangerous in the dark?

~

"Does anyone know where Kiku-hime-sama is?" Ellan asked Marlon. Marlon looked up from his desk at the envoy and nodded.

"Yes," he replied. "She took Mary for her appointment with Andersen-sensei in town."

"Alone?" Ellan asked with a touch of surprise.

"Yes," Marlon said as he returned to his work.

"You let her do that?" Ellan demanded, sounding very worried.

"Ah, yes." Marlon smiled, looking back up. "I'm sorry, Ellan-san. One does not 'let' Kiku-hime-sama do anything. She just does it. Did you perhaps forget that she is the High Princess of the Empire?"

"Leader Dessalen has asked for her." Ellan paled.

"Then tell Leader Dessalen she'll be along shortly," Marlon said.

~

"Ah, yes, Ellan. Where is the princess?" Dessalen was looking the latest reports from the Tazer sector. He made a note on the handheld imagedeck to redeploy a battle group of five ships. Pirates and slavers seemed to be a growing problem in that sector. He frowned. He would have his liaison speak to the local magistrate. If they continued to do business with criminals then he would make sure they understood that the Garlon T'zen were going to take a far more active role in their system.

"I was told she would be along shortly," Ellan said. Dessalen looked up sharply.

"That was not what I asked." Leader Dessalen put down the tablet and regarded his envoy, who looked too nervous for the Exalted Leader's liking.

"Kiku-hime-sama escorted Mary-hime to a physician's appointment," Ellan said. "It was to the native Andersen-sensei. Her office is in town."

"I take it they went alone?" Dessalen sighed. They must have, for Ellan to have worked himself up into such a state.

"Yes, my lord," he said. "I don't know what she could be thinking—"

"Stop," Dessalen ordered. "Kiku-hime is not like the other princesses. She is a Garlon T'zen officer who has earned her ascension. No one gave it to her."

"Yes, Leader Dessalen," Ellan said quietly.

"It doesn't mean I am happy about it," Dessalen muttered. Tamarik's warning seemed to be ringing a prophecy of doom in his ears.

~

A note was passed to Kiku shortly after she stepped through the front entrance of the Manor House. She glanced at its contents and nodded curtly to the messenger.

"I'm sorry, Mary-chan," she apologized. "Leader Dessalen has asked for me."

Mary frowned as she shrugged off her short green jacket and gave it to a nearby attendant.

"But you said we would eat dinner with Devon," Mary protested.

"I know." Kiku bit her lip. It was going to be difficult to juggle her obligations to Leader Dessalen while still caring for Mary-chan. And now that her other sisters were there as well . . . She put a hand to her head. One thing at a time. "Tell Devon-kun I'm sorry and I'll make it up to you both soon."

Mary still looked cross as Kiku brushed a kiss against her forehead and hurried toward the library where Leader Dessalen was probably still working. Kiku knocked politely and entered the large shelf-lined room. A small fire burned in the fireplace, and Leader Dessalen was looking over numerous imagedecks and sheets scattered across the desk. He glanced up, and a small smiled touched his lips.

"Ah, Hime-sama." He turned his attention back to something on the desk. "I heard you had gone out."

"Hai," she said. "Mary-chan had an appointment with Andersen-sensei."

"The brother couldn't take her?" he asked, still surveying his documents. Kiku fidgeted a little, wondering if Leader Dessalen was unhappy with her. She knew she was supposed to be available for him, but she had only been gone a few hours.

"No, Leader Dessalen," she said contritely. "Devon-kun works at the American Embassy. His job makes doing these sorts of things for Mary difficult. So that's why I do them."

"Devon-kun?" Leader Dessalen looked up, irritated. "Works?"

"Of course." Kiku smiled, cocking her head to one side.

He regarded her for a long moment and then motioned for her to come closer. "We've had these requests come from the Rilli envoy." He motioned to a large stack of enveloped papers. "The American government is trying to start independent negotiations with them without our counsel."

That didn't surprise Kiku much. The Americans were the most unhappy of any of the Earth's governments with the Garlon T'zen incursion. But from what she could see, they had been the biggest bully on the planet. Besides, they were still smarting over her New York City raid when she rescued Mary-chan.

"The Rilli, not wanting to endanger their lucrative trade treaties with the Garlon T'zen, have asked us to review what these Americans have sent them and advise them on their best course of action." He smiled.

"Just tell them no," Kiku replied stiffly. She didn't like the Americans much. A feeling that was mutual. Last she heard, she was being called a war criminal.

Leader Dessalen's lips twitched. "Then we wouldn't know what the Americans were trying to negotiate without our knowledge. Really, Hime-sama," he chided.

"Ugh." She made a face. The Exalted Leader of the Garlon T'zen smiled indulgently.

"It is in their Earth language," he continued. "You know this one?"

"Of course." She sighed.

He rose and led her to a long wood table and pulled out a chair for her to sit. Dessalen's golden eyes glittered in the light. "Then this is an excellent use of your talents, Lieutenant." He leaned close until his nose almost touched hers. Kiku's heart beat wildly. His fingers ran along her jaw and moved a strand of hair behind her ear. "Read through the materials and give the Rilli your recommendation."

"You're cruel, Ouji," Kiku managed to whisper.

"Mm." He closed eyes and smiled. Kiku's breath caught as his lips touched hers. A knock at the library door interrupted the moment, and Leader Dessalen straightened up with a sigh of irritation. Kiku felt both relief and disappointment. She immediately started to dig into the papers the Americans had sent the Rilli, studiously ignoring the presence of her prince and the two sub-commanders who had entered to give their reports.

~

Dessalen quietly entered his bedchamber by way of the main door. The large window was open halfway, and a soft breeze blew through. Kiku-hime had gone up to bed hours before, her eyes watering from reading page after page of the Americans' small typed proposals. He was pleased with that one. He could have gotten their idiot documents translated and ordered Tamarik to handle the issue. But this worked out much more nicely. It could easily keep the princess occupied and out of mischief for a week.

Closing the bedchamber door stirred the air, and the curtains around Kiku's bed gently billowed. Without thought, he moved closer and silently pulled the curtain aside. His eyes were drawn to Kiku's sleeping figure, breathing softly against her pillows. Her long neck and shoulder lay exposed as her short chemise slipped off a little to the side.

He forced himself to turn away and go to his own bed. He quickly undressed and pulled on a pair of loose bottoms. Lying down, he threw an arm over his eyes. He took a deep breath and tried to will himself to sleep. Soon, he promised himself. Soon the waiting would be over.

But sleep didn't last long. A heartwrenching scream echoed from one of the nearby bedrooms. It sounded like Kaori. Even before his feet could touch the floor, Kiku had flown out of bed, a weapon held low in her hand. Only a few times in his life had real fear gripped him, and seeing his princess running headlong into unknown danger was one of them.

"Kiku!" Her name tore from his throat as he leapt up to follow her. The doors to the other bedrooms opened, and frightened girls ran out. All but one room—that door stood open already.

The scene inside the room chilled his blood. Kiku was standing off with a man in black. The intruder had a hold of Kaori, holding her in front of him by her throat, her arm twisted around her back. Kiku had her hand cannon leveled evenly at him.

"Let my sister go," Kiku ordered in one of the Earth languages.

Shouts came from the garden below and from the inner suite as soldiers poured into the Manor. The black clad intruder must have realized he was going to be overwhelmed in moments. He threw Kaori in Dessalen's direction. Dessalen caught her as the man jumped out through the broken balcony doors.

Kiku growled in frustration and sped after him.

"Kiku! Stop!" Dessalen ordered. Kiku flew out the balcony doors. Dessalen let go of the hysterical Kaori and followed closely behind. He grabbed her arm before she could leap over the railing and continue the chase. "Kiku!"

"No!" she cried in frustration. "He's getting away!"

"He won't get far." Dessalen clenched his jaw. Weapon fire rang out all around them, stray shots pinging against the wall behind them. Dessalen pulled Kiku back as his golden eyes swept the darkness. Kiku stiffened with shock, and he caught her in his arms.

Crimson spread across her shoulder and arm.

He pulled her tightly against him as her eyes began to flutter. "Kiku!"

"Gomen, Ouji," she said softly as she reached up and touched his lips with two fingers.

Irrational fury boiled in his veins. Carefully cradling the princess's pale form, he tried to shield the sight of her wounded body from Kaori's view. But when he stepped into the bedroom her arm fell forward, and blood ran freely down it, pooling on the floor, as he carried Kiku past the throng of soldiers back to his bedchamber.

"Kiku!" Kaori went into hysterics, screaming after him. Someone must have stopped her from following after as he carried Kiku to his bedchamber.

War-hardened soldiers balked seeing Kiku limp in his arms. Leader Dessalen wouldn't fault them for it. Kiku-hime's chemise was soaked with blood and her face still, her breath ragged and uneven against his chest.

"Get Marlon," he growled laying her down on his bed. Grabbing a shirt, he put pressure on the free-flowing wound. Akane ran into the chamber behind him.

"Kiku!" she gasped, her dark skin turning ashen. She turned and closed the door to lean on it.

"Stay out!" Dessalen ordered.

"But—" she protested. He shot her a look that brooked no further argument, and she darted back out the door.

The room quickly filled with soldiers and medics. Marlon entered at a flat run, looking like he had been pulled from his bed. Leader Dessalen stepped out of the way to make room so they could work to save Kiku's life. He ground his jaw as he looked down at his hands covered in her blood.

He caught a nearby soldier by the collar. "Find Lysis."

Leader Dessalen grabbed a white shirt and pulled it over his head. Then he yanked on a pair of boots. He had coddled this planet long enough, and it was high time the general started to earn his keep.

It didn't take long for General Lysis to appear in the hall outside of Leader Dessalen's bedchamber.

"The Manor has been breached," Leader Dessalen told him. Lysis eyed him warily.

"Whose blood is all over you?" Lysis asked. Leader Dessalen offered a bitter smile.

"It's not mine," he said. He was unsure why he didn't want Lysis to know Kiku-hime was lying wounded in the next room, other than that the fewer who knew the better. That, and he didn't like the general's interest in the princess. Leader Dessalen had a strong suspicion that Lysis had designs on the girl, and he did not approve.

"Use whatever means you care to," Dessalen ordered. "Take care of this."

Lysis was apt at this sort of operation. Given free rein, the general could have Manor Town cleaned out of spies and enemy agents by nightfall the next day.

Dessalen had every intention of giving the general free rein.

"Immediately, Leader Dessalen." Lysis bowed and left.

~

Kiku woke up hearing the soft snaps of a burning fire. At first she thought she was part of the fire. The pain across her shoulder and arm was an intense flame. The discomfort drove her to consciousness. Her eyes blurred and then refocused on Leader Dessalen sitting across from her in a chair next to the bed.

"You awake, Kiku-chan?" he asked softly, moving closer.

She tried to smile. "Hai." Her voice didn't sound like her own; she had to strain to speak.

"Hush," Leader Dessalen scolded gently, touching her face tenderly. "You were wounded."

"Did you find him?" Kiku asked hoarsely.

"Lysis will find him." Leader Dessalen's features darkened dangerously.

"Lysis? No!" Kiku struggled to sit up but was rewarded with excruciating pain. Tears filled her dark blue eyes as a small sob escaped her. Lysis would have the streets running with blood. He was merciless and unyielding.

"Hime-chan, Hime-chan," Dessalen soothed, leaning her back carefully, real worry reflected in his golden eyes.

He kissed her lightly on the forehead. Then he paused and slowly touched her lips with his. Kiku closed her eyes as she parted her lips to accept a small kiss. He drew back and breathed into her ear. "You frightened me badly, Kiku-chan."

"G-Gomen," Kiku stammered as her eyelids grew heavy once more. He drew up her fingers and held them while she lost the battle and slipped back under the heavy waves of unconsciousness.

Kiku drifted.

~Eyanna.~ Kiku called. ~Eyanna! Hear me!~

Silver Eyanna appeared, translucent and beautiful in Kiku's mind's eye. Her presence was as cool and refreshing as it had been the first time she had come five years before. Even before Kiku could say it, Eyanna knew what Kiku wanted. Kiku's Celestial patron offered her a reproachful expression.

~What you ask is perilous, my daughter,~ Eyanna warned.

~You promised, Eyanna,~ Kiku said. ~You promised me the power to protect my sisters.~

~It is folly,~ Eyanna replied. ~But I would deny you nothing, dear one.~

CHAPTER 3

Dessalen woke with a start, blinking and rubbing his eyes. How had he fallen asleep? He turned to where Hime-sama was lying in the bed, or at least where she should have been lying in the bed. He jumped to his feet and looked around the room. The window overlooking the garden was open, but the room was otherwise unchanged, other than that his princess was missing.

He walked purposefully to the chamber's main double doors and yanked them open. The guards looked at him with surprise. Obviously she hadn't come this way. Scowling, he slammed them closed and crossed back toward the center chamber. How could she have even gotten out of bed? His blood froze for a moment at the thought: perhaps another intruder. He hurried to open the door to the center suite.

Akane was sitting in one of the wide wingback chairs with a tearstained face.

"Have you seen Kiku-hime?" Leader Dessalen demanded. Akane shook her head. He started to turn away.

"Wait Onii-san," she said. "I know what she did."

"What do you mean?" Leader Dessalen's voice hardened. "What did she do?"

"S-she . . ." Akane's voice shook with fear.

Dessalen moved over to Akane's side. He knelt on one knee next to her. He didn't believe that Akane was afraid of him. He softened his tone and bit down on his anger. "What is it, Akane-chan?" Dessalen coaxed the girl to speak.

"She invoked Eyanna," Akane whispered.

Dessalen felt the blood drain from his face.

~

<u>6 months ago</u>

The bell on the glass door chimed softly as Kiku pushed it open. The smells of warm food assaulted her senses as she stepped through the door. Kiku paused for a moment, feeling an odd stir of emotions catching in her throat. The face of a boy, from long ago, who wore her features, flashed brightly in her mind; but only for a moment. Kiku put her hand to her head and frowned. It wasn't an unpleasant memory, just disconcerting. Being in this place—these smells, this Earth—was stirring long-forgotten images and feelings that she'd rather just stayed buried.

All that had little to do with the task at hand. And this particular task had to do with another young man. A young man named Devon Blackwood.

It had been two months since she'd seen him last. In that time the Garlon T'zen had come to terms with most of this world's local governments. Many were unhappy with the Garlon T'zen incursion and howled they would not be enslaved by an alien race.

Kiku rolled her eyes. As if they knew anything of enslavement. With the back-trading many of the countries were doing with Tirelli and the Xoned, the planet would have been stripped bare of its natural resources and its population sold into slavery by the end of a generation if the Garlon T'zen hadn't intervened. It was in their best interests that the Empire had made this a preserve to protect it. Most governments had kept their dealings with these other spacefaring races secret, for obvious reasons. They weren't acting in the best interests of their people, often trading children for technology. Now that the Empire had discovered and exposed this, many were doing everything they could to try and keep those dealings undisclosed. The hypocrisy turned her stomach.

The Garlon T'zen founded its holdings on an island country in the southern hemisphere. That land's government entity deeded over a vast territory in the mountains on the promise of Garlon T'zen protection and lucrative trade agreements with the guilds. It was a fair bargain, and the secure settlement of Manor Town was established—named for the sprawling three-story manor set near the center of town. It was where Kiku had stayed with General Tamarik since they'd completed construction. The plan was for her sisters to join her once Leader Dessalen felt the sector had been fully secured.

Leader Dessalen had spared no expense in its construction. The holding could even be entirely shielded in times of war, making it nearly as impenetrable as any of their warships. Many of the planet's governments had petitioned to have embassies in Manor Town, along with representatives of many of the different races from off-planet. It was a good community, and Kiku was happy there.

Being happy didn't stop her from thinking of the first native she'd met. It had taken a lot of investigation to find him. Jace-kun had steadfastly refused to help. He had told her to forget about the man, saying any involvement with her would be dangerous for them both. Devon was from a place that was still unhappy with the Garlon T'zen, this "United States." General Tamarik had to institute a continuous military presence there to ensure their good behavior, but their truce was tenuous at best. Kiku's captain warned her that any interest she took in Devon could endanger his life, from either the Garlon T'zen or his own government.

Still, Kiku couldn't let it go. There was something about his honest and soft demeanor that drew her to him. And his heartbreaking worry about his lost sister touched something in her soul. Again, for half a heartbeat, she saw the face of that other young man. More and more lately she was getting glimpses of her past. Perhaps that drove her to find Devon Blackwood.

It had led her to this restaurant in a city they called New York. She remembered he'd said he was going to go there to look for his sister. It was one of the clues she'd used to find him.

"Yeah," she heard from behind the counter, in the kitchen. "I'll be there in a second."

Kiku nodded with a smile. It didn't matter that she couldn't see him. She recognized his voice. The young princess resolved to repay her informant handsomely. It was another lieutenant in her squad. When the lieutenant had seen her struggling with the Earth databases, he'd reluctantly agreed to help her. Usually Captain Jace assisted her with this sort of thing, but this time he wasn't of a mind to, telling her instead that it was dangerous and irresponsible for her to be obsessed with this Earth person. She had been rather unhappy when Captain Jace and Marlon-sensei had left the young man in the first place. Marlon had told her that Jace was right and to let it go.

"Okay." The voice moved closer, and the doors from the back pushed open. "What can I get for you?"

He froze when he saw her. Kiku glanced down at herself with a frown. She didn't look that odd. She had gotten normal native-type clothes before coming to see him. She was wearing a pair of black jeans and a white t-shirt. She was wearing her black leather Garlon T'zen jacket, with practical interior pockets with half a dozen different kinds of weapons in them. Her black military boots were the only item she thought looked a little odd. She should be passing for a native easily.

"Oh, hell," he whispered softly. Kiku smiled brightly and leaned against the counter.

"Hello! I finally found you," she said. "I wanted to thank you for helping me."

"Yeah?" Devon picked up a towel and wiped off his hands. His green eyes watched her warily. "Sure."

"You were very brave." Kiku frowned. He didn't seem very pleased to see her.

"I guess," he said. "What are you doing here?"

"I said, to thank you," she said. "And I told you I would help you with your sister."

"Yeah, well," he said. "I'd do it for anyone. Even them."

"Them?" Kiku asked.

"You know." He looked a little nervous. "The Garlon T'zen."

"Oh, us." Kiku stood up and sighed. "Does that matter?"

"A little," he admitted. "We're not really happy about the invasion."

"Our mission is acquisition and preservation." Kiku crinkled her brow. "Not domination and annihilation. Besides, they shot at us first. "

"Ugh," he said. "You make it sound like you do this all the time."

"Well, not all the time," she admitted. "Ouji-sama makes me go to diplomatic functions too."

"Who?" He frowned.

Before Kiku could answer, four men in loose, baggy clothes entered the restaurant. Something about their manner put her off. Especially when the last one, a short man with blond hair, turned over the sign on the door and locked the door. She leaned back and hoisted herself to sit on the counter facing them, watching with suspicion, her eyes appraising. Two of the men were armed under their jackets. The other two probably were too, but Kiku couldn't spot their weapons.

"Hey," Devon said. "We're still open."

"I don't think so," one of the men said. His skin brown, and he had white peppering his black hair. He walked over to the counter. His dark eyes dismissed Kiku as no threat. A faint smile played on her lips.

"If you're here to rob me, you're really going to be disappointed." Devon opened a drawer under the counter.

The man shook his head, leaning on the counter and splaying his hands.

"This joint?" He smiled, showing all of his teeth. "Not worth my time. No, you're the one in trouble here."

Kiku crossed her feet at the ankles and slid her fingers into her jacket pocket around her small hand-cannon. She glanced back at Devon with a nod. He swallowed and shook his head. She snorted softly. The man flicked his eyes in her direction. She met his gaze evenly.

They were here for a fight. She'd been on enough drops to know that they had hardened their resolve to do violence. Kiku steeled her own resolve for the same.

"Me?" Devon asked turning his attention back to the man. "Why?"

"All your questions." The speaker turned his attention back from Kiku to Devon. "Nosing around Club Felicity."

"I'm not doing anything wrong," Devon said as he stepped back from the counter.

"That's where you're wrong." The man shook his head with an oily smile. "You're causing all sorts of problems with your questions. Police kind of problems."

"The police don't have time to care." Devon drew in a deep breath. His eyes moved to Kiku for a moment. "Not when we have those aliens around."

"Yeah, well they are making the time to ask questions too," the man said, pointing a finger at Devon. "And that is bad. Bad for everyone. Bad for you."

Silence hung in the air. Then Devon spoke.

"Let the girl go," Devon said. Kiku jerked her head around and offered him a withering glare. As if she'd leave him alone. Gods, there were only four of them! "She has nothing to do with this."

"Maybe we'll have a little fun with her when we're done with you." The man's eyes felt like oil against Kiku's skin. He moved closer to her and put a hand on her thigh. He looked up at her with a smile. "You'd like that, wouldn't you, baby?"

"Hands off, cur!" Kiku spit out in Garlon T'zen. He cocked his head to one side as if trying to make out the language. But before he could speak, she swung her leg around and kicked him hard on the side of the head. He dropped to the ground, bleeding from the temple. His companions looked at her in shock before they started to grab for their small handheld weapons. She looked back at Devon. "Get down."

"What?" he said. Then she realized she was still speaking her own language. That was the trouble with English. She had to work at using it. But she didn't have time to translate. Two fired their weapons in her direction, but missed. Kiku was more accurate with her own. She fired off two hot rounds with her small hand-cannon—hit the blond man in the leg and the shorter man in the shoulder—dropping them both. The blond fired in her direction, missing her but hitting Devon in the midsection. Blood spread quickly through his shirt and apron.

"Damn it!" Kiku cursed. She sprang forward off the counter and immobilized the blond with a hard knee in the crotch and a clout on the side of the head, then swung herself back over the counter. She caught Devon in her arms as he started to collapse. She eased him down slowly against the wall, shaking her head. "You were supposed to get down."

"Yeah," he mumbled, wincing in pain. Kiku drew in a deep breath as she heard the bell bang on the door as two made their escape. The other two were bleeding on the floor. Kiku grabbed a handful of napkins from under the counter and pressed them against Devon's side. "It hurts," he whispered.

"I'm sorry," she offered. "I know it does. Keep pressure on it, it'll slow down the bleeding. What did they want?"

"It's my sister," Devon said. "This place called Felicity has been selling the videos. I did try and talk to the police, but they can't do anything."

"Because of the Garlon T'zen?" Kiku asked.

He nodded. "They're too busy worrying about them to be worrying about a bunch of kids," Devon said bitterly.

"Hrm." She frowned.

"I have to get to a hospital," he said. "Can you help me?"

"No." She shook her head. "You shouldn't move until the bleeding is stopped."

"Kiku," he whispered. His green eyes held heartbreaking worry. She smiled and pushed her fingers though his long brown bangs. If those men knew something about his sister, she had to find out more. She pulled a transponder from inside her jacket and thumbed it before sliding it into the front pocket of his jeans. "What's that?" he asked.

"Help," she said simply. "Jace-kun makes me carry these."

"Who?" Devon asked bleakly. Kiku smiled and touched his forehead with her lips. Then she stood quickly.

"Someone will be here to help soon," she said. "I'm going after them."

"Wait," Devon tried to push himself up but failed.

"Stay still. I promised I'd help with your sister," she said as she moved around the counter, tucking the hand-cannon back into the pocket of her jacket. "And that's what I am going to do."

~

Present

"Devon-kun!" Kiku banged on his apartment door. Rain poured around her out of the night sky. It had opened up with a crack of thunder just after she had left the Manor House. Kiku wondered if it was Eyanna voicing her displeasure, both with the events at the Manor and at Kiku's stubborn determination to take care of it herself. Kiku banged again on the door, louder this time. "Wake up, Devon-kun!"

"Kiku!" Devon opened the door, wincing at the light from the porch. "Kiku? It's one in the morning!"

"I'm sorry," Kiku said. She was sure she looked like a pale drowned rat. Devon looked at her with confusion. Kiku knew she didn't have much time. If General Lysis had been set loose by Leader Dessalen, all of her leads would be dead before morning. She had to find answers fast. "Get dressed. I need your help."

~

Dessalen paced back and forth inside the library. He didn't know whether to be angry or impressed. He was a little of both. Kiku had not only managed to slip out of the chamber undetected but off the Manor grounds as well. And when they were under full alert from the intruder. It was hard not to find that impressive.

Oh, he was going to kill her when he got his hands on her.

"Leader Dessalen." Marlon entered the library. The physician looked strained, but that was to be expected from the night they had had. Dessalen was about to make it worse.

"Hime-sama is missing," he said, straight to the point.

"What?" Marlon said with shock. "How?"

"Let's say she didn't approve of the way I was doing things." Leader Dessalen quirked a sardonic smile. Kiku always tried to avoid wholesale killing. She'd complained about Lysis's methods on more than one occasion. While Dessalen wholly approved of the general's results, Kiku was not so inclined. "She went out on her own. I've already spoken to Captain Jace, and he's not heard from her. Do you have any idea of what she may do?"

"I'm sorry, Leader Dessalen," Marlon said. He tipped his head back with a frustrated sigh. "I have no idea what that girl would do."

"Go find her, Marlon," Leader Dessalen ordered. "No one knows she's missing and no one knows she's wounded. Let's keep it that way. I'm sending her captain out as well. He can be trusted."

"Yes, Leader Dessalen," Marlon said, looking ill.

~

"Where are we going, Kiku?" Devon asked as she led him up through the narrow streets of Manor Town. They paused under an eaves trough as the rainwater poured down heavily around them. In some of the narrow alleys there was only room to walk. A horse and cart would never fit through them.

"The Rillian Embassy," she said. Kiku closed her eyes and leaned heavily against the wall. Her breath was short and caught in her throat. Eyanna had told her it wouldn't be easy, and she could feel the wound taking its toll on her. It felt hot and wet. Kiku wondered if maybe it was bleeding again. Shaking her head, she started to walk back out, but Devon put a hand on her arm and looked at her with worried eyes.

"What's going on, Kiku?" he asked. "You look like hell."

"You can't see anything in the dark," she half-teased and pulled away. He stood behind her for a moment.

"You're moving slow too." He slowed his step to match her pace. "I can't help you if you don't tell me."

Kiku smiled and touched his arm briefly.

"The Manor House was attacked," she said. "Someone got in."

"Is Mary—" he started. Kiku nodded.

"Mary-chan and the others are fine," she said. "And I'm going to keep it that way. I read some trade agreement that was sent by the Rillians last night. I think I know who might be behind all this, but I have to know for sure before I—"

"Before you what?" he asked urgently.

Kiku lifted her head, and her eyes glinted bright silver in the moonlight.

"I will take care of this," she vowed. "But I need to know for sure that it's who I think it is."

"You're still not telling me anything," he said.

"Not yet," she agreed. "I'm still figuring it out. I'll tell you everything as soon as I'm sure."

~

6 months ago

Captain Jace had already been out looking for her when he got the transponder alert on his wrist communicator. He and the rest of the unit were in combat uniforms walking the streets of New York City.

He'd gotten word she'd left Manor Town too late to stop her. The lieutenant who had helped her with this bit of rebellion told him where she'd gone. Jace was considering having the man whipped for his hand in it. He had rousted a detail and ordered a transport from one of the orbiting battle platforms to follow her. Captain Jace then informed Marlon-sensei that Kiku-hime was on the move. The physician had met them at the transport wearing a combat uniform. Now Marlon was waiting at the nearest Garlon T'zen station while Jace worked to recover the truant princess.

Hopefully not wounded this time. The young captain swore he was going to make the girl pay for this in training. Gods! Did she have no common sense whatsoever?

Jace worked to cool his temper when it became clear that she had activated a transponder. He tightened his jaw as he had his men secure a street where a small restaurant was located. He stepped in and quickly scanned it. Two men lay on the floor bleeding from various wounds. The smell of the laser discharge and burning flesh in the air were testimony of the princess's violence. No Kiku in sight. He looked behind the counter and felt his temper ignite.

He'd told her to let this go. But had she? No. She was being as infuriatingly stubborn as only she could.

Jace moved around the counter and crouched down next to the unconscious man. He pulled the activated transponder out of his pocket and clicked it off. Damn her anyway.

Jace shook the man's jaw gently to wake him. Devon Blackwood opened his eyes slightly and groaned.

"You," Blackwood said. Clearly Blackwood was as happy to see the captain as Jace was to see him. "She said help would come."

"Mm." Jace nodded. "The lieutenant is not stupid, just idiotic. Where did she go?"

"She chased after some guys." The man struggled to sit up. That only caused his wound to start bleeding more freely. Jace pushed him back down, feeling a bite of resentment. Like it or not, the princess had left the man with an active transponder. And while Jace was more inclined to slit his throat than help him, he knew Kiku would never forgive him for it.

"Don't move," he ordered. "I'll get a medic."

"What about Kiku?" Blackwood asked.

"How many men was she hunting?" Jace asked.

"Hunting?" Blackwood made a face.

Jace had only done a fast study at this language and it wasn't his best, but that was the word for what the princess was doing.

"Two," Blackwood answered.

"She's fine," Jace said. "She's armed."

"She's just a girl." The young man dropped his head back and closed his eyes. "They'll hurt her."

"Not likely." Jace stood up and indicated for the medic to move forward. "Once he's stable take him to Marlon-sensei."

"Yes, Captain," the man said. Jace turned and left the restaurant, looking at the darkening sky.

"Here, Captain," one of his men called to him. He'd found a fresh blood trail. He looked at Captain Jace with concern. "You don't think the princess is wounded, do you?"

Jace shouldered his weapon and indicated for the men to follow.

"Hard to say," he told them. "This is Kiku-hime after all."

~

Present

Marlon groaned as General Lysis approached on horseback in the rain. Lysis was the last person he wanted to see at the moment. But the general had spotted him and was heading right for where he was sitting on his own horse. Lysis nodded when he got close.

"What are you doing out this time of night, Sensei?" General Lysis asked.

The general was suspicious. Marlon knew Lysis could smell a lie, so decided to stick with the truth. Just selected pieces of it.

"Leader Dessalen sent me on an errand," Marlon said, peering out from under the hood of his rain jacket. Rain poured down around them. General Lysis narrowed his dark eyes, his strong features even more angular in the dim light. Marlon let a small smile play on his lips. He did enjoy annoying Lysis when he could. Like Kiku, Marlon didn't wholly approve of his methods of operation.

"What sort of errand?" Lysis demanded. He pulled his horse's head around and sidled closer to the Marlon's mount. "And why would he send you?"

"I was told to be discreet," Marlon replied evenly. "As to why he ordered me to do it, do you question the Exalted Leader when he gives you an explicit order?"

"Not usually." Lysis's lips twitched. The general turned to scan the area, perhaps to determine whether Marlon was alone. "Very well, Sensei. I'm sure we'll run into you again tonight. And I will, of course, speak to Leader Dessalen about your wanderings this evening."

"I wouldn't recommend it, General," Marlon replied. "He's in a very, very bad mood."

~

6 months ago

"There's activity on a back channel," the major at the communications panel told General Lysis. They were standing in the command center of a heavy dreadnaught class cruiser, high above the Earth. The general scowled and looked at the reading over the major's shoulder.

"The High Princess?" General Lysis asked. "Kiku-hime?"

"Yes sir." The major nodded.

Lysis rolled his dark eyes expressively in irritation. Gods, the girl was sloppy. Bad enough she was on this backwater with little protection. But she had to go out and play? That would only lead to trouble. The general was all too aware of just how much trouble she could find or cause—usually both. He pointed at the screen as he moved to leave the operations center. "Destroy that communication. And clear any back trail to it."

"Yes sir," the major said as his fingers flicked against the screens. Lysis knew his man would be able to bury any information that could lead back to the High Princess's location.

Lysis moved quickly down the corridor of his ship toward one of the launch bays. He'd make a drop with a unit to see if they could find and secure her. He had meant to speak to Tamarik about his incursion first, but given the reason for Lysis to be in this system, he wasn't so inclined.

There was a plot inside the royal house of Garlon T'zen. He had nosed it out three systems back. And all of the strands led back to the Earth. Who was behind it, he couldn't be sure. To be honest, all indications were that it was the High Princess herself. Every informer he had spoken to so far said the orders were coming from inside the highest-ranking house of the empire. To a casual observer it looked like the girl was setting Dessalen up for a leadership challenge. He rubbed the back of his neck, taking a seat in the transport, quickly buckled in, and then nodded to the pilot.

The thing was, Lysis knew the girl. She was infuriating, stubborn, and had a dangerous temper. But she was also sweet, innocent, and guileless. The image being painted for him by his spies contradicted everything Lysis knew firsthand. Lysis didn't believe she had the heart to betray Leader Dessalen. And he couldn't see her moving to take control of the Empire either. Her only real interest involved the safety of her sisters. Even the Exalted Leader fell second to that.

Dessalen was obsessed with her. Lysis had been there at Discovery. The Exalted Leader's golden eyes followed her with hot possession. If not for the curse, Dessalen would have made her his long ago.

The general closed his eyes and felt the pressure around him as the skiff plummeted through the atmosphere. This latest intelligence was actually helpful to him. He hadn't wanted to appear in Manor Town. If the town was being properly run—and there was no reason to doubt that it was—Tamarik would know the moment he landed. Lysis couldn't be sure where Tamarik's loyalties lay in this mess.

Yes, Tamarik had been unquestionably loyal to the old queen, but Lysis wasn't certain that loyalty carried over to her son. It was possible Tamarik was acting on the High Princess's behalf as her guardian, which could account for a portion of Lysis's intelligence data.

A faint smile crossed his face. This gave him a chance to maybe see the princess too, without her guardian hovering.

He didn't doubt Kiku-hime would be aggravated by his presence. The two of them got along like oil and water. She was reckless, and he had exacting standards. The general grunted, shifting positions. Too bad, that. Kiku was not only a beautiful woman, but her good heart charmed him. He'd already made up his mind that when the time came, he wasn't going to let Leader Dessalen be the only one to play suitor. He didn't delude himself that it would be easy. Dessalen wasn't going to take having competition well.

It also wouldn't hurt, he thought, if the girl just didn't dislike him so much.

~

Captain Jace found the High Princess sitting, leaning against a narrow back alley wall. All around her was the carnage she had wrought. Six bodies were bleeding their lives out on the ground. It looked like a fierce fight; the girl looked drawn out and exhausted. He motioned with his fingers and had the men fan out to guard and make sure all the bodies were dead. Shaking his head with frustration, he knelt next to her and gently touched her shoulder. Her weapon came up fast, and she held it on him for a moment. Then her eyes recognized him. She dropped it heavily to her side.

"Gods, Jace-kun," she said. "I could have shot you."

"Wouldn't be the first time," he reminded her. That earned a hint of a smile. She closed her eyes and tipped her head back against the wall. He turned and looked around. "What was this?"

"A mess," she admitted. "But I did find out where Devonkun's sister is."

"Didn't I tell you to let that go?" Jace drew in a deep breath and turned back to face her. She hadn't opened her eyes.

"Can't," she whispered.

"Are you injured?" he asked as he started to look her over. He didn't see any blood, but that didn't mean much. She could have a broken bone or an internal injury.

"Mm." She shook her head. "Just tired."

"You didn't invoke Eyanna-sama, did you?" His voice was low and harsh. A smile crossed her face, and she opened her eyes to regard him. He relaxed, seeing they were her depthless blue rather than the steely silver they turned when invoking her celestial gift. But there was glint of power that made him wary. He'd been witness to it enough times to know her celestial patron had manifested.

"Didn't have to," she said. He tightened his jaw.

That just meant the celestial had taken it upon herself to interfere. That was no good in anyone's estimation.

"Gods," he muttered. He turned to help hoist her onto his back. "Let's go."

She would be exhausted from the possession. When Eyanna manifested it always took a physical toll on her. He could carry her this way and still be able to draw a weapon if needed. He hooked her legs over his arms and started back to the station. Her arms wrapped around his neck, and her head leaned heavily against his shoulder.

"We need to rescue her." Kiku's voice was soft in his ear. He lifted an eyebrow and glanced back at her.

"Because you like the boy?" he asked.

"Because she's been chosen," Kiku whispered.

He paused midstep and felt a chill steal over his heart.

"Chosen for what?" he asked, but he knew. Just as well the princess didn't answer. He could feel her go slack on his back. He was sure she had been fully possessed and the carnage they found was the result. From the amount of death involved, that it wasn't just the princess's hand acting in the action. Kiku let men live, Eyanna did not.

Jace recognized General Lysis outside the station as he walked up. That was puzzling. Lysis was leaning against the door, obviously waiting for them. What was the general doing here?

General Lysis was the commander of Leader Dessalen's special operatives—the spies and the assassins. Mostly Lysis put down rebellion and insurrection, and he did it very well. Then Jace remembered some of the chatter he'd heard of late: a rebellion was brewing. Given that, he shouldn't really have been surprised to see the man after all.

But he was. This planet was far removed for Garlon T'zen politics and scheming. It was young, rough, and wild. Much like their High Princess.

"General." Jace inclined his head as he walked past. Lysis frowned, seeing Kiku-hime sleeping on his shoulder.

"She hurt?" Lysis asked, his sharp brown eyes looking the princess over. The general stepped close enough that Jace could feel his breath. Lysis was one of the Exalted Leader's most trusted generals. He was also one of his most beautiful, with a body practically chiseled from stone. His brown hair, cropped short, curling around his ears, framed the face of an angel.

"No," Jace said as he continued past him.

"Then what's wrong with her?" Lysis demanded as he followed.

"Nothing a nights sleep won't fix," Jace said. He moved into one of the bunkrooms and laid Kiku on a cot. She muttered something in her sleep as he pulled a blanket over her. The young captain felt uneasy as the general's eyes lingered a bit longer on her face than what was appropriate, given the Exalted Leader's unspoken claim on the princess. Jace remembered the last interaction between General Lysis and Kiku-hime. The princess was investigating a potential threat to her sisters on a holiday. General Lysis had his own way of dealing with the insurgents, that the High Princess did not approve of. It ended in a way that surprised Jace, and he suspected Lysis harbored feelings for Kiku-hime. Feelings that could earn Lysis execution at the Exalted Leader's hand.

Jace motioned for the general to follow him out of the bunkroom and then turned to face him, crossing his arms.

"Insubordinate as ever, I see. You're supposed to be keeping her out of trouble," the general said in a low, controlled voice. "Don't think I don't know where you came from, Captain."

Jace nodded. He had been under the general's command at one time, so Lysis was aware Jace was out of Leader Dessalen's Elite. It was where the general had come from himself. It was still open to speculation whether or not the Exalted Leader had released him from that oath when he promoted him to general. That was just one of the many secrets the two men kept together.

"Leader Dessalen does not care for that to be open knowledge," Jace said. Leader Dessalen had been very specific about that. His entire unit was Elite, but not even General Tamarik knew that particular. It was for the High Princess's safety. A good move, considering the girl's talent for trouble. Still, that had little to do with the general's appearance now. "What brings you planetside?"

"A plot," Lysis answered. He jerked his head in the High Princess's direction.

"Which one?" Jace asked. Plots and schemes were a staple of Garlon T'zen life. The captain couldn't be sure which one the general was speaking of, and he wasn't inclined to give him any more information than what was necessary.

"One against House Garlon T'zen," Lysis answered.

Jace frowned. "The one I know of only targets the Exalted Leader," he said.

"He is House Garlon T'zen," Lysis said in a cold voice. Jace shook his head.

"Not anymore," he corrected. "Kiku is the High Princess of the Empire. The political implications are not lost on you, I'm sure."

"Is Kiku-hime behind this?" Lysis's voice hardened. "Is she going to stand against Dessalen?"

Jace looked at him for a moment before he laughed outright.

"You give the girl too much credit," Jace answered with scorn. "It wouldn't even occur to Kiku-hime to betray the Exalted Leader."

"I didn't think so," Lysis admitted. "But everything points that this is coming from inside the house itself. Every order, every code, and it's originating here. From this planet."

"Mm." Jace nodded. He knew where it was coming from. He was really surprised that the general hadn't put it together yet. "Sadar-sama."

"What?" Lysis asked, blinking a couple of times. He drew his brows together. "That house rat? He's not even in the military."

"Doesn't mean he doesn't have supporters," Jace said. He started back down the hall to the security center, and Lysis followed behind. Jace nodded to the watch captain. "I'll take watch. Can you go check on Marlon-sensei's charge for me?" he asked the captain.

"Hai." His counterpart inclined his head respectfully to Lysis as he moved out of the small room. Once the door closed and sealed, Jace turned to Lysis. This was the only secure place to really speak.

"The plot is against Leader Dessalen by his brother," Jace told him. "And Kiku-hime is not in any danger from it."

"What do you know?" Lysis asked.

"Enough to know it doesn't involve the princess," Jace said, "so it's not my problem."

"Dessalen-sama is the Exalted Leader." Lysis's voice went cold with anger. "Where is your loyalty?"

"My orders come directly from the Exalted Leader," Jace said with little emotion. "Leader Dessalen made Kiku my only priority. He doesn't want me involved with anything that would take my attention away from her."

Lysis crossed his arms and scowled. "A Fidelity Oath." It wasn't a question, just a flat statement. Jace shrugged in an offhand manner. Lysis eyed him with irritation. "Well, that explains a lot."

Again, Jace shrugged.

A Fidelity Oath could only be sworn to a member of House Garlon T'zen. By taking it, Jace swore his total loyalty to the High Princess. His life belonged to her. It was Leader Dessalen's own request that he do so. And even with all the aggravation the young princess caused him, it wasn't a thing Jace regretted.

"I need to do some investigation," Lysis said. "I need Tamarik distracted. I am not sure of his loyalty."

"How distracted?" Jace asked as he started to flip though the screens. They lit for a moment on the infirmary where the young man was lying under Marlon-sensei's care.

"Pretty distracted," Lysis said. "This planet is the core of this. I'm going to plant some men. This thing is bigger than I thought, if Sadar has ties to the military. I need to root this out."

"The princess has an operation in mind," Jace admitted.

"The princess isn't a distraction," Lysis said. "She's a walking hazard. I don't want her involved."

"She can't get into too much trouble here," Jace told him. Lysis snorted. Jace didn't believe it much himself. "But this is something she's adamant about doing. We could do it quietly or create a sizable altercation."

They both stood in silence for a long time before General Lysis nodded once.

"All right," Lysis said. "Let Kiku have her way. Just make sure she doesn't get shot this time."

Jace inclined his head with respect as General Lysis turned and left the small security center.

~

Present

Dessalen had gone back to his chamber to change into a clean shirt. He decided to check on the girls before he made his way back to the library to wait for news of Kiku. Akane sat watching Dido, Toki, Kaori, and Mary sleep tangled together in a large bed as Leader Dessalen reached the room. She startled at the sound of his footsteps. He watched her take a deep breath and relaxed as he leaned against the doorframe watching them worriedly.

"Are they sleeping?" he asked softly.

"Finally," Akane murmured. "Mary-chan sobbed herself to sleep. She's terrified with Kiku-chan gone."

Dessalen nodded knowingly. He'd read the reports from when Kiku-hime had rescued their youngest princess. The abuse Mary-hime had suffered had been tremendous. It was hard to believe that a child so small could have been through so much. For that reason, Dessalen approved Kiku's small act of war, even if his generals had been less inclined.

Still, most hadn't been there at Discovery, when the Garlon T'zen found Kiku and the others as had been promised by prophesy. Dessalen knew well the unseen scars Kiku and the other princesses carried. They too had been treated in unspeakable ways. Once he understood the full circumstances of Mary-hime's ordeal, he knew there would be no chance that Kiku could be persuaded from action.

"Mary-chan truly believes only Kiku can keep her safe," Akane said. "I thought maybe Devon-san would be of help. But there was no answer at his apartment. I even sent a steward to try and find him."

Dessalen looked up sharply.

Devon Blackwood.

"Thank you, Akane-chan," he said softly. "Send word to me if you need anything."

"Kiku is hurt, Onii-san." Akane paused and then stepped near him and dropped her voice. "And I worry what Eyanna-sama will do. She is rash and unthinking."

Dessalen nodded, well aware of Kiku's celestial patron's temper.

"I will have her found, Akane," he said. "I swear, Kiku-hime will be unharmed."

"But how much death will follow?" Akane shook her head and crossed her arms about her. He offered her shoulder a light squeeze. He didn't honestly care if Eyanna decided to exterminate the entire town, as long as Kiku came back to him whole and safe.

"Send for me if you or the others need anything," he told her. She nodded in quiet assent.

Turning on his heel, he went to send a message off to Marlon. At least he had a direction for the physician to search.

~

"I'm sorry, but the ambassador is asleep," the man at the front door told Kiku wearily. Devon started to pull on Kiku's arm.

"C'mon, Kiku," he said. "This is insane, even for you. We can come back tomorrow."

"We won't," Kiku said with some force, pulling her arm away. She lifted her chin and banged the door open with her fist. She stepped inside and pointed at the stunned attendant. "I am the High Princess of the Garlon T'zen, and I will see the Rilli ambassador now."

"Wait! Wait!" One of the small, child-size Rillians came running out, bowed, and knocked the human attendant in the knees. "Fool! This is Princess Kiku of the Garlon T'zen! Go light a fire! I'll wake the ambassador."

Devon wore a stunned expression as they were quickly ushered into a large, opulent study. Kiku was sat on the couch and covered with blankets, which she politely accepted.

A tray of steaming hot beverages was brought by an attendant, and Kiku gratefully used a towel to wring out her sopping hair.

"You look pretty terrible," Devon said.

"I'll be fine," she said. Her shoulder was aching. "When this is over."

He was about to ask something else when a small alien woman hurried into the study with a low respectful bow. It was the Rillian ambassador. Like the other woman, she was about the size of a human child of ten, but with the proportions of a grown woman. Most of the other spacefaring races were humanoids of one type or another. Kiku's tutors had tried to explain the interrelated genetic histories, but it had only made her head ache.

"Sit, please," Kiku said. The ambassador pulled her robe tighter around herself and sat across from Kiku. "In the documents you sent to the Manor," Kiku began, "I read some things that didn't make sense. But I think there is something not right. I need to know more about these dealings you've had with the Americans."

"No. No dealings." The ambassador shook her head firmly. "Not until Garlon T'zen say. That's why we forwarded the agreement to you first. We have no interest in crossing the Empire."

"Yes, I'm sorry." Kiku closed her eyes. She wasn't good with diplomats. General Tamarik had been trying to give her more experience with them, but she couldn't help but speak her mind. She would rather take on a straight firefight than try to dance around with words. This sort of thing fell to Akane's gift, not Kiku's. "My mistake. I don't think the documents told everything. I need to know more."

"No they don't, Hime-sama," the ambassador said solemnly. "Not because you are Garlon T'zen, but because you are the avatar to a heavenly celestial, we will tell you all we know."

"Heavenly celestial?" Devon asked.

"Hush," Kiku murmured as she leaned in to listen to the Rillian envoy. She switched to Garlon T'zen to make it easier for the ambassador to communicate. "Who are the Americans working with to help negotiate this trade agreement with you?"

"The Garlon T'zen," the ambassador answered. She leaned over and poured herself a steaming cup of tea. "A high noble."

"Which House?" Kiku asked sharply. This was not going to be tolerated.

"Garlon T'zen."

"My house? No," Kiku said. "Wait. No. Sadar? Leader Dessalen's brother?"

"So it is." The Rilli inclined her head. "He and a few generals are working very closely with the Americans to secure these trade agreements. They tell the Americans that Prince Sadar has full power to negotiate."

"But that's not true!" Kiku exclaimed. Devon looked at her curiously.

"What is it, Kiku?" he asked.

Kiku set down her cup carefully. "Which generals?"

"I do not know that," the female Rilli told her. Kiku scowled. "But we do know where our contacts are staying here in town. Would that help?"

"It's a start," Kiku said. She turned to Devon. "I think I know who attacked the house. We're going to go take care of it."

"Just you and me?" His eyebrows crinkled over his eyes. "That a terrible idea."

"True." Kiku nodded. "I'll call Jace-kun."

"Ugh." Devon shook his head unhappily.

Kiku turned back to the Rilli. "Thank you, Ambassador. I will make sure that Leader Dessalen knows you helped us. May I use your communication unit before we leave?"

~

Marlon tugged the horse's head around and sighed heavily. The longer the princess was missing, the more he worried. Kiku-hime's wounds were too serious for this nonsense. How the girl had found the physical reserves to leave the Manor astounded him. But there were a lot of things about the Garlon T'zen princess that astounded him.

Not the least of which was her ability to charm their domineering leader with a blush and a smile. Leader Dessalen had sent him along when she had deployed with General Tamarik for her military training. On more than one occasion Marlon had the opportunity to tend to assorted injuries the princess managed to acquire. He had also seen his Exalted Leader dote on her when his schedule allowed opportunities to check on her progress.

The physician did not care to think about the consequences if something dire befell Kiku-hime. He didn't believe there would be any room for mercy in Dessalen's cold heart. Marlon closed his eyes for a moment, wondering if the people of this planet had any idea the kind of power they were tampering with. Leader Dessalen could easily order the destruction of the planet with a flick of his finger and turn his back, never to think on it again. The thought left Marlon colder than the rain falling around him. He had come to care very much for this place, and for the lovely Dr. Andersen in particular.

A flash lit up the black sky and the explosive boom followed close afterward. Marlon turned quickly around on the horse to look behind him. He sighed, rolling his eyes toward the heavens in frustration, and turned his mount in the direction he had just come.

Certainly Kiku-hime would be in the center of the mayhem.

~

6 months ago

"I remember you." The young man opened his eyes and sat up on his elbows. "You're that doctor that came for Kiku."

"That's right," Marlon answered. He went over to the bed with a handheld scanner. His patient was a sturdy, slim man. Other than his green eyes, he could pass for Garlon T'zen. "No fever."

"Fever?" Devon Blackwood said. He sat up a little more and winced.

Marlon nodded. "No infection. That'll be tender for a few days," he said. "Don't do anything strenuous."

Marlon pulled back the sheet and looked under the bandage. Where he had sealed the wound, it still looked white and harsh on the Earth man's skin. He nodded once with approval. "That'll fade in a day or two," he said, pulling the cover back over him.

"You kidding?" The young man peeked under the covers. "I was shot!"

"That tends to happen in the lieutenant's company," Marlon said.

"Is she okay?" the man asked.

Marlon drew his eyebrows together. He had learned their language, but some of its slang still eluded him. "Captain Jace found her before she could cause much carnage," he offered. Devon frowned.

"Is she crazy or something?" Devon asked, dropping back on the pillows. "I mean, she didn't even think about how dangerous that was."

"That does sound like Kiku-chan." Marlon's lips twisted. The lad had no idea how much trouble the princess could get into. "I heard she had a plan."

"What sort of plan?" Devon asked.

"I wanted ask him about that." Another voice came from the door. It was Kiku's captain. He inclined his head politely to Marlon. The physician acknowledged him with a flick of his eyes. "If I may speak to the man alone?"

"You hurt him, and Kiku-hime will be vexed," Marlon warned in Garlon T'zen as he started out of the room.

"I am aware." Captain Jace nodded.

Marlon didn't doubt the young captain would want to cause the young Earth man harm. Especially given Kiku's fascination with him. Still, the Garlon T'zen physician didn't believe Captain Jace would really do anything to harm him, if only for that very reason.

He headed to the mess. He hadn't eaten since the day before and was hungry. He was just relieved it wasn't Kiku herself under his care. All too often that was how these things turned out. He got a tray and sat at the table and picked at the food. Combat mess left a lot to be desired. He hoped it wouldn't be too long before they returned to Manor Town and its more civilized accommodations.

Marlon looked up to see General Lysis come in and look around, clearly looking for someone. Marlon made a face as Lysis pulled a chair around and straddled it across the table from him. The physician lifted an eyebrow in surprise. He hadn't heard Lysis was in this sector, let alone on the Earth. But he supposed he shouldn't be surprised. Lysis made it a habit to appear when he wasn't expected. That was part of his duty to the Exalted Leader.

"General," Marlon said. He lifted a hot native beverage and enjoyed the aroma with a faint smile. There were some things the planet had to offer that he did enjoy.

"I may need your services," Lysis said with no preamble.

Marlon frowned. He supposed he shouldn't be surprised by that either. "Trouble?" Marlon asked.

"Always," Lysis answered.

Marlon pressed his lips into a firm line and pushed his tray away from him. Just thinking on what he was being asked killed his appetite. "Not as much anymore. And not something I expected here."

"Can't be helped," Lysis replied.

"Does General Tamarik know you're here?" Marlon asked, looking at him sideways. Lysis shook his head.

"And I don't want him to," Lysis said. "He could be involved."

"You doubt the general's loyalty?" Marlon scowled. There were a lot of things he could believe. But that Tamarik wasn't loyal to House Garlon T'zen wasn't one of them.

"Maybe," Lysis said honestly. "It's better this way. I don't want the princess to know either."

"Planning murder?" Marlon asked.

"Probably." Lysis toyed with a spoon on the table and then looked up at Marlon. A faint smile crossed his features. "She's too softhearted."

"That's not a character flaw, Lysis." Marlon pointed out.

"No," Lysis agreed. "But it is bothersome."

"How do you suppose she won't find out?" Marlon asked.

"Captain Jace said she's got an operation in mind," Lysis said. "Something to keep her and Tamarik busy."

"Kiku does?" Marlon frowned. "That sounds problematic on its own."

"Not going to argue with that," Lysis grunted. Then he stood with a nod. "But it works for my purposes at the moment. I'll let you know where we'll be."

"Is Leader Dessalen aware of your actions?" Marlon asked.

General Lysis paused at the table for a moment.

"No," he said. "I don't have anything solid to take to him yet."

Marlon nodded and watched the general leave.

If the request for his services had come from anyone but Lysis, he would have sent an immediate dispatch to Leader Dessalen. But Marlon knew well that Lysis operated with a free hand at the Exalted Leader's behest. Marlon had been ordered to cooperate with his efforts before. There were any number of uprisings that the general put down that never earned Dessalen's notice. The Exalted Leader of the Garlon T'zen was far too busy for most minor insurrections to be brought to his attention. Lysis was apt at crushing them before most got past their infancy. Which was why he was so valuable to the man they both served.

Still, this thing with Kiku concerned Marlon. The girl could get into any sort of trouble if she wasn't watched carefully. He knew that her captain did his best, but the man had to sleep sometime. An example of this was their current predicament. The girl had a talent for disappearing when she had a mind to.

He left his uneaten food on the table and walked out of the mess. He went to the bunkroom where the young princess was still sleeping. Captain Jace had said she was just tired, but sometimes these were things that the physician had to see for himself. He moved to her bedside and ran a hand along the side of her face with a tender smile. She stirred and opened her eyes.

"Marlon-sensei," she said with a yawn. "How is Devon-kun?"

"Recovering," he said, sitting next to her. "But really, Kiku-hime, why are you so interested in this man?"

"His sister," she said. "She was abducted. Like me and my sisters. I have to help."

"There are probably thousands of children who go missing," he said. "It's the way of these primitive worlds. Why her?"

"There is something," she said and then paused. She shook her head.

The princess was keeping something more from him, but Marlon didn't push. He could always tell when she was being evasive. She'd tell him when she was ready.

"And he helped me when I needed it. I need to repay the favor."

"Not at the expense of your own safety," Marlon said. "What are you up to?"

She closed off her expression and blinked at him a few times. It was a look he knew all too well. He also knew that it was equally unlikely anyone save the Exalted Leader himself could talk her out of it. Maybe. Even Dessalen had trouble with the princess when she set her mind to something.

"I hope you aren't planning on doing something reckless," Marlon said. "Or on your own."

"She's not," Kiku's captain put in as he came into the bunkroom. Marlon glanced over his shoulder at him and frowned.

"Are you going to talk to General Tamarik about this?" Marlon asked the captain.

Kiku sat up and stretched her arms over her head. "No. Ji-chan would be mad."

"Isn't that an indication that whatever you're planning is a bad idea?" Marlon asked archly.

Kiku only regarded him with her large dark blue eyes. "You're not going to tell him," she said.

Marlon groaned inwardly. He had planned on telling the general. If only to save himself the grief he was sure to get from the man later. But now that Kiku expressed her wish for him not to, he couldn't without offering her disobedience. Even if she was only a lieutenant in the military, she was still the High Princess of the Garlon T'zen Empire. Marlon's loyalty had been sworn to her house years ago when he'd become Leader Dessalen's personal physician. A role he now shared with all the princesses.

"No, Hime-sama," he said. "If that is your wish, I won't tell him."

"Good." She smiled. Then she swung her legs around the side of the bunk and hopped off. "I need a shower, Jace-kun. Then I'll meet you in ops to work this all out?"

"Yes, Hime-sama." Captain Jace inclined his head in respect. "I've already started three sims. We can work out which one you believe is best when you're ready."

"I want to launch in . . ." Kiku paused ". . . two time parts?"

"I'll activate the men," Captain Jace answered.

Kiku turned her attention back to Marlon. "We're going to need you too. Sensei," she said. Worry crossed her features. "She's in pain. I'm sure she's in grave physical danger."

"I'll get a medpack." Marlon stood.

"Good," she said. When she had left the room, Marlon turned his attention back to the captain.

"I want it known that I find this ill advised," he said. "I am sure someone of your talents could make this happen without General Tamarik even being aware."

Captain Jace put a hand on his hip and then nodded slowly.

"I could," he admitted.

"But that's not what Lysis wants," Marlon said. The captain smiled.

"The general is looking into an issue that could spill over onto the High Princess," Jace said. "It's in her best interest to cooperate with him."

"Even if she doesn't know he's involved?" Marlon asked.

"It's better she not." Jace nodded. Marlon drew in a deep sigh.

"I'd argue that point if I didn't believe you were right," he said.

The captain put his hand to his chest and nodded in a polite salute, leaving Marlon standing alone in the bunkroom.

~

Present

It was still raining heavily, and Lysis was getting frustrated. So far, he hadn't had much luck. He was ready to call a house-to-house search to find the insurgents. If this were any place else, any other world, he would just evacuate the town and bomb it. He rubbed the back of his neck in frustration. He didn't believe that he could get permission from Leader Dessalen, given the importance of this particular holding.

And he still was damned curious to know what Marlon was up to. He didn't suspect the physician of any sort of subterfuge; it wasn't in his nature. No, Leader Dessalen had him out doing something, but what? Lysis wasn't inclined to ask. The Exalted Leader was furious over this whole mess. And a furious Dessalen was a very dangerous Dessalen.

"General," a soldier called. "We have news from the Manor House."

"What?" Lysis barked, yanking his hood off his head. The rain washed over his short brown curls and cooled him off.

"Someone ordered reinforcements out to an undisclosed location," the younger man said with annoyance. "We can't get any details."

"Order them to tell you on my authority," Lysis snapped, frowning fiercely. Marlon was out, but the physician didn't have the authority to order a squad deployment.

"I tried, sir." The soldier looked up at him, with a confused look.

"What?" How in nine hells was that possible? Lysis's codes should have been high enough to get any information from the Manor House.

Then came the ear-shattering explosion just a few blocks away. General Lysis swung back onto his horse and clattered off in that direction, his men hard after him. As he came around a corner he could see the burning inferno of a building, flames licking high into the storm-ridden sky.

When he got closer he could see that Kiku-hime was standing in front of the building, watching it burn with her arms wrapped around her sides. Near her were the Earther brother of Mary-hime and a small group Garlon T'zen soldiers who looked satisfied with themselves. General Lysis immediately recognized Captain Jace and briefly considered having the man whipped. Well, that was why he couldn't get information out of the Manor House. Obviously, the princess ordered a strike.

Idiot girl.

Anger flared as he thought of all the dangers to her safety. Was the girl mad? She was far too valuable to be running around in the middle of the night. Jumping off the horse, he strode forward and grabbed her by the shoulder, yanking her around to look at him.

"What are you doing out at this time of night?" he demanded. She gasped in pain and began to crumple in his hands.

"What are you doing?" the Earth boy shouted, jumping forward. Captain Jace grabbed hold of the lad before he could do anything foolish.

Blood started to seep through Kiku's jacket where Lysis had a hold of her. He shifted his hold lower. She looked like she was ready to drop, pale and breathing hard.

"How did this happen?" Lysis demanded. How had the insane girl managed to get herself wounded? Marlon came into his field of view and extricated Kiku from his grasp.

"Leader Dessalen appreciates you finding his lost princess." Marlon clipped his words while trying to get Kiku to lift her chin to look at him.

"His princess?" Lysis retorted. But his mind was working quickly as the pieces fell together. How would Leader Dessalen know to have Marlon out looking for the girl unless she had already been wounded to begin with? Remembering the Exalted Leader's fierce visage and bloodstained hands from early in the evening, Lysis snarled inwardly. Damn Dessalen to hell for withholding this from him.

"You can take that up with him," Marlon said smoothly. "For now, Hime-chan, we've got to get you some attention."

"No, Marlon," she said wearily. "I've got to see Ouji."

"Sorry, Princess," Marlon said softly, "but you're done. I'll take you to Andy-chan's. It's closer."

General Lysis watched as the Garlon T'zen physician carefully picked Kiku up. Marlon jerked his chin toward the Blackwood man. "I need him too," Marlon said.

"Why?" General Lysis snapped. He had planned to get some answers out of the boy. Marlon threw one of his oh-so-superior looks in Lysis's direction. Lysis growled under his breath, clenching his fists.

"She's lost too much blood, General," Marlon said. "He is a matched donor."

Lysis waved to let the Earth boy go and then sent word back to the Manor House that Kiku-hime had been found.

~

"Oh my God, Marlon!" Dr. Andersen pulled on her robe as he came in carrying a semiconscious Kiku. "What happened?"

"Where should I put her?" Marlon asked.

"My bed in the next room." Dr. Andersen grabbed handfuls of sterilized instruments and bandages before following him in. Kiku's breathing was very shallow and irregular. Marlon cut off her wet jacket and then started on her clothes.

"What did you need me for?" Devon asked helplessly from the door.

Marlon flicked his eyes over to him. He could hear soldiers filling up the outer room and outside of the building. Captain Jace stepped in behind Devon and looked at Kiku with concern.

"Kiku-hime needs blood," Marlon told Devon. "Will you give yours?"

"My blood?" Devon looked unsure, but then nodded. "Yeah, if it'll work."

Dr. Andersen frowned. "A transfusion? That could be dangerous."

"Not as dangerous as the alternative," Marlon stated. He nodded to Captain Jace. "You, get out. And secure the area."

~

The sun was coming up when Leader Dessalen arrived at Dr. Andersen's residence in the town. The rain hadn't stopped; it was still coming down in a drenching downpour. He swept past the armed guards standing all around the house and into the office. Waiting inside were General Lysis and a few other men. Dessalen looked at him with a stony expression.

"Where's Marlon?" the Exalted Leader asked.

"Back there with Hime-sama and Andersen-sensei," Lysis said. Dessalen turned away and strode to the back room. The first thing he saw was his princess lying pale on the bed. He couldn't take his eyes from her until he saw her chest fall and rise with a few breaths.

Next was the Earth man, Devon Blackwood, lying on the bed next to her asleep, Kiku-chan's head pillowed against his shoulder. Marlon and Dr. Andersen were wrapping bandages around Blackwood and Kiku's arms. Leader Dessalen felt an immediate stab of jealously seeing them together on the same bed. He shot Marlon a poisonous look of anger.

"Was that really necessary?" he snapped.

Marlon's eyes darted to the couple on the bed, and he nodded almost imperceptibly.

Leader Dessalen ground his jaw in fury. "When will she be ready to go?"

"Shortly, Leader Dessalen," Marlon said.

"No," Dr. Andersen protested. "She really shouldn't be moved."

"Kiku-hime is going with me," Leader Dessalen told the doctor firmly. Dr. Andersen looked for a moment like she was going to protest, but she backed down under Leader Dessalen's hot gaze.

He returned to the outer room where Lysis was waiting.

"I heard you put your hands on Kiku-hime-sama," Leader Dessalen said with a deceptively soft voice.

"Yes, Leader Dessalen," Lysis said. "I was—"

Before he could finish Dessalen had him shoved against a wall, his forearm against Lysis's neck. Both men were formidable opponents in hand-to-hand combat, but Dessalen had the advantage. He put pressure on Lysis's neck, choking off his air.

"Don't ever touch Kiku again, General," Dessalen said softly. "Not in anger. Not in any way. Ever."

He pulled back and slammed a fist into Lysis's jaw. The general crumpled to the floor, gasping for air. Dessalen stepped away from him—and saw Marlon and Dr. Andersen watching him from the bedroom door. Marlon had wrapped an arm around her waist, drawing her back.

"Is the princess ready, Dr. Andersen?" Dessalen asked politely.

"Y-yes," she stammered as she and Marlon moved out of his way. Kiku was wrapped in a blanket. Dessalen tenderly brushed a hair off her cheek and then picked her up carefully. The girl stirred a little but did not wake. He walked passed General Lysis without sparing a glance in his direction.

CHAPTER 4

Going down the side steps of the Manor, Kiku skipped down them two at a time. It had been over a week since the attack on the Manor, and she felt fine. Kiku had begged to return to duty, and Marlon reluctantly agreed as long as she restricted her activity. It hadn't been that long, but she credited it to lots of rest and healing sleep under Leader Dessalen's sharp eyes. Today she was back in uniform and running errands for the Exalted Leader.

It had taken more than a day before she had been able to tell Leader Dessalen everything she'd learned from the Rillian ambassador.

Anger had flickered in his golden eyes, and he kissed her forehead.

"I will handle it," he told her. "You will rest and heal."

When he took such a tone, it was clearly an order. And truly, it was for him to handle. It was his half-brother stirring up the trouble with the Americans. All of it got into house politics that Kiku never really understood. She didn't spend time at court like her sisters, having deployed to the frontier with General Tamarik. The games the nobles played were confusing and stupid.

Kiku didn't know what Ouji-sama would do, but she did have every confidence the problem would cease to exist.

True to his reputation, General Lysis had cleaned out Manor Town in short order. Her stomach turned when she scanned the list of the dead. Lysis ordered too many immediate executions, many in front of their neighbors. Over a hundred bodies were stacked and burned outside of the border of the town. Kiku didn't approve of his methods. Manor Town had always been a little rough around the edges. Its underside had provided many opportunities for contacts that Kiku would have never gotten had they not been there. Kiku worried that General Lysis's net of martial law would stifle the free trade enterprise of the town that General Tamarik had fostered to create.

She shuffled the latest imagedecks from the Capital in her hands and knocked on the library door to announce her arrival. Leader Dessalen was expecting her, so she went in. He was in council with generals Tamarik and Lysis. Kiku threw a hot glare of resentment in General Lysis's direction, and he arched an eyebrow in return.

"It was bound to happen," Tamarik said. Leader Dessalen grimaced.

"Yes," he agreed. "But I had hoped it would hold off for a few more months."

"Any particular reason, my lord?" Lysis asked pointedly.

"Lysis." General Tamarik sighed. Kiku politely handed the imagedecks to Leader Dessalen.

"Do you need anything else, Leader Dessalen?" she asked. He looked up at her with a faint smile.

"Please find your sisters and have them meet me on the garden patio in an hour?" he asked.

"Certainly." She offered an incline of her head and left the library. Kiku didn't ponder the conversation further.

Often she had no idea what Ouji-sama and the generals were speaking of, and more often she didn't care.

~

Leader Dessalen's golden eyes followed Kiku's figure as she walked out of the library. Of course, he had he reasons why he had hoped the wholesale invasion of suitors had held off a few more months.

Lysis was watching him.

"You are so obvious," General Lysis said flatly. General Tamarik made a noise of frustration and went to pour himself a drink. Dessalen's arguments with Lysis were nothing new. But this particular contention was getting bothersome.

"What if I am?" Leader Dessalen retorted. He wished Lysis wasn't so damned valuable to him. Perhaps he could start a war halfway across the quadrant and have the general redeployed.

"You can't keep her hidden away forever, Leader Dessalen." General Lysis crossed his arms. "Or any of them for that matter. Or are you planning to keep them all for yourself?"

"Lysis!" Tamarik said sharply.

"No, Tamarik," Dessalen said with good nature. "General Lysis forgets that I am legal guardian to four of the princesses. I am nothing but a protective older brother."

By being their guardian, kinship laws forbade him from acting as a suitor. That would be a wholly inappropriate.

"Too bad you're not Kiku-hime's guardian as well," Lysis growled.

Leader Dessalen nodded with a smile. Exactly right, which was why he had Tamarik be Kiku's guardian in the first place. Tamarik knew Dessalen's intentions towards the High Princess and hadn't blocked him. The real challenge was making sure that Tamarik wouldn't approve of any other suitors for the High Princess. Leader Dessalen didn't care to compete for her affection.

"There are four others, Lysis," Dessalen said as he got up to leave. "Three of whom are of age. See if one of them will have you. But stay away from Kiku."

~

"Damn him!" Lysis exploded after Leader Dessalen left the library. General Tamarik sat down heavily in a chair near the fireplace.

"Lysis," the older general said wearily. Tamarik was starting to show his age. His face, once handsome enough to attract the attention of the late queen, was lined and worried, his dark hair peppered with gray. "Why do you push him?"

"He can't do this." Lysis gritted his teeth, starting to pace. "He can't just keep her for himself. He's never allowed her any choice!"

"Of course she's got a choice," Tamarik said. "Leader Dessalen hasn't forced himself on her. He doesn't have her chained to his bed."

"He might as well have," Lysis ranted. "He moved her into his damned bedchamber!

"Yes, he did do that," Tamarik agreed. "But I think that was more to keep anyone else out of her bed than him in it."

"Don't be naïve." Lysis made a face.

"I'm not!" Tamarik shot back. "Listen to me, Lysis. I know far more about Leader Dessalen and how he feels about Kiku-chan than anyone else in the Empire. He wouldn't ever do anything to hurt her."

"How he feels about her," Lysis mocked. "She's a conquest, a possession, just like anything else to him. I know how he is from personal experience, General."

"You're an idiot." Tamarik took a long drink out of his glass.

Lysis paused and then moved to sit across from Tamarik. He lowered his voice and looked at him seriously.

"I am for asking this." Lysis nodded. "Allow me the right to court Kiku-hime-sama."

Tamarik snorted and set his drink down and leaned back in the chair. His eyes glittered with amusement.

"You, Lysis?" Tamarik asked. "Even if I wouldn't question this because of your history with the Exalted Leader, Kiku hates you."

"Hate is a strong word. And I don't think the girl hates me as much as she claims," Lysis said. He ignored the jab about Dessalen. Even if they hadn't been lovers for years, Lysis felt confident in his standing with him. "Besides, I am probably the only man that Dessalen won't kill outright for even asking."

"Don't be so sure of your standing." Tamarik drew in a deep breath and let it out slowly. "I'll put it to Kiku. If she is inclined, I'll allow it."

"Let me ask her," Lysis said impulsively.

"You're dueling death on this one, General," Tamarik said. Lysis nodded.

"She's worth the risk." Lysis smiled, relaxing. Tamarik hadn't denied him outright. He had a chance. "I can handle Dessalen."

~

The bell on the outside door to Dr. Andersen's office rang, and she looked up from her desk in the back with surprise. She glanced at the clock, noting her next appointment wasn't for another hour. She got up and found two men in suits in the waiting room. Their hair was clipped military tight, one a blond, the other a redhead. They didn't look to be the casual occupant of Manor Town nor the typical diplomat. If she were to guess, she would say some government's flunkies, just a matter of whose.

"Are you Dr. Michelle Andersen?" one of the men asked.

"Yes," she said.

"We've come to speak to you about the Garlon T'zen," the other said.

"Really?" she asked. "And why would I discuss them with you?"

"Please, Doctor," the redheaded one said. "Your government has agreed to fully cooperate with our investigation."

Dr. Andersen looked back and forth between the two men. Bloody Americans. She knew why Kiku disliked them so much and agreed with the sentiment.

"Listen," Dr. Andersen said. "Maybe my government is cooperating, but you didn't ask me. And I don't even know who you people are."

"Sorry." The blond shook his head. "That's classified."

"That's funny," she said. "Get out."

"We don't want to do this the hard way, Doctor," the redhead said.

"Are you threatening me?" Dr. Andersen asked in a shocked voice. "You've got to be kidding!"

"Doctor," the one said taking her elbow firmly. "Why don't you get your coat?"

"I will not!" She yanked her arm away. "This is ridiculous. Where do you people get off—"

And that was the last thing Dr. Andersen remembered until several hours later.

~

"Good afternoon, ladies," Leader Dessalen said, stepping into the garden. Akane was sitting next to little

Toki helping her with some Earth-type needlework. He paused a moment and took in these beautiful young women, the princesses of the Garlon T'zen. By their appearance, they were nothing alike, but their bond had been forged by the stars themselves. He smiled, setting his hand on Toki's head affectionately. "What are you making, Toki-chan?"

"A kitten!" She held up the half-finished piece. Toki hadn't yet reached her majority of sixteen years old; that was still a few months away. With her bright blond ringlets and sky blue eyes, she was easily the most indulged and spoiled by them all. "Isn't it cute, Onii-sama? Can I have one? Please?"

He laughed indulgently and held up his hands. "We'll talk about that later. Right now, there is something else."

"What is it, Onii-san?" Dido paused braiding Kaori's hair. She was long and lean with brown skin and straight copper-colored hair. Kaori's complexion was a slightly lighter shade, but her hair black with long extravagant ringlets. Kiku stood behind them, her pale skin a stark contrast to their coloring. She was leaning against a tree.

"Where is Mary-chan?" he asked her, noting the absence of their youngest princess.

"With Devon-kun," Kiku said. "Do you need her as well?"

"No." He shook his head, irritated hearing Mary-hime's brother's name. He sighed, watching them. He hadn't lied when he said he was an older brother to them, an overprotective older brother at that. He loved each one of these girls, not only for who they were but because they were the saviors of his people. He detested the position they were being put into. But it was inevitable, necessary even. "Do you all remember why we had to find this particular planet?"

"Because it's where we're from," Kaori said. "Right?"

"That's part of it," he said.

"Because the Celestials said we had to come back here," Toki spoke up.

"That too." Dessalen nodded.

"It's because of the curse," Kiku said quietly. "Isn't it, Ouji-sama?"

"Yes." Dessalen looked at Kiku. "To break the curse on the Garlon T'zen, a new Origin world for the Celestials had to be found. Since each of you is an avatar of a Celestial, and this is the world of your birth, the Celestials should accept the Earth as their new Origin world and forgive the curse."

"That's wonderful, Onii-san!" Dido beamed. "So the curse is forgiven?"

"Perhaps," he said looking at them pointedly. "But we won't know until the first one of you conceives."

"Hm." Akane made a sound, looking back down at Toki's work. Dido and Kaori stared at him dumbfounded. And Kiku wouldn't look at him at all.

"So," he said, drawing a deep breath. "Word has spread that we've secured this world and that you five are holding court here. Because of your unique status, you will soon be plagued with suitors."

"But we don't accept suitors," Kaori said.

"That," Dessalen said, "was before we found this planet. Now you're free to choose whoever you wish."

Their reaction was less than enthusiastic. Dessalen couldn't fault them for that. How they came to the Garlon T'zen was a travesty in the first place, the abuses they suffered unimaginably cruel. Sometimes the door to his room would open in the night, and one or more of the girls would crawl into Kiku's bed seeking comfort and protection.

Had he realized how much they missed her he wouldn't have kept Kiku so much apart from the others.

Each Princess had been chosen by a patron Celestial. And to each a particular gift went along with it. With gentle Akane, it had been wisdom, and there were many times he was grateful for her gift of insight. Dido was love, and not only did she have an extraordinary capacity for it, but she was able to almost magically inspire it in others. The youngest, Toki, was the healer. Dessalen knew Kiku's wounds were far too grievous to have healed in such a short time. But just living with Toki had miraculously shortened Kiku's healing to a week when it should have been a month. Sweet Kaori had brought music back to their lives with her inspired voice and talent. Music had faded from the Garlon T'zen's lips and hearts the day the curse fell up their people. The first sign of it lifting was the gift of each one of their princesses. The day of their discovery was celebrated as the highest holiday in the Empire.

And lastly Kiku. His eyes fell upon her as she lifted hers to meet his. Kiku carried the most extraordinary gift out of them all. One the Garlon T'zen would never think to get from the Celestials. Kiku was the sworn protector of her sisters, fierce and brave; throwing herself headlong into any danger for the sake of her sisters. In her blood sang the gift of war.

Dessalen needed to speak to her. He was running out of time before Manor Town would be overrun with officials from minor houses to curry their favor. Before that happened, Kiku had to choose him.

"Kiku-chan," he said in a low voice, stepping toward her. Immediately she looked alarmed.

"I-I'm sorry Ouji-sama," she stammered out hastily. "But I promised Mary-chan I would eat dinner with her and Devon-kun."

And she darted away. Dessalen stared after her for a long moment, drawing a deep breath and holding it, grinding his jaw.

"You need to breathe, Onii-san," Akane said, having moved to his side; her hand lightly touching his back.

He let out the air, rubbing his forehead in frustration. Akane pulled him by the arm away from the others with a smile.

"Kiku-onee is just frightened," Akane said soothingly.

"Of me?" Dessalen asked with shock.

"Not you especially, but certainly the circumstance." Akane shook her head. "Just be patient. With coaxing, she'll come to you."

~

"Ah, there you are now. How are you feeling, Michelle?" a friendly voice asked. Dr. Andersen fumed silently in the pleasant sitting room. At least it wasn't a cold white-walled interrogation room like in the movies. Instead, it was parlor with warm furniture and fire burning brightly in the fireplace.

"I'm mad as hell," she snapped, pushing her brown hair out of her eyes. "How dare you kidnap me?"

"Would you care for some tea, dear?" asked an older lady carrying in a silver tea service. She was grandmotherly down to her gray hair and half-moon spectacles perched on her face.

"I would certainly not," Dr. Andersen said. "I want to leave."

"All in due time," the first voice and along with it, its owner came into view. It was an older man wearing a tie and sweater, probably near his late fifties from Dr. Andersen's guess. He was balding, but his eyes looked kindly enough. "I am terribly sorry about the boys just grabbing you like that. Sometimes they don't think things through."

"Damn right they don't," Dr. Andersen said indignantly. "What is this about anyway? And who the hell are you people?"

"We're from the Central Intelligence Agency," the man said. "My name is David Smith."

"I'm sure it is," Dr. Andersen muttered. Mr. Smith's lips twitched.

"This is my wife, Amanda." He motioned to the lady pouring the tea. "We've been living in Manor Town since its foundation. And again, I apologize for the boys. They're new and don't understand about good manners."

"Meaning if the Garlon T'zen knew you kidnapped me it wouldn't go very well for you?" Dr. Andersen asked.

"Let's just say Amanda and I have been here long enough to know that it wasn't a very smart thing to have done." David shrugged. "So, why don't we start again?"

"Why don't we not?" Dr. Andersen smiled.

"Before you say that," Amanda interrupted as she handed Dr. Andersen what looked to be a middle school yearbook, "why don't you take a look at this?"

Amanda Smith fingered the pages to where there were several sticky notes and then pointed out a picture in the middle of a row of others. Dr. Andersen wrinkled her brows and pulled the book a little closer. That was damned odd. The picture was several years old and in black and white, but the likeness to Kiku was striking. Under the photo, the name read "Jennifer Davis."

"Huh," Dr. Andersen mused. "Everyone has a double, they say."

"Don't you find that interesting?" Mr. Smith asked with surprise.

"Not terribly," Dr. Andersen said.

"Would you find it interesting that that girl has a brother?" Mr. Smith pressed on, pointing to a picture to the immediate left of the first. "A twin? His name is James Davis, Jimmy."

"I don't see the point of any of this." Dr. Andersen shook her head, closing the book and handing it back to him.

"Princess Kiku is Jennifer Davis, Doctor." Amanda sighed. "It's a terrible story."

"Jennifer Davis was kidnapped from her home five years ago when she was thirteen," Mr. Smith continued. "She and the other girls, these princesses, are all originally from the Earth. Our sources have told us they are part of a Garlon T'zen breeding program."

"That is the most lame-brained crackpot thing I have ever heard," Dr. Andersen snapped out. "And that's saying something, because I've heard a lot!"

"We can prove it," Mrs. Smith said. Then she paused and looked at Dr. Andersen seriously. "Well, we can with your help."

"I wouldn't help you prove the sky is blue," Dr. Andersen said.

"Oh?" David Smith said. "I was under the impression you cared about Princess Kiku."

"Of course I care about her." Dr. Andersen fumed, crossing her arms, looking away.

"Then you should want to help her," Mrs. Smith said kindly. "If we're wrong, we're wrong. It's been known to happen. But I don't think we are. But if we're not, then Jennifer, and the others, should be returned to their families."

"You're wrong." Dr. Andersen rolled her eyes.

"Jimmy Davis will arrived in Manor Town tomorrow morning," Mr. Smith said. "He's a well-mannered eighteen-year-old lad. We'd like him to stay with you."

"With me?" Dr. Andersen asked.

"He's here on a cultural work study for high school. At least that's what we told him. It was a little tricky, but it worked out," David Smith said.

"You mean the boy doesn't even know about this?" Dr. Andersen asked.

"Of course not, Michelle," Mr. Smith said. "That would violate national security."

"You people." Dr. Andersen felt a headache coming on. She drew in a deep breath and rubbed her temple with her fingers.

"What we need you to do, is run a DNA comparison," Amanda Smith said. "Totally independent of what we have. You have access to Princess Kiku, so I don't suppose it would be a problem for you, would it?"

Dr. Andersen paused for a few moments looking back and forth between the two of them. How could they be serious? Kiku wasn't from the Earth. And they drag this poor boy from America over to be a test subject to their schemes with no thought to his feelings in the matter either?

"You have no way to get Kiku's DNA." Dr. Andersen smirked, realizing exactly why they needed her.

"We could." David Smith made a face. "But it would be rather risky. And potentially dangerous to the princess herself."

Dr. Andersen paled thinking of all the ways they could get Kiku's DNA, and she didn't like any of them. Better that she agree with their silly plot, prove them wrong and send them packing. She sighed deeply in annoyance.

"All right," she said, closing her eyes. "I'll do it."

"That's a good girl." Amanda beamed. "Now have some tea."

~

It was late when Kiku finally returned to the Manor House. Leader Dessalen could hear her quietly put Mary-chan to bed and then make her slow movement through the rooms checking on each of her sisters. Then she slipped into the bedchamber they shared with a click of the door. He waited a few moments before doing anything.

He got out of bed and slowly made his way to her. Her back was toward him. They still needed to talk. And if he had to corner her in their bedchamber, dressed in only his sleeping shorts, to do it, then so be it.

"Kiku-chan," he said in a low voice. She whirled around with her muscles taut, ready for an attack. He hadn't expected that, but he shouldn't have been surprised. Dessalen did note her form was far better than the last time he had observed her spar. He grabbed her arm and pulled it around her back and wrapped his other arm around her waist, pulling her tight against him. It wasn't what he had planned, but it would serve it if was the only way he could hold her attention. "Kiku-chan," he admonished playfully in her ear.

"Ouji?" She relaxed against him as she realized he wasn't an intruder. "Sorry."

He released her arm but kept a firm hold on her waist, keeping her tight against him. With his free hand, he tilted up her chin, running a finger along her jaw, his bright golden eyes never leaving her dark blue. She returned his gaze steadily. "What are we going to do about this thing between us?"

Her cheeks colored, and she swallowed. "I don't know."

"Is there someone you favor more, Hime-chan?" he asked, softly lightly tracing her lips with his finger. Her breath caught, but she shook her head.

"N-no," she stammered.

He leaned down close and gently kissed her lips. "Not the Earth boy?" he teased with a smile, inches from her mouth. Her eyes held confusion as her head tipped back, and she leaned forward.

"Mm?" she murmured softly returning his kiss. Dessalen kept a tight rein on his reaction. He longed to divest her of her uniform and—

He had to stop those thoughts right there. Instead, he carefully matched her pace, not wanting to frighten her again.

"Hime-chan," he breathed into her ear. "Let me…"

"Ouji." She stopped him, touching his face with her hand. Her face glowed bright red. "I . . . I don't know what do. I've never…"

Her voice trailed off. Amused, Dessalen smiled gently down at her. He cupped her face and kissed her, this time slipping his tongue into her mouth. He stopped to look at her, nose to nose.

"Don't worry, Princess," he whispered. "I know what to do."

Dessalen paused for a moment, if she wanted to stop, she had to do it now. She held fast in his arms and leaned up on her toes to find his mouth with her own. He groaned in anticipation, feeling his pulse quicken. He started to unbutton the top of her uniform shirt as he nibbled along her jaw. Her hands splayed on his bare chest.

A sharp knock on the main door broke the moment, and he was torn. Gods! He was so close! Dessalen swore under his breath as he gave Kiku a longing kiss. He yanked the door open full of fury.

"My pardon, Leader Dessalen," said the lieutenant, looking very uncomfortable under his ruler's hot gaze. "The proxy alarms are going off in the system. General Tamarik is calling the command council."

"Fine," Dessalen snapped, slamming the door shut. He turned back to Kiku, who was hurriedly refastening her shirt and heading to his closet to find him a clean uniform. He was going to kill someone for this; he just had to determine who.

"Kiku-chan." He grabbed her hand, stopping her motion. She looked up expectantly. He kissed her wrist with glittering eyes. "We will finish this later."

"Hai," she answered, dropping her eyes.

~

When Jimmy Davis appeared on her doorstep the next day, Dr. Andersen was immediately shocked by his uncanny resemblance to Kiku. His hair was the same honey shade of blond, and the shape of his face and nose could have been stamped out of the same mold. But even more so were the same striking deep blue eyes that looked like they could see into forever. Only, Jimmy's eyes held a pain that seemed to simmer just under the surface. But other than that, the lad was a sturdy boy with an easy smile.

"Hi, Dr. Andersen. Nice to meet you," he said when he shook her hand. "Thank you so much for having me. I'm looking forward to my stay here. The whole place is pretty cool."

"You think so?" Dr. Andersen asked with an amused glint in her eye. "You'll get tired of the horses soon enough."

"No way!" he enthused. "Not having cars around is nice, and the air is so clean. How do they do that? Is it an alien thing?"

"Not having cars is a start," Dr. Andersen said. "Come along. I'll show you your room. I enrolled you in the high school here in town. You'll start on Monday, so you'll have a couple of days to explore the town."

"You mean I can do that?" Jimmy asked with surprise.

She looked up as she led him into his room. "Sure. Why not?"

"Well, at home they said Manor Town was like under martial law, and you had to have passes and stuff." He dropped his duffle bag on the bed. "The news said the Garlon T'zen didn't allow anything to go on here. That's why the media aren't allowed in."

"No." She made a face. "I mean, nothing like that. I'm not sure why they don't let the press in but I think it's mostly for the privacy of the off-world ambassadors. It does make it rather more pleasant. But no one will bother you if you go exploring. Just stick to the main roads and be polite. You shouldn't have any trouble."

"Okay." He grinned. "Wait until I tell my friends when I get back home. Oh, unless I can e-mail them. Do we have internet here?"

"No, sorry," Dr. Andersen called over her shoulder. "That is for security. The Garlon T'zen have some pretty strict communication rules when it comes to Manor Town. They call it a 'secured settlement.' All telephone communication in and out of Manor Town is restricted to the embassies. But you can write letters to your friends and family."

"You can't even call home?" he asked following her out to the main waiting room of the office.

"No," she said. "I write my Mum often. She understands. I do call her once a week from the British Embassy. There are public phones at the American Embassy that you could use to call home if you needed to as well."

"Oh," Jimmy said. "No one told me that. What about inside Manor Town?"

"Old-fashioned telephones." Dr. Andersen pointed at the phone sitting on the desk. "Although, I don't think they use actual wires. They just made them look that way."

"No cell phones?" he asked.

"No," she replied. "And only the Garlon T'zen military have portable communicators at all. If you have something like that, you could get yourself into trouble. "

"So the Garlon T'zen are pretty strict?" he asked worriedly.

"Very much so." Dr. Andersen looked at him. "But don't worry about it. Listen, before you go, I need to get a blood sample from you."

"Why?" he asked. Dr. Andersen led him back to the examination room and had him hop up on the table.

"To get a baseline of your current blood count and antibodies," she replied. "You're going to be exposed to a lot of new things. If you come down with something I want to know what you didn't have before you got here."

"I guess that makes sense." He winced as she expertly inserted the needle and handily drew out two vials of blood.

"There you go." She put a cotton ball and piece of tape over the draw point. "Now, why don't you wander around a bit and learn your way around?"

"Sure!" He hopped off the table and strode out the door while rolling down his sleeve.

Later, Dr. Andersen stared at the vials of blood for a long time before she did anything. The whole thing was ridiculous. She couldn't even believe she was being made a party to it. She didn't have to collect any samples from Kiku. She still had plenty from the night Marlon had brought her in bleeding to death. Prior to her transfusion with Devon, Dr. Andersen did a hasty type match between the two of them even though Marlon had assured her that there would be no problem. How Marlon had the foresight to have done so was beyond her thinking. But then he had been Kiku's physician longer and, given Kiku's propensity for trouble, probably had a ready list on hand of anyone who could give blood to the princess if required.

She was also lucky in that she had a small DNA lab at her disposal. Because of the wide variety of patients she was now attracting and because of the communication prohibitions she had to have the equipment to run her own tests. Something the American spies surely knew. Dr. Andersen doubted they would have any more luck getting communication out of the town than anyone else. There would be no way they would get this sort of material out of the town for analysis. They were using her for their dirty work, and she resented it. At least she had the satisfaction of knowing she would be able to tell them they were flat wrong.

Or at least she did until she stared at the results of the tests in dumbfounded shock three hours later. Her heart pounded in her ears as she looked over the results for the fourth and fifth time. She swallowed hard so not to be ill and looked around the small lab. Making her up mind, Dr. Andersen went into action.

She took the remaining vials of Kiku's blood and dropped them into her pocket while she zeroed out the results on the machine. Then she set fire to the results and dropped them in the sink. Dr. Andersen washed the ashes down the drain and drew a deep breath, trying to ease her shaking hands.

The streets of Manor Town were crowded at this time of day. Dr. Andersen wasn't sure if she was thankful for that or not. She was worried she would run into Blondie and Red as she started to make her way up to the Manor House. She had the distinct feeling she was being watched and it would only be a matter of time until one or the other of them made an appearance.

Sure enough, she spotted the blond standing on a nearby corner watching her. Dr. Andersen felt her heart leap up into her throat but continued with her brisk, purposeful walk. He fell into step beside her, and she pointedly ignored him.

"Going somewhere, Doctor?" he asked.

"I do have a life," she snapped.

"Mr. Smith is waiting for the results of your tests," he said tightly.

"Mr. Smith will have to wait until I've collected all my samples," she replied. She paused and looked at him.

"We don't have a lot of time, Doctor," he said touching her arm. She jerked it away from him.

"Don't touch me," she said.

"Don't be that way." The blond smirked. "You know we can always…"

"Is everything all right, Sensei?" a Garlon T'zen patrol officer asked in a clear tone from behind them. The blond CIA man composed his face instantly and tried to move off into the crowd but was immediately stopped by another uniformed officer.

"No." Dr. Andersen wasn't sure if she should be relieved or more worried. But the officer noted the glare the blond was giving her and with a jerk of his chin had him taken farther out of earshot. Dr. Andersen's hands were shaking. "I need to get to the Manor House. I need to see Marlon-sensei."

"Of course, Sensei," the Garlon T'zen officer said crisply. "Immediately."

He spoke into his wrist communicator and said something to his companions. Then he offered his arm to her with a smile. "I would be most honored to escort you there."

~

"Andy-chan!" Marlon said with surprise when Dr. Andersen fled into his arms and started to shake. "What is it?"

He nodded politely to the guard captain, who bowed and left the two of them alone in his office in the basement infirmary of the Manor House. He held her for a long time before she shoved him away and looked at him with accusing eyes.

"Why didn't you tell me?" she demanded. Marlon looked at her with bewilderment.

"Tell you what?" he asked.

"That Kiku is really from the Earth," she said with hot anger.

"Oh," Marlon replied. He was surprised it took so long for the Earth doctor to figure it out. "That."

"Yes, that!" Her voice shook with anger. "Don't you think that was worth sharing? Do you want to know what her real name is?"

"Kiku-hime-sama of house Garlon T'zen," he replied.

"No!" Dr. Andersen shouted back, near hysterical. "No! Her name is Jennifer Davis. Kidnapped from her home in America some five years ago!"

"Hm," Marlon mused. "That's probably about right."

"You knew!" Dr. Andersen's cheeks turned red. "You knew! She was kidnapped by the Garlon T'zen—"

"Don't." Marlon cut her off with a flash of temper. "Don't ever say we abducted them."

"Then how?" Tears dropped from her eyes.

"There are other spacefaring races, Andy-chan," he said. He moved forward and pushed her tears aside tenderly. He had been there at Discovery, and had treated Kiku for the first time then. Even now, he was still furiously angry over the treatment of their princesses before the Garlon T'zen found them. "Kiku-hime and the others were stolen, or even possibly traded, by slavers."

"No." Dr. Andersen shook her head. "We never had any contact with anyone outside Earth before the Garlon T'zen."

"That's not true," Marlon replied quietly. "I'm sorry, it's a painful picture. But it's true. That's why the Garlon T'zen established the Special Earth Preservation Zone. It created a guarded perimeter around your system that keeps the slaver ships out and makes trading in any of your domestic products illegal unless a treaty has been ratified and approved by the Garlon T'zen."

"But—" Dr. Andersen sat down in a chair, speechless.

"That's why Manor Town was established," Marlon continued. "Many races that had been previously trading with your governments, without the benefit of a treaty, are being forced to obey the same laws that are enforced by most civilized cultures. This is to protect your people. Otherwise your planet would be stripped bare and left as a husk with your people enslaved inside twenty years."

"And the Garlon T'zen enforce these treaties?" she asked slowly. Marlon nodded. "Why? What do you get out of it?"

Marlon drew a deep breath and sighed. There was only so much he was willing to reveal to the doctor, as much as he cared about her.

"We got Kiku-hime and the others," he said, which was true. "And since this is their home planet we have a responsibility to protect it."

"That's it?" she asked skeptically.

"For the most part." Marlon shrugged.

"There's a problem." Dr. Andersen dropped her eyes. "The American's believe that Kiku and the others are from the Earth. The said they had it on good authority that it's true."

"They do," Marlon said coldly.

"You know?" she said with surprise.

"We know who their authority is," he said with a frown. "And Leader Dessalen is not amused."

"They found out who Kiku really is," she continued. "And they sent her brother."

"Hime-chan has a brother?" Marlon asked with delighted surprise.

"I ran some tests," she continued. "I think they know I ran the tests, but they don't know the results. Oh no!"

"What is it, Andy-chan?" Marlon asked with concern.

"It's Kiku's brother," Dr. Andersen said with worry. "He's wandering around Manor Town. He doesn't know. If the Americans find him, I don't know what they'll do."

Marlon frowned in thought. "Well, then we'll have to find him first."

~

Jimmy Davis walked through the center of Manor Town taking in the sights. He wished he had a camera with him, but the only one he had been part of his cell phone. He'd been told not to bring his phone, and he didn't have the money to get something before he got on the alien transport for Manor Town. He sighed wistfully and shoved his hands deeper into his pockets.

Manor Town was amazing, sort of a cross of a medieval town and the Star Wars cantina scene. The streets and walkways were paved with smooth stones. There were shops, and aliens, and humans, and black-uniformed men patrolling the streets. He could smell strange foods as he walked by restaurants sporting names in a foreign script he could only assume was in an alien language.

True to Dr. Andersen's word, no one said a thing to him. He thought for sure someone would have stopped him and demanded he explain what he was doing there. But most folks offered polite smiles with a nod. It was like the small town his grandparents still lived in. His heart did drop to his stomach first time he saw a Garlon T'zen patrol. Tall, muscular dark-haired men wearing simple black uniforms. They were terrifying.

Jimmy drew a sigh of relief when the Garlon T'zen barely flicked an eye over him and moved on. He would probably piss himself if they spoke to him. He shook his head with disgust with himself.

He didn't think he would have been as afraid of them if the news at home wasn't full of horror stories about the ferocity and unbending will of the Garlon T'zen. There was no end of television specials with accounts told by traders of the other races about the Garlon T'zen and their stranglehold on the galaxy. Things he only dreamed of in cheap sci-fi movies seemed to be coming true in the guise of the malevolent aliens who had taken up residence on their planet.

This was an unbelievable opportunity for a kid from Southfield. He didn't even know how he had been picked for it. He'd been told it was a lottery-type program.

His mom hadn't liked the idea of him coming. She begged him not to go, but he had to. Jimmy tried to help her—and he got it, he did: losing his sister had destroyed him too. But maybe this was his chance to make a change. This was his break away from her endless rounds of drinking. She was killing herself. Jimmy hadn't even bothered to tell his dad he was going. Why should he? He was eighteen. He didn't have to tell him shit.

Jennifer had just got on the school bus one day and ever came back. Unlike his mother, he carried no illusion she was alive somewhere. That sort of thing didn't happen. When he was packing his bag, his mother begged him not to go, that she couldn't lose another kid. He promised her that she wasn't going to, and he'd be home in three months.

He stopped in front of the American Embassy and looked at the tall wood-framed building. It had a flag proudly waving from the roof. Here there were no gates or walls to protect it as there were at the embassies in other countries. He supposed that the Garlon T'zen had more to do with the architecture than the Americans. He also noted there were no armed soldiers to be seen either; another oddity that wouldn't probably be found at any other American embassy.

Remembering what Dr. Andersen had said about telephone calls outside of Manor Town, he opened the door to the public waiting room and stepped inside. It wouldn't hurt for him to give his mom a call and let her know he had made it there safe and that he would only be able to write her letters for the next few months. A young dark-haired man was speaking on the phone. He nodded to Jimmy and held up a finger, mouthing, One minute.

"Yeah, I know," the man said to the phone. He was wearing a white shirt and black tie. He looked Hispanic to Jimmy and sort of young to be working in an embassy. Jimmy didn't think he was much older than he was. "C'mon, Mary, don't be like that. Listen I have to go. Yes, now. I'll talk to you later tonight. Yes. I promise."

The young man hung up the phone, rolling his eyes. Jimmy couldn't help but smile.

"Your girlfriend?" he asked.

"Worse." The young man grimaced. "My sister. What can I do for you?"

~

"We need to handle this carefully," Marlon told Dr. Andersen, leading her upstairs. "General Tamarik should be advised before we do anything."

Marlon stopped an attendant to ask where the general might be. Learning he was in command council with Leader Dessalen, Marlon made a face. He motioned for Dr. Andersen to follow him through a narrow hallway that led to a small security center.

"Captain Jace." Marlon nodded as they came in. The young captain looked up expectantly. "Dr. Andersen is trying to locate a new arrival. What did you say his name was, Andy-chan?"

"James Davis," Dr. Andersen said hesitantly. "He's just a lad of about eighteen years."

"Can you get his likeness from the arrival disbursement?" Marlon asked the captain.

"Certainly," Captain Jace said. He typed a few things on what looked like a flat table to Dr. Andersen. Then a holographic image of James Davis floated in the center of it.

"Use surveillance and locate the boy," Marlon said. The captain nodded, typing out the commands.

"And then?" Captain Jace paused looking back at Marlon.

"Observation," Marlon said. "For now."

"Yes, Sensei," the captain said. The image of Jimmy disappeared. Marlon then led Dr. Andersen back out of the small room.

"You can do that?" she asked.

"Do what?" Marlon asked as he tapped out a note on an imagedeck and passed it off to a nearby attendant.

"Just order that someone be watched, or something?" She looked at him pointedly. He rolled his eyes with a sigh.

"Don't be dramatic," he said.

They went to the library to wait for the general to join them. When he did, he looked at the two of them with a stern expression.

"This had better be important, Sensei," General Tamarik growled. "The session is likely to go on for many more hours, and Leader Dessalen is in a foul mood."

"I'm sorry, General." Marlon bowed with a hand on his chest. "But this is urgent, and it has to do with Kiku-hime."

The general sighed heavily and poured himself a drink. "What has she done this time?"

"Believe it or not, General, it's nothing like that." Marlon's lips twitched. "Andy-chan, please tell the general everything you told me."

"I-I'm not sure where to start," Dr. Andersen stammered under the general's hard gaze.

After Dr. Andersen had explained her tale, Marlon sent her off to the gardens to wait for him. He stood with General Tamarik in silence for a long moment.

"What do you want to do about this, General?" Marlon asked.

"Send the boy back to America." General Tamarik nodded. "Have him collected and deported."

"You think that wise?" Marlon asked. "The Americans already believe he's Kiku's brother."

"But they have no proof," General Tamarik said. "Andersen-sensei said she destroyed the evidence. The lad has been brought here under false pretenses. We would deport anyone under those circumstances. Honestly, it's the best way to keep him safe."

"Is that fair to him or Kiku-hime?" Marlon felt a pang of pity. Kiku valued her sisters as her family. How would she feel to know that she had a blood brother still alive?

"He is not my problem," General Tamarik said gruffly.

"And Kiku-chan?" Marlon asked softly.

"Kiku-chan carries too many scars to face this." General Tamarik dropped his head. "I'll not put her through it."

"Yes, General." Marlon nodded, turning away to carry out the general's orders.

~

When General Tamarik returned to the command center, three levels down in the Manor House, Leader Dessalen noted his arrival with irritation.

"Good you could rejoin us, General," the Exalted Leader snapped. "Since you called this proceeding in the first place."

"My apologies, Leader Dessalen." General Tamarik inclined his head. "There was a matter that required my immediate attention."

Leader Dessalen tapped the imagedeck he had in hand against the table and narrowed his eyes. He wanted this over. He thoroughly resented being yanked into a command council when he had very nearly—

Dessalen clenched his fist in frustration.

"We're done," he announced pushing himself away from the table to stand.

"But, Leader Dessalen, what about these unregistered ships entering the system?" General Kassius protested. "We need to decide how to proceed."

"Oh, that is very simple, gentlemen," Leader Dessalen said coldly. "Destroy them."

~

"Onee-sama?" Mary crept quietly into the small study where Kiku was napping on the couch. Kiku hadn't had much time to sleep, having spent most of night in the command chamber with Leader Dessalen, and then the rest of the day running errands for him. She had been dismissed earlier, and she was desperate for just a little sleep. "Kiku-onee?"

"Mm?" Kiku opened one eye blearily. "What is it, Mary-chan?"

"It's dinner time, Onee-sama," Mary said with a smile. "Devon called and asked if we could meet him at the Ivey's Gate."

"Oh gods, Mary," Kiku groaned. "I'm dead. Can you see if someone else will take you?"

Mary crossed her arms and stared at Kiku. Kiku tried to ignore the child but it wasn't working.

"Captain Jace would be happy to take you." Kiku sat up with a yawn. "So would any fine officer in the Garlon T'zen military. Would you like me to find you a general?"

"I want Kiku-onee," Mary said stubbornly.

"Hai, Hai." Kiku smiled, shaking her head. She gave Mary a playful shake. She paused, seeing Leader Dessalen standing in the doorway. Mary turned and smiled brightly at him.

"Good evening, Leader Dessalen," Mary called out.

"Hello, Mary-chan," he said, giving her shoulder a light squeeze as he walked by.

"Leader Dessalen." Kiku felt her face color and nervously dropped her eyes. He stepped close, and Kiku had to crane her head to meet his eyes. "I'm sorry."

"I heard," he replied. "Very well, Kiku-chan. Don't be too long."

Leader Dessalen drew up her chin with two fingers and leaned down to kiss her. Kiku honestly thought her legs were going to turn to rubber as her heart began to race. She swallowed with difficulty.

"I'll be waiting," he whispered, and Kiku nodded.

~

"So you're staying with Dr. Andersen?" The young man working at the embassy was Devon Blackwood. He was a friendly sort, with an easy smile. When he learned Jimmy was new in town, he offered to take him to dinner with his little sister and one of his friends. Dr. Andersen hadn't said he had to be home at any set time, so Jimmy agreed.

He figured a guy from the States could tell him a lot more about Manor Town than Dr. Andersen could.

"Yeah." Jimmy nodded. "You know her?"

"Sure." Devon smiled. "She's my sister's doctor. Nice lady too. You know, you look kind of familiar to me. You ever been to New York City?"

"Never," Jimmy said. "Maybe I have that kind of face? So how come you're here in Manor Town? You seem pretty young to be a diplomat."

"Yeah," Devon answered. "It's complicated. I'm not a diplomat; I just work at the embassy. Let's go to the restaurant, and I can try to explain. It's a crazy story."

Ivey's Gate, Jimmy learned, was a Garlon T'zen style of restaurant. Devon thought that Jimmy would like to try the food as long as he was staying in Manor Town.

"Is it crazy different?" Jimmy asked. They were offered patio seating outside. The sun was just setting, and there was a light nip in the air. "The weather is so different in this part of the world. At home, the leaves have just started to change, here it's spring."

"That's not a Garlon T'zen thing," Devon said. He turned to the waiter, who appeared human, but was he? Jimmy had to admit, he couldn't tell the difference between the Garlon T'zen and humans. "Can we get an English menu?"

"Of course," the waiter said and moved off.

"Is he human?" Jimmy asked dropping his voice. Devon met his eyes for a moment and then he nodded.

"Yeah, but he's probably Garlon T'zen." Devon said. Jimmy looked confused.

"I don't understand," he said.

Devon nodded and thanked the waiter as he brought their water and two menus. He set his aside.

"They are just a different race," Devon said. "But we're the same species. At least that's how one of their doctors explained it to me. They come from a different planet, but somewhere, somehow, nearly all the aliens are really human at their core. Just certain traits are more common with some than others because they don't intermarry too often."

"But what about evolution?" Jimmy asked. "Does that mean that everything originated on Earth? We've got like bones and stuff from thousands of years ago."

"I tried to get Dr. Marlon to explain that, and he said that goes too far back in their historical records." Devon looked troubled. "But he did say that Earth is not unique in having evolution. I'm not sure he was using the right word, though. Sometimes their English is iffy. He told me to study up on Garlon T'zen, and he'd see if he could get me enrolled at their academy on their Capital world. It's like college."

"Oh?" Jimmy asked with surprise. "Really? Why would they let you?"

"They kinda adopted my sister," Devon said. "It gets even more crazy than that, but that's as good of an explanation as any. They saved her in New York City. That's another long story too."

"How old is your sister?" Jimmy asked with interest. "And what about your folks?"

"Mary is eight," he said. "And our parents were killed in a car accident three years ago. It's just me and her."

"I'm sorry," Jimmy said. Devon shrugged, but then brightened and pointed.

"There they come," he said moving to stand. "That's Mary and Kiku. Kiku is one of the Garlon T'zen princesses."

"Here?" Jimmy stood and turned around. He looked at the two approaching figures and felt like his world was drawing in around him. His heart froze in his chest.

She was older. She'd filled out a lot since she was thirteen. But she still had the same face. His face. But she was wearing a black military uniform. She hadn't been paying that much attention to them as she came, and she froze when her eyes fell on Jimmy.

"Oh my God." His voice sounded a hundred miles away. "Jennifer!"

~

The blood drained from Kiku's face when she saw the young man standing next to Devon. From the wide-eyed stunned look on his face he recognized her too.

"Oh my God," he said. "Jennifer!"

He grabbed her in his arms and hugged her. Kiku stood frozen for a moment and then shoved him away, feeling stark terror.

"No!" she said with ferocity. Mary stepped closer to Devon and took his hand, looking between Kiku and the newcomer worriedly. "Don't ever call me that!"

"But—" The young man looked bewildered. Out of nowhere, men were trying to take hold of both Kiku and him. A redheaded man sneered near her ear as he pulled a weapon. Kiku felt the familiar rush of adrenaline as her training took over her actions.

"That's all we needed to know," he said, menacing her with a handgun. Kiku immediately yanked the man's hand around and deftly broke his wrist. "You bitch!"

Kiku swung her legs under him, knocking him to the concrete, and yelled to Devon, "Get back to the Manor!"

Devon hoisted Mary into his arms and turned to run with his sister when the shots rang out. Kiku looked wildly around, and her eyes went wide with terror as she watched Devon drop to the pavement.

"No!" she screamed, fighting her way to make it to his side. "Devon-kun!"

Blood was pooling around his body, and he had multiple wounds in his back and head. Tears welled up in her eyes as she touched him and knew he was already dead. Mary had been shielded by him but had taken a hard hit to the head from the fall and was unconscious. Bullets continued to fly, and the street was filling with Garlon T'zen soldiers. Kiku knew there was nothing she could do for Devon, and her priority was Mary.

She pulled the child into her arms, shielding her as best she could. Seeing a nearby horse she snatched the reins from its owner with a yank and swung up into the saddle with a mighty heave. Her legs protested with pain, and she was sure she pulled a muscle from Mary's extra weight. She gripped the girl to her body tightly as she leaned into the horse, holding on with the strength in her knees.

Kiku took to the streets of Manor Town at a full gallop, going to the Manor House. She could hear the sirens warning the citizens off the streets as soldiers deployed to the center of the disturbance.

When she clattered into the courtyard at the Manor House, it was already chaotic with activity. Someone yanked the head of her horse to bring it to a stop. Kiku nearly fell out of the saddle. She was pulled down off the horse by the yard officer, who looked at her and Mary's bloodstained clothes with troubled eyes. He bellowed orders into the air, and it was only moments before Marlon was trying to pry Mary out of Kiku's arms.

"Let her go, Kiku-chan," Marlon said urgently. "I need to take a look at her."

When Kiku's eyes focused, and she realized who he was, she released her death grip on the child, and Marlon pulled Mary away swiftly to give her attention. Kiku knelt there for a long moment. Tears fell from her eyes and she made no attempt to stop them. Clenching her hands into fists she got up and turned on her heel and headed toward the barracks.

"Captain Jace!" Kiku yelled at the top of her lungs. A corporal stopped and looked at her.

"Hime-sama?" he asked.

"Find him," she ordered.

"Hai!" He hurried off. Kiku turned and ran directly into General Lysis.

"What are you doing?" he demanded. Kiku stepped around him. "Don't ignore me!"

"Hime-sama!" Captain Jace came running out of the Manor House. The young captain's eyes raked her over for a moment and then he nodded, seeing the blood on her uniform.

"We have a mission, Captain." Kiku kept walking, still ignoring the general.

"What's the mission, Hime-sama?" Captain Jace asked.

"Search and destroy," Kiku said with little emotion.

"Belay that," General Lysis snapped at Captain Jace. He stepped in front of Kiku. "You will do no such thing."

"Get the men ready, Captain," Kiku ordered over her shoulder.

"Yes, Princess." Captain Jace inclined his head and turned on his heel, walking away.

"You can't do this." General Lysis pointed a finger in her face. There was a commotion at the gate and a wave of grief nearly overwhelmed Kiku as she watched Devon's body being brought into the compound. She pushed the unbidden tears roughly from her cheeks.

"You can either help me," Kiku said evenly. "Or get out of my way."

CHAPTER 5

Leader Dessalen moved his horse up next to General Lysis's. It was full night, and Kiku had waged her private war against the insurgents, setting their holdings in the town on fire. Captain Jace had been keeping the Exalted Leader informed of her progress. Kiku had taken most of the opposition into custody, and they were being held in the landing field outside of town under heavy guard. Leader Dessalen would have executed them immediately, but Kiku hadn't made that decision. The Exalted Leader would take care of that detail for her soon enough.

"Are you going to let her burn down the whole town, General?" Leader Dessalen asked. General Lysis turned in the saddle to acknowledge his arrival. Firelight flickered on Lysis's attractive features, and he nodded politely.

"If she wants to," General Lysis replied. Leader Dessalen's lips twitched into a half smile. He'd let her do the same at this point. But her sisters were desperately worried about her, and letting Kiku go on like this wasn't doing her any good. It was time for his princess to come home.

"My thanks for keeping her out of trouble," Leader Dessalen said, kneeing his horse forward to where Kiku was farther down the hill.

"I didn't do it for you," Lysis retorted.

"Hm." Leader Dessalen smirked. It didn't matter. He knew he would be Kiku's choice when she was ready. However, in light of these events, Kiku was going to need time to grieve. His horse clip-clopped as it got closer to her. "Kiku-chan."

"It's my fault, Ouji," she said not taking her eyes from the flames as they licked the sky. She was sitting on her gray mare. "I got distracted. It would have never happened if I hadn't—"

"That's enough, Kiku." Dessalen cut her off shortly. She turned and looked at him with eyes that held heartbreaking pain. Dessalen immediately resolved there would be swift retribution for it. He drew in a deep breaht and continued. "Mary-chan is safe and alive. That is the most important thing."

"But—" she protested.

"Wouldn't Devon Blackwood want the same?" he asked. Kiku choked back on a sob and dropped her head, her loose hair obscuring her face. Dessalen sighed and slid off his horse. He walked purposefully over to hers and pulled her down into his arms. "Kiku-chan, you didn't do anything wrong. You protected your sister. Leave the rest to me, ne?"

Kiku broke down as heart-wrenching sobs racked her body. She clung to the front of his uniform burying her head into his chest. Dessalen held her tightly, pressing his forehead against the top of her head.

~

It was a slow ride back to the Manor House. Kiku sat in front of Leader Dessalen on his horse. Armed soldiers surrounded them on horse and foot. Captain Jace was still in town on Leader Dessalen's orders. Manor Town on high alert and Jace-kun was conducting a house-to-house search for other insurgents and agents. Kiku didn't want to come back, but Ouji-sama had been firm.

He swung off the horse first and then pulled her against him in a lingering hug before he stepped away from her, his face grim.

"I will take care of this, Kiku-hime," he assured her in a quiet voice. The men were filing in around them. Kiku lifted her eyes to meet his. "Go and stay with your sisters. Mary-chan, especially, needs you here tonight. Do you understand?"

"Yes," she said. She understood, but agreed to nothing. She would see to Mary-chan and then find Jace-kun. He looked at her with wary eyes and took her arm by the elbow and started to pull her toward the house.

"Lysis," Leader Dessalen said over his shoulder. "Find Tamarik and Makiellen and tell them I want their time."

"Yes, Leader Dessalen." Lysis was leading both his horse and Kiku's towards the barns. She looked in the general's direction and felt a flutter of emotion.

"Wait." She pulled away for Leader Dessalen and went after General Lysis.

"Kiku!" Leader's Dessalen's tone was sharp, but she ignored him.

"I should take care of Dolly." Kiku put her hands on the reins to take them, but General Lysis refused to let them go. He glanced back at Leader Dessalen first and then looked down at Kiku.

"No, Hime-sama." Lysis's voice was gentle, but firm. Kiku's face heated as she looked up at him. He looked at her with a serious expression. "I will take care of your horse myself. You need to see to your sisters."

His eyes met hers and she felt . . . what? Something.

He'd been . . . kind. Usually, he argued with her. Or worse, was coldly indifferent when she expressed her disapproval of his actions. Tonight, he was supportive. Stayed close. Didn't countermand her order to spare the prisoners. Tonight, he had been what Kiku needed him to be.

"Thank you." Her voice was whisper-soft. His face softened, and he leaned down to speak quietly in her ear.

"Go to Dessalen before he has a stroke, Hime-sama," he said with light humor. "And please stay at the Manor until the town is secured?"

She wasn't going to make that promise to him either. She set her face in a stubborn expression. Lysis muttered a curse as she turned and returned to Leader Dessalen's side.

"Come, Kiku-chan." Leader Dessalen frowned fiercely in Lysis's direction before focusing his golden eyes on her face. He took her arm again and pulled her gently toward the house. He paused in the entryway and looked as if he was going to speak, but they were interrupted.

"Leader Dessalen." It was Marlon-sensei coming across the wide foyer, his boots sharp on the marble floor. "Ah, you found our princess."

Marlon smiled gently at Kiku and dropped a hand on top of her head. Kiku couldn't muster a smile and Marlon looked at her with sympathy. "You didn't get hurt, did you, Hime-chan?"

"No, Sensei." Kiku shook her head once. "How is Mary-chan? I asked Jace-kun to check, but no one would tell him anything."

"Come see for yourself," Marlon said. He nodded to Leader Dessalen. "I'll take the princess to her sisters."

Leader Dessalen looked torn and then nodded in agreement.

"All right," he agreed. The Exalted Leader offered Kiku's shoulder a light squeeze. "I expect your report after Kiku is settled, Sensei."

"Of course," Marlon said. Leader Dessalen turned on his heel and walked away with purpose. Kiku watched him go feeling conflicted. He was angry, but not with her. She hated him leaving her, but he had to. Marlon nudged her and offered his arm. Kiku wrapped her fingers around it as they went up the stairs. "Mary-hime had a head injury. It was very serious."

"Is she still in the infirmary?" Kiku stilled. Marlon shook his head and pulled her along.

"I said was, Hime-chan." Marlon's voice soothed. Kiku closed her eyes and let his calm wash over her. Marlon-sensei had been the first to care for her all those years ago. She trusted him as much, maybe even more, than Ouji-sama himself. "Toki-hime came."

"Ah." Toki held the gift of healing from her Celestial patron. She had only invoked it for Kiku or her other sisters before, but it made sense, Mary-chan was Celestial chosen too. Mary Blackwood was as much her sister as the others. "Is Mary-chan in her room, then?"

"I had to sedate her," he said, pausing outside of the wide double doors that lead to the outer room of the suite. "I know she's got a lot to face, but we needed you back before she did. Also, Andy-chan returned to her house. Mary doesn't like me to touch her."

"Yes," Kiku nodded. "I know."

~

"How did this happen?" Leader Dessalen demanded. He had generals Tamarik, Lysis, and Makiellen in the library. Marlon-sensei stood nearby, having returned after settling Kiku in with her sisters. The physician gave his report on the Americans activities prior with Dr. Andersen. Leader Dessalen was furious this could have transpired in Manor Town at all.

"I'm not certain," General Makiellen replied.

"That's not good enough!" Dessalen raged. "Do you know how lucky you are that it's not Mary-hime or, Gods help you, Kiku who is dead?"

"Yes, Leader Dessalen." General Makiellen paled.

"I don't think you do," Leader Dessalen said, his voice cold and fierce. "We have a security breach. For all I know, we have insurrection from inside the Manor House itself."

"That's not possible," General Makiellen denied. "Everyone here is loyal, my lord."

"You think so?" Dessalen replied. He flicked his eyes in General Lysis's direction. "Lysis?"

"It's probable," Lysis agreed with a nod. "I want to start interrogating the captured combatants. With your permission, I would like to use Marlon-sensei."

"Ugh." Marlon grimaced.

"Use your discretion," Leader Dessalen said. And then he looked at the physician. Marlon looked unhappy but composed his features under Leader Dessalen's hard gaze. "And you cooperate with the general."

"Yes, Leader Dessalen." Marlon inclined his head.

"When you are finished," Leader Dessalen said. "Execute them all. Not one of them lives for this, Lysis."

"Yes, Leader Dessalen," Lysis answered. His dark brown eyes met Dessalen's with a slight nod. Lysis was insubordinate and aggravating, but unfailingly loyal. Dessalen could trust him with this.

"My lord, if I may," General Makiellen interrupted. "That may be a bit harsh! They are acting under orders of their superiors. Surely—"

"Ah, that is correct," Leader Dessalen agreed. "Lysis, find out who issued those orders so we may take appropriate action."

It wasn't difficult to discern Leader Dessalen's meaning. General Makiellen stood stiffly with his hands clenched at his side.

"I protest," he said. "This is a preserve, your orders have been—"

"I'm giving you new orders, General," Dessalen interrupted. "I am done playing games with these savages. This place will be safe for our princesses."

General Makiellen dropped his head and refused to meet Leader Dessalen's eyes. The Exalted Leader shook his head with frustration.

"Makiellen and Lysis, get out," he ordered. He pointed at Tamarik. "You, I'm not done with."

After the others had filed out, Tamarik stood under Leader Dessalen's hard stare for several moments before he spoke.

"Is something on your mind, my lord?" Tamarik asked politely. Dessalen growled under his breath, longing to do violence.

"Why didn't you tell me about this brother of Kiku's?" Dessalen demanded.

Tamarik paused for a moment and then squared his stance, and raised his chin.

"Because it was not your concern," Tamarik informed him. Dessalen's blood burned with hot anger. "It is a matter for me, as her guardian, to decide. Not you as a potential suitor."

"Everything to do with Kiku is my concern," Dessalen yelled.

"I don't agree," Tamarik retorted. Dessalen came dangerously close to lashing out at the general but restrained himself. As Kiku's guardian, Tamarik did have oversight in her affairs. Dessalen himself couldn't be both Kiku's guardian and suitor. The conflict for Kiku's best interest would be apparent and unacceptable to the house nobles. Dessalen had always known where his relationship with the princess would lead, which was why the general was Kiku's guardian.

"Damn you!" Dessalen slammed both his hands against the desk. He began to plot the swiftest way to remove Tamarik from the equation. Kiku was precious to him, and he detested someone else having more control over her welfare than him.

"Where is the boy now?" General Tamarik asked.

"I sent him home with the Earth physician," Leader Dessalen said.

"I want him deported," General Tamarik said.

"I don't," Leader Dessalen replied.

"You can't do this." General Tamarik clipped out his words. "You're interfering."

"I have always interfered, General," Leader Dessalen snapped back at him pointing a finger. "You may be her guardian, Tamarik, but make no mistake, Kiku is mine."

~

"Do you want to talk about it?" Dr. Andersen asked Jimmy. He was staring out the window listlessly. They were sitting in her small kitchen. She made him a cup of hot tea, and it was cold in front of him. It was late, but he wouldn't be able to sleep. Her words drew his attention, and he refocused his eyes on the doctor.

"I'm sorry," he apologized. "Did you say something?"

"I asked if you wanted to talk about it," Dr. Andersen repeated. "This has to be overwhelming."

"I don't even know where to start." Jimmy shrugged, returning his dark blue eyes back out the window. "How did this happen? Why does my sister act like she doesn't even know me? Why is she being treated like some alien princess? How is she even alive? I don't understand."

"I'm sorry, James," Dr. Andersen said with sympathy. "I can't answer those questions. But I can tell you that Kiku is—"

"Her name is Jennifer," Jimmy said. His face flushed with anger.

"All right, then," Dr. Andersen said calmly. "That Jennifer is a princess of the Garlon T'zen and—"

"That's not possible." Jimmy ground his teeth. He shook his head. "She's just a girl. An American girl. And my sister. She doesn't belong with them."

"I don't know the details," Dr. Andersen admitted. "But I do know a lot happened to your sister these past five years she's been missing. She's made a life with the Garlon T'zen, and she is happy."

Jimmy tightened his jaw. "I don't believe it," Jimmy said. "They've brainwashed her or something."

Dr. Andersen sighed and leaned back in the chair.

"I'm sure we'll learn more tomorrow," Dr. Andersen said. "Come along. Let's try and get some sleep."

~

The door opened with a gentle swing, but the room was dark and still. Leader Dessalen frowned with concern and went to Kiku's bed to find it empty. Shaking his head he went to the other set of double doors and quietly entered the sitting room shared with the princesses. There he found

Akane and Dido sitting on a long couch speaking to each other in soft tones.

"My pardon, ladies," he said softly. "But where is Kiku-hime?"

"She's sleeping with Mary-chan, Onii-san," Dido said, dropping her eyes. Her long brown hair was pulled back into a long braid that went nearly to the floor. She looked somber and serious. Dessalen closed his eyes in brief thanks, feeling his stomach unclench. He knew Kiku hadn't intended to stay at the Manor tonight. He didn't think to send Marlon to sedate her until after the physician had left with General Lysis.

"Toki-chan went in to join them just a bit ago." Akane pointed toward the younger princess's door.

Leader Dessalen went to Mary's room, quietly opening the door to look in. Until he saw Kiku himself, he would worry all night. Toki raised her head to look at him when he entered.

"Onii-sama," she whispered.

"Shh," he responded. Toki dropped her head back down on the pillows. She was on one side of Mary and Kiku the other. They all looked pale and drawn out, and Kiku seemed to be sleeping soundly. Toki was running a hand along Mary's head. Dessalen suspected the girl was using her Celestial gift to ease the child's emotional pain. He wondered if she had done the same for Kiku.

"Onee-sama won't wake up until morning," Toki said as if answering his question. His golden eyes met hers of pale blue. He felt the echo of power. Ah, so they were taking a more active role in this matter. Not that Dessalen minded. Anything that would ease his princess's pain would be welcome, even Celestial interference.

"Thank you, Toki-hime." Dessalen inclined his head and left the room. There was little he could do. And if Toki said Kiku would sleep the full night, he ought to try and do the same.

~

The knock had come painfully early in the morning. Dr. Andersen wrapped her robe around herself and opened the door. A uniformed Garlon T'zen soldier bowed and handed her a bright white linen envelope.

"Thank you." Dr. Andersen stepped back into the small house, toward the kitchen. She found James still sitting where she had left him the night before. "James, didn't you go to bed?"

He shook his head and leaned his forehead into his hands. She sat across from him and opened the envelope warily reading the contents.

"We've been invited to the Manor House for tea." Dr. Andersen folded the envelope closed. James jerked his head up looking both terrified and angry.

"Why?" he asked.

"Well," Dr. Andersen said. "You are the princess's brother."

"Can we not go?" James blurted out.

"Don't be silly," she said eyeing the envelope. She had never been so summoned by Leader Dessalen, and she didn't feel that comfortable with it. The few encounters she had had with the Exalted Leader of the Garlon T'zen had been brief and unpleasant. "I don't think it's something we can decline."

James paled. Maybe that hadn't been the best way to put it. The lad had been understandably shaken up by the events of the night before.

"This may be your chance to learn about what happened to Kiku," Dr. Andersen said. He raised his eyes to meet hers and clenched his jaw.

"Jennifer," James said.

"Yes," Dr. Andersen said. "About that. Where we're going, don't correct anyone about her name."

James looked pale and stubborn, and Dr. Andersen offered a silent prayer the boy had more common sense than it looked.

~

General Lysis was leading his horse into the barn when he saw Captain Jace returning with his men across the compound. Lysis needed to wash the stink of death away, but first he needed to speak to the young captain.

"Captain Jace," he called out. The captain's combat uniform was covered in soot and he carried his helmet in one hand. He looked in the general's direction and started forward with a nod.

For his part, Lysis had been out most of the night with Marlon, and his own uniform was splattered with blood and bile. The physician hated the work, but his skills were required. Lysis learned disturbing details about the Americans and their allies. Internal factions in the Empire were nearly ready to move against Leader Dessalen, and they didn't have much time. At least one unknown general was going rogue, and if experience had taught Lysis anything, it was no one acted alone.

General Lysis handed the reins of his horse a stable hand as Jace came to stand in front of him.

"General," Jace said.

They stood off from each other. Jace was a strong, well-built soldier. He was also resourceful and cunning. It was unfortunate Leader Dessalen had tied him to the High Princess. Lysis could have used him.

"Captain," Lysis acknowledged. "Good hunting?"

"Moderately so." Jace nodded to a few of his men who were passing by with their horses and weapons. "I need a clean uniform and then to report to the High Princess. We still need to take the American Embassy, and she wanted to be part of that action."

Lysis frowned sharply.

"I don't believe Leader Dessalen will approve of her involvement," Lysis said. And neither did he. Gods.

"I don't believe the High Princess cares what the Exalted Leader approves of." A faint smile crossed the young captain's lips. Lysis ground his jaw and shook his head angrily.

"You can't be serious," Lysis retorted, but Jace only arched an eyebrow. "I want the embassy left alone today; it'll give the rats time to scurry there, thinking they're safe. I'll take it tomorrow before the funeral."

Jace nodded slowly, but then—"Hime-sama could still order us out," he said.

"That's why you're not going to be at the Manor," General Lysis said. "I want you to take a detail and see to Dr. Andersen's security."

"The Earth physician?" Jace asked.

"And her charge." Lysis nodded, and then realized that Jace didn't know that particular bit of intelligence. "He's Kiku-hime's brother. The Americans found him and brought him here to confirm her identity."

"Brother?" Captain Jace looked at him sharply. Lysis nodded. "Kiku-hime is going to go out whether I go with her or not. I need to be here when she does."

"No," Lysis said. "She won't. I'll keep an eye on the princess and will contact Leader Dessalen to intervene if she tries. I don't have a bothersome oath in my way to make sure she behaves herself."

Captain Jace drew in a deep breath and looked off for a long moment, refusing to meet the general's eyes. Lysis wasn't certain the captain would agree, and his oath to the princess made it impossible for Lysis to enforce any order. Damn Dessalen anyway. This complication could be laid wholly at the Exalted Leaders feet.

"You underestimate the princess, General," Captain Jace said. "I also don't believe your interest in her is healthy."

"Don't be insolent," Lysis said with mild humor.

"Hime-sama—" Jace started and then shook his head. "There is much you don't understand, General. I'll go and guard her brother's life, for her."

"None of us will get much sleep for the next few days, Captain," Lysis said and relaxed a little. Lysis's plan would work as long as Captain Jace went along with it.

"We just came off three tours in the frontier fighting the Ma'gaar." Captain Jace offered a look of scorn. "Are you getting soft, General?"

Lysis eyed the captain as he turned and walked away from him. Gods, the man was insubordinate. He'd have to take it to Dessalen sooner than later. Jace's oath protected him from Lysis, but not necessarily the Exalted Leader.

Lysis turned to get a shower, and a clean uniform. Then he would find the High Princess and try to keep her from mischief.

~

At breakfast, Kiku nodded politely to her sisters as she sat down next to Mary. The girl was only staring listlessly at her plate.

"Come on," Kiku coaxed. "Eat a little toast and drink some juice?"

Mary shook her head without speaking. Kiku felt her heart sink. She had no words of comfort. She looked up at Akane, who offered a gentle smile.

"Mary-chan needs time," Akane said.

"I don't understand," Mary whispered. Her brown hair fell around her face. "Why did Devon have to die?"

Kiku looked at her helplessly. He didn't have to die, he just did. But the last thing her eight-year-old sister needed right now was Kiku trying to explain that.

"I can take Mary back to her room," Dido offered. "Would you like that Mary-chan? I'll read you a story if you like."

"Will you come too, Kiku-onee?" Mary asked, her light green eyes pleading. Kiku had wanted to find Jace-kun. But she should report to Leader Dessalen first.

"In a bit," Kiku said. "I need to speak to Leader Dessalen first."

"About what, Hime-sama?" Leader Dessalen came striding into the dining room. He took a seat across from Kiku. Dido was getting Mary up from her chair, and Kiku waited until they left before she spoke. He looked after the young princess with concern.

"Are you going to need me today, Leader Dessalen?" Kiku asked. Akane made a noise, and the Exalted Leader flicked his eyes in her direction first. Akane shook her head once, and Kiku felt a flare of resentment. Were they all plotting against her?

"I think you should stay at the Manor House today, Hime-chan," he said.

"Do you need me then?" Kiku asked. She pushed her plate away and looked at him.

"No," he said. "You are released from duty until after the funeral."

"Thank you, Leader Dessalen." Kiku pushed herself away from the table. He stood when she did. Akane put her hand on his forearm, and he shook it off and followed closely behind Kiku. They were in a narrow hall, and he pulled her around by her shoulder. She looked up at him feeling another wave of resentment.

"You may not leave the Manor House today," he told her sternly. Kiku's dark blue eyes flashed with hot temper.

"Ouji-sama!" Kiku exclaimed. "I have work to do."

"Not today." He stepped back and let out a deep breath. "Until Lysis cleans this up, I want you here."

"Lysis," she hissed. "Do you know what he will do?"

"It is my will," Leader Dessalen said mildly. His expression softened, and he moved closer, tipping up her face with a light finger. "Oh Hime-chan, I know you're in pain. You need time. Let me take care of this. Swear you'll stay at the house."

"I—" Kiku paused and bit her lip. She turned her eyes away. "Please don't make me."

"Swear," he whispered leaning forward to touch her lips with his. Kiku's eyes flooded with tears. She blinked them away with a little nod.

"I promise," she said quietly. "I'll stay at the house."

He drew in a deep breath and pulled her into his arms. "Thank you, Hime-chan."

~

It was half past one o'clock when Dr. Andersen and Jimmy arrived at the Manor House. An attendant bid them welcome with a deep bow. Next, they were ushered into a large sunroom that looked out over the gardens. Dr. Andersen marveled at the beauty of the house once again.

It was hard to believe that the Garlon T'zen had it all built without help from any Earth architects, because it looked like an old estate house out of somewhere in Europe.

"Ah, Andy-chan." Dr. Andersen turned to see Marlon smile as he entered the sunroom. "Thank you for coming today."

"Marlon," Dr. Andersen said with surprise. "I didn't think I would see you."

"Mn." He made a noncommittal sound. He turned to James Davis and inclined his head politely. "And you must be James-san."

"Just James," the lad replied. "Or Jimmy."

"I'm honored to meet you," Marlon said. "I am Marlon and have had an opportunity to know your sister quite well."

"You could say that," Dr. Andersen said dryly. Marlon snorted softly with a nod.

"Andy-chan." Marlon smiled winningly. "Please join me for a walk in the garden?"

"But I'm supposed to meet Leader Dessalen," she said.

"Yes," Marlon said. "I know."

"But—" she protested even as he wrapped an arm around her waist and led her away.

"Don't worry, James-san," Marlon said over his shoulder. "I'll return her later."

"Marlon!" Dr. Andersen tried to pull away, but Marlon held her firmly and steered her towards the gardens. "Let go."

"But I like holding you." He teased her with a smile.

"But Leader Dessalen," she said, looking over her shoulder with worry.

"Now, Andy-chan," Marlon scolded. "Do you really believe I would do something Leader Dessalen didn't wish to happen?"

Dr. Andersen felt a sharp pang of worry, her eyes widened with fright.

"What about James?"

"Leader Dessalen wants to speak to the boy alone," Marlon said. They were standing close together. "And to be honest, I wanted some time with you."

Dr. Andersen paused, looking up into Marlon's dark eyes. He was troubled behind his smile. She reached up and touched his face. He closed his eyes and leaned into her hand.

"What is it?" she asked.

"I—" he started and then stopped. He caressed her cheek with two fingers. "I need you."

Dr. Andersen could feel her heart race, and her mouth went dry. He watched her face seriously. She had been attracted to him from the first time they met. Marlon was tall, slender, but still well built, his features sharp and smooth, with dark hair. Everything any woman would be attracted to. Being this close to him filled her with a need for more. It seemed like an eternity since they had last shared a kiss. All they had ever shared were promises that never came to anything.

Maybe now it was time?

She leaned up on her toes and kissed him gently. Was she ready for that something more? God! Was this the time to even be considering it? But when she paused and opened her eyes to see his hunger, her heart answered before her head had a moment to stop her.

"I'd like that," she whispered.

~

The boy was waiting alone for Leader Dessalen in the sunroom as he had ordered. Marlon-sensei had done his work and the Earth woman wasn't to be found. It was better this way. Dessalen didn't need her in his way.

The boy looked up expectantly when Dessalen entered and looked at him with a mixture of alarm, and perhaps a hint of anger. What struck the Exalted Leader first was his resemblance to Kiku. The same honey-colored hair, but his short cropped. The same features in the face; only with Kiku's they were softer and more muted. But most of all, they had the same dark blue eyes. The boy was certainly her brother; just by looking at him there was little disputing it.

But how much was he really like Dessalen's princess? That was the real question.

"Good Afternoon," Leader Dessalen said. "I am Dessalen of the Garlon T'zen."

"Hello." The boy shifted uncomfortably under Leader Dessalen's steady gaze. "My name is James Davis. Um. Thanks for inviting me."

"I wanted the opportunity to meet you," Leader Dessalen said. "Princess Kiku is very precious to me."

"Jennifer," James Davis said, his voice low and stubborn, his face pale as he raised his dark blue eyes to meet Dessalen's golden. "Her name is Jennifer Davis, and she's my sister."

Leader Dessalen regarded the boy for a long moment. He had generals that wouldn't speak to him in such a manner. But as he watched James, the young man's stubborn eyes wouldn't falter even though he was clearly frightened. Dessalen decided the boy was far more like Kiku than he had anticipated.

"That may be true, James Davis," Leader Dessalen replied with a small smile, "but Kiku is my princess. Now, shall we have some tea?"

~

Her consent made his heart sing. Marlon started to avidly kiss Dr. Andersen's jaw working his way down her neck, his dark eyes darting around wondering where they could go for some privacy. He decided they could go back to his small room in the Manor House. He was fortunate enough to have a private room on the first floor. Leader Dessalen had decided that the physician needed to be near when Kiku had been recovering and thought it prudent to keep him close on hand for any other mishaps as well.

Marlon tugged on Dr. Andersen's hand with a smile, drawing it to his lips for a quick kiss before leading her back into the house. Together they moved quietly through a few halls. It only took moments to be inside Marlon's small room with a click of a lock.

Marlon pulled her red hair loose of its clip and let it cascade around her shoulders. Gods, he wanted her. Marlon leaned down and tasted her lips, losing himself in the touch of her flesh. He needed this badly; after his long night, he needed her. She didn't smell of fear and urine. She wasn't afraid. Marlon started to unbutton her blouse while he slid his hand under to touch her soft skin. He would bring her pleasure instead of the pain he had dealing so much in of late. Dr. Andersen's fingers undid the buckle and slipped her hand down the front of his pants.

"Andy-chan!" He gasped into her neck. She offered a throaty chuckle.

"C'mon, Marlon," she said, her voice laughing in his ear. "Can't you take it?"

Marlon smiled, forgetting his troubles, and pulled her onto his bed.

"I can." He grinned as she moved to straddle him. "But I plan to give back as well."

"Oh, I do hope so," Dr. Andersen replied as she leaned down to kiss him once again.

~

Jimmy sat stiffly in the chair across from the leader of the Garlon T'zen. He couldn't believe he was actually sitting with the head person himself. The President couldn't even get in to see this guy, and he, Jimmy Davis, was having tea with him.

And he was scary. Why hadn't Dr. Andersen come back before this Dessalen person had shown up? Where had the other Garlon T'zen guy taken her? Why was she being kept away? And why was the leader of the Garlon T'zen having tea with him in the first place?

Leader Dessalen sat back and regarded Jimmy with those strange golden eyes and an impassive expression.

"Kiku and the others had been sold to slavers in a system very far from here," Leader Dessalen said, toying with the spoon on the table. "How that came to be is unclear. We don't know if they were stolen, sold, or traded from your planet."

Jimmy stared down at the table and swallowed hard. He didn't know if he believed him or not. He had thought the Garlon T'zen had taken them. Now he didn't know what to believe.

"We found them on a trade planet known as Slarlis, approximately three of your years ago. I don't know how many times they were sold or passed along." Dessalen's voice grew cold. Jimmy looked up and he could see real anger flicker over Leader Dessalen's features. "They were brutalized and their treatment horrific. We don't even know the full extent of what happened to them. But it is heinous and illegal in any of the Garlon T'zen territories. And as a result, they don't have all of their memories from their past lives. They are all, still, deeply scarred from the ordeal."

Jimmy felt a cold pit in his stomach. Was that why Jennifer didn't recognize him? She didn't remember him?

Leader Dessalen dropped the spoon on the table angrily and looked away for a long moment before he continued.

"Kiku, Akane, Dido, Kaori, and Toki managed to stay together and survive," Dessalen said.

"How?" Jimmy asked, his voice breaking with emotion.

"No one knows outside of the Garlon T'zen," Leader Dessalen said. "And it is not information we share."

"I don't understand," Jimmy said.

"You don't need to," Leader Dessalen said. "What you do need to know is that the five princesses, six now with Mary Blackwood, are very precious to the Garlon T'zen. And their welfare is our foremost concern."

"But they're from here, Earth," Jimmy protested. "How can they be Garlon T'zen royalty?"

Leader Dessalen looked at him for a long moment, and then ignored the question.

"I would like you to attend Devon Blackwood's funeral tomorrow," Leader Dessalen said. "And I'm going to have you and Dr. Andersen moved to the Manor House today. I am not satisfied with the security of Manor Town."

"What?" Jimmy looked at Leader Dessalen with pure shock. "I-I can't live here!"

"You will," Leader Dessalen said. "Now why don't we find your sister? Hm?"

~

It took little time for Leader Dessalen to discover Kiku-hime's whereabouts. He questioned a nearby attendant and got an answer that made him frown. When he had released her from duty, he had hoped she would take some time to rest, perhaps spend it with her sisters. And while he appreciated she hadn't left the house grounds, sparring in the exercise yard was not what he had in mind.

James Davis followed sullenly. The boy wasn't happy about being moved into the Manor House, but Dessalen didn't care. Part of the reason Devon Blackwood was dead was because he had lived outside the Manor, making it necessary for Kiku and Mary to leave the house more often than was wise. In hindsight, Dessalen should have had Blackwood moved into the Manor House as well. Then perhaps they wouldn't be burying him tomorrow. However, in his fierce jealousy, he hadn't wanted Mary-hime's brother so close to Kiku.

It would be a simple thing. Andersen-sensei already spent a good of time at the Manor House. Moving her here would eliminate the need for Mary to go out for appointments. And as for Kiku's brother—Leader Dessalen knew Kiku would be resistant. But his princess was not whole. Perhaps her brother could help heal the emotional wounds that lingered.

The exercise yard was nearly empty, with only a handful of officers in attendance. Kiku was in the middle of a round with a fresh-faced captain. To his credit, the young officer wasn't offering Kiku any quarter. Kiku looked exhausted but continued to beat back the other's attacks with fierce determination. She was wearing shorts and a cropped top. Her body glistened with sweat, and her damp hair was pulled back away from her face in a tail.

Leader Dessalen frowned, looking around for Captain Jace, but he wasn't to be found. Then he spotted General Lysis leaning against a wall watching the match with a veiled expression. The general stood up and offered Leader Dessalen a small bow.

"How long has she been at that?" Leader Dessalen asked. James Davis looked on with shock.

"A few hours," Lysis replied, his eyes going back to where Kiku was continuing her match. "Captain Jace needed some sleep, so I am keeping an eye on the princess. She's not lost yet."

As little as Dessalen liked the idea of Lysis watching Kiku-hime, he felt confident the general wouldn't allow her to indulge in any of her signature antics.

Dessalen wasn't surprised to find her here. Kiku was driving herself to take out her anger and frustration on her opponents. Not an unworthy notion, but she was tiring and wouldn't stop until she was injured. This, Dessalen could easily put an end to.

"Enough!" Leader Dessalen commanded as he strode forward purposefully. The men bowed in immediate respect, and Kiku's opponent dropped his staff to his side and stepped back. Kiku turned angrily, breathing hard from the round.

"Ouji-sama!" she protested. Then her dark blue eyes swept behind him and noticed James Davis. She immediately colored with anger. Kiku swallowed hard, and she stood stiff with temper. Her hands betrayed her agitation as she worked the staff back and forth. "What is he doing here?"

"He is my guest, Lieutenant," Leader Dessalen said mildly. Kiku looked away for a moment and then back to Dessalen. Her eyes smoldered with heat.

"Fine," she said. "If you'll excuse us Leader Dessalen, the captain and I are going to finish the match."

Dessalen could feel the tension in the yard start to rise as the men shifted restlessly. Clearly they were not comfortable with this battle of wills between their Exalted Leader and High Princess.

"No, Kiku," Dessalen said. "You are finished here."

Kiku's face was set in stubborn lines.

"Not until I lose," Kiku said. Leader Dessalen lips twiched into a half smile. Gods, she was enchanting; and enticing, and everything he desired.

"Very well, Hime-chan," Leader Dessalen said as he unfastened his uniform jacket. "I will be your opponent."

"Ouji!" Kiku protested.

"What's the matter, Kiku-chan?" Leader Dessalen offered a wicked smile ,throwing his jacket to a nearby soldier. General Lysis straightened, frowning unpleasantly. Leader Dessalen idly wondered how much he could irritate the general. He deftly took the pole from the captain she had been sparring with and warned him off with a look. He turned and met her with a smile. "Don't you want to fight me?"

Kiku looked at him angrily for a long moment and gritted her teeth. "Fine," she said again and stepped aggressively into an attack.

Dessalen deftly blocked it and countered with enough force in his blow that she dropped her pole, shaking her hands from the sting. She immediately took a defensive position, but he turned and leveraged his pole with one hand and used it to twist her arm around her back. He pulled her tightly against him keeping pressure on her arm. He caught her wrist with his other hand. Dessalen smiled down at her, pulling her wrists to his lips as she struggled to free herself.

"Do you yield, Princess?" he teased. She scowled and tried to use her legs to leverage herself. Dessalen added pressure on her arm, and she winced in pain. The curves of her form along his body heated his desire. Dessalen deliberately leaned down and nibbled on her ear. "Hm? Hime-chan? I could enjoy this for hours if you like."

"Ouji," she protested turning her face toward him. Dessalen took the opportunity to firmly kiss her, expertly coaxing her to respond. It only took a few moments before she was equally returning his attention. He pulled away, lingering near her lips.

"Do you yield?" Dessalen murmured. She swallowed and nodded even while tears dropped from her eyes.

"Yes, Ouji-sama," she whispered. "I yield."

Leader Dessalen offered a gentle smile as he released her. He wiped her tears and kissed her forehead.

"Go on, Kiku-chan," Leader Dessalen told her. "I'll see you at dinner with your sisters."

"Hai," she said. Kiku didn't even spare her brother a glance when she turned and walked away.

"So you can take a girl, Exalted One," Lysis sneered. "How would you fair with an equal opponent?"

"You're welcome to try, General," Leader Dessalen replied, feeling satisfied his demonstration had angered the general. Lysis had to learn that Kiku was out of his reach. Permanently.

Lysis stepped out into the yard, tossing his jacket backward carelessly. He grabbed a pole from one of the bystanders and immediately drove a hard attack. The ferocity and speed demonstrated was nearly unnatural. Both had been trained to fight since they could walk. Leader Dessalen, however, had been drilled by the most rigorous instructors the Garlon T'zen had to offer. There had been no uncertainty about his destiny, and he had been trained to reign with absolute power since before he could remember. His well-muscled body housed an indomitable will. Given this, there was no doubt in the outcome. Lysis lay on the ground with Dessalen's pole angled at his throat.

"I could kill you." Leader Dessalen pulled in on his fury.

"Then you had better," Lysis replied without fear. "Because that's the only way you will stop my pursuit of Kiku-hime-sama."

Dessalen felt his blood run cold as he looked down at the general. His golden eyes glinted as he considered driving the pole through his general's neck. And Dessalen may have if he didn't feel confident with his position in the princess's affection. Still, Lysis was valuable to him. He was loyal without question. He could hardly be blamed for desiring Kiku when Dessalen knew the ache of wanting her so much himself. Still, he swung the pole and knocked Lysis hard across the side of the head.

"The girls already have one funeral to attend this week, General," Dessalen said, his tone cold and calm. "I'll not put them through another."

He threw the pole down at him and stepped over Lysis's prone body to retrieve his jacket. He noted James Davis had watched the events unfold with a stunned expression and nodded curtly to the boy. "Come along, James. It's time we found Andersen-sensei."

~

"Good Afternoon, Dr. Andersen," Leader Dessalen said as he strode into the library. Dr. Andersen and Marlon were waiting there for his arrival. While she had enjoyed her adventure with Marlon, she had been worrying about James. The lad was following behind the Exalted Leader of Garlon T'zen looking pale and shaken. Leader Dessalen was pulling on his black uniform jacket over his plain white shirt as he came in.

"Good Afternoon, Leader Dessalen," Dr. Andersen replied. "It was good of you to invite us."

"Marlon." Leader Dessalen turned to the Garlon T'zen physician. "Please assist Dr. Andersen and James Davis in moving their residence to the Manor House."

"What?" Dr. Andersen choked out. "I can't just—you're not serious."

Leader Dessalen's lips twitched as he gazed down at her. There was something in his gold-colored eyes that made him look almost more unworldly than he already was. Most of the Garlon T'zen could easily pass for Earth men. But Leader Dessalen was more alien, powerful, and frightening than any other she had met.

"Coordinate with General Tamarik on the details." Leader Dessalen flicked his eyes way with a faint smile, addressing Marlon again. "I will see you all at dinner."

"Yes, Leader Dessalen." Marlon inclined his head as the Exalted Leader exited the library without a backward glance. Dr. Andersen looked helplessly at Marlon. Marlon raised his eyebrows.

"Marlon," she said, "someone has to talk to him. I can't just move into the Manor House."

"I'm sorry, Andy-chan," Marlon said. "It is his will."

"Don't you people ever argue with him?" Dr. Andersen asked with frustration. James cleared his throat and nodded.

"Uh yeah," James said. "It didn't work out very well."

"Ah, yes. General Lysis, I'm sure," Marlon said. James shook his head with a shrug. Marlon rolled his eyes. Dr. Andersen felt a chill remembering the last altercation between Leader Dessalen and General Lysis all too well. If James witnessed one of those encounters, it was little wonder he looked terrified.

"What about my patients?" Dr. Andersen said. "Marlon!"

"We'll work something out with General Tamarik," Marlon assured her. "Listen, Andy-chan, Leader Dessalen has spoken. You and James-san are moving to the Manor House."

~

Dinner was probably delicious, but Jimmy didn't remember much of it. He didn't think he ate much either. He and Dr. Andersen were ushered into the dining room at half past six and were joined by all of the Garlon T'zen royalty. Marlon introduced them, and in the back of his mind Jimmy wondered what their real names were. Were their families grieving for them too?

The one that surprised him the most was Princess Toki. She was only a few years younger than he and was breathtakingly beautiful. She had long blond ringlets down her back, and her eyes were the color of the pale sky. Toki was kind to him, shyly asking him questions all through dinner. Jennifer completely ignored him.

About halfway through the meal, Leader Dessalen joined them, offering his apologies for being late. Jennifer refused to look at him too. The Garlon T'zen leader tried to make conversation with her, but she barely glanced in his direction. After their fight, Jimmy wasn't surprised. He colored remembering Leader Dessalen making his sister kiss him. Jimmy was more shocked she kissed him back!

Ugh. He didn't know how he was going to explain any of this to his mom. Leader Dessalen was really into Jennifer. Jimmy didn't know the Garlon T'zen rules about that sort of thing, but he see they were a couple. He wondered if they were sleeping together, and knew that would probably kill his mother.

Jimmy picked at his food, wondering how he could get Jennifer to talk to him. He had to convince her she needed to come home. This place, with that crazy alien leader, wasn't any place for his sister.

~

Leader Dessalen was inclined to allow Kiku her petulant behavior for a day or two. The princess was still overwrought over the death of Devon Blackwood. They still had to get through the funeral, and reception afterward. The funeral itself was a private affair of the Garlon T'zen. The reception, in the evening, would allow the ambassadors from both on and off world to offer their condolences to Mary-hime.

While Kiku was polite to Dr. Andersen, she pointedly refused to look in her brother's direction. Leader Dessalen sighed inwardly. Just by her closed-off reaction he knew he was right and Tamarik wrong. Kiku needed to move past this bitterness for her happiness and wellbeing. The general was trying to protect the princess, but in this case he was crippling her. It was painful for her, but nothing could be done about it. With the sort of power Kiku's patron gifted, anything less than her being whole was dangerous. And Dessalen knew well exactly how dangerous, as did every Garlon T'zen man living.

"Kiku-hime," Leader Dessalen said, "do you have everything prepared for tomorrow?"

"Hai," she said not looking up from her plate. Akane offered a sharp glance in his direction. Kaori looked up sadly.

"I found the funeral song," Kaori-hime said. Leader Dessalen smiled.

"I'm sure it will be wonderful," he replied. Kaori colored with a shy smile.

"I'm tired," Mary announced. The child had hardly eaten. Dessalen made a mental note to have Marlon check on her. Kiku rose immediately and went to her side.

"It's all right, Mary-chan," she said. "I'll take you up to bed."

Mary nodded and pushed away from the table, and the two of them left. Leader Dessalen watched them leave with a neutral expression. He excused himself and got up from the table as well. New dispatches had come in from the Capital for him to review. It would be a long while before he could find his own bed for the night.

~

It was late when the door to the bedchamber opened and Leader Dessalen slipped in. Kiku was awake. She hadn't been able to sleep, instead crying most the night. Guilt burned her soul. Devon-kun was dead and it was her fault. Even worse was he had been in love with her and she hadn't acknowledged it. She couldn't! Ouji would not have understood. She tried to protect him with her silence, and he was dead anyway. And worse, dead not knowing that she had loved him a little too.

She could hear Leader Dessalen change out of his uniform and move across the room. He came close to her bed.

"Kiku-chan." Leader Dessalen's voice was soft as he touched her shoulder. She turned, looking up at him with her eyes wide, ashamed he had caught her crying again. He settled on the bed next to her and pulled her into his strong arms. She pressed her head into his chest. There was no place Kiku felt safer and, truly, no one she loved more. Kiku could feel the beating of her heart as she looked up into Dessalen's golden eyes. He nuzzled the top of her head, holding her close.

"Ouji?" she asked, pulling away a little. Leader Dessalen kept a firm arm around her waist.

"What is it, Kiku-chan?" He tenderly caressed her jaw with two fingers. Kiku leaned forward, closing her eyes seeking out his lips. He returned her kiss gently.

"Please stay with me tonight," she whispered. "And hold me. I don't want to be alone."

Leader Dessalen sighed and shifted around on the bed so he could cradle her in his arms. Kiku leaned her head against his chest, wrapping her fingers around one of his arms. Sighing with contentment, she was finally able to close her eyes and almost immediately drop off to sleep.

CHAPTER 6

Sleep did not come for the Exalted Leader of the Garlon T'zen that night. For him, it was a restless night of keeping his heated lust in check. It was agonizing torture to gaze down at Kiku's sleeping form cuddled in his arms. Every ounce of will was employed not to roll her gently over and take her. Her soft breath against his chest was a taunt. Teasing, trying to provoke him into action. In truth, he didn't know how much longer he was could wait.

When morning came and the sun was just rising through bedchamber windows, Kiku began to stir. She opened her eyes to slits with a small smile.

"Good morning, Ouji-sama," she murmured.

"Good morning, Kiku-chan," he returned quietly.

He stroked her cheek with his thumb and leaned down to kiss her. Kiku closed her eyes and rolled over on top of him continuing to kiss him sweetly. Dessalen's body responded and his hand wandered down her back to her round bottom. He moaned, pulling her tighter against him, deepening his kiss.

"Please, Hime-chan?" Dessalen murmured into her ear. "Let me?"

Kiku responded by kissing him with more urgency, wrapping her arms around his neck. Dessalen closed his eyes and rolled her over on her back. His lips went to her neck while his hand found its way to her round, firm breast. She responded eagerly, and Dessalen slipped his fingers under her light top to touch her bare flesh. Kiku drew leg up and arched against him.

Dessalen allowed himself to sink into the oblivion of need. He fumbled with the buttons at his waist all the while continuing to kiss Kiku tenderly. No words could express how he'd longed for this.

"Onee-sama?" Mary's soft voice called from nearby as the door to the outer suites swung open. Both Dessalen and Kiku froze. He clenched his hands against the pillows, groaning against her neck. Dessalen cursed himself silently for not locking the doors the night before.

"M-mary-chan?" Kiku stammered trying to disentangle herself from her prince. Dessalen kissed her deeply a last time before rolling off her, utterly frustrated. "What are you doing up so early?"

"I had a bad dream," the child said, breaking down into tears.

"I'm sorry, Mary-chan." Kiku got out of bed, pulling the curtain around so the girl wouldn't see Dessalen lying in her bed. "Come on, I'll take you back to bed. You need to get some more sleep. It's going to be a long day."

"Will you stay with me, Onee-sama?" Mary-chan pleaded. Dessalen groaned again, throwing an arm over his face. He knew where this was going to lead, and it wasn't to the end he had planned. "Please?"

"Of course," Kiku agreed, and Dessalen closed his eyes in abject frustration.

~

The sun was just coming up when General Lysis was rapping on Marlon-sensei's door. Getting no answer, the general frowned and tried the handle. The door swung open, but the small room was empty. The bed hadn't been disturbed, and it appeared the physician hadn't been there all night. Lysis raised an eyebrow. Marlon-sensei was the model of responsibility. He certainly wouldn't have left the Manor House without leave. The general's first thought was something had happened that required Marlon's skills. Given the temperament of their High Princess, it was a likely possibility.

The small security center on the first floor was just around the corner from Marlon's room. "Where is Marlon-sensei?" General Lysis asked. He didn't have time for Dessalen's games this morning. He planned to go to the American Embassy early, before the funeral. He already had Captain Jace preparing his men, and he wanted Marlon to go with them. Oh, he knew the sensei detested his role in Lysis's operation, but he was too skilled not to use. Under normal circumstances, Lysis wouldn't be able to ask Marlon to do anything, as the physician answered to Leader Dessalen alone. But the Exalted Leader had ordered Marlon to cooperate with Lysis's operation, and he had been performing his tasks to perfection.

"He spent the night with Andersen-sensei," the officer on watch replied. "He left word in case he was needed."

"He did," Lysis said with surprise. "Why would he do that?"

The watch officer raised his eyebrows and looked at the general. "Sir?"

General Lysis frowned. He didn't know if he should go retrieve the physician himself or have him sent for. It would be terribly rude to Andersen-sensei to pound on her door at this hour of the morning. She was at the Manor House as the personal guest of Leader Dessalen. Offending the

Exalted Leader over something like this was not something the general was willing to do. Especially not when Lysis was already skating on the edge of good judgment regarding the High Princess. He didn't need to offer Dessalen a reason to move against him.

"Call her room and inform Marlon I have need of his services," Lysis ordered. "Tell him I want him now."

"Yes, General," the watch officer said as he dialed the nearby comm unit.

~

The French-style telephone was ringing near Dr. Andersen's head. It seemed rather absurd as she woke blearily from sleep. She reached toward the nearby nightstand and fumbled with the receiver. Marlon was lying next to her under the covers, and they were both nude. After Marlon had joined her for the night, she had to admit that perhaps living in the Manor House would have its advantages.

"Hello?" she mumbled.

Dr. Andersen hadn't been woken up by a telephone in years. The only phone she had at her house in town was in the office.

"I'm sorry to disturb you, Andersen-sensei," came the polite voice on the other end, "but may I speak to Marlon-sensei?"

"Um—" She passed the phone over to Marlon. Of course, they knew he'd spent the night there. Dr. Andersen felt embarrassed, but then quickly dismissed it. They were both adults, after all. And she doubted anyone would say anything. The Garlon T'zen were pretty closed-mouthed about most things.

Marlon sighed next to her. "Yes, of course."

He handed the receiver back to her, and she hung it on the old-fashioned hook. He leaned over to kiss her.

"I've got to go," he whispered. She looked up into his face and dark eyes. She leaned forward and kissed him with more urgency. When had she fallen in love with him? She pulled away, and he smiled meeting her eyes. She didn't even have to ask. He loved her too.

"Right now?" Dr. Andersen asked, glancing at the clock. It wasn't even 6:00 A.M. yet.

"Yes," he said. Marlon wore dark expression as he got out of bed and pulled on his uniform. "I'm sorry, Andy-chan. I'll be back in time for the funeral."

"What's going on?" she asked. He shook his head and kissed her lightly on the forehead.

"It's not your worry," he told her. "Try to get some more sleep."

~

"So?" Lysis asked when Marlon made his appearance coming down the main staircase. "You're not sleeping in your own room these days?"

"I would think you would have better things to do than worry where I sleep," Marlon replied. Marlon, and he, were both dressed in the standard uniform of the Garlon T'zen. Lysis's rank gleamed on his cuff and collar, as did Marlon's. Only Marlon's rank held the personal insignia of the Exalted Leader.

"Really, Sensei," General Lysis mocked as they walked out the front door of the Manor House. "An Earth woman? You're not going to play suitor for a princess?"

"It's not your concern, General," Marlon replied with no emotion. Lysis raised an eyebrow in amusement. He did enjoy baiting Marlon. Marlon was never candid about what he thought of General Lysis's actions. His moral superiority irritated Lysis more than anything else. "Why did you drag me out of bed at this hour of the morning?"

"We're going to pay the American Embassy a visit," General Lysis said.

"Just the two of us?" Marlon asked. General Lysis laughed humorlessly. Captain Jace and his men were standing outside in combat uniforms. Marlon-sensei flicked his eyes to General Lysis.

"Using Kiku-hime's men?" he asked. His words held volumes of disapproval. "Did you get her out of bed too?"

"They are Tamarik's men," General Lysis said swinging himself up on his horse. Marlon did the same. Marlon offered a scathing look, and Lysis shrugged. "At least officially. And Leader Dessalen's order gives me a free hand in this."

"And Hime-sama?" Marlon asked. He looked at Captain Jace. "Is the princess aware of what you're doing?"

"The princess is aware we are securing the town," Captain Jace answered. "Leader Dessalen has removed her from the duty roster until after the funeral."

Marlon nodded, and they started toward the embassy.

"She is going to be very unhappy," Marlon remarked.

"I don't happen to care," Lysis answered.

~

As operations go, it was hardly challenging. There was only a minor risk of injury, and their adversaries weren't well trained. It wouldn't have been a bad one for Hime-sama to participate in, had she known about it. But then, had she known about it, she would have certainly disapproved of it.

Jace understood why General Lysis was acting as he was. Manor Town, now that all of the princesses were in residence, needed to be the most secure holding in the Empire. It wasn't just Kiku-hime now, but all of her sisters.

He was walking along a line of kneeling prisoners. One tried to get up and Jace kicked the back of his knee.

"Stay down," he ordered.

They had taken twenty-two prisoners, five of them armed with weapons of Earth origin. Most looked to be clerical staff, older, untrained, afraid. The ones who had weapons were younger and in better physical condition. Captain Jace motioned for two to be sent to Marlon-sensei for interrogation.

A private hurried over to him and leaned close.

"General Lysis wants the ambassador," he said. Captain Jace nodded in acknowledgment.

"Who is the ambassador?" He raised his voice and stepped in front of the line. They were all silent, no one answered. "Come now. One of you is."

"This attack is illegal," an older man spoke.

"Are you the ambassador?" Captain Jace asked, his tone quiet and controlled. The man nodded slowly. Jace moved forward and yanked him to his feet by his collar, pulled him away. He walked him inside of the building. It had been swept for explosives, and specialists were now going through all of their communications and records. After they were finished, the demolition team would move in and destroy the building. "General Lysis has asked to speak to you."

"Who?" The man looked pale and shaken. Jace didn't answer.

Jace nodded to the man at the door.

"Where is General Lysis?"

"Third door on the left," the corporal replied. Jace flicked his eyes around the flurry of activity. They wanted to get this done fast, before the funeral, which was happening just past the noon hour, as tradition dictated. Blackwood may not have been Garlon T'zen himself, but his sister held enough standing that his funeral rated full honors.

He entered the room without knocking. General Lysis was sitting at a desk in the middle of the room, scanning an imagedeck in his hands. Marlon-sensei was standing nearby, looking unhappy.

"Ah, yes." General Lysis looked up with a smile. "Thank you, Captain. You are the ambassador?"

The man pulled away from Jace. His blue eyes burned with hostility. He was a tall, thin man, well past his prime, his hair nearly silver. He drew in a deep breath and spoke.

"The embassy is considered American soil," the ambassador said. He stepped away from Jace and clenched his hands at his sides. "This unprovoked attack is an attack on our country itself!"

"Unprovoked?" General Lysis asked. He set the imagedeck down and got up and moved around the desk. "Devon Blackwood is dead and American agents are responsible."

"If that is true, then they acted on their own." The ambassador lifted his chin. Jace snorted softly, and General Lysis met his eyes for a brief moment, before turning his attention back to the ambassador. "Your actions are going to lead to war. Washington will not tolerate this act of aggression."

"War?" General Lysis laughed at him outright. The ambassador flushed with bright anger. "That could be amusing."

"The Garlon T'zen's position with the United States has been precarious at best since the New York incident," the ambassador said with heat. "Are you aware of how close diplomatic relations are to breaking off completely?"

"You would think," General Lysis mused, crossing his arms across his chest, "that after this 'New York incident,' which was nothing more than a raid by a rogue lieutenant, you would have a better understanding of your position."

Jace nodded with a faint smile.

~

6 months ago

Kiku-hime had looked over all of the options and decided the plan using a net would be the best way. Jace agreed, as it was the surest one for her personal safety.

Their target was a child, a little girl. Kiku had taken a picture from the young Earth man's wallet, and Jace had imaged it. All of their men had a copy. He wasn't unmoved by her desire to help this child, and if the girl was Celestial chosen as Kiku-hime said, they had no choice.

Captain Jace had two full units ready to move when he ordered the city of New York to be cut off from all power. They dropped their units near the target coordinates.

They met resistance, and it didn't take long for the country's government to go into action against the Garlon T'zen. Jace monitored the channels as they escalated their howls of protest up the Garlon T'zen chain of command.

Soon General Tamarik was demanding to know who ordered the incursion. Captain Jace easily ignored him for the moment and used Kiku's command codes to continue the operation. Like it or not, guardian or no, the general didn't have the authority to counteract her, and the mission continued.

In the end, Tamarik had little choice but to throw in behind them. It wasn't long before the whole east coast of the country erupted into a war zone. But by that time Kiku had the small broken girl child in her arms and was taking her to Marlon-sensei. Jace felt ill as he realized the extent of her injuries and abuse. It put him immediately to mind of when the Garlon T'zen had found Kiku and her sisters. Jace had been there too. It had been the first time he had ever met Kiku-hime, an encounter that changed his life forever.

The child was nearly catatonic until she saw Marlon-sensei, and then she went into screaming hysterics. The physician couldn't get near her without her wailing in fear. Kiku held her and did everything she could to reassure her that she was safe. Finally, Marlon sedated her and began to treat her injuries as they lifted the transport out to Manor Town.

"She's terrified of men," Kiku explained in a pained voice.

"That will make treatment problematic," Marlon told her. Kiku bit her lip with worry.

"We'll find a female physician," she said. "Is there one in Manor Town?"

Jace went to a screen at the side of the transport and started through the roster of inhabitants in Manor Town. He nodded and called back.

"A woman named Andersen," he said. Marlon moved forward to look at the screen and then nodded in approval.

"Have her taken to the Manor House before we land," he ordered. "I can help her with what she doesn't know."

"Yes, Marlon-sensei," Jace said as he issued the order, again using Kiku's codes. He flicked through screens reading about the escalating conflict between the Garlon T'zen and the forces of the United States. A faint smile crossed his lips.

General Tamarik was furious, and General Lysis sent a one-word acknowledgment. The general was going to use the turmoil to do what the general did best.

~

Present

It was true, relations were strained with that government since the operation that rescued Mary-hime, but Jace never expected they would try and move against the princess here in Manor Town. For that alone the Exalted Leader ought to call for the extermination of the entire country.

Even as he thought it, Jace knew that Leader Dessalen would not, if only because it would upset Kiku-hime.

"What do you mean? Our position?" the ambassador asked. He was shaking with either anger or fear. In this situation, it was difficult to tell the difference.

"Do you think we don't flatten your country because we can't?" General Lysis asked.

"I-I don't understand," the ambassador stammered.

"Obviously," Lysis retorted.

"We don't have time for this," Marlon interrupted. He turned to look at the ambassador with a frown. "What the general means is that the Americans have no means to wage war with us, let alone have any hope of winning. You are no threat. You have been allowed your freedom out of courtesy."

"So what then? What happens now?" The ambassador swallowed hard, looking around to each man.

"That will be up to Leader Dessalen." General Lysis inclined his head. "But first, we have questions that you will answer."

~

"They didn't have any other family?" Leader Dessalen asked. Kiku shook her head. They were standing in the library while the rest of the house was getting ready for the funeral. Generals Tamarik, Lysis, and Makiellen were also present. Marlon-sensei was standing next to Kiku.

"It was just the two of them," Kiku answered. "Their parents died in an accident a few years ago."

Leader Dessalen turned to the generals.

"Then I will be Mary-hime's guardian," he said.

"Do you think that wise?" General Makiellen asked. "You're already guardian to four."

Kiku's face colored, knowing full well why Leader Dessalen wasn't her guardian as well. As if he could hear her thoughts he flicked her a smile. She hadn't understood that at first, but he had explained it to her.

"So?" Leader Dessalen asked to dismiss the concern. "I see that makes no difference. Mary-hime needs someone who is going to keep her best interest in mind."

"Of course, Leader Dessalen," General Makiellen said. "I just mean that with the responsibility of the others, especially now, that perhaps General Tamarik—"

"Thank you, no." General Tamarik shook his head. "I've got my hands full with Kiku-hime."

"Ji-chan!" Kiku retorted, and Leader Dessalen smiled.

"Well then, perhaps I could—" General Makiellen started.

"Absolutely not," Marlon interrupted. "She doesn't even know you and Mary-chan is terrified of most men."

"You have no say in the matter, Sensei," General Makiellen said.

"He has more say than you." Leader Dessalen's voice was mild. He looked to Kiku, raising his eyebrows. "Kiku-hime?"

"Leader Dessalen is an appropriate choice," Kiku said. It was true that Mary-chan was terrified of men. But she was comfortable with Ouji-sama. At least he wasn't a stranger to her.

"You can't seriously be going on the word of this girl." General Makiellen turned on Leader Dessalen with a look of disbelief. Both generals Tamarik and Lysis regarded Makiellen with shock.

"Kiku-hime-sama is the High Princess, General." Leader Dessalen turned and faced him with a cold expression. "And she is her sisters's sworn protector, chosen by the Celestial Eyanna. I am most certainly going on her word."

"I didn't mean—" The general put his hands up and stepped back.

"We're done." Leader Dessalen dismissed them. "I will make the announcement tonight at the reception."

"Yes, Leader Dessalen," they politely murmured as they filed out of the library. Kiku nodded to him and met his eyes. She had to change into a dress uniform. It was nearly time to bury Devon-kun.

~

The interment took place halfway up the mountain, outside of town. A small monument had been erected on the far side of a large clearing. The wind blew through roughly while the five princesses stood surrounding Mary. Kiku was standing just behind her as she watched her brother's casket being lowered into the ground. The Garlon T'zen officers in attendance wore black dress uniforms, which were very similar to their regular uniforms but with an extra accent of thin silver piping that ran around the collars and down the pants legs. Leader Dessalen stood just away from the girls watching as his red cape fluttered in the breeze. Kiku had also chosen to wear her dress uniform. Her face was an emotionless mask. Leader Dessalen tightened his jaw unhappily. He would do anything to spare her this pain.

Dr. Andersen and Marlon-sensei stood close together, their heads hanging in grief. Dessalen knew both were close to the Blackwoods, and this death touched them deeply. Captain Jace and the rest of his unit were ringed around them, wearing combat uniforms, for security. Dessalen wondered if either General Lysis or Tamarik had figured out young Captain Jace's assignment, and the Exalted Leader's role in it. Lysis probably had. He wasn't as sure about Tamarik. Leader Dessalen was having concerns about the competency of that general these days.

Farther on the mountain, Leader Dessalen had enough security for him to feel comfortable with letting all six princesses out. They couldn't see it, but he had ordered an energy shield to cover the airspace above their heads before they stepped out of Manor Town. He had no intention of being careless with the Garlon T'zen's most precious assets.

Kaori's mournful funeral dirge began. It was an old song, about their bodies being given back over to the stars. Leader Dessalen listened with a heavy heart. He hadn't particularly liked Devon Blackwood, but it wasn't because he wasn't a good man. If anything, it was because he was a good man. If anyone had a chance to threaten his standing with Kiku, it would have been him. But Dessalen hadn't necessarily wanted him dead, if only for Kiku and Mary.

Dessalen stepped forward as Kaori's last note echoed down the mountain. Mary was crying quietly, leaning against Kiku. He reached over and picked the small child up into his arms. Mary wrapped her arms around his neck and cried against his shoulder as they all turned away and walked down the mountain.

~

Hundreds had lined up at the Manor House to offer their condolences. Delegations from every embassy, both from the Earth and off-world ambassadors, and the trader guilds were in attendance.

Kiku stood in the reception line feeling self-conscious in the dress that Akane and Dido had cornered her into wearing.

"You are not going to wear a uniform tonight." Dido's eyes flashed. Kiku had tried reminding them she was a Garlon T'zen officer, but they pointed out she was their High Princess too. Sometimes she had to play the part.

Kiku wore a sheer formal dress of dark blue, it being as close as to black they would allow her. It was sleeveless with small straps on her shoulders. The dress was impossibly tight and the bodice clung to every curve. It had a slit up to her thigh, making it easy for her to move in, should she have to fight. But it also revealed her shapely legs.

Except for Toki and Mary, all the princesses dressed more provocatively than Kiku would have expected. Akane shrugged off her concern, saying it was appropriate court dress for formal functions. But Kiku wasn't so sure. They were causing a good amount of talk, and more than one lingering appreciative glance, and not just from the Garlon T'zen.

"You look lovely tonight, Kiku," Dr. Andersen told her. She was coming through the line with Marlon-sensei. He respectfully inclined his head to each of the princesses as he moved through the line.

"Thank you, Andersen-sensei." Kiku felt her face color again, longing for the endless line to finally end.

~

"The princesses are lovely this evening," General Rohlon remarked. Leader Dessalen nodded, not taking his eyes off the reception line. As the Exalted Leader, he did not participate with that. No one on the planet had the status to meet with him. He had declined every request for meeting with the leaders of the Earth's nations, instead delegating

General Tamarik to take care of those matters. "Kiku-hime especially so. We don't see her out of her uniform enough to appreciate what a beautiful young woman she is."

Leader Dessalen frowned at the general and walked away saying nothing. He didn't care for anyone else to appreciate Kiku-hime; and it was obvious she was appreciated by many. He clenched his hand into a fist in frustration. It didn't help he was driven to distraction by what she was wearing. Gods. Who had chosen that for her?

"Leader Dessalen." General Tamarik stepped close to speak in a low voice. "Delegates from the United Kingdom and Canada wish to speak to you on behalf of the Americans."

Dessalen narrowed his eyes and shook his head.

"You and Lysis handle it," Dessalen muttered.

"They are concerned you plan to strike the United States itself," General Tamarik replied. "Neither of us can speak to that."

Leader Dessalen raised an eyebrow and walked away. When would that damnable line end? He longed to whisk Kiku to his side and warn off her would-be admirers.

~

"Leader Dessalen is occupied," General Tamarik told the delegates. General Lysis stood nearby and snorted. He'd been watching the Exalted Leader all evening. The only thing occupying Leader Dessalen was Princess Kiku.

"Please," the woman from Canada said. "This is very urgent. We share a border with the United States. We have a vested interest in what is going to happen."

"And we've also been asked by Washington to inquire about the well-being of the Americans in Manor Town," the British man continued. "They lost all contact with their embassy in the early hours this morning."

"I can answer that," General Lysis replied. He moved forward and offered a nod to General Tamarik. The older general stepped aside. Both operations had been under Lysis's direction. "Leader Dessalen ordered all the insurgents we captured the night Devon Blackwood was murdered to be executed. The residents of the embassy will be deported once we've finished with their debriefing."

"They're to be executed?" The Canadian woman paled.

"No," General Lysis clarified. "Leader Dessalen ordered it and it was done."

"Oh God." She covered her mouth with her hand and fled the room. General Lysis looked after her with a bemused expression and shrugged.

~

"Dr. Andersen." Ronald Fitzroy was the ambassador for the United Kingdom. He stepped forward and greeted Dr. Andersen, and she offered a faltering smile. "You look well this evening."

"As well as I can be, Minister," Dr. Andersen said, her posture rigid and straight. "Considering I buried a dear friend of mine today."

"Of course." The Minister coughed and had the good manners to look embarrassed. "Very rude of me not to offer my condolences."

Dr. Andersen glanced around wondering where Marlon went. She didn't want to be on her own long. She had the feeling she would be eagerly picked apart by many of her countrymen given the chance over the current state of affairs in Manor Town.

"You should offer them to Princess Mary," Dr. Andersen replied.

"I mean to do that. The line has been impossibly long," Minister Fitzroy said. "And about that, Andersen; how is it she's considered a princess?"

"I really don't know, Minister," Dr. Andersen answered. "But she is, and it's something the Garlon T'zen take seriously."

"Right about that." He coughed again. Dr. Andersen was tempted to offer him a lozenge so he would go away. "I heard you've moved into the main house here?"

"That's true." Dr. Andersen bit her lip. Don't ask, she thought silently to herself.

"What's that about then?" The Minister pinned her with a glare. Dr. Andersen looked at him helplessly. She doubted he would understand that Leader Dessalen announced she was moving, and so she did.

"Dr. Andersen is a guest of Leader Dessalen," Marlon said from behind her. He set a hand on her shoulder and offered a light squeeze. Dr. Andersen looked up at him gratefully. He offered her a quick smile before he cleared his features to look at the ambassador. Marlon was wearing his Military Dress uniform, so there would be no misunderstanding whom exactly he happened to be representing. The Minister turned a cold eye to the Garlon T'zen physician.

"Do you mean a citizen of the United Kingdom is a prisoner here?" he asked.

"Not at all." Marlon narrowed his eyes. "And rumors saying such will not be tolerated."

"Are you threatening me?" Ronald Fitzroy seemed to be working himself up into lather. It would have been funny if it weren't so serious.

"Not I." Marlon smiled. "But I could easily find someone who would."

~

When Kiku finally divested herself of the receiving line, her nerves were frayed. She went to a nearby table and found a glass of wine and downed it quickly. She then took another as she mingled with the crowd.

"Don't get drunk, Kiku-chan," General Tamarik scolded, coming up from behind her. Kiku pushed her loose hair back over her shoulder, sticking her tongue out at her guardian. "Charming."

"I hate this." She scowled, looking at the crowded reception hall.

"I know." He stood next to her for a moment and then sighed seeing yet another delegate weaving their way through the crowd to speak to him. "My pardon, Hime-sama, but duty awaits, and it's nothing you want a part of."

Kiku's eyes followed his and she nodded, taking a sip of the wine and moving off again into the crowd. She looked around for Leader Dessalen, wondering where he had gone. When she was in line, she had seen him and felt his watchful eyes. But she couldn't find him and paused at a nearby captain to ask his whereabouts. The captain nodded.

"He took Mary-hime up to bed," the captain replied to her inquiry. "She was overwrought."

"Oh," she said. Why didn't he call her? She could have helped with Mary-chan. Sighing, she wondered if she ought to follow or if she should stay. But quickly she was surrounded by a pack of admirers from the various embassies. They all smiled and vied for her attention. Kiku looked bewildered between them. "I'm sorry, I need some air."

She practically bolted out the side door to the gardens, pressing her head against a tree. Ugh. She looked back over her shoulder with a shake of her head. Kiku disliked that kind of attention. If that was typical of court, then she wanted nothing to do with it. She drew in a deep breath and let it out slowly, trying to resettle her nerves.

The garden was full of damp, moist smells, and Kiku took another deep breath. Her dress moved with her like a second piece of skin, and the second glass of Earth wine seemed to go right to her head. But after the noise and pressure of the reception inside, the garden was a welcome oasis.

"What are you doing out here alone, Hime-sama?"

Kiku turned with a start to see General Lysis leaning against a tree watching her with a glint in his eye. "I needed some air." She felt immediately uncomfortable under his gaze. His eyes lingered a little too long on her form before returning to her face. Kiku flushed with color. While she wasn't comfortable with his gaze, she felt a thrill of— something, when he looked at her. "I didn't like it in there."

"I agree. I don't like these things either," Lysis replied. "But you shouldn't be out alone."

"I'm fine alone." Kiku's temper flashed. She went to step around him but instead stumbled in the dark. General Lysis caught her as she fell against him. He looked down at her with a pleased smile.

"Hime-sama," he whispered, leaning down to seek her lips with his. He kissed her gently, teasing her lips.

Kiku pulled back in shock, blinking several times, touching her fingers to her lips. "What?"

"You are very beautiful, Kiku." His voice was whisper soft. "I've desired you for a long time. I've asked General Tamarik for permission to pay you court. He said I could, if you agreed."

Kiku stepped back confused, bumping into a tree. She was stunned by his words. Kiku was at a loss. She felt her face heat. General Lysis stepped closer, leaning to kiss her again.

"General," the Exalted Leader of the Garlon T'zen said from behind. "Am I interrupting something?"

General Lysis stiffened and turned slowly to meet the gaze of Leader Dessalen. "Maybe you are."

"I suggest you find something safer to do, General." Leader Dessalen's voice was cold. The general looked like he was going to challenge him for a moment and then thought better. Glancing back at Kiku he bowed and headed back to the reception at the Manor House.

~

Leader Dessalen watched General Lysis leave with narrowed eyes. He refocused his hot gaze back onto the princess, who was standing still in shock. Dessalen pulled in on his fury and took her by the elbow to go back to the house.

He had only left for a moment to put Mary-chan to bed. The child had broken down in tears and wouldn't let anyone but him close to her. When he came back, Kiku was being hounded by a pack of would-be suitors. Before he could get to her, General Makiellen interrupted him. When he looked again, she was gone. Gritting his teeth, he tried to think of suitable retribution for Lysis having dared touch what was his.

"Wait, Ouji-sama." Kiku stopped and touched his chest with the palm of her hand. He froze. not trusting his reaction, closing his eyes breifly before reopening them. She stood in front of him looking up at him earnestly. She reached up to touch his cheek. "Are you angry with me?"

He leaned into her hand and felt his body heat. Dessalen was near murderously angry with Lysis and could have happily wrung the life out of the general with his own hands. But looking at Kiku troubled and beautiful . . . "No Kiku-chan," he whispered. "I could never be angry with you."

She stepped closer, pressing her body against his as she buried her face in his chest. He could feel every curve of her slender form through the thin dress, and it drove him to madness. Dessalen's need for her had become a living thing. His arms wrapped around her back and he pulled her tighter against him. Dessalen stood frozen, trying to regain his shredding self-control before he deliberately lifted her chin to kiss her. When he leaned down into the kiss, it wasn't the gentle kisses they had shared before but one full of heat and possession. His heart was racing. His hand went to her neck and cradled her head as he leaned her back. Hearing her moan stoked the flame inside of him. The hunger he had long denied came roaring out of control. There would be no stopping this time. He would have her. This night would be the end of it.

Dessalen paused lifting his eyes to scan the garden. Prying eyes were starting to take note of their activity from inside the Manor House, but he didn't care. Let them all know. Dessalen easily scooped Kiku into his arms and strode purposely back to the security of the Manor.

"Ouji?" she whispered, burying her head into his chest to avoid questioning eyes. He could feel her trembling in his arms.

"Shh," he said. The reception would carry on without them, and he saw no reason for a social obligation to keep him from his prize. He took the side stairs back to their chamber. A servant hurriedly opened the door. He asked no questions at the warning look from Leader Dessalen's eyes, instead closing the door quickly behind them. Dessalen carefully set her on his bed, unfastening his collar all the while kissing her pushing her against the pillows.

"Ouji-sama," she said. "What are they going to say?"

"Nothing," he murmured. He pulled the strap of her dress off her shoulder and ran his lips along the curve of her collarbone and shoulder. His lips made their way down to the top of her small round breast, and he pushed on the bottom with his hand, trying to work it free of the dress. His mouth latched on the exposed nipple and his teeth teased it until it stood up hard.

"Oh!" she gasped. Her back arched, pressing her body against him. He cupped a hand under a buttock pulling her tighter to him.

Yes, this was what he had longed for. Kiku's fingers fumbled on the clasps of his uniform dress shirt. It took a moment for it to slip away off from his shoulders and fall to the floor. Her hands ran up his bare chest and gripped his back, her eager mouth kissing his and nuzzling his neck.

Dessalen inched up her dress and ran his hands along the inside of her thigh. She shuddered, and her nails bit into his shoulders. His member was tight against his breeches to the point it was painful. He loosened the buttons and it shot free of its restrictions immediately. The princess gasped, feeling the hard throbbing man-part against her stomach. Shyly, she touched it, sending a chill of pleasure through Dessalen. His sharp intake of breath made her draw back.

"Did I hurt you?" she whispered. He chuckled and pulled her hands back to where they had been and nosed the side of her ear.

"You could never hurt me." His words were spoken like a prayer against her skin. Dessalen quickly slid his pants off and was naked against Kiku's form. His fingers tore at the offending dress that was between him and the flesh he so desperately had to join. But it clung stubbornly to her form. Frustrated, finding no easy way to take it off he tore at a side seam and the garment ripped away.

Finally there was nothing between him and her. His hands wandered over her body and his kisses drew deeper, more demanding. Mad with desire he drew her leg up and slid between. He looked down at his princess, who was damp with sweat breathing hard. Dessalen wrapped his arms around her shoulders tightly. He saw Lysis in the garden trying to take what was rightfully his with a jealous stab of heat. No, Kiku belonged to him. Closing his eyes, he clung to her as he drove deep into her with a hard thrust. The princess cried out in pain. He felt something give inside of her, and it was wet and soft. Kiku's fingers dug into his flesh as he pushed deeper into her.

"Gomen, Hime-chan," he murmured, faintly regretting the pain he was causing her. Dessalen covered her mouth with his to smother her sobs, probing deep into her mouth with his tongue. Her body responded against his. He pulled her rear tighter to him as he rocked slowly against her, losing himself in her scent and touch. Her soft cries turned slowly into moans, and she started to push herself against him. The effect on the Garlon T'zen prince was immediate as his pulse quickened. It wasn't long until his voice mingled in with hers as they pushed harder, faster, each driving the other where there was only passion and heat. Dessalen held his seed as long as he could; he wanted Kiku to peak first, but he was certain would die he if he didn't let go. Just as the urgency in his loins became too much to bear the princess cried out with a mixture of lust and agony. There was a rush of wetness that soaked the bed around them. The onslaught of pleasure Dessalen felt broke the last of his control, and he spilled. He pushed with several sharp thrusts and stilled. He panted, clinging to her with his head against her shoulder.

The two of them lay tangled together for a long time. When Dessalen started to pull himself away, Kiku clung to him desperately.

"No, please," she begged. Dessalen lifted his head and ran a thumb along her jaw. "Not yet. I don't want it to end yet."

"Silly one." He chuckled kissing her tenderly. "It's never going to end."

"Promise," she said, grabbing his face with both hands, looking at him. Tears stood in her eyes, stark terror showing in her face. "Swear to me Ouji. Swear you'll never leave me."

"I swear," he promised, moving to comfort her silent tears as they slipped down her face. How could the girl not realize what she did to him? How could she not know that without her he didn't think he could live?

~

"So?" General Tamarik said when Leader Dessalen emerged from his chamber later. He was waiting in the shared sitting room of the suites. "It is done?"

"You make it sound so technical," Dessalen said.

"Lysis spoke to me." Tamarik ignored the Exalted Leader's sarcasm. "He is interested in courtship."

"I don't think so." Dessalen's eyes narrowed dangerously. He poured himself a drink.

"That's not for you to say," General Tamarik replied. "I am Kiku-hime's guardian, and I am the one who approves of her suitors. Of which, I may add, you are not one."

"An oversight on your part, I'm sure," Dessalen said. "You've always known my intention."

"I've known." Tamarik nodded. "But you've never formally declared your intention."

"Oh please." Dessalen snorted. "Everyone in the Empire knew my intent. Besides, I think the point is moot now."

"I'm not sure you're a suitable suitor," Tamarik remarked.

"What?" Leader Dessalen looked at the general as if he had lost his mind.

"You grab her out of the garden and ravish her?" Tamarik crossed his arms and looked at him critically.

"She was a willing participant, I assure you," Dessalen growled. "This is ridiculous."

"Perhaps." Tamarik nodded. "But you need to be reminded of the law, Exalted One."

"I know the law." Dessalen frowned, his temper catching fire.

"There are only five princesses," Tamarik continued.

"Six." Dessalen corrected. "I am well aware of how many there are! I am guardian for the others, or had that slipped your senile brain."

"Humph." Tamarik groused.

"I couldn't be Hime-sama's guardian and lover." Dessalen was rather satisfied with the way it worked out for him. "Now could I?"

"No," Tamarik agreed. "You couldn't. But—"

"What?" Dessalen snapped.

"You can't be her only lover, either," Tamarik told him. His face colored with fury.

"Leave me," Dessalen ordered. General Tamarik bowed and left the room. Leader Dessalen looked at his half full glass and threw it against the wall, watching the glass shatter with satisfcation. Damn him!

"Ouji-sama?" Kiku stood in the doorway wearing one of his white shirts, her honey hair cascading around her shoulders. His heart ached to look at her. He would happily destroy planets to possess her. He was easily considered the most dangerous man in the known galaxy, and this girl had taken his heart. "Is something wrong?"

"No, Hime-chan," he said, tenderly going to take her hand. He didn't care. He would find a way around it. He had played the Celestial's game long enough. He would not be cheated out of the only thing he ever truly wanted. Dessalen would not share his princess with another. "Let's go back to bed."

CHAPTER 7

The Exalted Leader of the Garlon T'zen woke slowly with his princess still curled in his arms. Kiku's honey-colored hair tangled across the pillows and his arm. Dessalen closed his eyes and drew in a deep breath, enjoying her scent and allowed himself to feel utter contentment for a little longer. Soon he would have to tear himself away and deal with what might be a minor uprising below.

Dessalen knew all along there would be bitter rivalries for the attention of the princesses. This hadn't been an issue before. The Celestials had provided the Garlon T'zen with a test. The girls were not to be touched until their home world was found. However, now that it had been, the princesses were free to entertain the affections of suitors.

So Dessalen had a real issue. He didn't need his military killing each other for the ladies' favor. Or worse, murdering the men they did choose out of jealousy.

Even though he had adored and desired Kiku from the first moment he had picked her up in his arms three years ago, there was an urgent political reason for him to consummate his relationship with her. His position as the Exalted Leader made him untouchable. If Kiku chose him first, then he could set a hard precedent. The princess's choice was hers alone and not to be tampered with.

Dessalen's heart had claimed her years ago. It was only a matter of time before she was lying in his arms. The waiting has been nearly unbearable at times but finally it was done. Now he had to deal with those foolish enough to challenge his claim.

Giving her shoulder a last caress, he pulled himself away and out of bed. She stirred and opened her eyes.

"Ouji-sama?" she mumbled. "Is it time to get up?"

"For me." His tone was full of regret as got out of bed and pulled on a pair of trousers. Leaning down, he wrapped a hand around the back of her neck and kissed her slowly. She responded with a hand around the back of his head. Dessalen closed his eyes with a sigh and pulled away. He had to stop, or he wouldn't make it out of the chamber. "Gomen ne, Hime-chan."

She sat up and looked at him with her large dark blue eyes. Then she smiled.

"I'll get dressed," she said, pulling back the covers. Dessalen laughed. He grabbed them and firmly pulled them back over her.

"No." He grinned. "I want you to wait right here for me."

"Ouji!" she exclaimed. Kiku's face flooded with color. "I can't just lie in bed waiting for you all day!"

"Mmmm." Dessalen smiled, buttoning his shirt. "I like the picture that paints in my mind."

Kiku made a noise of frustrated embarrassment and pulled the covers over her head. Grinning Dessalen pulled them away to kiss her quickly on the forehead before striding out of the room.

He took the main steps down into the expansive foyer and looked to the men gathered. There was a small crowd of generals, captains, and a few retired officers who had traveled to the Earth to make their case for courting the princesses.

"How is the Princess this morning?" Lysis bit out the question as the Exalted Leader came down the stairs.

"Kiku-hime is very tired." Dessalen smiled, feeling smug. "But that is none of your concern."

"Kiku-hime's welfare is all of our concern, Leader Dessalen." General Makiellen stepped forward. "And I must protest you whisking her off before the event had a chance to begin last night."

There were murmurs of agreement and voices got louder. Leader Dessalen let them go on for a few moments before he raised his hand.

"Quiet," he ordered. "Kiku-hime chose. Leave it at that."

"And we're to take your word for it?" General Lysis retorted.

"Yes." Leader Dessalen dropped his voice dangerously. There was a loud outburst of anger from the growing crowd. Dessalen felt his temper start to rise. He hoped this wouldn't lead to violence, but was ready to take that tack if necessary. He'd made arrangements with Tamarik and had men ready to act at a gesture.

"Silence!" A sharp feminine voice rang through the hall. They all looked up in stunned silence to see Kiku dressed in an impeccably perfect black uniform coming down the stairs. Her chin was held high, and her eyes glinted with a silver hue. Dessalen could feel the raw power radiating from her form. His eyes swept the room, wondering if these fools had any idea who they were dealing with. "You dare question my choice?"

General Makiellen stepped forward with a small bow.

"Not at all, Princess," he said. "We just wish you to make more than one."

Leader Dessalen felt a jolt of rage, clenching his fists at his sides. Kiku looked at the general and the rest of the assembly with contempt.

"You are not worthy." Kiku's voice was cold and unemotional. Makiellen looked at her with stunned shock. Dessalen wanted to laugh, but restrained himself as relief washed over him. Lysis looked like he had swallowed a rock, and the rest didn't know how to react. Kiku turned her back on them and stepped toward Dessalen. He felt the hair on the back of his neck rise. She looked up and held him with her otherworldly eyes.

"Lady Eyanna," he murmured. A smile played on her lips.

"You are worthy of my Kiku," she told him, low enough so only he could hear. "Because my golden Mathias chose you first."

Her words startled him. Dessalen nodded, hearing his heartbeat in his ears. He hadn't realized before that Eyanna wanted him for Kiku. He hadn't thought the Celestials would interfere that much in their affairs. Clearly, he was mistaken.

Now he had to worry about the others. What if their suitors didn't meet their patron's approval? That did not bode well for the curse to be forgiven. As if Eyanna could hear his thoughts, she smiled. Kiku's eyes faded back from the sharp silver to her natural deep blue. She blinked a few times in confusion.

"Ouji?" she whispered.

"It's all right," he said. Dessalen wrapped an arm around her waist, leading her from the expansive foyer. He threw a look of warning at the would-be suitors. They didn't know how lucky they were. Had Eyanna not intervened their blood would be running on the marble floor.

~

Dr. Andersen was having breakfast with James when Marlon joined them. He offered a smile to the boy and a wink to the doctor. Dr. Andersen frowned and continued to eat. Marlon pulled out a chair and sat down. He knew she was unhappy about having to move to the Manor House, but he agreed with Leader Dessalen about it.

"What are your plans today, Andy-chan?" Marlon asked.

"I am enrolling James in school," Dr. Andersen replied. "I'm going to take him over there today. If he's staying on, he needs to continue his studies."

"He should be tutored here at the Manor House," Marlon offered. Her frown deepened.

"He needs to be with children his age," Dr. Andersen said.

"I'm not a child," James put in with a frown.

"I'm sorry, dear," Dr. Andersen apologized. "Young people his age. Actually, it wouldn't hurt to have Toki-hime and Mary go to school as well. I don't think keeping them isolated here is good for their development and socialization."

Marlon cleared his throat. "I don't think Leader Dessalen would approve."

"What wouldn't I approve?" Leader Dessalen came into the dining room with Kiku. Kiku took one look at James and immediately closed up emotionally. Marlon's face creased with worry.

"I'm enrolling James in school today," Dr. Andersen said. She met Leader Dessalen's gaze evenly and Marlon smiled. He had utterly lost his heart to the woman. "And I suggested, perhaps Toki-hime and Mary should go to school too. Both could benefit from spending time with young people their own age."

Leader Dessalen looked thoughtful for a moment and flicked his eyes to Kiku. "Kiku-chan?"

"Mary-chan needs some normality in her life," Kiku admitted. She let out a long breath and looked troubled. "And Toki-chan has no friends her age."

"Work with Captain Jace and secure the education facilities," Leader Dessalen ordered. "It needs to be done for James-kun even if the others don't attend instruction."

"Yes, Leader Dessalen." Kiku-hime's face colored and she abruptly left.

"Why does she hate me?" James asked. Marlon looked over at the young man with sympathy. The lad didn't understand how hard all this was for the princess. But she didn't understand this was hard on him too.

Leader Dessalen looked at the boy in a not-unkind way. "Sometimes you have to be patient with Kiku-chan. She'll come around."

"Jennifer," James muttered, his jaw set in a stubborn line. Marlon's eyes darted to the Exalted Leader's, but his reaction wasn't what Marlon expected.

"Hm." Leader Dessalen offered a benign smile. He turned, leaving the dining room without another word. James got up and pushed his chair back in.

"I'll get ready," he said, leaving Marlon alone with Dr. Andersen. She craned her head after James for a moment, before turning her attention back to Marlon.

"He's in a frighteningly good mood," Dr. Andersen said. Marlon shook his head with irritation. The physician wasn't entirely happy with the developments of the night before. Kiku was dear to him, and the Exalted Leader would not be the suitor Marlon would have chosen for her.

"He's got good reason to be," he replied. "But stay clear of General Lysis. He's in an equally foul mood for the same reason."

Lysis's mood, however, Marlon approved of. Neither man was good enough for the princess.

"What?" Dr. Andersen frowned. "Something happen with Kiku?"

"Yes," Marlon answered.

"Is she all right?" she asked with worry. "She looked a little off color this morning."

"She's fine," Marlon said. Dr. Andersen continued to regard him with a frown. He lowered his voice. "What do you think, that he brutalized her?"

"Well." Dr. Andersen wrung her hands a few times. "Maybe."

"Don't be ridiculous." He got up and pulled Dr. Andersen's chair out for her. They started to walk out of the dining room together.

"Are you going to talk to them about using contraceptives?" she asked in a low voice. Marlon looked down at her with open shock.

"Not that attached to me, are you?" Marlon retorted.

"Kiku is too young," Dr. Andersen said. "She shouldn't be having babies already. I mean it, Marlon, don't your people—"

"No," he replied. "We don't. Stay out of it."

"But—" Dr. Andersen protested. He pulled her around a corner and kissed her tenderly.

"Andy-chan, Andy-chan," he said with a gentle tone. "I mean it. Don't meddle in this."

~

Leader Dessalen dropped the latest imagedecks on the table with irritation and started to pace. None of it was news he wanted from out system. General Catensen had done his best to quell the Ma'gaar pushing to expand into Imperial territory, but he needed reinforcements. Leader Dessalen was needed at the Capital to have the necessary armaments redeployed. He also had to meet with the ambassadors from the Geis system to confirm a trade treaty. If he didn't hold the borders in the Ma'gaar sector, they would lose those systems. He rubbed his forehead.

He had stayed too long. But he couldn't leave until he and Kiku had—

Dessalen sighed and threw himself into his chair. He promised Kiku he wouldn't leave her, and he briefly considered taking her. However, he knew the princess, and her sisters, need to be here. Like it or not, the Celestials had made their will clear. For the curse to be forgiven, this was to be the order of events.

Dessalen was utterly frustrated with his predicament. He couldn't let the Empire fall apart, but he couldn't bear the thought of leaving his princess either. Not when it had taken so long to get to this point. And not when there were dozens of eager suitors waiting for an opportunity to take his place. He ground his jaw and threw an imagedeck across his desk in anger.

"Because golden Mathias chose you first," Eyanna had said. Leader Dessalen's gold-colored eyes glinted remembering her words to him. Perhaps she was telling him something as well?

Leader Dessalen stood up and closed his eyes. He reached inside to the hidden power he knew dwelt in there and touched it.

~Mathias,~ he called. ~Hear me.~

~

"The whole town is designed with the infrastructure already in place." Lieutenant Midin stood next to a table in a command chamber deep in the sub-basement of the Manor House. The table was displaying a full holographic layout of Manor Town with the two buildings in question lit brighter than those surrounding. Captain Jace was standing next to Kiku with his arms crossed in thought. "We just need to activate the imagers in those particular buildings and assign men to watch them."

"How many men would we need for that, Jace-kun?" Kiku asked.

He sighed, clearly unhappy.

"Can't the princesses just be tutored at the house, Hime-sama?" He leaned forward on the table and looked everything over with a shake of his head and then turned to meet her eyes. "This is an unnecessary security risk."

"No." It wasn't that Kiku disagreed with the captain, but rather that she agreed with Andersen-sensei more. While Toki was completely spoiled, she carried the deepest scars from their captivity, before the Garlon T'zen rescued them. Maybe if she did things like a normal girl, made friendships outside of just her sisters, she would be able to heal. And as for Mary-chan, Kiku knew the depths of her shattered heart. What it was like to lose a brother.

Kiku hit the table with frustration and immediately stopped that line of thought.

Jace straightened and looked down at her.

"Hime-sama?"

"It's nothing," she lied. He continued to regard her, and she relented. "Leader Dessalen said we'd have to secure the school for that boy anyway."

"You mean your brother, Kiku-hime?" Captain Jace regarded her with a hard look

"He's not—" and she stopped herself and shook her head. "You don't understand."

"I'd say I do," Captain Jace replied. He looked over to Lieutenant Midin and gave a curt nod. "That'll be all, Lieutenant."

Lieutenant Midin nodded to excuse himself politely. Kiku crossed her arms and looked at Jace with belligerence, but before he could speak, Akane was pushing her way into the chamber as Lieutenant Midin was making his way out.

"What is it, Akane-chan?" Kiku asked.

Akane frowned and shook her head, looking around.

"It wasn't you, then?" Akane huffed and looked troubled. Kiku felt immediate apprehension. "It's nothing. Maybe."

Kiku jerked her chin toward Jace, and he inclined his head, leaving Kiku and Akane alone.

"Tell me." Kiku softened her voice. She went over to Akane's side and could see she was shaking. Kiku put a hand on her arm and smiled reassuringly.

"A Celestial was invoked," Akane said, her voice shaking. One of Akane's gifts was to be able to sense that sort of activity. Usually, it was Kiku doing something Leader Dessalen didn't approve of, but this time, it wasn't her. "But it wasn't one of us. I already looked in on the others. I don't know—"

"Thank you, Akane," Kiku said, pressing her lips together. If it wasn't them, Kiku knew who it was. "I'll take care of it."

"But, Kiku-chan, who—" Akane asked.

"It's all right," Kiku assured her and then hurried out of the chamber.

She took the elevator back up to the regular basement of the house and then climbed the wide stone stairs to the main floor.

Where would Leader Dessalen be at this time of the day? Her eyes flicked to the library, and she quickly crossed the foyer and opened the door.

Kiku hadn't wanted to be correct but knew she was when she saw his prone body on the floor. "Oh, Ouji-sama."

Akane and the others didn't know. She only knew because Eyanna had told her. Kiku quickly locked the door behind her and knelt next to him, pulling his head into her lap.

"Ouji-sama?" Kiku called softly. "Ouji?"

Leader Dessalen stirred and opened his eyes to slits. Kiku was both relieved and angry. Why would he have done this? He knew it was dangerous for him!

"Kiku?" He tried to sit up, but winced in pain and dropped back down, closing his eyes.

"You shouldn't do that, Ouji-sama," she admonished.

"Mm." Even in pain, his mouth twisted into a small smile. "What's that, Hime-chan?"

"You know," she accused. He nodded with a moan

"Don't scold me, Kiku," he murmured. "You've done far worse."

"Hai," she sighed. There was little arguing that point. She pressed her fingers to his forehead. "You need to sleep. I can't get you up to our room alone."

"Get Marlon," Leader Dessalen said as he slipped back to unconsciousness. "He can be trusted."

Kiku leaned down and kissed him gently. "Baka."

"Hai," Leader Dessalen agreed.

~

Marlon was let into the library by Kiku-hime and looked at Leader Dessalen on the floor with alarm. He moved quickly and knelt at his side to check his breathing and pulse.

"He's all right," Kiku assured him.

Satisfied that the Exalted Leader didn't seem to be in immediate medical peril, he breathed a sign of relief. "What happened here, Kiku-chan?" Marlon asked. Kiku looked uncomfortable and bit her lip.

"Ouji-sama did something foolish," she said. Rising to his feet, Marlon gave Kiku a hard look.

"I can't help him unless you tell me," he said. She bit her lip. "Kiku-hime, tell me."

"I'm sorry." Kiku shook her head. "If he wants you to know, he can tell you when he wakes up."

"If he wakes up," Marlon muttered. Kiku smiled.

"Ouji will be fine," she said. "I promise. We just need to get him up to bed quietly so he can sleep. No one can know."

"If you say so, Hime-sama." Marlon didn't like being kept in the dark. But he didn't have any reason to believe Kiku was lying to him.

But he would most certainly be taking this up with the Exalted Leader when he woke.

And Marlon had a long time to wait. It was close to twenty hours before Leader Dessalen lifted his eyes. Marlon had trouble keeping the generals at bay. Finally, he just told them that Leader Dessalen was busy with Kiku-hime and he wasn't to be disturbed. It rankled them, but it ceased the inquiries of when the Leader was going to be available for conference.

Only General Lysis hadn't bought the story. The general looked at him with hard eyes. The man was too good at what he did.

"What's really going on?" he demanded.

"You can take it up with Leader Dessalen later," Marlon told the general. Which was pretty much the same answer he had gotten from Kiku-hime.

When Leader Dessalen finally woke, Marlon looked him over critically. He was sweating and pale. He'd been feverish while he was out, but Marlon hesitated to treat him not understanding exactly what his malady was. Kiku had been stubbornly unhelpful in the matter.

"You don't look well, Exalted One," Marlon remarked.

"Hm." Dessalen closed his eyes again.

"Would you care to explain this?" Marlon asked with some bite in his voice. Leader Dessalen sighed and opened his eyes, sitting up.

"I would like a drink of water," Leader Dessalen said. Kiku immediately got up and got it for him. She gave him a reproachful look while he gratefully swallowed it. "Gods, my head hurts."

"Good," Kiku snapped. Marlon raised his eyebrows in surprise. Kiku was genuinely vexed with the Exalted Leader. Leader Dessalen smiled at her with a shrug.

"You'll get over it," he told her. Kiku scowled and walked out, slamming the door. Leader Dessalen winced at the sound, dropping his head back against the pillows.

"She is unhappy with you," Marlon remarked. He had noted that the entire time Leader Dessalen had been unconscious, Kiku had been both worried and angry.

"Yes," Leader Dessalen answered.

"I would like to know what laid you out for a full day," Marlon said. "One should tell one's physician these things."

"There's nothing you can do for it," Dessalen muttered, struggling to sit up. He put his head in his hands. "Ugh."

"I'll be the judge of that." Marlon lifted Leader Dessalen's chin and looked at his eyes. One was more dilated than the other. He frowned. He wanted to get him into the basement infirmary so he could run a few scans.

"A Celestial," Dessalen muttered.

"Pardon?" Marlon said with surprise. He thought he heard Leader Dessalen say something about a Celestial?

"It was a Celestial," Leader Dessalen said a little louder. "Mine, to be exact."

~

"You look like hell," General Lysis remarked coming into the Leader Dessalen's bedchamber. Dessalen was up and dressed, wearing a white shirt and black uniform pants. He had Marlon summon the general as soon as he could stand on his feet.

"Thank you," Leader Dessalen answered. General Lysis crossed his arms and looked at him critically. "Don't you start. Kiku has already thoroughly scolded me."

"She should," General Lysis retorted. Marlon looked at Leader Dessalen with a touch of surprise. "You're an idiot."

"He knows?" the physician asked.

"Of course I know," General Lysis said with irritation. Dessalen smiled with a nod. General Lysis had been part of the Exalted Leader's inner circle for years. The men who stood in it knew Dessalen's greatest secret. That he, himself, had been Celestial chosen since he was a young child.

"We've got a problem," Leader Dessalen interrupted. There was little time, and they had to act fast. "There are defiantly traitors in the Manor House."

"Who?" Lysis asked.

"He's not that helpful," Leader Dessalen answered with a roll of his eyes. "But there's more than one, and they're getting ready to move."

"They're after the princesses, then?" Lysis asked. The general looked concerned.

"Most likely." Leader Dessalen nodded. "I wouldn't have been given the information otherwise."

"Do you have a plan?" General Lysis asked.

"I do," Leader Dessalen admitted. "But I don't like it. I'm going to send Kiku and her sisters away until this thing is put down."

General Lysis folded his arms and nodded. Dessalen could see his mind working quickly. Then Lysis looked up.

"But where?" he asked. "Manor Town is the most secure facility we have on the planet."

"No," Leader Dessalen said. "There's a holdstead we built before the founding of Manor Town. It's three days ride into the mountains if you use horses. Once its shields are activated, it is impossible to breach."

"Who are you sending with them?" Lysis asked. Dessalen made a pained expression. This part of the plan he disliked the most. However, his patron had been specific. Little as he liked it, he knew he had to comply.

"No one," he replied.

"Are you insane?" Lysis spit out. He threw his arms up in the air and shook his head.

"I agree with the general, Leader Dessalen," Marlon interjected. "Sending the five of them—"

"Six," Dessalen corrected. He looked back and forth between the general and the physician. "Mary-chan must go too. There's no helping it. No one can be trusted."

"I can go," Lysis retorted. Leader Dessalen felt an immediate stab of irritation. Like he wanted Lysis alone with Kiku for any number of days. But even as he thought it, he knew the general was genuinely concerned about the safety of all the girls, rather than some misguided attempt to spend time with the High Princess.

"No, I need you here," Leader Dessalen said. And it was true. Lysis was one of the few who, while bothersome, was utterly loyal. "I don't like sending them off alone either, but I've got to trust Kiku with this."

General Lysis looked at Marlon-sensei in a calculating fashion. "Send him."

"No." Leader Dessalen shook his head. He'd already considered it, but— "Andersen-sensei will go with them if they need a physician. There is a good chance we'll need the sensei's skills here. Kiku-hime's brother will go, too. It'll only keep him out of our way here, though. I doubt he will be much help to her."

"That is something that needs to be addressed in the future," Lysis remarked. Dessalen nodded. He'd been giving a lot of thought on what to do with James Davis.

Then he pinned Marlon with his sharp golden eyes.

"What do you think about Dr. Andersen going?" he asked. Marlon looked at him with surprise.

"If it's what you desire, Leader Dessalen," Marlon replied. "But staying here would be more dangerous."

Leader Dessalen smiled. He'd gotten more information from his patron that he hadn't expected.

"I have other news," Leader Dessalen said. "The curse has been forgiven."

"What?" Lysis eyes flashed with annoyance. "Already?"

As much Leader Dessalen enjoyed his general's discomfort, he knew he couldn't let that pretense stand. "It's not Kiku-chan."

"It's not?" General Lysis paused, looking troubled. "One of the other princesses, then? You haven't approved suitors for any, have you?"

"Sensei?" Leader Dessalen turned to look at the Garlon T'zen physician.

"I assure you, Leader Dessalen, I have not entertained the affections of any of the princesses," Marlon denied.

"What about the lovely Andersen-sensei?" Leader Dessalen raised an eyebrow.

General Lysis laughed, relaxing with a nod. And Dessalen had to agree, had it been one of the other princesses, there would be trouble over it. Marlon looked back and forth between them.

"That's not possible," Marlon whispered, looking stunned. But to be fair, finding out you were about to be a father, when you had no hope of such an event for over half your life, would do that.

"Oh, I wouldn't say that, when the Celestials take an active interest in our affairs," Leader Dessalen remarked. "Especially living under the same roof as Toki-chan. Really, you shouldn't be surprised."

Marlon closed his eyes for a few moments and then looked back at Leader Dessalen.

"What should I do?" he asked.

"This is your affair, Sensei," Leader Dessalen said. "She is not Garlon T'zen, and she doesn't have a guardian for you to negotiate with. Likely she's still unaware herself. She can, of course, live under our protection as long as she wishes."

"My thanks, Leader Dessalen." Marlon bowed, his face flushing with bright color.

~

Preparations were made quietly that night. Kiku had listened seriously to Leader Dessalen as he explained what they had to do. She nodded, remembering the old holdstead. She had made the ride back and forth from there a few times with Captain Jace, so she was confident she could find her way there with a map to guide her.

They told the yardmaster to pack horses for a small scouting party that would be out for a few days. Packs and horses were made ready. Captain Jace supervised and had a handful of men acting as decoys. Kiku and the others were to meet them at a secure point away from the house. They chose the pavilion at the park in the center of town.

Kiku was disappointed that she couldn't stay and help with the insurrection, but understood that her priority was the safety of her sisters. The house wasn't going to be safe, and it was her responsibility to take them where they would be.

Captain Jace was unhappy he wasn't going with them and had taken it to Ouji-sama himself. He'd come back stiff and angry. Leader Dessalen told him in no uncertain terms that the captain was staying behind.

Marlon-sensei and Leader Dessalen had come to bid them safe journey at the park; Captain Jace was nearby watching the deserted park with wary eyes.

"Be careful, Kiku-chan," Leader Dessalen admonished. He hugged her fiercely. Kiku nodded, not trusting her voice. She was determined not to cry. He cradled her face with one hand, kissing her gently. Kiku opened her lips to kiss him ardently. She hated leaving him but knew she had to for the sake of her sisters. Looking up into Leader Dessalen's eyes, she knew he felt the same.

"You take care too, Ouji," she whispered. "You're going to be in more danger than me."

"Never fear, Hime-chan," he said with a twist of a smile. "I will make sure they pay dearly for this."

At the same time, Marlon was saying good-bye to Dr. Andersen. They were close enough that Kiku could hear their quiet words. Marlon-sensei looked troubled.

"Can't you tell me what's happening?" Dr. Andersen asked.

"Andy-chan." Marlon pressed his cheek against hers. "Just please be careful and do everything Kiku-hime says.

She's young, but she's an excellent officer. She'll keep all of you safe."

"Or die trying," Dr. Andersen said worriedly. Kiku stifled a small giggle. Dr. Andersen worried too much sometimes.

"Don't even say that, Andy-chan," Marlon scolded. "You'll be safer where you're going."

"I would still rather stay with you," she said.

"I would rather you go." He kissed her lightly and stepped away. She looked at him wistfully with a sigh and turned to follow Kiku and the rest out. They quietly pulled themselves up on their horses and made their way out of the park, and then out of town.

~

"Gentlemen," Leader Dessalen said as he sat down in the command chamber. He and Lysis had prepared as much as they could without knowing who was to be trusted and who wasn't. General Lysis had sent off a priority order to General Catensen to have his battle group redeployed to the Earth sector immediately. Leader Dessalen doubted Catensen would make it in time for anything other than mop up. But knew he could count on the general to be loyal and planned to put him in command of the sector once he arrived. General Tamarik had clearly lost control of his command and needed to be replaced.

There were five generals assigned to the system and they were in attendance along with Lysis and Marlon. Dessalen glanced around and took stock. He doubted Tamarik was disloyal but couldn't be sure. The general had been unhappy with his handling of Kiku and as her guardian was in a position to make things difficult for him. He hadn't in the past, but Tamarik was determined that Dessalen live to the letter of the law and allow multiple suitors. That was something Leader Dessalen had no intention of allowing. And now that he was armed with the knowledge that any Earth woman could conceive a Garlon T'zen child, he was even more determined.

"I have decided to move the Capital to Earth," he announced without preamble. There was a mixture of shock and surprise from around the table.

"You can't be serious!" General Makiellen drew in a sharp breath. "The Capital has been the center of culture and commerce for over a thousand years!"

"More like two thousand," General Kassius corrected. "Our allies will not tolerate moving it to this backwater."

"The Capital is a stagnant and dying planet," Dessalen stated. "We all know that. The curse has made sure of it."

"But with the princesses having founded this new Origin world—" General Makiellen tried his best to sound reasonable "—it was to be forgiven. Their children are to be sent back to reseed the Capital."

"The Celestials will never allow that," Leader Dessalen said. "You know that."

"So you've said, but I don't believe it." General Makiellen frowned. "There is nothing to lead us to believe that is true."

"Other than the fact it is?" General Lysis retorted.

"You're siding with him on this, Lysis?" General Rohlon asked.

"When the Exalted Leader makes a decision you live with it." Lysis folded his arms and regarded the other general with a cold glare.

"Why?" Makiellen sneered. "Did he offer you a place in Kiku's bed for your support?"

General Lysis leaped from his chair with his face full of fury. Leader Dessalen put his hand on Lysis's forearm and gave Makiellen a dangerous look.

"That's not my place to offer," Leader Dessalen said softly. "And you are out of line."

"How much does this have to do with Kiku-hime-sama?" General Tamarik looked at Leader Dessalen critically. "I believe it has to do with you not wanting to leave her bed."

"General," Leader Dessalen warned.

"You cannot let your infatuation with that girl keep you from your responsibilities!" General Tamarik pounded the table with his fist.

"Don't." Leader Dessalen's eyes flashed.

"I will accept as many suitors as necessary for her to find someone she'll have other than you!" General Tamarik stormed.

"I forbid it!" Leader Dessalen spat out, jumping to his feet, full of fury.

"You can't stop me." General Tamarik stood and slammed hands hard on the table.

That ended the meeting.

"That went well," Lysis said sarcastically as he and Leader Dessalen walked out of the command chamber. Dessalen was enraged. He hadn't planned on losing his temper, but he also didn't plan on Tamarik's open rebellion. But rebellion wasn't betrayal.

"It's not him," Dessalen growled angrily.

"I don't think so either," Lysis remarked. "I'm leaning toward Makiellen, myself."

Leader Dessalen paused. He was so angry with Tamarik he hadn't thought much about the other generals. He gave Lysis a curt nod. "Find out."

"Yes, Leader Dessalen." Lysis inclined his head and moved away. Marlon continued to follow behind him as Dessalen made his way to the library.

"I'm going to have a drink," Dessalen muttered. "You?"

"No, thank you," Marlon said as he eyed Leader Dessalen. "And you shouldn't drink much, either."

"Worried?" Dessalen brought the glass to his lips and, closing his eyes, let the burning fluid drain down his throat.

"Concerned," Marlon replied. "They're going to learn the Princesses are gone soon, and that will spur them into action."

"Dessalen! Where the hell are they?" Tamarik bellowed as he thrust open the library door. Marlon raised an eyebrow, and Leader Dessalen shrugged.

"Ah, General." Dessalen smiled genially. "Care for a drink?"

"What have you done with Kiku-hime and the others?" Tamarik demanded. "You have no right—"

"I have every right," Leader Dessalen interrupted. "You seem to keep forgetting that I am the guardian of the others."

"Not of Kiku!" Tamarik yelled.

"Lieutenant Kiku," Leader Dessalen smiled, "who is my aide and under my direct command, is on a mission that happens to involve her sisters."

"Very convenient." General Tamarik offered the Exalted Leader a withering glare.

"And it happens to be true." Leader Dessalen sat down, relaxing into his chair.

~

"How much farther is it, Kiku-onee?" Toki asked. "I'm so tired."

Jennifer smiled over her shoulder at Toki. They had been riding all of the night and half of the day. Mary was asleep in the saddle against Dr. Andersen, and the rest were taking the trek with stoic determination. But Toki, being the next youngest next to Mary, was wearing out. They would have to stop soon or she would drop out of the saddle.

"Toki-chan can ride with me if she wants," Jimmy offered. He wasn't used to riding either, but he was holding up better than the young princess. His sister met his eyes for the first time in days. He didn't understand her open hostility. His face flushed with bright color. "If that's okay."

Jennifer pressed her lips into a firm line and glanced around.

"We need to get more distance between Manor Town and us," she said. She pulled her horse back, and it fell into step next to Jimmy's. "Are you sure? Have you ridden before?"

"Well, yeah." He drew in a deep breath. How could she not remember all of the summers they had spent up north on their grandparent's farm? "You don't remember?"

"I don't remember anything before the Garlon T'zen." Her tone was clipped and short. Toki looked at her pleadingly, and Jennifer relented. "All right. Yes, if you could, James-san."

"Can't you call me Jimmy?" he asked. Jennifer looked at him with irritation.

"No," she said kicking her horse forward.

They stopped and shifted around. Jimmy helped Toki up on his horse and then threw his leg over and settled in with the princess behind him. She wrapped her arms around his waist, and they continued their trek. He tried to make conversation a few times with his sister, only to be soundly rebuffed. He had no idea what he had done, but knew one thing for sure.

"She hates me," Jimmy mumbled. Toki was lightly dozing leaning on his back. He felt her pull away and yawn.

"Who?" she asked.

"Jennifer," he replied.

"Onee-sama?" Toki asked with surprise.

"What does 'Onee-sama' mean?" he asked, turning to look at her over his shoulder. Toki smiled. She thought for a moment.

"Most honored big sister," she said. "Onee is 'big sister.' Sama is like 'lord' or 'lady.'"

"Uh huh," Jimmy said. He didn't know a lot about their language, but he had a mind to learn more. If he sister was going to be here, he needed to. "Can you tell me more?"

"Of course," Toki looked up at him with a bright indulgent smile. "Jimmy-chan."

~

"Leader Dessalen." General Makiellen stepped in front of him in the front hall of the Manor. "I insist you divulge the whereabouts of the princesses."

"No," Leader Dessalen replied with a cold voice. He flicked his golden eyes around the room. It looked like the standoff was about to get under way.

"You are not putting the concerns of your people before your own—" General Makiellen started, but Leader Dessalen cut him off with a sharp movement.

"Don't start, General," Dessalen said. "This has nothing to do with that. What did Sadar offer you?"

"Lord Sadar is a full blooded prince." General Makiellen straightened his shoulders and met Dessalen's eyes with a sneer. "Unlike you, he will see to it that the Princesses fulfill their duty. Our people will survive this catastrophe your mother left us."

"That old prattle again," Leader Dessalen dismissed. "It's nothing but the whining of old men. You've lived too long on the frontier, General. No one cares anymore."

They were drawing a crowd, which was what Dessalen had planned. Lysis had carefully seeded it with his handpicked operatives ready to move when the signal was given. The order was to immediately kill any who even looked as if they were going to support the uprising. Dessalen had no tolerance for traitors and was going to make a hard example here. If he had to kill most of the garrison to do it, so be it. Dessalen didn't care if all he ended up with was Lysis's specialists and Kiku's personal unit. It would be enough to hold Manor Town until Catensen's battle group arrived.

"You will tell me where you've sent them," General Makiellen growled, starting to feel superior. He seemed very self-assured in his victory. "Generals Rohlon, Kassius, and Jasxon all stand with me."

"I don't," General Tamarik said stepping forward. "There is no excuse for betrayal, General."

"You're an old fool." General Jasxon pointed a finger. "He'd be rid of you as soon as he could just to keep possession of Kiku-hime-sama."

"I doubt that," General Tamarik replied.

"Tell us where they are, and we might send you back to your father's people." General Kassius smiled at Leader Dessalen. "They've long wanted an alliance. Prince Sadar thinks it would be a suitable use for you."

"Now he's choosing my bed partners?" Leader Dessalen mocked.

"We will find them," Makiellen said, his tone laced with menace.

"You'll have to get through Kiku-hime to get them," Leader Dessalen said.

"That shouldn't prove too difficult." Makiellen made a distasteful face.

"You obviously don't know our princess very well." Tamarik let out a short laugh.

"We'll get what we want out of you." General Makiellen made a gesture. But things didn't happen the way he had anticipated. Rohlon and Kassius dropped on either side of him immediately, and Leader Dessalen offered a predatory smile and he took two steps and quickly disarmed Makiellen.

"Shame on you, General," the Exalted Leader mocked wrapping his fingers around his throat. "You should never have let me get my hands on you."

He squeezed and quickly yanked his wrist, snapping Makiellen's neck with a powerful twist. The room had erupted into chaos with men fighting and dying. Dessalen stepped over a body and looked for Lysis. The general had just dispatched two more soldiers when he saw Leader Dessalen motion to him.

"Find Jasxon," Leader Dessalen ordered.

"He got away?" Lysis scowled.

"I don't see his body," Dessalen snapped with anger. "I want him dead."

"Of course, Leader Dessalen." General Lysis nodded.

~

In the end, casualties weren't as bad as anticipated. Only half of the garrison at Manor Town ended with their blood pouring out on the Manor House floor. Leader Dessalen still wasn't certain they'd gotten them all. He issued an order that only Kiku's unit was to remain in Manor Town due to the breach. The rest would be rotated out with fresh troops from General Catensen when he arrived. Until then everyone was being watched very carefully, and they knew it.

Lysis hadn't found General Jasxon, much to Leader Dessalen's displeasure. Marlon hoped the general had enough good sense to get off-planet rather than look for Kiku and the others, but they couldn't be sure. And with the situation still not totally stable, Leader Dessalen had no inclination to send for their return.

Marlon-sensei was looking over a few minor wounds Dessalen had managed to take in the failed coup. The physician was silent as he wrapped his arm, sensing that the Exalted Leader's mood was not the best. Dessalen couldn't help but look longingly towards Kiku's bed.

"She'll be back soon enough, my lord," Marlon remarked. Leader Dessalen flicked a glance up at Marlon.

"That obvious?" he asked.

"About Kiku-hime?" Marlon smiled. "Always."

"Hm." Dessalen smirked. "Well, it could be worse."

"Yes. You could be dead and then she would be very vexed," Marlon said with dry humor.

Leader Dessalen snorted. Marlon continued to dress Leader Dessalen's wounds with a small twisted smile.

A knock came at the door and Captain Jace stepped in with an incline of his head.

"I'm sorry, Leader Dessalen," he said. "But there is an urgent call for Marlon-sensei. The lady is quite insistent."

"An Earth call?" Leader Dessalen frowned looking at Marlon, who shook his head unknowingly.

"Yes sir," Captain Jace continued. "She says she is Mrs. Jane Andersen from Great Britain, Andersen-sensei's mother. She's hysterical and insists she speak to Marlon-sensei immediately."

"Go take it," Leader Dessalen ordered. Marlon offered a slight bow to the Exalted Leader and followed Captain Jace out to a nearby telephone in the hallway. Manor House, having been built to match Earth standards, had merged both types of communications through the odd devices.

"Hello, Mrs. Andersen," he said. "Yes, it's Marlon."

He paused listening to the woman on the other side of the phone, feeling the blood drain from his face. He closed his eyes and swallowed with difficulty.

"Yes, I understand," he said feeling his blood freeze in his veins. "Thank you. Please tell her not to call again."

He hung up the phone and tried to quiet his racing heart. Looking back at the double door bedchamber his legs felt like lead as he walked back slowly. He re-entered with a polite knock, and Leader Dessalen looked up expectantly.

"What was it?" Leader Dessalen asked.

"Andy-chan contacted her mother from the holdstead," he said using quiet, measured words. "Calling the Manor directly would be too dangerous. She said all didn't make it to their destination."

"Tell me," Leader Dessalen demanded in a low voice with his golden eyes glinting dangerously.

"They were chased—" Marlon closed his eyes. "Kiku-hime led their pursuers off in another direction, sending the others on. The others made it. Kiku never arrived."

CHAPTER 8

"Where are the others, Kiku-hime?" General Jasxon demanded. Kiku turned her head away and refused to look at him. She had been beaten and was sore from her capture. It was a good they wanted her alive, but Kiku hadn't felt the same about her captors. She didn't enjoy killing the general's men. If anything, she felt angry he'd put her in the position where she had to defend herself from her own people. "If you cooperate things will go better for you."

"I'll not cooperate with a traitor." Her blue eyes flashed with heat. She glanced around the small conference room they had brought her to after pulling her off the transport. They tried to get her to talk, but she steadfastly refused to speak. The cuffs bit into Kiku's wrists, but she didn't give them the satisfaction of seeing any discomfort. "How dare you even touch me? Leader Dessalen will have your head."

"You shouldn't count heavily on Leader Dessalen, Princess," General Jasxon told her. He came around and stood over her. He was dark haired, but balding. His nose was crooked, probably having healed from a bad break. Kiku longed to break it again. "His days of power aren't for long."

"You wish." Kiku threw a fierce frown in his direction. General Jasxon shook his head, rolling his eyes. He tossed down an imagedeck and looked at her sternly.

"You are aware, we can make you talk," he threatened. Kiku laughed at him.

"Go ahead and try," she said. "I've already been through the worst the Xoned could do to me. I'm not afraid of you."

He lost his temper.

"You are a stubborn, spoiled, willful child!" he raged at her.

"Come now, General," said a new voice. "Is that any way to speak to the High Princess?"

Kiku looked sharply at the newcomer. She knew him but they had never met. Sadar was Leader Dessalen's older brother by a different father. Both Ouji and Sadar were children of the late High Queen, but Dessalen had been his mother's heir. Kiku didn't know who Sadar's father was; no one ever spoke of it.

His hair was black and cut short against his head. His eyes were very dark; his features reminded her somewhat of Ouji-sama's, only softer. He was heavier than her prince, but that was probably from living the soft life outside the military. Ouji had explained it before. Sadar was the elder, but not the son of his mother's sworn consort. The High Queen decided between the boys, when they were children, who would rule after her. Not all were satisfied with the High Queen's choice.

"Sadar-sama." General Jasxon bowed with respect.

"Ah, Kiku-hime-sama." Sadar cocked his head to one side and looked at her appraisingly. Kiku returned his gaze evenly. "I am very pleased to finally meet you."

Kiku met his eyes with a frown. She wasn't pleased to meet him at all! So he had been behind all of this?

Sadar laughed, circling her. "I heard you could be difficult," he said.

"You have no idea," General Jasxom muttered. Sadar silenced him with a wave of his finger. The general shook his head with frustration.

"I want you to tell me where the other princesses are, Kiku-hime," he said.

"I won't," she said.

"That's fine too," Sadar replied with a wide grin, "because I can certainly make do with just you."

Kiku jerked her head up, unsure of what he meant. He smiled in an unfriendly manner. She drew in a deep breath while flicking her eyes around the room. She'd figure a way to escape, and then she would also figure out a way to take care of Sadar.

~

Leader Dessalen was enraged. And worse, there was no handy target to take it out on. He was angry with himself for sending Kiku off without additional men. He was furious with Lysis that Jasxon got away. He was near blind with fury that anyone would dare touch Kiku-hime.

"Do you know anything yet?" he demanded, cornering the watch officer in the small security center. The young lieutenant paled and shook his head.

"N-no, Leader Dessalen," he stammered out. "We're still trying to bring the systems back up after the uprising."

"It was a failed exercise in disobedience," Leader Dessalen corrected. He pointed menacingly. "I want those systems back up. I want downlinks from the orbiters. And I want it now!"

"Y-yes, Leader Dessalen." The lieutenant's hands trembled as he continued to work studiously under the Exalted Leader's hard scrutiny.

"May I have a word with you, Leader Dessalen?" General Lysis leaned into the room. Leader Dessalen snarled but followed the general out.

"What?" he demanded.

"You're going to give the lieutenant heart failure," General Lysis told him. "Standing over him staring isn't helping."

"Have you heard from Catensen yet?" Leader Dessalen asked. General Lysis crossed his arms and offered a sidelong look.

"The systems are down," General Lysis reminded him.

"Damn it!" Leader Dessalen exploded.

"That's not helping either," General Lysis said. Dessalen looked at him with hostility.

"Then what do you suggest, General?" Dessalen ground his jaw.

"That you have a little patience," General Lysis replied.

"I have no patience!" Leader Dessalen stormed striding through another door, slamming it.

"I've noticed," Lysis muttered from behind him.

Dessalen marched through the lower level of the house to the mid-size command chamber. He found Captain Jace working on a projector with three other men. He moved around to try and get a better look. The young captain met his eyes with a hard look.

Dessalen nodded and threw himself into a chair. He knew Jace was angry with him but was wise enough not to voice his unhappiness. Dessalen's guilt was biting at him hard enough. But neither knew if Kiku wouldn't have disappeared had the Exalted Leader sent her captain with her. But one thing was certain: Jace would have died before Kiku was taken into enemy hands.

"You have it, then?" Captain Jace asked the corporal assisting.

"Yes sir," the man answered.

Captain Jace turned to the Exalted Leader. "We're ready," he told him.

"Lysis!" Leader Dessalen roared. Captain Jace arched an eyebrow and move around the table, pulling out a control pad.

It was only a moment before General Lysis entered with Marlon-sensei following close behind. Good, Dessalen wanted both of them here.

"The systems are back up," Captain Jace said. The captain flipped on the holographic projector and started to scroll through what looked to be hours of orbiter data before he came across what they were looking for: Kiku and her sisters riding their horses in a single line through the snow.

Leader Dessalen didn't move as he watched the events unfold without sound on the projected holo image. Kiku and the others were making their way through a small wooded area; the replay was hard to see through the trees. She paced her horse up and down their line of riders a few times before she turned and nudged the animal into a gallop in the opposite direction of the others, going back over their trail.

"Good thinking," Lysis muttered. Leader Dessalen didn't respond. He was frozen in fear of what he would find at the end of this. Either she would be dead or she wouldn't. He held his breath.

Kiku was intercepted in a clearing, so the orbiters offered a clear view of what happened. She killed two men with a hand cannon before they yanked her from her horse, knocking the weapon away. Then it was a clean unarmed fight. She didn't surrender even though it was clear she had no chance of winning or escape. Still it looked like she did make one, possibly two, more kills before they knocked her roughly to the ground and overpowered her.

Leader Dessalen closed his eyes, willing his heart to start beating again as he drew a deep breath. "She's alive."

"Yes sir," Captain Jace said, sounding relieved as well.

"Get an energy trail on their transport," Leader Dessalen ordered.

"We already have it," Captain Jace said. "I've got the coordinates of where they went. Still on the planet, the United States."

"Really." Leader Dessalen narrowed his eyes coldly. Jasxon was more stupid than he thought. It looked like they were taking Kiku right to Sadar. If that was the case, then Dessalen finally knew where he was lurking as well. He turned to Lysis. "How many men do you need?"

General Lysis frowned. "I need more information."

Leader Dessalen shook his head. "We don't have time."

"I disagree," General Lysis replied, his voice low and serious. "With the systems back online we can grid the planet so a ship can't leave. We use the orbiters to get more surveillance, possibly send in drones."

"Sadar has Kiku." Leader Dessalen clenched his jaw and ground out the words.

"He's not going to harm her or she would already be dead," General Lysis pointed out.

"You know what he wants from her." Leader Dessalen dropped his voice. General Lysis nodded.

"Kiku-hime is strong, Leader Dessalen." General Lysis easily looked as troubled as Dessalen. "We'll be in a far better position to take her back once Catensen gets here. We can't afford to act rashly. Her safety is at risk."

Dessalen met Lysis's eyes. The general wasn't being disobedient; he was advising him as an officer. The Exalted Leader also knew that Lysis genuinely cared for Kiku's safety and would give him the best recommendations based on that. Even as Dessalen longed to go rashly after her, he knew Lysis was right. He closed his eyes briefly and nodded once. He stood up from the table and nodded to Captain Jace. "Assist General Lysis."

"Yes, Leader Dessalen." Captain Jace inclined his head as the Exalted Leader swept angrily out of the room.

~

Kiku found herself in a sparsely decorated bedroom; she was rather surprised her cell wasn't a little more prisonlike.

First, she had been roughly undressed by two Earth women who didn't seem too interested in what they were doing. They didn't speak to her, and she didn't speak to them. Then she had been shoved into a shower room. Kiku wanted to resist her captors, but she couldn't help herself there. She was filthy from days in the saddle and smelled like horse and sweat. She was also sore and bruised. The hot water pouring over her felt heaven-sent as she scrubbed herself clean.

Then she was given a short, thin robe along with a pair of shorts and escorted to the bedroom, shoved in, and she heard the door lock with a solid click. Kiku thoroughly inspected the room, looking for anything she could use as a weapon. But the mirrors were bolted to the walls and the only objects portable were the pillows and blankets. An adjacent bathroom yielded nothing as well. Kiku went back to the bed and dropped her head into her hands dejectedly.

The door lock clicked, and she looked up expectantly. Sadar let himself in and leaned against the door appraising her through narrowed eyes.

"Kiku-chan," he purred.

"What do you want?" she asked, unnerved by his appearance. He didn't seem to be wearing much more than a robe and light pair of pants. Kiku immediately felt self-conscious in the small robe she had been given and pulled it tighter around her. Sensing her discomfort he smiled.

"I just came to make sure you were comfortable," he replied stepping away from the door. "Are you comfortable, Kiku-chan?"

"I'm fine," she said, getting up from the bed.

"That's good." He continued to move close. Kiku watched him warily. "Now what can I do to make you more comfortable?"

"You can leave," she said. Sadar laughed.

"What I heard about you is true." He shook a finger at her.

"Don't come any closer," Kiku warned.

"What do you think you're going to do, Kiku-chan?" he asked mockingly. "Fight me?"

"Count on it," Kiku said shifting her feet into a defensive stance.

"Come now," he said. "Don't you tire of playing warrior? Why don't we play princess instead?"

"I'm not playing." She lifted her head and glared at him. Sadar smiled and reached for her. Kiku knocked his hand away and blocked his next immediate attempt. She swept her leg under his and knocked him hard in the middle of the chest. Sadar landed on the floor, scowling up at her.

"You don't wish to fight me," he warned. "It won't go well for you."

Kiku glared at him back angrily. "So you have to beat women into going to bed with you?"

"Don't speak to me like that," Sadar snarled. "I am a prince of House Garlon T'zen."

"And I'm the High Princess," Kiku snapped back. "So don't you come in here and think I'll lie down for you!"

Sadar looked at her with glittering eyes before he backed up slowly.

"Very well, Kiku-chan." He smiled unpleasantly. "We will do this another way."

~

"Do you think Kiku-onee is all right?" Toki asked Andersen-sensei. She swallowed hard, fearing the worst. Toki had tried to talk to Akane-onee first, but Akane had been snappish with worry herself.

"I'm sure she's fine, Toki-chan." Andersen-sensei's words were far more confident than her eyes. Toki began to tear up.

"I'm afraid," Toki said. Her voice shook with emotion. "What if something happened to her? What if she's dead? What will we do without Onee-sama to protect us?"

"Oh, Toki-chan." Andersen-sensei pulled the young princess into her arms, hugging her tightly. "It's all right. Really it is. Kiku is smart and brave. I'm sure she's alive."

Toki wiped her eyes, looking around their barren surroundings. The holdstead was little more than a small base carved into the side of the mountain. It had been an abandoned base of operations. It had taken Akane and Dido a few hours to get its systems and shields back online. But once the shields were erected they were fairly secure inside. Unless someone blew up the entire mountain, they would remain safe inside.

"Do you really think so, Andersen-sensei?" Toki asked.

"I think . . ." Andersen-sensei paused and then continued, "I know that whoever is after you girls wants you alive, and that includes Kiku. I'm hoping that my mother's call to Manor Town was able to let Leader Dessalen and the rest know that she's in danger. Don't you think he would take care of it?"

"Hai." Toki's voice broke.

"Why don't you see if James needs anything," Andersen-sensei told her. The doctor looked pale. "I'm feeling a little ill all of a sudden."

"Oh, isn't that expected?" Toki blinked a few times in surprise. From what she had learned, from Kaori and Dido whispering, pregnancy often made you ill. It was one of the worries weighing on their minds. Toki wondered if she might be able to ease it with her Celestial gift.

"You mean with the stress?" Andersen-sensei asked. "I'm sure that's it. This has been hard on us all."

"No, no." Toki shook her head. "It's because of the baby, right?"

"What baby?" Andersen-sensei looked at her with genuine surprise. Toki frowned. How could she not know?

"Your baby," Toki whispered, dropped her voice. "You know, you and Marlon-sensei's."

"Don't be ridiculous, Toki-chan." Andersen-sensei choked out a laugh. "That's not possible."

"But, Andersen-sensei," Toki protested.

"You go find James." Andersen-sensei shook her head with a smile.

"Hai," Toki said, leaving the Earth doctor still shaking her head.

Toki found James down with the horses. He was feeding them. Toki noted the worry line across his brow.

"Jimmy-chan?" Toki said softly.

"Oh, it's you, Toki-chan." He turned to face her with a halfhearted smile. "Is everything okay?"

"Hai," she said. "Are you all right?"

"I'm just worried about Jennifer," he said. Toki cocked her head to one side. She thought it was cute the way he called Onee-sama by her Earth name. Onee-sama didn't find it cute at all, but that sort of made it cuter.

"I know, Jimmy-chan." She bit her lip. "We all are. You do know she's our sister too, right?"

"I guess," he said. Then he turned to her and looked at her. Toki marveled at how much he looked like Kiku. Even being near him made her feel like she was closer to Onee-sama—the same dark eyes and troubled features when worried. "Why is that, Toki-chan? How is it that Jen and the rest of you are sisters?"

"Oh." Toki felt a cold grip of fear steal over her. She didn't like to remember that. But Jimmy-chan deserved to know. "We made a promise when we were still with the Xoned. It—it was before the Garlon T'zen came. We were all we had, so we became family."

Toki began to shake, and Jimmy looked at her with concern. He moved closer to her, and Toki curled against him. He wrapped his arms around her. Toki drew in a deep breath, drawing strength from his nearness.

"Kiku-onee swore she would protect us," Toki whispered. "And she did, Jimmy-chan. But it was hard. Eventually, we were traded into a Death Circle. It was a place you didn't come out of."

"What happened?" Jimmy-chan asked.

"I don't remember it all exactly," Toki said. "But there was a big fight, and somehow the Garlon T'zen were there. Kiku-onee was hurt. We had been with the Xoned about two years then, maybe, I think."

"How did the Garlon T'zen fit into this?" Jimmy-chan asked looking down at her. "I still don't understand why you were made princesses."

"That was because of the Celestials," Toki answered. "They made a promise to the Garlon T'zen. We were the first part of the promise. Because of that, each of us was made a princess. Kiku-onee is the High Princess."

"That doesn't clear much up. What is this promise?" Jimmy-chan said with confusion. Toki dimpled a smile up at him.

"That we'll break the curse," Toki said. "Without us, the Garlon T'zen would be a dead race. But because of us, there will be another generation."

"What?" He looked at her with confusion.

"Toki-chan!" Andersen-sensei yelled, sounding panicked. "You had better come and explain something to me!"

Toki giggled.

~

General Lysis paused outside the door to Leader Dessalen's bedchamber. He could hear Dessalen's restless pacing. Sighing, he knocked and entered at hearing the irritable assent.

"You really should try to sleep," Lysis told Leader Dessalen. Dessalen was standing near the window leaning against the frame, looking outside. His light hair was tousled and he was shirtless. Leader Dessalen flicked a glance over his shoulder and said nothing.

Lysis stopped for a long moment, torn with indecision. He silently moved closer to the Exalted Leader and touched him in the middle of the back. Dessalen stiffened but didn't move.

"It could be days yet, Dessalen," Lysis said softly. "You have to be rested and prepared."

"I can't sleep," Leader Dessalen said over his shoulder. "All I can think about, worry about, is what he's—"

"Don't torture yourself," Lysis whispered. "There are plenty of us that will do that for you."

"Hm." Dessalen smiled looking back out the window. Lysis ran his hand up to Dessalen's shoulder and squeezed it lightly.

"Let me," he offered, feeling his heartbeat hammer in his chest.

Leader Dessalen turned and caught Lysis by the back of the head kissing him fully on the lips. Lysis twined his arm around Dessalen's and felt his body begin to respond. It had been years since he had shared Leader Dessalen's bed, but he remembered the Exalted Leader of Garlon T'zen was a skilled lover. Lysis wanted to keep Dessalen's mind from Kiku if only for a few hours, allow his exhausted prince the peace of sleep.

Dessalen pulled away, caressing his cheek against Lysis's, and looked at him with his otherworldly golden eyes—eyes that were so unlike any other Garlon T'zen. Most credited them to his father's heritage, but Lysis knew better. Those eyes came from his deep early childhood bond with the Celestial Mathias. Lysis had been in Dessalen's inner circle since the beginning, and he knew all of these things. Sometimes lovers. Often bitter rivals. Always unfailingly loyal.

"A worthy offer." Dessalen smiled sadly and pushed him away. "But no."

"Good night, Leader Dessalen." Lysis offered a small bow, quelling a feeling of disappointment. Dessalen turned back to the window.

"Good night, General," he replied.

~

It didn't take days for General Catensen's battle group to arrive, much to Leader Dessalen's consolation. Catensen barreled into the system with seven warships. That meant he had left four to secure the Ma'gaar sector. Dessalen would consider where he was going to shift resources around once he got Kiku away from his brother. Until then he couldn't think of much else.

General Catensen's visage appeared on the holoview in the command center. The General hadn't changed much. He was still straight and rigid, looking thinner than he had been, his grey eyes sharp and a sardonic twist to his mouth.

"So, my lord," General Catensen spoke smoothly with a cultured tone, "you can't even manage to hold a backwater hole like this?"

"Catensen." Leader Dessalen's voice was a sharp growl. "You took your time getting here."

"My apologies." General Catensen offered a smirk. "But I had to take care of some stragglers you missed. They thought to offer a challenge when I entered the system."

"There had better not be any pieces left," Dessalen replied.

"You wound me," Catensen mocked.

"Send a full troop deployment to Manor Town, General," Dessalen ordered ignoring the general's insubordination. "We'll drop the net. Make sure nothing leaves the planet. However, do not, and you'd best be listening to me this time, destroy any outgoing vessels. There's a good probability Kiku-hime-same would be captive on board."

"You managed to lose the High Princess too?" General Catensen replied coldly. "Just the one princess, or all five?"

"General," Leader Dessalen snapped angrily. General Catensen bowed curtly, and the holo went blank.

"He's charming as ever." General Lysis remarked near the door.

"He's a bastard," Leader Dessalen said, grinding his teeth. "But he's exactly what I need at the moment. You'd better be ready to move."

"Yes, Leader Dessalen," Lysis said. "I plan on taking Marlon and Captain Jace's unit."

"You can have Marlon but not Kiku's group." Leader Dessalen shook his head, striding out of the chamber.

"But we know they're loyal," General Lysis protested.

"Right." Leader Dessalen nodded, stepping out into the sunlight, watching the ships drop out of the sky. They would hit the landing field outside of Manor Town in moments. "And that's why they're to go after the other princesses. You get operatives from Catensen."

"Ugh." Lysis made a face. Leader Dessalen flicked a glance in his direction.

"You two will have to play nicely together," he remarked.

"I will try, Leader Dessalen," Lysis said with a sigh.

~

Sadar wasn't foolish enough to try and escape on a ship to space once he saw Dessalen had pulled in seven warships. He looked over at General Jasxon.

"Any idea who that is?" he asked. Jasxon nodded, frowning.

"Catensen," he replied. "Those are his ships. I can't believe he would bring him here."

"Seems a bit much doesn't it?" Sadar agreed. General Catensen was usually used in the big battles, in the sectors that counted. Sadar smirked. "Dessalen must be desperate."

"No," General Jasxon disagreed. "He's just angry."

"Bah," Sadar dismissed.

"My lord," General Jasxon said. "I would recommend we evacuate this location. We'll probably be under siege soon."

Sadar nodded. "Get the princess."

"Is that wise?" General Jasxon asked. "You'll have a far better chance of escape if you leave her."

"I just got her to the point where she's pliable enough for me to bed her without losing a limb," Sadar retorted. It had taken a few days of drug treatments to get the mix just right. First it was too much, and she wasn't even conscious, and then too little and she was still too violent.

Weapons fire suddenly exploded somewhere in the complex.. General Jasxon shook his head and grabbed Sadar's arm.

"I'm sorry, your Excellency," he muttered. "But if we get away, we get another chance. If they catch us, we are all dead."

Sadar paled. He knew the general was right. He allowed him to lead him out of the command center.

~

General Lysis had ordered limited weapons fire and no explosives. He didn't know where they had Kiku-hime, and he didn't want to risk her injury. Marlon was nearby with a medpack slung over one shoulder and a small hand canon in his hand. Lysis tried to talk the physician out of coming in the first wave, wanting to secure the base first, but Marlon-sensei had been insistent. Lysis gritted his teeth wishing, he had the ability to outrank him.

At least Lysis wasn't the only one dealing with minor insubordination. Captain Jace had only flicked a glance at Leader Dessalen before he walked away to prep his gear to go with Lysis. The young captain said there was no chance that he wasn't going to recover the high princess. He'd sent his unit to retrieve the other princesses, under the command of Lieutenant Minden. Dessalen had been furious, but Lysis was grateful for even a few men that could be utterly trusted.

It didn't take much to take and secure the small base Sadar had been using. It was somewhere in the territories belonging to the troublesome nation state. There was a mixture of Garlon T'zen and natives staffing it. Lysis ordered the immediate execution of the Garlon T'zen traitors. The natives looked on pale and shaken by the swift brutality. He was torn at what to do with them. Their fate would be decided by the condition he found Kiku-hime in; or if he found her at all.

Lysis hadn't found Sadar or Jasxon either. He worried they had spirited her off along with them. He checked the energy level in his weapon. Well, he supposed it didn't matter. There was no chance he was returning to Leader Dessalen without her. If it took taking this country apart to find her, he was more than willing to start.

"General." An officer going through the surveillance cameras called him over. Lysis let out a long breath at seeing Kiku-hime on a monitor. She was lying on a bed in loose-fitting top and bottoms. Lysis nodded.

"I'm going to get her," he said. "Start demolition."

"Yes sir," the officer said, pulling explosive charges out of his side packs. Lysis used his wrist comm to tell Marlon he had found the princess. Marlon was demanding details of her condition.

"You'll get them," Lysis growled, "when I have them."

He closed the link abruptly. This whole situation had them on edge. It would be better once they got Kiku-hime-sama and the others back to Manor Town where they could be best protected.

He found the room and twisted open the lock to let himself in. He walked over to the bed and first looked her over carefully. She hadn't woken when he opened the door, and that was surprising. Her dark blond hair was loose around her face, and she was breathing evenly. He knelt down next to the bed.

"Hime-sama?" General Lysis said quietly. She slowly opened her eyes and smiled with a stretch and a sigh, looking very much like an Earth kitten just waking from a nap. Not at all like a captive being rescued. Lysis frowned.

"General . . . Lysis," she said and then giggled. "L-chan."

Lysis raised both his eyebrows. No, this was not typical behavior at all. He reached down and pulled her to her feet.

"Kiku-hime," he said. "Are you all right?"

"I'm fine." She slurred her words, stepping closer to him. Kiku slid her fingers deftly under his shirt, teasing along the edges of Lysis's well-defined muscles. He stiffened in surprise. Her other hand reached lower, and he caught it tightly. She leaned up to nibble along his jaw.

"Kiku," he said, his voice hoarse. "Don't."

"Why not, L-chan?" She giggled, taunting him further with her lips. "I know you want me."

He tried to catch her face so he could get a good look at her. Her dark blue eyes were glazed and unnaturally bright. He caressed her cheek, looking down at her with worry.

"What did they do to you?" he murmured. She smiled beatifically and leaned to kiss him. He leaned up higher out of her reach. General Lysis had had to do many difficult things in his career, but trying to resist the princess's advances may have been the most physically grueling. He didn't even know if he could. "Kiku, stop this."

"Kiss me," Kiku said in a singsongy voice. Her hands went to his face, caressing his jaw, tugging at his neck, pulling him toward her. He knew this was wrong. Gods, yes, he wanted her! But like this? She would despise him later, and Dessalen would rightfully gut him.

"Kiku, please," he begged. "I can't."

"Shh," she murmured. He moved forward closer against his will. "Say 'Kiku-hime-chan, please kiss me.'"

"No," he denied even while his mouth sank hungrily onto hers. She tasted so sweet and responded so sincerely. He could almost convince himself that she really wanted this. His hands moved around her body of their own volition, eagerly exploring the soft curves he had only been able to observe. With new alarm, Lysis felt her tugging at his waist, unbuckling his belt. He moaned in her ear. "Oh, Kiku."

He reached down and gently took her hands into his and met her eyes.

"Please don't," he asked. She smiled at him widely and shook her head. She leaned forward to kiss him again.

"Hime-sama." Captain Jace's voice was sharp from the door. The young captain had his helmet in his hands and was looking at the two of them in sharp disapproval.

"Jace-kun!" Kiku said brightly, turning quickly. She swayed on her feet and put a hand to her head just as her eyes rolled back. Lysis caught her before she dropped to the floor. Captain Jace started forward to take her, but Lysis shook his head.

"General." There was both warning and hostility in Captian Jace's tone, but Lysis decided it was best to ignore it for the moment.

"Tell Marlon to meet us at the transport," Lysis ordered as he moved around the captain for the door. He looked down at Kiku and shook his head. And he softly murmured, "You will be my death for certain, Kiku-chan."

~

Dessalen sat slumped in a chair leaning his head on his hand while he watched Marlon examine Kiku with rapt attention.

Nothing terrible had happened to Kiku while she had been in Sadar's possession; nothing that Marlon could find, anyway. There was no evidence he had forced an intimate encounter with her. Both he and Marlon were sure they would find something if he had. If Sadar's goal had been to impregnate her, he left nothing behind for that to happen. Dessalen closed his eyes as a wave of unquenchable anger ran over him again. Even the thought of anyone touching . . . taking . . . Kiku enraged him.

Marlon stepped away from the bed and pulled the blanket up around Kiku's chin, and lifted his eyes to meet the Exalted Leader's. Dessalen nodded and got up to follow Marlon out of the chamber.

"How is she?" Dessalen asked as they stepped into the hall outside of the wide double doors.

"The princess will make a full recovery," Marlon said.

Leader Dessalen nodded.

Lysis told him what had happened when he found Kiku. Leader Dessalen was not pleased but could see the general was in an untenable position. Kiku had been drugged. Marlon was keeping her sedated while he worked to flush the foul contents from her system. The last thing Dessalen needed was Kiku seducing anyone who happened by. Even if it was himself; Dessalen couldn't stomach the thought of joining with her that way. He supposed he should be grateful to Lysis for not taking advantage of the situation, and for having the courage to come to him and admit it happened at all. But he wasn't. He was angry, bitter, and jealous. At least he could admit his flaws. He smiled to himself.

"When are you going to let her wake?" Leader Dessalen asked.

"I'll step down her sedation tonight," Marlon answered. "I'd rather she wake on her own. This could trigger a—"

"I am aware," Dessalen cut him off shortly.

Kiku and the others had been slaves when the Garlon T'zen found them. They were controlled by both drugs and by implants to cause pain. Leader Dessalen had seen Kiku lose hold of her Celestial gift before. They were very fortunate she hadn't had a psychotic break in Sadar's care.

It could have destroyed the planet.

"I'll stay with her," Dessalen said. "I am not to be disturbed."

"Of course." Marlon inclined his head, and Dessalen returned to the chamber.

Kiku stirred softly in her sleep. Dessalen tenderly caressed her cheek with his hand and then tucked the blankets around her a little more.

Later he would deal with Catensen and Lysis. Hopefully they hadn't killed each other yet. Both generals were valuable to him, but they got along like oil and water. He smiled softly and settled himself back into his chair to watch his princess sleep. Kiku would likely wake by morning. His smile widened. He supposed he should be grateful for the respite, knowing Kiku-hime couldn't possibly get into any trouble at the moment.

~

"You let them escape?" Catensen mocked critically from a chair in the library. General Lysis scowled in his direction. He was waiting, hoping Marlon would come and give them an update on the High Princess's condition. But he had the feeling he'd have to corner the physician downstairs later.

"The mission was to recover Kiku-hime-sama," Lysis said.

"Always the underachiever." Catensen smirked. "You should have gotten the princess and killed the traitors. Really, Lysis, being out here is making you soft."

"Go to hell," Lysis snapped. Why did Dessalen put up with this bastard?

"And didn't you execute General Tamarik?" Catensen continued.

Ah yes, that's why. He was probably as brutal as the Exalted Leader himself.

"He's not a traitor," Lysis replied.

"No, but he's incompetent, which is almost as bad." General Catensen flicked a finger. "He was in command of this sector, and all three generals under him go rogue? Plus, he's got another plotting behind his back? This whole situation can be laid at his feet."

General Lysis crossed his arms with a frown. He couldn't dispute Catensen on that one. Clearly Tamarik didn't have a handle on things. The situation should have never gotten to the point it did. Perhaps the stress of being Kiku-hime's guardian was too much of a distraction. Or the General just had seen too many years of service.

"He needs to be made an example of," General Catensen said with his eyes glinting.

"You should speak to Leader Dessalen before you do anything," Lysis warned. And the Exalted Leader took exception to killing those in command positions: not that Lysis hadn't done it himself before, but there was always political fallout from it. "The general is Kiku-hime's guardian. It wouldn't look good for Leader Dessalen if he ordered his execution."

"So?" General Catensen got up to pour himself a drink. "It shouldn't matter."

"It might," General Lysis remarked with a pained expression. "Leader Dessalen and General Tamarik are in serious dispute over Kiku-hime-sama."

"That's probably why the general failed so miserably," General Catensen said with a superior air. "And as to Dessalen and the girl—"

"What?" Lysis demanded.

"Meh." General Catensen sat back down. "It's nothing. Too much is being made of it."

General Lysis quietly kept his own counsel. He'd once thought the same of Dessalen's interest in the princess as well, but now he wasn't so sure. He and Catensen had known Dessalen since he had been a young man, little more than a boy. Both were part of Dessalen's inner circle of confidents, which gave them more insight into his behavior and motivations. Lysis thought the Exalted Leader's infatuation with the girl would be done once he had bedded her. But that certainly didn't seem to be the case, and Dessalen's hot look of possession still followed the princess everywhere. General Lysis probably knew the Exalted Leader better than most.

And he didn't think the general was right at all.

~

"I'm sorry to disturb you, Leader Dessalen." Marlon entered the bedchamber. "But there is a problem."

Dessalen sat up from the chair where he had been dozing. "What is it?"

"General Tamarik is dead," Marlon replied calmly. Leader Dessalen raised his eyebrows and searched Marlon's emotionless face. He looked over at Kiku's bed and motioned toward the door. He didn't wish Kiku to wake hearing of her guardian's death. Once they were out of the chamber he nodded.

"What happened?" Leader Dessalen asked in a low tone.

"I'd say the general was executed," Marlon said. "Old style, ceremonial blade. I could hazard a guess to who, but that would be rude."

Leader Dessalen sighed, rubbing his temple in irritation.

"He should have spoken to me first," he muttered. "Damn him."

"The general does come with a set of challenges," Marlon agreed.

"You stay with Kiku-hime," Dessalen ordered with steel in his voice.

"Of course, Leader Dessalen." Marlon inclined his head.

After an inquiry, Leader Dessalen found General Catensen was exercising in the yard. He had to admit the General was as graceful and deadly has he had ever been. Leader Dessalen watched him move. He was shirtless and working with a short blade in his hand. The general was slim and wiry, his chest crisscrossed with scars. Catensen stopped and offered Leader Dessalen a curt bow when he saw him.

"You look well, Leader Dessalen." Catensen smirked. "I was beginning to wonder if you ever left your bedchamber."

"And you are in your typically good mood after a murder." Dessalen's voice was like ice.

"Execution," General Catensen corrected. "It was a minor detail that I am sure you overlooked yourself."

"If I had wanted him dead, General," Dessalen snapped, "he would have been dead."

"Dessalen, you can't appear weak." General Catensen sighed with a shake of his head. He moved closer to the fence and looked at the Exalted Leader critically. "Letting him live was a grave error that would have only led to more insurrection. I merely corrected it for you."

"I am the Exalted Leader of the Garlon T'zen, General." Dessalen lifted his chin with his eyes flashing dangerously. "You may not kill my generals on a whim!"

"Of course, Leader Dessalen." General Catensen bowed. "I don't know what I was thinking."

"Don't mock me," Dessalen warned.

"I wouldn't think of it," Catensen replied.

A slow smile started to spread across Leader Dessalen's face. "I've just thought of a suitable punishment for you, General." General Catensen eyed the Exalted Leader warily, well aware of Dessalen's idea of revenge.

"What?" he asked suspiciously.

"I had already planned on appointing you to Tamarik's post in this system and territory," Leader Dessalen said. "But you've left me in a very awkward position, so it's only fair you assume all of the your predecessor's responsibilities."

"So—" General Catensen prompted.

"You'll be made Kiku-hime-sama's guardian." Dessalen nodded with satisfaction. Dessalen wasn't in a position to take on her guardianship himself, and there were few others he could trust with it.

"That girl!" Catensen exclaimed.

"The High Princess." Leader Dessalen nodded.

"I don't want to," Catensen retorted.

"Too bad," Dessalen replied.

"I refuse!" General Catensen yelled.

"You can't." Leader Dessalen smirked. "There is something to be said for being the Exalted Leader, General. Now, I'm going back up to the princess. You should probably go review Kiku-chan's records since it's now your job to keep her out of trouble."

Leader Dessalen walked away laughing.

~

"Lysis-kun!" There was a banging on his door. "Lysis-kun! Wake up!"

General Lysis pulled himself out of bed and opened the door to find General Catensen standing outside. Catensen pushed his way in.

"What do you want?" Lysis asked irritably.

"You have to talk him out of it," Catensen demanded.

Lysis wondered if he was dreaming.

"What are you talking about?" Lysis threw himself back on the bed.

"Dessalen," General Catensen replied. "He was angry about Tamarik."

"Told you to talk to him first," Lysis mumbled from under his arm.

"He made me that girl's guardian," Catensen said with disdain.

"Better you than me." Lysis grinned, lifting his head. "For more than one reason."

"Tell him I'm a rotten bastard and no good," Catensen offered.

"Oh, he knows that." Lysis smirked. He did admit he was enjoying this.

Catensen glowered at him. "You're no help!"

And then he stormed out, slamming the door behind.

~

Even before she opened her eyes, Kiku could tell she wasn't in the same place. The texture of the sheets, the smell of the cool breeze, it had to be a dream of home. Sighing, she reluctantly opened her eyes, sure she would be back in the plain-walled prison that she last remembered.

But it wasn't that place; it was the bedchamber she shared with Leader Dessalen.

"H-how?" she stammered out, her voice hoarse and raw. Leader Dessalen came into her view with a brilliant smile and caught her up in tight hug, kissing the side of her head.

"Kiku-chan," he murmured. "You have to stop worrying me like this. You're taking years off my life."

Kiku closed her eyes and relaxed against him, finally feeling safe and warm for the first time in a long time. "I'll try, Ouji-sama," she said.

CHAPTER 9

Princess Kiku was standing in front of him in the solid black uniform of the Garlon T'zen. She was a lovely young woman, and Catensen could understand why Dessalen was attracted to her. Her features were soft, and she certainly did things for her uniform that none of his men could.

He cleared his throat and looked down at her. What did Dessalen expect of him, anyway? Being her guardian entailed what? He didn't know. Had he known he was going to be saddled with her, maybe he would have asked Tamarik before he cut his throat.

"Ouji-sama said to meet you," the princess said in a low voice. She dropped her eyes off to the side looking—what? Sad?

"Ouji?" he questioned.

"Leader Dessalen." She bit her lip. "Sorry."

"Nothing to be sorry for," he remarked, mildly amused. He supposed she couldn't very well call him the Exalted Leader in bed; Dessalen's ego was already big enough. Still, calling him a prince wasn't much better.

"Leader Dessalen told me that General Tamarik was killed." She dropped her eyes again. "And that he appointed you as my guardian in his place."

"Did Dessalen tell you how he died?" General Catensen inquired.

"No." Kiku-hime shook her head. "But there was much confusion when the rogue generals tried their trap. A lot of people died."

General Catensen felt a pang of sympathy but shrugged it aside easily. General Tamarik was a fool and needed to be removed. Catensen would make the best of the situation with the princess and this guardian role, whatever that happen to entail.

"What is your current assignment, Lieutenant?" he asked. She stood up a little straighter. She nodded and raised her eyes to meet his. Ah, there, she was an officer after all.

"Currently, I'm assigned as Leader Dessalen's personal aide," she told him. "Under his direct command."

"So you're available to him and act on his behalf when needed?" He nodded and then he paused with a frown. Typically aides to a superior officer either bunked with them or near them. But typically one's aide wasn't an impossibly attractive young woman.

"Yes, General," she replied. "I also help with my sisters. Walk Mary-chan and Toki-chan to school. Help with after school functions. But Leader Dessalen releases me for those responsibilities."

"I see," he replied. "Thank you, Lieutenant Kiku. I need to review your records, and we'll speak again later."

"Yes, General," she said and exited.

It was later after he had gone through her records and current orders that he frowned.

Catensen had known Dessalen nearly his entire life, and this smelled of one of his plots. The Exalted Leader was up to something with this girl and the handling of her affairs, but what, Catensen couldn't quite discern.

He got up and made and inquiry as to where he could find the Exalted Leader. With Dessalen it was better to confront these things head on. If Catensen was going to be dragged, unwillingly, into one of his games, he wanted to know exactly what it was.

The Exalted Leader was in his favorite spot it seemed, the library on the first floor of the large Manor House. Catensen went to the door, straightened his uniform and offered a polite knock. He heard an assent and let himself inside. Dessalen was on the far side of the room, sitting at a desk with imagedecks piled around. General Catensen closed the door behind him and crossed the library.

"Funny how you never mentioned that you moved her into your bedroom," General Catensen remarked, coming closer to the desk. Leader Dessalen was reading an imagedeck, and looked up with a frown.

"What?" Dessalen asked.

"There were reasons why you and Tamarik were having issues over the princess," Catensen said. Dessalen tossed the imagedeck aside.

"I never said there weren't," the Exalted Leader replied. His golden eyes met Catensen's, and a faint hint of a smile crossed his features.

"You, my dear Exalted One," General Catensen said smoothly, "are making it impossible for little Kiku-chan to receive any other suitors."

"There will be no other suitors." Dessalen's eyes flickered with heat.

"You make her your aide." Catensen ticked off on his fingers. "You keep her at your side and under your eye. You move her into your bedchamber. When she's not doing for you, she's taking care of one of the other princesses."

"I don't see your point," Dessalen said.

"Hm," Catensen mused. "Yes, you do."

"Catensen," Dessalen said in a low voice edged with menace, "I will tell you once, out of courtesy. Kiku. Is. Mine. Don't interfere."

"You made me her guardian," Catensen pointed out.

"Because she has to have one." Dessalen's countenance darkened.

"The reason she has to have one is to prevent things like this from happening." Catensen shook his head. "She's just a girl, Dessalen. You need to get back to the task of running the Empire."

"Fine." Dessalen drew a deep breath. He stood up and leaned on the desk and met Catensen's eyes. "I want us to be sworn. I want Kiku as my wife-consort."

"You can't be serious," Catensen scoffed with a short laugh.

"Once we're sworn and I don't have the constant threat of someone trying to steal her—" Dessalen clenched his fists at his side "—I will be able to get back to managing the Empire."

Catensen crossed his arms and regarded him. He didn't care much for the law, and he didn't care if she took one or a hundred lovers to her bed. Catensen's concern was Dessalen. The Exalted Leader did have to get his mind off this girl and back to the Empire. Bedding her certainly hadn't done it. Now he was ridiculously guarding her against all other seekers. That was keeping him distracted. Perhaps Dessalen did have the best solution after all. And even more likely once he did have complete possession of her he would lose interest.

"Only you can make that happen," Dessalen said pointedly, coming around the desk. He motioned toward the general with a finger. "You can accept my offer. She can't."

"Dessalen," Catensen groaned, "why do you want her?"

"She is mine."

Dessalen's golden eyes glinted with a flicker of hidden power. Catensen only caught it because he had seen it before. And then the realization hit him like a cold shower. A small shudder of fear ran up his back, and he realized he must refuse Dessalen's offer outright. Putting two powerful Celestials together would be very dangerous.

"I will have her, Catensen. I will do whatever it takes for it to happen."

General Catensen thought of everything he knew that the Exalted Leader was capable of. Truly, there was little he wasn't. And Catensen felt sincerely uncomfortable staring down a Celestial. He had heard of such things as what he suspected was happening here, in stories they were told as children. But until this moment, he hadn't thought anything like that was really possible. Dessalen himself would be hard pressed to explain it.

"I'm sorry, Leader Dessalen." Catensen bowed. "I have to decline your offer. I don't believe it's in the best interest of the Garlon T'zen."

"Damn you!" Dessalen shouted, hitting the desk hard with a fist.

"In fact," Catensen started, "it's high time the princess received other suitors. I will require Kiku-hime three evenings a week. That shouldn't interfere with her duties."

"You will not!" Leader Dessalen raged. General Catensen looked at Leader Dessalen with far more confidence than he felt. The ground he was treading was far more dangerous than any battle action he was ever likely to see. It wouldn't take much more for Dessalen to have his head removed from his body, and likely with his own hands.

"Have a good evening, Leader Dessalen," General Catensen said as he moved toward the door.

"We're not done!" Dessalen spat angrily.

"Yes, Dessalen," General Catensen said firmly. "We are."

~

Midday the next morning Lysis was called to General Catensen's office. Lysis noted it hadn't taken him long to move Tamarik's things out and impose his own self-styled stark pretension. He was met by Marlon-sensei, who looked at the general with curiosity.

"Do you know what he wants?" Marlon asked. Lysis shrugged.

"Hard to say," Lysis replied. They both stepped into the office together. General Catensen was standing looking over some imagedeck reports. He nodded curtly to the two of them.

"How long has this thing been going on with that government state?" he asked.

"The Americans?" Marlon asked. Catensen nodded absently, going through another deck. "Most of the trouble started after Kiku-hime's raid of one of their cities. But they were complaining before that. It was only an excuse to be more vocal."

"The princess?" Catensen looked up. "Why would she do that?"

"It had to do with Mary-hime," Marlon replied.

"And . . ." the General prompted. Marlon raised his eyebrows. "Explain."

"No," Marlon answered.

"You really are annoying." General Catensen scowled at Marlon-sensei.

"So I've been told," Marlon said. He offered a curt nod. "Have a good day, General."

Then the physician turned and left the office. Only
Marlon would be able to get away with such an act of open
insubordination.

"What the hell is he doing assigned to this backwater
hole?" General Catensen snarled. Lysis rolled his eyes as
he sat down in a chair. Marlon was the highest-ranking
physician in the military and answered only to Leader
Dessalen. He always had, always would. Both Catensen and
Lysis knew it all too well.

"Kiku," Lysis answered. "Marlon-sensei has been
detailed to Kiku-hime since Discovery. Where she goes, he
goes. Because Leader Dessalen couldn't be there, Marlon
was."

"Dessalen's been obsessing over the girl since the
beginning." Catensen pinned Lysis with a glare. "Hasn't
he?"

Lysis immediately felt uncomfortable. Kiku-hime wasn't
a subject he cared to discuss with Catensen. And he certainly
didn't want to talk about Leader Dessalen's relationship
with her. It left him feeling too raw and vulnerable. Neither
of which he would ever admit to Catensen.

"The girl needs to find someone else," General Catensen
announced.

"Dessalen will never allow it," Lysis replied.

"That is exactly the issue." General Catensen crossed
his arms and looked pensive. "I don't believe it's Dessalen
who's claimed Kiku-hime. It's the other."

"What?" Lysis scoffed. "That's ridiculous."

"No, it's not." General Catensen came closer and sat in a
chair and looked at him earnestly. "This obsession runs too
deep and for too long to just be Dessalen longing for a girl.
The Celestials are the driving force behind it."

"Then why would you interfere?" Lysis asked.

"Kiku holds Celestial power as well?" General Catensen asked.

"Of course," Lysis replied. "All the princesses do."

"You've seen her use it?" he asked.

"Perhaps." Lysis shrugged. "It's hard to say."

"It doesn't matter," General Catensen said. "The Celestials are not our allies. They cannot be trusted."

"And yet you trust Dessalen," General Lysis stated.

"I do." Catensen nodded. "But that's why he can't have Kiku-hime. It will give the Celestials too much power; too much power over him. The best way is for her to find someone else. He'll never give her up on his own."

"What makes you so certain she'll give him up?" General Lysis raised his eyes to meet Catensen's.

"She's only a woman, Lysis." Catensen smiled. "A girl, really. She can hardly know her own mind. She'll be easy to confuse and manipulate."

"I wish you luck," Lysis said, moving to stand.

"You're going to help me."

"I will not hurt Kiku for you, Catensen," Lysis said in a low voice.

"I've already listed you as one of her suitors. General Tamarik made note of your inquiry before, and I decided to approve it," General Catensen said. "It will be you along with Lieutenant Tello and Captain Sangra. Each of you will have one evening a week with the princess. I thought to give her a wide variety in rank and position as well as temperament."

"You're insane," Lysis muttered. "Dessalen will kill you. And likely me along with you."

~

"I told you—" Leader Dessalen glowered at General Catensen. He had ordered not only General Catensen to his presence when he got his outrageous proposition, but Lysis and Marlon as well. If you were planning to murder someone, it was best to have a few witnesses. "—No."

"I'm very sorry, Leader Dessalen," General Catensen replied. "But in this matter, you have no say."

The library seemed to be taking on an ominous shadow as Leader Dessalen felt his temper slip further out of his control. Marlon and Lysis shifted uncomfortably. Each moment the air grew heavier around them. Dessalen worked his jaw and glared at Lysis.

"I'm sure you had nothing to do with this?" His voice harsh and angry.

"Leader Dessalen—" Lysis started to speak, but Dessalen cut him off with a quick gesture. He didn't want to hear anything Lysis had to say at the moment. He didn't care if he was involved in the planning of this or not. The fact the general's name was on Catensen's list was enough to infuriate the Exalted Leader.

"You still have Kiku-hime four nights a week," Catensen said reasonably. "Plus most of her days. Each of the others only gets one evening. You are certainly still the most favored suitor."

"This is unacceptable," Dessalen replied angrily.

"She doesn't even have to accept them." Catensen shrugged. "She gets to know them. If there is no attraction, we move on to the next."

Leader Dessalen glared at Catensen.

"So you plan to keep throwing men at her until she beds one?" Dessalen felt his body grow cold.

"Or two." Catensen lifted his chin and looked at Dessalen narrowly. "Perhaps more. It is what she should be doing."

"I'll find a way to stop you," Dessalen said in a low dangerous voice.

"Perhaps it's time for you to consider taking another lover yourself." Catensen smirked. "You might get lonely those nights she's gone."

Dessalen moved blurrily fast, reaching for the General's throat, but Catensen anticipated his action, knocking his hand away and stepping back. Dessalen got a hold of the edge of his uniform jacket and yanked him close to his face.

"You've reached the end of your life, General," Dessalen murmured.

"Leader Dessalen," Marlon interrupted, "perhaps you should consider before you kill the general?"

Dessalen flicked his golden gaze back at Marlon for a moment. The physician regarded him calmly. Dessalen released Catensen, shoving him backward. Marlon was right to remind him not to act too rashly, no matter how much he longed to. Another reason that he'd called Marlon and Lysis to the library along with Catensen.

"As much as I loathe to say it," Dessalen remarked, "you are correct, Sensei. I can always kill the general tomorrow."

And he turned and walked out of the room.

~

General Lysis let out a sigh of relief. For a moment, he was sure Catensen had pushed Dessalen too far. He had to admit he didn't think the general had the stones to do it. Yes, Catensen was always pushing the edge of insubordination, but this was different. This was dueling with death himself.

"Thank you, Sensei." General Catensen straightened out his uniform. Marlon tossed him one of his infuriatingly superior looks.

"I didn't do it out of kindness, General." The physician's tone was like ice. "You're in a valuable position strategically for this sector. So you happen to be more valuable alive than dead. Perhaps Leader Dessalen will feel the same if his temper cools."

"If." General Catensen snorted. "Not very likely, is it?"

"No," Marlon replied. "I also don't agree with what you're doing with Kiku-chan. This will be frightening and hurtful to her."

"Then maybe he should have made you her guardian," General Catensen retorted.

"There's no chance of that, General." Marlon narrowed his eyes. "Because I don't think he's good for her at all."

Marlon turned and walked out of the library. Catensen looked after him with a little surprise.

"Hm," Lysis mused to himself. "I had wondered about that."

"You think it's true?" Catensen asked, turning to face him. Lysis laughed.

"Oh, yes," Lysis replied. "Marlon is . . . Marlon. Leader Dessalen respects him and offers him more courtesy than he does any of us. But Marlon genuinely cares for Kiku-hime and would put himself between her and any harm. That includes Leader Dessalen himself."

"Then perhaps he should court her," Catensen said, looking after Marlon-sensei with speculation.

"Marlon would have your heart for even suggesting it." Lysis shook his head. "It's not like that. Besides, he has the Earth woman, Andersen-sensei."

"I'd heard rumors." Catensen nodded. He turned to meet Lysis's eyes. "Is that why she is living here at the Manor House?"

"Sorry, General." Lysis stood up to leave. "That is not for me to say."

Besides, General Lysis had no intention of giving General Catensen any information that he could leverage against Marlon in his games of manipulation.

~

"He can't make me do that!" Kiku's blue eyes stormed. Marlon sighed. He thought he had better speak to Kiku-chan before Leader Dessalen or General Catensen had a chance to. Either one would certainly make a mess of it. Leader Dessalen would get angrier than he already was, and General Catensen would shrug and tell her she was doing it and would only infuriate her.

"Kiku-hime, he is your guardian and he makes these decisions," Marlon said, trying to reason with her. "General Tamarik just had never done so because the opportunity never presented itself."

Which was true. General Tamarik was getting ready to accept a reasonable list of suitors; he'd spoken to Marlon about that very thing. But Marlon was also certain that Tamarik would have discussed it with Kiku first. He didn't think the older general would have accepted any without her barest approval. Unlike Catensen who, other than Lysis, seemingly picked men that she had never even laid eyes on before.

"I'm fine with Leader Dessalen." Kiku dropped her eyes, coloring. Marlon sighed; she was still so young and naive. "I don't want anyone else."

"I'm sorry, Kiku-chan," Marlon said. He wanted to make sure she understood the rules they were all operating under. Yes, General Catensen could approve suitors for her time, but, ultimately, it was Kiku's decision on how far she decided to take things with them. "But all they have is the right to court you. You do not have to take any of them to your bed unless you wish to."

"Marlon-sensei!" Kiku-hime's face turned scarlet. "I wouldn't! I-I can't! Ouji—"

"Leader Dessalen has no say in this, Kiku-chan," Marlon told her firmly. "This is the law. Unless you're sworn, you may take as many lovers as you desire. Leader Dessalen knows this. He doesn't like it, but he knows it."

"But," Kiku protested tearfully.

"General Catensen cannot force you to take any one of them as your lovers either," Marlon continued. "Do you understand, Kiku-chan? He can't make you do anything. He can only approve of worthy suitors for courtship. You decide if you want them or not."

Kiku nodded with tears running down her face. Marlon sighed. "Let's find Andy-chan for lunch. Leader Dessalen is bad company right now. Why don't you wait a bit before discussing this with him, hm?"

"All right, Sensei." Kiku wiped her eyes with the back of her hand.

~

The atmosphere around the library was as dark as his mood. Dessalen tried to concentrate on the latest batch of reports from the Capital, but his mind refused to let him spend more than a few moments on them before he would think of Catensen's refusal of his proposal. He tossed the latest imagedeck on the desk with frustration. And worse, this list of "suitors"? Dessalen snorted. He'd have their throats cut if they even tried anything with Kiku. He'd make damn sure every one of them knew it, too.

"Leader Dessalen?" Marlon opened the door politely. Dessalen looked up and waved him in.

"What is it, Marlon?" Dessalen asked. He wasn't in the mood to speak to anyone at the moment. And he was sure he didn't want to talk to Marlon about what Marlon probably wanted to talk about.

"Why did you make him her guardian?" Marlon cut right to the point. In another man, Dessalen may have taken offense. But in Marlon's case, Dessalen knew he wasn't critical of him but concerned for Kiku. Still, this wasn't a conversation he cared to have. "Lysis would have been a better choice. Not only would you have put a stop to his pursuit, but also he genuinely cares about her well-being."

"I considered it," Dessalen said. "But Lysis wouldn't have gone along with my plans. Catensen didn't have an agenda with Kiku-hime, so I didn't believe it would be an issue."

"Plans?" Marlon asked, his eyes watching the Exalted Leader critically. Dessalen scowled. "I'm sure it has nothing to do with flouting traditional law."

"Possibly." Leader Dessalen turned away. "Well, it doesn't matter because Catensen flatly refused my proposal. And then he draws up a list of suitors!"

"So you're going to kill him?" Marlon asked. The physician crossed his arms and looked at Dessalen critically. "That would be bad form considering General Tamarik's recent demise."

"I didn't kill Tamarik," Dessalen muttered. "Or order it."

"No one would believe that," Marlon replied. Dessalen shrugged in an offhand manner. He'd ordered enough deaths for less. The house nobles would never believe that the Exalted Leader didn't have a hand in Tamarik's death. "I'm afraid you're stuck with him for awhile. You could have him redeployed to an active combat zone and hope he gets killed."

"He's too damned good for that. And he'd probably take Kiku with him," Dessalen grumbled. "I already considered it."

They heard the loud slamming of the front door and raised voices. One of them was clearly Kiku's. Leader Dessalen got up and opened the library door a crack so they could hear better.

"You have to be the most annoying idiot on the entire planet!" Kiku yelled.

"It was only five minutes, Jen!" James protested.

"Don't call me that!" she yelled back.

"Look. Just because you're having a bad day don't take it out on me!" James shouted. "I never asked you to walk me back and forth to school like a damned kindergartner! It's embarrassing!"

"Fine!" Kiku's voice cracked with emotion. "You can walk alone, and I'll just take Toki-chan and Mary-chan!"

"I won't go unless I walk with Jimmy-kun!" Toki's voice added to the mix. "Onee-san, stop being mean!"

"Toki-chan, I have to walk you," Kiku protested.

"Then you have to walk Jimmy-kun too!" Toki said matter-of-factly.

Their voices started to move away.

"Baka Otouto!" Kiku yelled as she stormed away out of earshot.

"Who are you calling baka?!" Jimmy retorted after her. And they were gone. Marlon smiled.

"They seem to be getting along better," Marlon said dryly as Leader Dessalen closed the library door.

"At least they're talking." Dessalen shrugged. "Siblings fight. She did just call him 'little brother.' That's progress."

"Yes." Marlon nodded. "Idiot little brother."

Leader Dessalen paused for a moment and looked back at Marlon, his mind working quickly. He might not have thought of it if not for the small altercation in the front hall.

"James Davis is Kiku-hime's full-blood brother, correct?" Leader Dessalen asked.

"Her twin," Marlon replied, obviously not getting the significance of where the conversation was going. "Anyone can tell by looking at the two of them."

"But Andersen-sensei ran tests," Leader Dessalen continued.

"She did." Marlon nodded. "They came out full positive. She destroyed the results."

"You could run tests of our own?" Leader Dessalen nodded with a slow smile.

"I could," Marlon agreed. "But why? Do you doubt he's her brother?"

"Under Garlon T'zen law, my dear Sensei—" Leader Dessalen started to relax for the first time since General Catensen's outrageous announcement "—it is a full-blooded male relative who is guardian the unattached female. Father, uncle . . . brother."

"He's not Garlon T'zen." Marlon frowned. "And still a boy."

"Not so much a boy. He's Kiku's age," Dessalen said. "He's an adult by law."

"Leader Dessalen." Marlon started rubbing his temple. "He's still not Garlon T'zen."

"Why not?" Leader Dessalen asked. "Kiku-hime certainly is. He would fall into our house, House Garlon T'zen."

"Ugh." Marlon made a face. "Kiku-chan would be very unhappy with you. And I am not saying she's wrong."

"She'll get over it." Dessalen dismissed Marlon's concern. "This is a way out."

"You're going to have that boy challenge General Catensen?" Marlon retorted. "That's just cruel."

"You don't think he can do it?" Leader Dessalen smiled.

"No," Marlon replied. "And I can't believe you do, either."

"He is Kiku-hime-sama's brother, Sensei." Dessalen nodded. "You are underestimating him."

~

"Explain this to me again?" Dr. Andersen looked at Marlon. "First he gives Kiku to General What's-his-name. Then the general decides Kiku needs to date. He lines up a list of gentlemen. Leader Dessalen is unhappy, so he's going to make James—a child, mind you—Kiku's legal guardian?"

Marlon watched Dr. Andersen explain all this with expressive gestures in the garden. He had his head resting on his chin, smiling indulgently. He adored this woman.

"And now you want me to make James understand all this?" Dr. Andersen blinked at him a few times.

"I had hoped you would," Marlon said, straightening. "I don't know him that well, and Leader Dessalen scares him."

"Hell, Leader Dessalen scares me," Dr. Andersen muttered. Marlon grinned.

"He would never harm you, Andy-chan." Marlon reached over and pulled her hand into his and ran a tender thumb along her wrist.

"I'm not so sure of that." She looked pensive.

"I am," Marlon assured her. Dr. Andersen sighed.

"Can't he just make someone else her guardian?" she asked. "I am surprised this is a problem for him."

"This is a very delicate issue," Marlon replied. "When it comes to the princesses, the law is very clear. Even he has to abide by it."

"There's more to this," Dr. Andersen mused. Marlon was again struck by her uncanny intuition. Of course there was. Not only did Leader Dessalen want to remove General Catensen as Kiku's guardian, but also he planned to use James for some unknown plan. Marlon wasn't certain of the plan, but he had an idea of it.

And truly, if Andy-chan could bear Marlon's child, there was no reason the princesses needed to reseed their race alone. Only a few knew of Andy-chan's pregnancy yet. She had only found out from Toki-chan at the holdstead. Leader Dessalen felt it best to keep it quiet for a bit. Knowing the political climate of the Empire, Marlon was inclined to agree. Both men were working to protect her and her unborn child.

"That may well be," he agreed. "But for now, I agree with him. I don't like what General Catensen is doing with Kiku-hime either. He is not looking to her best interests and is not a suitable guardian."

"And you think James would be?" Dr. Andersen said with shock.

"At least he cares about her, Andy-chan," Marlon said. "And he wouldn't do things for political expediency. He can learn the rest."

"I don't know, Marlon." Dr. Andersen bit her lip. "Dragging another Earth child into the Garlon T'zen world. Is it ever going to stop?"

"Probably not," Marlon said. "We're not going anywhere. If Leader Dessalen gets his way, the capital of the Empire is going to be relocated to the Earth. There's not much to do but get used to us."

He smiled at her winningly, and she rolled her eyes, leaning over the table to kiss him. Marlon enjoyed the thrill of pleasure until he heard someone clear his throat.

"Excuse me, Marlon-sensei," General Catensen said. Marlon groaned inwardly. Dr. Andersen pulled away and looked at the general with large, frightened eyes. Marlon squeezed her hand gently.

"Why don't you do what we spoke about?" Marlon suggested. She nodded and got up and left the patio.

"Lovely woman, Sensei," General Catensen remarked. "I can see why you've taken her."

"Did you need something, General?" Marlon asked.

"I was wondering why Andersen-sensei lives at the Manor House." Catensen sat down at the table without being invited. "As the new head of the Special Earth Preservation Delegation, I need to understand the political nature of my house."

"Your house?" Marlon arched an eyebrow.

"Of course," General Catensen replied. "My system, my planet, my command, my house. And everyone in it, my guest."

"Are you saying that Andersen-sensei is no long welcome at the Manor House?" Marlon narrowed his eyes.

"I'm sure you like having her here." Catensen smiled silkily. "But I just don't see the point."

"Both she and James Davis are guests of Leader Dessalen, General." Marlon leaned back in his chair. "My liking her here has nothing to do with it."

"Really?" Catensen said with mock surprise. "And here I thought he was only interested in Kiku-chan."

"Tsk." Marlon smirked. "You can't bait me so easily."

"Well then, if Leader Dessalen isn't interested in her, perhaps I'll entertain the Earth sensei's affections," Catensen mused.

Marlon laughed outright. "Feel free to try, General. But it will hurt your legendary vanity when she refuses you."

"You can't know that for sure, Marlon-kun," General Catensen teased softly. "Any woman who isn't sworn is free to exercise her desires and is free to be pursued. Why do you suppose even the great Dessalen is so mad with jealousy over little Kiku-chan, who practically worships him, hm? It's because he knows that no woman is immune to the right moment."

"Oh, you are pathetic." Marlon sighed with a shake of his head as he rose to his feet. "You must be getting dull, because I cannot be moved by your manipulative drivel."

General Catensen scowled. "Maybe you should move out of my house too."

"Yes, yes." Marlon nodded. "I will be sure to ask Leader Dessalen where he would like me to move the next time I see him."

Marlon laughed at the frustrated look the general threw him when he walked away.

~

James was studying in the sunroom with Toki-hime when Dr. Andersen found him. He was helping the princess with her Algebra homework. The young princess didn't have an aptitude for it. James was a senior in the same high school in Manor Town where Toki was a freshman. He was long past Algebra and into what looked to be second-year Calculus. Dr. Andersen couldn't help but be impressed by that. She hoped he didn't come to her for help with that. It had been a long time since she had completed the required maths for pre-med.

"There you are, James," Dr. Andersen said. "How are you coming with your lessons, Toki-chan?"

"Badly." The princess scowled.

"She's doing fine," James said. "She can do it. She just doesn't like to."

"I don't see why I should have to," Toki complained. "When am I going to need this in real life?"

"It's good for you to learn things, Toki-chan," Dr. Andersen explained. "It broadens your mind."

"None of my sisters had to go to high school," Toki said with a pretty pout.

"They didn't get any schooling with the Garlon T'zen?" Dr. Andersen asked with surprise.

"Well, yes." Toki bit her lip. "They did. We all did. We had to learn how to read and write. And there was history, law, and other stuff. Kiku-onee had to learn more because she was in the military. But it wasn't high school."

"Sounds like it was its equivalent." Dr. Andersen's lip twitched. "But do be a dear and study upstairs for a bit? I have something I need to discuss with James."

"What is it, Dr. Andersen?" James asked, turning to her with polite interest.

"Oh, I don't mind." Toki smiled. "You can go ahead and talk."

"It is a little private." Dr. Andersen couldn't believe the audacity of the little scamp. Toki frowned.

"It won't matter because Jimmy-chan will tell me later," she said, collecting her books.

"Probably," Dr. Andersen agreed. Toki walked out of the sunroom with a sniff.

"She doesn't mean anything by that," James apologized for her. "I think the Garlon T'zen have spoiled her a bit."

"You think?" Dr. Andersen asked drily. "They have spoiled all of them, if you haven't noticed."

"Not Jennifer," he replied. "The rest of them are treated like royalty, and she runs around like Leader Dessalen's servant or something."

"Oh, James." Dr. Andersen groaned. "She does it because she wants to. She made the choice about being in the military. And to be quite frank, she's not treated like the typical foot soldier."

James scowled. Dr. Andersen knew this was going to be difficult to explain. And James wasn't going to like it, probably not any of it.

"Did you hear that Leader Dessalen named General Catensen Kiku's new guardian?" Dr. Andersen asked. He looked at her with a confused expression.

"Why does she need a guardian?" he asked.

"Something in their laws say that unmarried girls and women have to have a male guardian to look after their legal affairs," she explained. "From what Marlon explained to me, it's a little different than what we think of as a guardian. Typically it's their father, but if a family member isn't available one is appointed."

"But why?" James asked. "That seems pretty backward. Are women like second class citizens or something?"

"Quite the opposite, actually," Dr. Andersen continued. "This is the most information I've been able to pry from Marlon about their culture at all. It seems that the women hold most of the power. Because of that, their guardian makes certain that only the most suitable men are allowed to court their favors."

"Huh?" James asked.

"One role of the guardian is to choose, or approve, the men she'll date, so to speak." Dr. Andersen paused for a moment. This was the tricky part. And she wasn't sure she fully understood it either. "A Garlon T'zen woman may have multiple suitors, or boyfriends, at the same time. I guess it's encouraged."

"That disgusting!" James made a face. "My sister is involved in this?"

"Well, that's the thing, you see." Dr. Andersen's hands fidgeted in her lap. How does one tell a person's brother these things? "Leader Dessalen isn't inclined to share your sister, if you know what I mean."

James' face turned bright red. Dr. Andersen prayed she wouldn't have to go into detail on that. The lad wasn't an idiot, and he surely had spoken to Toki about it. He dropped his eyes and looked away.

"I know about Jennifer and Leader Dessalen," he said quietly. "And I don't like it."

"I'm sure you don't." Dr. Andersen bit her lip. "But here is the thing. I guess General Catensen doesn't like it either."

"Good," James said, looking up. "Then he can put a stop to it?"

"No," Dr. Andersen answered. "What he decided to do is draw up a list of suitable suitors. He's insisting that she spend one evening a week with each one."

"What for?" James asked.

"Weren't you paying attention?" Dr. Andersen asked. "He wants Kiku to take one or more of these others as a lover as well and—"

"Ew!" James exclaimed. "No! Ick! Are you kidding?"

"No, it's quite true." Dr. Andersen nodded. "It's the way they do things. And as her guardian, he can do it."

"Why doesn't Leader Dessalen stop him?" James asked. "I mean, he's the most powerful guy, right?"

"He can't," Dr. Andersen said. "I guess, in this one thing, he just plain can't. It's their law."

"Wow," James said with a little awe. "I didn't think there was anything he couldn't do."

"But, as I said," Dr. Andersen continued with her story, "he's not happy with this development. So he believes he's devised a way to thwart the general's plan."

"How?" James asked.

"Funny you should ask." She offered a winning smile.

~

General Catensen was rather surprised when he got the summons to see Leader Dessalen in the command chamber. He supposed it was better than meeting him in the dueling yard. Catensen hadn't thought Dessalen would speak to him for days yet.

What even worried him more was the Exalted Leader's genial expression. That didn't make the general feel particularly comfortable. At least General Lysis and Marlon-sensei were also in attendance, so perhaps Dessalen wasn't planning on murdering him outright.

"Good evening, General," Leader Dessalen said, sitting at the head of the large table.

"Leader Dessalen." General Catensen bowed with respect.

"Aren't you curious to know if I'm going to kill you or not?" Leader Dessalen's lips twitched.

"I'm sure it doesn't matter, Leader Dessalen." General Catensen smiled bitterly. "You've already made up your mind one way or the other."

"True," Dessalen replied. "I'm not going to kill you today. Does that please you?"

"I suspect it may be easier if you did," General Catensen said. Leader Dessalen shrugged.

"You have a very bad attitude, General," Leader Dessalen chastised. "Telling Marlon-sensei he would have to move. You think the Manor House is yours?"

"It is my command, Leader Dessalen," General Catensen said. "The House is the center of operations. Of course the house falls under my jurisdiction."

"With all six princesses in residence?" Leader Dessalen made a pained expression.

"They are my most esteemed guests," Catensen said graciously. Marlon-sensei rolled his eyes.

"This house," Leader Dessalen said, "this whole town was built for them. This was to be their primary residence once they returned. It is their home. They are not guests. You, on the other hand, have no standing in the house."

"Leader Dessalen," General Catensen said, "you are still angry—"

"No, I'm not," Leader Dessalen interrupted. Catensen glanced at General Lysis, who was wearing a carefully guarded expression. "In fact, I have decided to take your recommendation and journey back to the Capital world."

"I'm glad to hear it, Leader Dessalen," General Catensen said.

"I have important business there concerning Kiku-hime-sama," Leader Dessalen said mildly. General Catensen froze.

"What business would that be?" he asked.

"Does he know James-kun?" Leader Dessalen asked General Lysis.

"I don't know, Leader Dessalen," Lysis replied.

"Do you?" Leader Dessalen pinned Catensen with his golden eyes.

General Catensen hurriedly tried to think. Hadn't Marlon mentioned someone named James was also a guest of Leader Dessalen's, along with the Earth woman?

"Kiku-hime-sama's brother from here. On Earth, same mother and father," Leader Dessalen explained.

"I haven't met him, Leader Dessalen." General Catensen's mind was quickly trying to calculate what Dessalen was doing.

"You probably won't before we leave. In fact, I'm sure of it." Leader Dessalen tapped his finger against the table. "James-kun is accompanying me to the Capital to be confirmed in Kiku-hime-sama's family house, our house. House Garlon T'zen."

"I don't understand, Leader Dessalen." General Catensen frowned. "What interest would an Earth man have in being made a member of a Garlon T'zen family house?"

"Because then he becomes Kiku-hime's guardian by default, General." Leader Dessalen lifted his fierce eyes to meet Catensen's. Catensen felt the jaws of the trap clamp tight around him. Leader Dessalen smiled slowly. "And, then, I will most likely kill you."

"Yes, Leader Dessalen." General Catensen felt a chill run through him. Dessalen meant it.

"Still, while I am gone," Leader Dessalen continued, "you are Kiku-hime's guardian and the commander of this regional system. However, you are to move out of the Manor House before my departure, and you are not to stay here."

"Of course, Leader Dessalen." General Catensen closed his eyes, trying to quiet his fiercely beating heart.

~

"Did you know about this?" General Catensen asked Lysis later. Lysis was drinking a bottled Earth beer in the garden. Catensen was pacing back and forth. Lysis watched him with faint amusement.

"About what?" Lysis asked.

"Kiku-hime's brother!" General Catensen snapped.

Lysis nodded. "I knew she had a brother. But I didn't know what Leader Dessalen was going to do. Actually, I'm surprised the boy is going along with it."

"Boy?" General Catensen stopped and looked at Lysis.

"Mm." Lysis nodded, taking a drink. "He's Kiku-hime's twin."

"Dessalen thinks he can control him, then," Catensen mused.

"Perhaps." Lysis grinned wryly. "I just think he wants rid of you."

"Do you know where this boy is?" General Catensen asked. Lysis shook his head.

"I wouldn't try anything, General," he warned. "He's probably with Toki-hime or Andersen-sensei. You get near either of them, and you'll have real trouble."

"Even the Earth woman?" Catensen retorted. "What is so important that she's living under Garlon T'zen protection?"

"Not for me to say." Lysis decided he needed another beer and walked away from the general. Maybe he would find one of Kiku's squad to go keep an eye on Andersen-sensei as well. Lysis wasn't particularly concerned if Catensen happened to kill Kiku's brother, but if he harmed the first woman to carry a Garlon T'zen child in twenty years, Lysis would have the General's blood himself.

~

At the end of the day, Leader Dessalen sent word for James Davis and Kiku to come to the library. He had begun the preparations for the trip back to the Capital, and they would be leaving as soon as winter break started at James-kun's school. Andersen-sensei had been insistent that the young man not be absent from classes. It was only a week away, so Dessalen decided he could afford to give the doctor this boon. Really, it was a little thing for what she was doing unwittingly for his people. It wouldn't hurt to indulge her a bit.

The first one to arrive was James. Leader Dessalen nodded to him.

"Kiku-hime will be here shortly, and then I will explain," he said.

"Dr. Andersen said you wanted me to go to your planet or something for Jennifer," he said. The Exalted Leader flicked his eyes over the young man and nodded once. Again, he was impressed with his courage and deameanor.

"Something like that," Dessalen replied just as Kiku slipped into the library. She noted James's presence with a snort of irritation. "Good evening, Princess."

"Good evening, Leader Dessalen," she replied. Dessalen noted her formality as a sign she was irritated. Well, he thought, it's only going to get worse.

"Kiku-chan, have you spoken to General Catensen about your suitor prospects yet?" he asked. Kiku turned red but shook her head no. "Do you know what he has in mind?"

"I've heard," she muttered, crossing her arms.

"Is it what you want?" he asked. Kiku had to set this in motion. And truly, her wishes had to be heard by her brother. Kiku looked up at him sharply with hot angry eyes.

"How can you ask that?" she demanded.

"Because it is about what you chose, Kiku-hime," he replied in as neutral a voice as he could find. Dessalen longed to rage, but at this point, right now, it wasn't what should be done. "Not about what I may want."

"This isn't fair!" Her temper flashed. "I can't believe he's just doing this without even asking me! I don't know any of them except for General Lysis. Lysis!"

"What do you think about it, James-kun?" Leader Dessalen asked, flicking his eyes back to Kiku's brother. James startled a little and swallowed.

"I don't think it's fair if Jennifer doesn't want to," he said.

"Then we're agreed." Leader Dessalen smiled. "Kiku-hime, James-kun needs to be confirmed in our family house, under Garlon T'zen law."

"W-what?" She looked confused. "What are you talking about, Ouji-sama?"

"Then James-kun, as your brother, will become your guardian rather than General Catensen." Leader Dessalen continued to smile, watching Kiku's face carefully.

"No!" Kiku's eyes widened. She shook her head and paled. "You can't do that!"

"I think it's an excellent solution," Leader Dessalen replied. "I'm sorry, Kiku-chan, but it must be done. James? Do you understand?"

"Yes sir." He nodded. "Dr. Andersen explained it to me."

"So, then, you're prepared to journey to the Capital?" Leader Dessalen asked.

"Yes sir," James answered.

"No!" Kiku's voice twisted with anguish. "Ouji!"

"We will leave at the beginning of your winter break." Leader Dessalen nodded. "Thank you."

Leader Dessalen walked purposefully from the library. He was finished with the discussion, but he was certain Kiku wasn't. Sure enough, she was following him out.

"Ouji-sama! You can't do this!" She stormed at him. Leader Dessalen kept walking, leading her unwittingly back to their bedchamber. She continued her protests as he steadfastly ignored her until they were both inside of the chamber. Once the door was closed he turned to her and quickly took her into his arms before she had a moment to resist.

"Don't scold me, Kiku-chan," he whispered into her ear as he held her tight.

"You can't," Kiku continued to protest. Leader Dessalen leaned down and nibbled on her lips even while she tried to continue to speak. She squirmed in his arms, but he persisted in his efforts and was rewarded when she began to kiss him back. Her body melted against his as he ran his hand along the soft curve of her waist.

"Come love me, Kiku-chan," he said as he began to unbutton her shirt. He couldn't, wouldn't allow anyone else to taste her lips or feel the soft curves of her body. Dessalen felt the strength of his resolve harden as he slipped his fingers under her shirt to touch her soft bare skin. Her hair smelled of wildflowers. His body ached for her, and his soul longed for her. How could she not understand that he would do anything, anything, to keep her?

"Ouji," she groaned against his neck. "Why? I don't understand—"

"Oh, Kiku-chan." He kissed her softly. "It's the only way. And if I have to brave the hell of your temper to keep you, I'll do it."

Kiku looked at him seriously for a moment and then giggled against his chest. He smiled, kissing her forehead.

"I'm not that bad." Her voice held a hint of amusement. Dessalen grinned and pulled her toward the bed. She may not have forgiven him, but she wasn't still angry. And perhaps by morning, he thought smugly, she'd have forgiven him as well.

~

"You want me to move into the Manor House?" General Lysis looked at Leader Dessalen like he had lost his wits. Dessalen looked at him balefully.

"I trust you more than Catensen at the moment," Dessalen said.

"That's not saying much." Lysis rolled his eyes. "No thank you, Leader Dessalen. I'd rather stay in the barracks. It'll be better for my longevity."

Dessalen's lips twitched with an amused smile. He had to admit moving General Lysis into the Manor House while he was gone didn't sit comfortably with him either. But Sadar and Jasxon were still at large and were a threat. He had real concerns about all of the princesses' safety, not just Kiku's. He couldn't leave the house empty of ranking officers in good conscience. Given the current choice between Catensen and Lysis, it fell to Lysis. He had to put aside his jealousy for the safety of all six of the princesses.

"It's not an invitation, General," Dessalen told him. "It's an order."

Lysis groaned, closing his eyes. "Do you understand the position you're putting me in?" he demanded.

"Stay away from Kiku and you'll be fine." Dessalen smirked.

"I'm not going to do that," General Lysis told him pointedly. Dessalen felt a flash of anger and tightened his jaw.

"Lysis," he hissed.

"I won't." Lysis glared at him stubbornly. "And it's the one thing you can't order me not to. In his insanity, Catensen made me one of her suitors, and I plan on taking advantage of the fact."

"General, if you try anything," Dessalen warned, "I'll have your head on a pole."

"Is it not Kiku-hime's choice, Exalted One?" General Lysis narrowed his eyes.

"Of course it is." Leader Dessalen drew in a deep breath, trying to calm himself. "But if I come back and find you in her bed, there's nothing that will save you."

"I think it's well worth the risk, Leader Dessalen." General Lysis smiled.

CHAPTER 10

"A what?" Kiku looked back and forth between Toki-chan and James-kun. Kiku was walking with them back to the Manor House. Captain Jace was walking a bit behind, his eyes watching their surroundings warily. He had told her that if she was insistent about walking her sister back and forth to school, that she was going to have a detail with her. Kiku was walking between James-kun and Toki.

"A dance, Onee-sama," Toki-chan explained excitedly with a small hop to her step. She put a hand on Kiku's arm and looked up at her earnestly. "It's to celebrate the end of the semester. Jimmy-chan and I want to go."

"That sounds like a security risk," Captain Jace said from behind them. She looked over her shoulder and nodded to her captain. Jace-kun shook his head once. Kiku herself could think of a half a dozen reasons why it was a bad idea, but Toki-chan was looking at her pleadingly.

"I suppose you put this idea in her head?" Kiku shot a glare at James.

"He did not!" Toki stomped her foot before James could reply. "Onee-sama, stop being mean to Jimmy-chan!"

"Toki-chan," Kiku groaned.

"You could make this work if you wanted to," Toki said stubbornly.

Kiku frowned. Well, she could. But she didn't want to.

"Please, please, please!"

Kiku threw up her hands in surrender. "Fine!" she exclaimed. "I'll see what I can figure out."

They were coming up the steps of the house.

"Thank you, Onee-sama!" Toki threw her arms around Kiku and hugged her. Kiku grimaced.

"I didn't say it would work," Kiku protested.

"I know you'll figure it out!" Toki beamed happily. "You always do!"

Kiku shrugged her way out of the embrace and shot James-kun a venomous look. He raised his eyebrows with a helpless shrug. She couldn't blame him entirely, as much as she'd like to.

"This is a terrible idea," Captain Jace said to her after they were alone on the steps of the house. He let out a long sigh and crossed his arms, tipping his head back.

"I know," Kiku agreed. "But I said yes, so you and I are going to figure out how to secure the event."

He drew in a deep breath and nodded. "Very well, Hime-sama," Captain Jace agreed. "Let's go to the security center and see what resources we have to work with.

~

"Kiku asked if we could chaperone a high school dance," Dr. Andersen called out to Marlon from the bathroom where she was soaking in the tub. He was lounging on her bed flipping through a magazine. It was amazing what some of these Earth people seemed to be interested in. It amused him that his ever-serious Andy-chan enjoyed her gossip papers from back home. He wondered what the Globe would think of the Manor House's living arrangements. With a sarcastic grin, he closed the magazine and looked up.

"What is that?" he asked. Andy-chan came out wrapped in a towel, combing through her hair.

"It's a get-together for the youngsters," she said. "Sort of like what the reception was, only on a far scaled-down version."

"Why does Kiku-hime want us to attend?" Marlon frowned. It didn't sound like anything he wanted to be part of. Bad enough he had to face the events put on at the Manor House; it made little sense to seek them elsewhere.

"Toki is determined to go, and she's taking James with her." Andy-chan smiled. "It's cute, really. But Kiku is worried and is arranging security."

"Mm." Marlon nodded. "Well, then I should go and you stay here at the Manor House."

"Ha." Dr. Andersen flashed him a smile. "Nice try. But I was asked to be a chaperone by the school administration, as well. If anything, I'm going and you're staying."

"I don't think so," Marlon replied with no humor. Andy-chan came over and sat on the bed next to him and ran her fingers through his short black hair. She leaned forward and met his lips. He closed his eyes in brief contentment and then pulled back with a deeper frown.

She giggled. "Kiku said you'd be this way."

He caught her hands and pulled her against him and looked at her seriously. "Any public event outside the Manor is a security risk," he said. "You really shouldn't go."

"I really have to." Dr. Andersen smiled. "How the hell did all of you end up so damned paranoid?"

"Years and years of training." He smiled, leaning to kiss her again. She put her fingers on his lips.

"I'm going," she told him. Marlon sighed, pulling her wrist to his mouth.

"Fine," he muttered. "Then I'm going too."

~

A soft knock came on General Catensen's new office door. He was now firmly moved out of the Manor House and was established in a room in the barracks. Rather uncivilized of Leader Dessalen, truly. And then the Exalted Leader added to the insult by moving General Lysis into the Manor House? Catensen snorted. Well, hopefully, that would work to his advantage. Moving Lysis into closer proximity to Kiku-hime could only be a good thing.

"Enter," he called out. Lieutenant Telleo stepped into the small office with a bow.

"You sent for me, General?" the lieutenant asked.

General Catensen looked him over critically. He was young, nearer to Kiku-hime's age than either Leader Dessalen or General Lysis. Slim and soft-spoken, his official assignment was that of a translator. Something Catensen hoped the lieutenant and Kiku-hime would have in common. The young man's hair was dark brown and lay straight on his head.

Catensen also knew that Lieutenant Telleo had a few other hidden talents that the general hoped he wouldn't have to call upon.

"Ah yes, Lieutenant," he said. "Tonight will be your first evening with the princess."

"Oh." Telleo looked down. Catensen raised his eyebrows in surprise.

"Don't you want to be with the High Princess, Lieutenant?" General Catensen smirked. "You are getting quite an opportunity here."

"No." Lieutenant Telleo looked confused. "I mean, yes, I do. But I don't understand why. Kiku-hime-sama didn't look happy about it."

"This may well be the most important assignment you'll ever get, Lieutenant." General Catensen lowered his voice. "It is of critical importance for the survival of the Garlon T'zen that Kiku-hime choose another besides Leader Dessalen."

"Then why did you pick me?" Lieutenant Telleo asked in a bewildered voice. "I can't be the best choice for this sort of thing. How am I supposed to compete with the Exalted Leader for her affection?"

"You'll do well enough." General Catensen shrugged. "Besides, your true mission is to kill the princess should she not choose another before Leader Dessalen returns from the Capital."

"What?" Lieutenant Telleo choked out. "I can't do that!"

"You can." General Catensen smiled wickedly. "You're a very good assassin. Something I've kept quiet since we've been deployed to Manor Town. You never know when you're going to need a good assassin. I've also set up Captain Sangra as the other suitor, a known assassin, which will draw all eyes away from you."

"Sangra wouldn't kill her." Lieutenant Telleo frowned. "He wouldn't risk his position in his royal house."

"True," Catensen agreed. "Sangra is too political for that sort of thing. But few know his house affiliation, which could work to his advantage in this situation."

"I'm sorry, General, but there is no reason good enough to kill one of the princesses." Lieutenant Telleo shook his head.

"In theory, I agree." Catensen nodded. "And I truly hope it doesn't come to that. But I have to keep the option open. As do you, Lieutenant."

"I don't think I could do that, sir." Lieutenant Telleo looked pained.

"Then perhaps you should make a real effort to win the princess's heart." General Catensen smiled tightly. "And then the option needn't be exercised."

"Yes, General." Lieutenant Telleo bowed, looking pale and shaken.

~

"I have to start those things before Ouji-sama leaves?" Kiku wrinkled her forehead, looking at General Catensen. The general had called her out to his office in the barracks. He was a tall and stern-looking man with a long scar on the side of his face. He crossed his arms and frowned.

"Yes," he said firmly. "This isn't a game, Hime-sama."

"It's stupid." Kiku's eyes flashed with temper. "Leader Dessalen could be gone for months! I want to spend as much time with him before goes as I can."

"As much time as he is allotted," General Catensen told her coldly. "The other time belongs to your suitors. Besides, Leader Dessalen does have an empire to administrate."

"I'm busy tonight," Kiku said. "I have another commitment."

"Then take the lieutenant with you," General Catensen replied.

"He'll get in my way!" Kiku started to raise her voice. She was angry at this whole situation. Why was the general so determined to be difficult? "I've got to make sure Toki-hime stays safe at this dance of hers!"

"Your responsibility to the Garlon T'zen comes first," Catensen said coolly.

"What do you think keeping Toki-chan safe is?" Kiku's dark blue eyes flashed. "Or have you forgotten I'm their sworn protector?"

"That's what you have the military for, Hime-sama," Catensen drawled.

"It is my personal responsibility, General." Kiku spit out.

Catensen smiled. "Get over it, Princess, and just take the lieutenant with you."

The general nodded curtly, and Kiku turned and walked away. She stalked across the yard and slammed the back door to the house hard. She clenched her hands at her sides and let out a frustrated scream.

"Something wrong, Hime-sama?" General Lysis asked her when she shoved past him in the hall. She only threw him an angry look as she continued on. She didn't have time for any of this. Bad enough she had to deal with this dance. Now she had a damned escort!

~

"Problems?" Lysis motioned after Kiku, seeing one of her watchers. The corporal nodded.

"She and General Catensen had words," he replied. Lysis rolled his eyes as the corporal continued to make his way behind her without her notice.

General Lysis found General Catensen in the main compound between the Manor House and barracks. He went up to him, shaking his head.

"Arguing with the princess?" General Lysis asked critically. Catensen paused to look Lysis over before he answered.

"She's a charming girl," Catensen answered.

"You had to get her going?" General Lysis sighed. He knew Kiku well enough to know that Catensen was completely mishandling her. Tamarik had his faults. But he, at least, cared about Kiku's well-being. "You couldn't wait a few days before you started in on her?"

"The girl has to get used to the idea she's not in charge," Catensen said, his posture rigid and stiff.

"Uh, General," Lysis interrupted. "She's the High Princess of the Empire. Once Dessalen leaves, she is in charge."

"No, she is not!" Catensen looked scandalized. "I am. I was given command of this territory. That is, until the Exalted Leader decides if he wants to kill me or not."

"You don't outrank her," Lysis pointed out. He shook his head. "You can make her accept suitors. However, you need to remember where you sit in the command chain."

General Catensen glared at him. "That girl does not outrank me," he growled. Lysis laughed at him with a broad smile.

"General, please." Lysis shook his head. "You've lived too long in the frontier. The youngest, Princess Mary, outranks you! Marlon outranks you! And Kiku-hime-sama, the High Princess of the Garlon T'zen Empire, most certainly outranks you."

"You don't." Catensen frowned peevishly. Lysis narrowed his eyes.

"No," he agreed. "But you don't outrank me either. And that's something you had best not forget for your own health."

"I'm still in command of the territory," Catensen said like a spoiled child.

"You are an arrogant bastard, you know that?" Lysis retorted as he walked away.

~

"You look very handsome, James," Dr. Andersen told Jimmy as she straightened his tie.

Jimmy swallowed nervously as he stood in the middle of the front entryway of the Manor House's main hall waiting for Toki to come down the stairs.

"You think this is going to be okay?" he asked her, feeling like there were ten thousand butterflies in his gut.

"Of course it is." Dr. Andersen rolled her eyes and gave his shoulder a light shove.

"Jen is just making such a huge deal out of it, is all," he told her.

"Hime-sama is concerned about your safety," Marlon-sensei said as he stepped out from one of the back halls. He was wearing the dress uniform of the Garlon T'zen military. It was a black uniform cut tight to his form with a long silver piping that ran down the sides of both the jacket and pants legs. "It will be fine, James-kun."

"It's not me she's worried about," Jimmy muttered, rolling his eyes.

"Don't be silly. Your sister cares about you, James," Dr. Andersen chided. Jimmy snorted and looked up the stairs expectantly at the sound of movement at the top.

Toki was coming down with Jennifer. Toki was wearing a light green dress that hung to her knees. Her long blond curls were pulled back away from her face with a bow that matched the color of her dress. She was beautiful enough to take his breath away.

But she is just a kid. Jimmy groaned inwardly. But he couldn't help himself. She was very sweet and very beautiful. And, really, she wasn't that much younger than he was. There were other guys in his grade dating ninth graders.

However the hard look of disapproval Jennifer was throwing at him didn't help. He raised his eyebrows slightly in surprise, getting a full look at her. She was wearing a dress too, only a black one. It reminded him of her uniform in a way. It had a high collar but bared her arms. It was formfitting and came to her knees, with a long slit half up her side.

Jimmy turned his attention back to Toki with a smile.

"You look beautiful, Toki-chan," he told her with a smile.

"So do you, Jimmy-chan." She dimpled a smile at him and pulled on his tie, standing close to him.

Jennifer looked around the entry hall. "Anyone see Lieutenant Telleo?" she asked with impatience.

"Who, Kiku-hime?" Marlon asked. The physician's looked around the hall as well.

"My escort," she ground out. Marlon raised an eyebrow.

"You got a date for the dance?" Jimmy asked her. That was unexpected, to say the least. The only one that he could see she would want to go with would be Leader Dessalen. And not even in Jimmy's wildest imagination could he see the Exalted Leader of the Garlon T'zen going to a high school dance.

"It wasn't my idea," she said darkly. "And he's late."

"Ah, General Catensen." Marlon nodded. As if that made sense somehow.

Jennifer crossed her arms, looking irritated.

Then another hurried into the entryway and bowed nervously.

"I-I'm sorry, Hime-sama," the man said. He was slim and wearing a dress uniform much like Marlon's. He didn't look that much older than Jimmy was. "I was in the middle of some work, and I lost track of the time—"

"I don't want to hear it," Jennifer interrupted. "I believe we're ready, then."

They headed toward the front door where Jennifer had a carriage and an armed detail waiting to take them to the school.

When they arrived, they did cause somewhat of a stir. Jimmy felt more than a little uncomfortable feeling the eyes of several of the other students and teachers looking at him with apprehension. Like it was his fault! He didn't ask his sister to have combat troops escort them everywhere!

Thankfully, the "added" security didn't seem to be as obtrusive once they were inside of the decorated gymnasium. And Toki's delightful laugh and pleasant company distracted his attention from noticing them too much anyway.

~

"So," Lieutenant Telleo said nervously. "This is a 'dance'?"

"Mm." Kiku made a noncommittal noise and frowned, watching the people mill around them. Most were young, some close to her age, others younger. Also in attendance were school and staff administration. She and Captain Jace had put plenty of men around the building and entrances so it would be difficult for anyone who wasn't supposed to be there to get in or out.

She threw a glance in the lieutenant's direction and then looked back to where her twin was dancing with her sister. She wasn't exactly sure if she approved of that. Toki-chan seemed rather taken with him. Kiku had hoped for a better match for her truthfully; a Garlon T'zen officer at the very least.

Kiku crossed her arms thoughtfully. But if Ouji-sama was going to have her brother confirmed in their family house, then he was going to be as much Garlon T'zen as she. Maybe it was time she had a chat with her baka-otouto about his intentions regarding her little sister after all.

"Where are you going, Hime-sama?" Lieutenant Telleo asked.

Kiku glanced over her shoulder with irritation.

"Nowhere," she replied. Gods, this was maddening. The lieutenant sighed and looked in the other direction.

"Are you enjoying yourself, Kiku?" Dr. Andersen asked when the princess made her way by her. Kiku paused for a moment.

"Not really," Kiku said, edging closer to the dance floor.

"You should try and give that young man a chance." Dr. Andersen indicated Lieutenant Telleo. "He seems like a nice enough gentlemen."

Kiku offered the Earth physician a withering look. Dr. Andersen offered her a small shrug.

"You would think I could choose my own suitors!" Kiku fumed. "The general is being unfair!"

"I would have to agree with you there." Dr. Andersen nodded. "But I don't believe the lieutenant had any more choice in the matter than you. From what Marlon told me, General Catensen decided who it was going to be without speaking to the men first."

Kiku crossed her arms angrily.

"I don't care to discuss it," she said. Then she nodded toward her brother and Toki-chan. "What do you think about those two?"

"They're adorable." Dr. Andersen smiled. "Toki seems quite smitten with your brother."

Kiku frowned. "You don't think he's too old for her?"

"Isn't Leader Dessalen older relative to you than James is to Toki?" Dr. Andersen raised an eyebrow.

"T-that's different." Kiku glanced at Dr. Andersen with surprise.

"Is it now?" Dr. Andersen's lips twitched slightly as she moved away.

~

Working in the side study off the patio, General Lysis was going over some of the latest intelligence he had gotten from out system with a frown. Things were not going as well there as they should be. There was a light civil insurrection brewing. It looked like it may come to a low boil just about the time Leader Dessalen would be returning to the Capital with Kiku-hime's brother for him to be confirmed in her family house.

Gods. Lysis had no idea how Leader Dessalen planned on pushing that confirmation through the noble houses. Especially given the reports Lysis was getting. The nobles were unhappy the princesses were holding court on the Origin World at all. Many were of the opinion they should return to the Capital to choose their suitors among the "worthy" there.

Right, as if the Celestials were going to tolerate that. Even Lysis knew they wouldn't, and he was no priest. Idiots.

"General Lysis." General Catensen came walking into the study. "I'm surprised to see you here."

General Lysis looked up at him with a frown. Catensen had been moved out of the Manor House. Truly there was little he was supposed to be doing there. But there was the command chamber in the basement and much of the communication to and about the system could only be done from inside the Manor House proper. So the general did have reason to be in the house, even if it was irritating.

"Why is that?" Lysis asked. "Leader Dessalen did move me into the house when he moved you out."

"Hrm." General Catensen's grey eyes flickered with sharp irritation. "He did, didn't he. No, I was speaking about the event at Toki-hime's educational facility. Kiku-hime and Captain Jace were putting together a detail for it. I was sure you would have been brought in as well since you are in command of the special operatives."

"What event?" Lysis frowned.

"I believe Kiku-hime called it a 'dance,'" General Catensen said. "She was most unhappy when I told her she had to take Lieutenant Telleo with her."

"Why the hell did you do that?" General Lysis demanded as he rose to his feet.

"It is the Lieutenant's evening," General Catensen said in an offhand manner. "The princess is required to spend time with her suitors. Not to worry, general, I believe your night is tomorrow."

"That's not what I'm worried about." Lysis shook his head. "They couldn't have secured the school well enough. Damned Kiku! She's too reckless! I can't believe you let her do this!"

"Ah." General Catensen smiled. "As you pointed out earlier today, there is truly little I could do to stop her, even if I wanted to."

"Idiot," General Lysis growled at him as he walked by him. Well, he wasn't going to just leave her there. He would, at the very least, roust another full squad deployment for the event and make damned sure nothing happened to either princess at this 'dance' of theirs.

~

It had taken a little time, but Kiku had finally collared her brother and had him cornered without Toki around. Hopefully, her younger sister would make herself absent long enough for Kiku to set a few things straight with him.

"Geez, Jennifer." Jimmy pulled at his coat, straightening it. "You don't have to be so grabby. You know, you haven't changed one damned bit!"

"Shut up," Kiku growled at him. "Just what do you think you're doing with my sister?"

"Hey." He pointed a finger at her. "This dance was Toki's idea, so don't give me any crap."

Kiku swatted his finger away with indignation.

"I'm not talking about the dance," she said. "Toki-chan seems to like you an awful lot, James-kun."

"Can't you just call me Jimmy?" he asked, crossing his arms. "I swear to God, you are the most stubborn, mule-headed girl I've ever known! And that's not changed about you either!"

"I don't want to hear it!" Kiku's eyes flashed angrily.

"Too bad!" he yelled back at her. "I'm sick of you treating me like shit. I'm your goddamned brother!"

Kiku glared at him hotly and swallowed, turning her head away.

"I-I don't remember," she said.

"I think you remember something." He tightened his jaw, pushing his hair back out of his eyes. "Because you recognized me when you saw me and damned well knew who I was."

"No, I didn't," Kiku denied, refusing to look at him.

"And you've never been a good liar either!" he yelled. "Jesus!"

They were started to draw a little attention to them, and Kiku shook her head with frustration.

Well, she did remember him, perhaps a little. But it was so fleeting, confusing, and tangled up that it was impossible to sort out. Kiku drew in a deep sigh, relenting and opening her eyes to look at him.

"I don't remember much, Jimmy-chan," she admitted. "The Xoned were very cruel and used both drugs and torture to make us do what they wanted. It confused everything in my head. I don't know what memories are real, which are dreams, or nightmares. And—and it hurts too much to try and sort them out."

Kiku could feel the tears start to well up in her eyes and her throat tighten. Damn him! Damn him for making her feel this way!

"Hey," he said quietly, moving closer to her. He gently lifted her chin so she had to look into his eyes. Kiku hadn't truly looked at him, really looked at him. She searched his face and marveled at his dark blue eyes that were so much like her own. There was such a familiarity there. And, she did have a pang of empty loss inside of her. She knew somehow, even if she didn't quite remember, that she had lost her brother, her twin. Someone she had been closest to in the entire world.

"You had a pink blanket you had to sleep with," she said thoughtfully. "I—I always hid it to make you cry."

"Oh God." He rolled his eyes. "Out of all the things you had to remember?"

Kiku giggled and pushed an errant tear from her face, and then turned seeing Jimmy frown toward the door. Garlon T'zen soldiers were coming into the gymnasium. And then Kiku frowned sharply, seeing General Lysis enter next.

"What is he doing here?" She scowled and turned back to Jimmy. "You find Toki-chan and try to have fun. I'll tell the general to go away."

"You think he will?" Jimmy looked nervously in the general's direction.

"He'd better," Kiku said with a fierce frown.

~

The event seemed innocent enough, but it was these sorts of things that got people killed. It wouldn't surprise General Lysis if there were an assassination attempt here. It would be the perfect opportunity for one. On either Kiku or Toki, but more likely Kiku's brother. Lysis was sure

General Catensen was looking for an opportunity to kill the young man before Dessalen had him lifted off-planet. And to be honest, Lysis didn't care, other than there was too much risk for collateral damage to one of the princesses, or even to Dr. Andersen.

Still, it didn't look like his presence, or the additional men, were much appreciated by the attendees. Lysis shrugged slightly and made his way in farther only to be intercepted by the High Princess herself. General Lysis's eye wandered down her slim figure outlined in the black dress. Gods, she was beautiful.

"Princess," he said politely.

"What are you doing here?" Kiku demanded.

"I just came to add some additional security," he replied as he put his hands behind his back and looked down at her. "Really, Hime-sama. Even you know this is a huge security risk."

"Captain Jace and I secured the event." Kiku frowned at him. "So you can just go back to the Manor."

He shook his head. "No, I don't think so."

"That's an order, General." Kiku stomped her foot. He raised an eyebrow and quirked a small smile.

"I don't take orders from lieutenants," he said. Kiku's face colored brightly. Lysis knew he would pay for that remark, but he didn't care at the moment.

"You are unreasonable!" Kiku ground out. "Gods!"

"I'm unreasonable?" General Lysis asked, putting a hand on his chest. "Please, Princess. If it was just you here, then fine. But with your sister here? You should take the extra security as a gift."

Kiku closed her mouth and looked at him angrily. He knew he was right. And she knew it too.

"Fine." Kiku spit the word out. "You can stay for Toki-chan."

"Mm." He nodded. "I think you like me here too."

"I don't think so." And she stalked away while the general looked after her with amusement.

~

"What's he doing here?" Dr. Andersen whispered to Marlon. The Garlon T'zen physician shrugged.

"His duty, Andy-chan," he said. "As bothersome as the general is, he's probably right for coming."

"He's making the teachers nervous," Dr. Andersen said.

"Good." Marlon smirked.

"Marlon!" Dr. Andersen whacked his arm, and Marlon laughed softly.

"I'll worry if he drags someone out and executes them," Marlon said. "Other than that, he's fine."

"He—he wouldn't do that." Dr. Andersen paled.

Marlon shrugged. He wouldn't put it past Lysis, truly. Especially if he found a security threat to one of the princesses. And if that were the case, Marlon wouldn't be the one to argue against the action.

"Who said he could come?" Dr. Andersen groused.

"Heh." Marlon laughed softly.

~

"Kiku-hime?" Lieutenant Telleo asked shyly, moving closer to Kiku. She turned to look at him. "I-I mean . . . would you care to dance?"

"What?" Kiku looked at him with confusion.

"Well," the lieutenant started. He offered a faltering smile. "This is a dance, and you don't seem like you're enjoying yourself."

"I'm not here to enjoy myself." She frowned. "I'm here to keep Toki-chan out of trouble."

"But still," he said. "Wouldn't you be in a better position to do that if you were out on the dance floor where they are?"

Kiku frowned thoughtfully.

"I guess," she said. The lieutenant took her hand and pulled her out onto the gymnasium floor. He carefully set a hand on her hip and took her other hand. Kiku glanced around at the other couples out there. They were mostly students from the school and were dancing in far more intimate manners. Kiku colored and dropped her eyes. Gods, she wished the lieutenant was Ouji-sama.

"Kiku-hime," Lieutenant Telleo said, "what do you do as Leader Dessalen's aide? I mean, what's it like to know the Exalted Leader?"

"Ouji?" Kiku turned her attention back to Lieutenant Telleo.

"And why do you call him that?" he asked.

Kiku's face colored even further as her mind went back to that day.

"Well," she started, "it wasn't very long after my sisters and I were rescued from the Xoned."

"Discovery." Lieutenant Telleo smiled, giving the name to the day that was now celebrated as the high holiday of the Garlon T'zen: the day when Kiku and her sisters were found and liberated.

"I did call him Leader Dessalen then at first," Kiku said. Kiku remembered being confused at why he had been named her sisters' guardian, but not hers. But he took her aside and gently touched her lips with his saying it wasn't possible for him to be her guardian. "He told me that he wasn't the Exalted Leader to me, but, rather, my prince."

"That's a very sweet story, Kiku-hime." Lieutenant Telleo smiled at her. "I would have never thought the Exalted Leader would be like that."

Kiku nodded, dropping her eyes.

You should call me Ouji-sama, Kiku-chan, Leader Dessalen told her all those years ago as he kissed her gently. Because I am your prince, just as you are my princess.

~

General Lysis had his arms folded across his chest, watching the lieutenant dance with Kiku-hime with growing irritation.

So that was one of the other suitors? Ugh.

Damn Catensen anyway. Still, his madness had put Lysis on the list. Now, if Lysis could get the princess to not hate him quite so much. General Lysis grinned and moved forward onto the dance floor and interrupted the lieutenant and princess's dance.

"Excuse me, Lieutenant," he said. "But the princess really should dance with the ranking officer."

"Sir?" Lieutenant Telleo looked at General Lysis with confusion, but the general gave him a light shove.

"Go away," Lysis ordered. Lieutenant Telleo colored and inclined his head, moving off. Kiku looked at General Lysis with hot anger.

"What are you doing?" she demanded. General Lysis smiled and took her hand firmly and put his other on her hip and pulled her along.

"Don't make a scene, Hime-sama," he chided.

"That's what you're doing!" Kiku growled, but she didn't pull away. Lysis could see she was angry. She moved easily with him on the floor but refused to look up.

"James-kun seems happy," General Lysis remarked, glancing over to where Kiku's brother was dancing with

Toki-hime. The younger princess was smiling brightly up at him. The general doubted he would ever earn that sort of adoration from Kiku-hime.

"As long as Toki-chan is happy." Kiku frowned in that direction. "I guess it's all right."

"Really?" General Lysis said, looking back down at Kiku. "I would think Toki-hime could do better."

"Jimmy-chan is my brother, General." Kiku's eyes flashed with temper. "And when he and Ouji come back, he'll be a confirmed member in House Garlon T'zen. How can you do better than that?"

"He could be a general." Lysis smirked.

"Toki-chan's too young for you," Kiku said haughtily. General Lysis smiled and leaned down a little closer to her ear.

"I'm not interested in Toki-chan," he said softly. Lysis could see her face color brightly and heard a quick catch of her breath.

"I'm—I'm not interested in you, General," Kiku whispered. But General Lysis could feel her slight tremble, and he raised an eyebrow.

"That's all right, Hime-sama," he said, catching her eyes. Kiku looked at him with a mixture of apprehension and . . . what? Lysis couldn't say for sure, but it wasn't the open animosity that she had been throwing in his direction for the past month. He smiled.

But before he could do much else there was a commotion at the entrance, and he jerked his head around.

"Ouji-sama?" Kiku pulled away from General Lysis. Lysis groaned inwardly.

Wonderful.

And true enough: it was the Exalted Leader of the Garlon T'zen making his way through the entrance, looking around with a bemused expression. He was wearing a dress uniform and his red cape. Out of all of the arrivals, no one caused quite as much stir as him. His golden eyes swept the room until they landed on Kiku.

"Ah, there you are, Kiku-chan." Leader Dessalen smiled. He pulled her hand forward and brought her wrist to his lips. Kiku looked at him with dismay.

"What are you doing here, Ouji?" she asked.

"My princess goes to a formal event and you think I wouldn't attend?" Leader Dessalen scoffed. "Come now, Kiku-chan."

"But—" Kiku helplessly glanced around.

Lysis rolled his eyes as armed combat soldiers came in and lined the outer wall of the gymnasium. He shrugged to himself. At least Dessalen had taken care of the security issue, even if he was bothersome.

~

"Do you want another one?" Lysis asked as he reached into the basket for another beer. He had taken a liking to the Earth beverage. It was a particular brew made in Manor Town to which he was partial. He brought several bottles on this evening for his time with Kiku-hime. She nodded while making adjustments to the sim on the imagedeck. They had already had a few beers, and they were going to Lysis's head. He wondered how Kiku was faring.

The general had decided for his evening with the princess that he would try a little different approach. He appeared with a basket with their dinner and imagedecks for them to run battle simulations. He coaxed her to come out to the gardens with him to play war games with him. It didn't hurt that Kiku-hime was known to thrive on playing these sort of games, and it gave Lysis a chance to ease her defenses and evaluate her tactical skills at the same time.

Kiku finished her work on the imagedeck with a feral grin and handed it to him while taking the beer out of his hand. She dropped to her back on the blanket, staring up at the night sky. Lysis looked over the results of her sim and chuckled. Well, it was certainly creative. It beat his time by sixteen time parts, but with significant loss of capital.

"Kiku-hime," he started, "I don't think this one makes sense."

"Hm?" She looked back at him, her hair splayed loosely on the ground behind her. Lysis felt a pang of want as he looked at her glittering blue eyes. He leaned over on one arm and showed her the imagedeck with the other.

"Here," he said. "You took a 32% loss in armament. You could have covered with a deployment . . . here."

"Oh," she said. "I didn't see that."

"Maybe that's why I'm a general, and you're not," he teased, dropping the imagedeck and smiling down at her. She made a face.

"That's cheating," she accused. Kiku was close enough that he could almost feel her breath on his face. He couldn't help but smile tenderly, pushing an errant hair across her forehead. His hand wandered down the side of her face.

"You're very beautiful tonight, Princess," he said softly. Kiku grinned and pushed his hand away.

"Flattery is cheating too," she protested giggling. "It's not going to help your score with the sim."

General Lysis wondered if it was the beer that was relaxing her somewhat. He leaned down and kissed her on the lips. She stiffened immediately. Lysis knew he had to work this carefully or she would close back up and likely retreat. He did nothing to hold her down but teased her lips with his, coaxing her to respond. For a moment he thought she would, until she turned her face away.

"No," she said. "I-I can't. Ouji-sama . . . this is isn't right."

"You're doing nothing wrong." Lysis cupped her face tenderly. "Leader Dessalen knows this, Kiku."

"But," she protested.

"Did it ever occur to you," Lysis said softly, "that perhaps you need to learn for yourself if he is truly all you want?"

"What do you mean?" she asked.

"Kiku, if you don't taste other fruits," he replied carefully, oh so carefully, "you will always wonder if the one is all you ever wanted."

Lysis held his breath, wondering if she was going to get up and walk away. He expected she would. But instead, she lay there and watched him with confusion reigning in her beautiful eyes. Lysis longed to hold her tightly and reassure her, but that would only frighten her more. Having served in enough campaigns, he sensed this was time for him to try and press onward.

"You can," he assured her. "Leader Dessalen wouldn't be angry with you." Although, he may kill me. But Lysis was fully ready to take the risk at that moment.

"I—" She started looking even more confused. Lysis leaned forward and kissed her again, sucking on her lips gently. She parted hers, and Lysis eased his tongue into her mouth, teasing her as best he could without being too aggressive. She responded and he increased his urgency. Oh, gods. His heart began to race in his chest.

His hand trembled as it wandered down and slid against her hip. Kiku's hands first came up to his face and then around his neck. Lysis moved his lips along her jaw toward her neck.

"Kiku," he murmured. "Come back to my room with me."

"I don't know," she protested.

Lysis moved his lips to her ear. She squirmed under him even while his hands continued to wander her form—the perfect curve of her stomach and to the firm roundness of her bottom. Kiku was so tender, so sweet. Lysis felt like he would die for certain from the need aching between his legs.

"Please, Kiku," he begged. "Let me—"

"Gomen ne, Lysis-kun." She pushed him away. Lysis felt like the world just turned black. "I won't."

Lysis wasn't certain her resolve was strong. She may have refused him, but her body had responded.

"You want to," he told her. "It's all right, Kiku. You don't have to be afraid."

"The princess refused you, General," Leader Dessalen said coldly, stepping out of the shadows. Lysis felt a surge of anger. How dare he? This was his time. Dessalen knew it. Damn him for interfering.

"Ouji!" Kiku sat up with her face turning red.

"What are you doing here?" Lysis demanded.

"Just taking a walk, General." Leader Dessalen's eyes flashed with golden fire. "It's hardly my fault I ran into you."

"That's not what you're doing," Lysis snapped with righteous anger. Dessalen knew the law! Kiku was beginning to accept him!

"Come, Kiku-chan," Leader Dessalen said. "It's late."

"Hai," she said, immediately getting up. Lysis caught her wrist and looked back at Leader Dessalen.

"This is my night," he said flatly.

"Your evening," Dessalen corrected. "The nights are still mine."

"Damn you, Dessalen," Lysis hissed. Leader Dessalen smiled faintly.

"Good night, Lysis-kun," Kiku said quietly as she unwrapped his fingers from around her wrist. Lysis nearly moaned in physical pain.

She walked over to Leader Dessalen, looking down at the ground. Dessalen leaned down, lifted her chin, and kissed her deeply. Kiku leaned up on her toes, putting a hand on his cheek. Lysis watched with a mounting jealousy. Leader Dessalen flicked a look of satisfaction in his direction.

"Don't fret, Hime-chan," Leader Dessalen told her kindly. "I am not unhappy with you."

Lysis clenched his fists in impotent fury.

~

But it didn't mean that Leader Dessalen wasn't unhappy with General Lysis. Kiku walked in silence next to him, his arm possessively around her waist. He could smell the alcohol on her, and he wondered just how much Lysis had given her to drink. He had muddled Kiku's senses and judgment in hopes of entertaining her affections. Dessalen felt a jolt of fury at how close he had nearly gotten as well.

When they got to their bedchamber, he closed the door. Kiku stood next to his bed with her hand on the banister for a long moment with her head hanging.

"I'm sorry, Ouji-sama," she said softly. Dessalen thought he heart would break from the pain in her voice. For the thousandth time, he resolved to have his revenge on General Catensen for this. Not for himself this time, but for the pain and confusion Catensen was inflicting on Kiku. She was too young and vulnerable to have to contend with these things.

He walked over to her and wrapped his arms around her from behind, hugging her tightly to himself. "There is nothing to be sorry for, Kiku-chan."

"But," she protested.

"Shh," he said, turning her to face him as he leaned down to kiss her forehead. "You are the High Princess, Kiku-chan. There are going be many who will want to court your favor. You decide if you want them or not."

"I want you," she said quickly. Dessalen smiled with a warm glow of satisfaction.

"And you have me," he told her firmly, taking her face in his hands and lifting it so she would have no choice but to look in his eyes. "That is not going to change, dearest one. Even if you have the bad taste to choose that bothersome general of mine."

"Oh, Ouji." She giggled tearfully clinging to him. He kissed the top of her head.

"Of course," he told her, only half in jest, "I'd have to kill him when you were done with him."

~

Carrying the bag downstairs, Jimmy was surprised to see Jennifer standing in the front entry hall. She looked up at him.

"Are you ready?" she asked.

"I guess," he said. "Where's Leader Dessalen?"

"Ouji-sama is going to meet us at the landing field," Jennifer told him, motioning for him to follow. He followed her out back, where there were a few horses saddled waiting for them. Jimmy eyed the horses and then looked over at his sister.

"I'm not that good of a rider," he said. Sure, he'd ridden on their grandparent's farm, but he had hoped for a carriage, since he had a bag.

"Then you'll have to get better, won't you?" Jennifer told him crisply as she pulled herself up into the saddle. Another man was getting up on a horse behind them.

"What am I supposed to do with my bag?" he asked.

"Carry it," she said. "Gods, Jimmy-chan. Stop being so helpless. It's embarrassing."

"Jennifer!" Jimmy said crossly. The other man chuckled.

"Stop picking on your brother, Hime-chan," the man said. Jennifer threw him a look.

"He's bothersome, Jace-kun," she said.

"Mm." The man nodded. "And you're not?"

Jennifer stuck her tongue out at him. Jimmy pulled himself up on the horse, trying to keep hold of his bag at the same time. It was awkward, but he managed to do it. Then he set it in front of him and picked up the reins and glared at her. Jennifer shrugged slightly and urged her horse out of the yard.

The streets of the town weren't too crowded yet for the day. It was still pretty early. A few shops were open. Jimmy yawned, thankful his horse seemed to be following Jennifer's. He wasn't awake enough to trust himself.

Then they went through one of the town's checkpoints and made their way down to the landing fields.

"Nervous?" Jennifer asked, glancing back at him.

"Yeah," he said. "The idea that I'm going to another planet is kinda scary."

She frowned.

"Don't be like that, Hime-sama," the other man said. "It's better to admit he's afraid than not."

"Right." Jennifer rolled her eyes. Jimmy frowned at her and turned his head back toward the ships that were waiting for them. True to what Jen had said, Leader Dessalen was waiting while conferring with some other officers. Jimmy almost fell when he slid off the horse, and Jennifer snorted with irritation.

"There you are, James-kun," Leader Dessalen said. "We're about ready to lift out."

"Yes sir," Jimmy said nervously. Leader Dessalen turned his attention to his twin.

"And you be a good girl, Kiku-chan," the Exalted Leader told her. "Don't start any wars while I'm gone."

"I wouldn't do that, Ouji-sama." Jennifer frowned at him.

"Oh, I know better than that, Hime-chan." He smiled and then leaned down and kissed her. Jimmy looked away, feeling uncomfortable watching a man try to swallow his sister whole. "All right, then. Come along, James."

"Okay." Jimmy drew in a deep breath and started toward the open door of the transport.

"Wait, Jimmy-chan," Jennifer called out and then ran forward to hug him impulsively. Jimmy wrapped his arms around her with more than a little surprise. "Be safe, Jimmy-chan. Do what Ouji-sama tells you."

"I will, Jen," he said. "Don't worry."

"I will worry," she said, pulling away, looking at him seriously. "Really, Jimmy-chan. This is dangerous. You know that, don't you?"

"I guess," he said with confusion. Jennifer looked at Leader Dessalen with a pained expression.

"This isn't fair," she said. "You can't ask him to do this."

"He's doing this for you, Kiku-chan," Leader Dessalen said. "It's the only way to remove General Catensen."

"Don't." Jennifer turned to Jimmy. "It's not worth it, Jimmy-chan."

"How can you say that?" Jimmy asked with dismay. "God, Jennifer! I just found you again. I thought you were dead. Don't you understand that I would do anything for you?"

Jennifer dropped her head as tears slipped down her cheeks. Jimmy kissed her cheek quickly and pushed her away.

"I'll be all right," he assured her as he turned to follow Leader Dessalen into the transport. "I promise."

ABOUT THE AUTHOR:

Kyleen Valleaux writes because it's cheaper than therapy. She works as a telecom mercenary and takes the stress out on fictional characters. Never one to back down from a writing challenge, she will go without food or sleep to get the stories written. Her family and friends have adjusted to her complete withdrawal from the human race each year during the month of November. She resides in Michigan with three big German Shepherd Dogs, and a millennial.

Please feel free to connect with Kyleen to keep up with her latest releases!

https://twitter.com/kyleen66
https://www.facebook.com/kyleenvalleaux/

Chronicles of the Garlon T'zen
Book 2: Homecoming

The horse didn't look too bad, but she was unhappy. General Lysis went into her stall and ran his hands smoothly along her leg until she nickered and shifted her weight.

"There's a girl," he told her. He looked over his shoulder to a private that was looking at him with dismay.

"General?" the young man asked. Lysis shrugged.

"It's the High Princess's horse," he told him. "Get hot backs and some cold water."

"Yes, sir." The man moved away, and Lysis stood up and ran his fingers along the horses nose. She made happy noises and nudged him for more.

"If only your mistress felt the same," he said with humor.

He spent most of the night alternating hot and cold packs on the animals knee. He was sleeping leaning up against the wall when he felt someone touch his shoulder. General Lysis opened his eyes to slits and frowned.

"What are you doing out of the infirmary, Hime-sama?" he asked, stretching. Kiku stood back up on her feet. She wasn't in uniform rather wearing loose light blue pants with a matching shirt with ties running along her neck and shoulders. Typical civilian wear for the Garlon T'zen. Her hair was loose around her and fell about her shoulders in soft curls. She pushed a strand back over her shoulder.

"Marlon-sensei let me go back to my room," she said. "I got a shower and changed."

"I'm certain that's not what the sensei had in mind," Lysis said standing up. But he took her not being in uniform as a good sign. Marlon had restricted her from duty after all.

"I wanted to check on Dolly." Kiku's eyes reflected worry. "It was my fault she got hurt."

"It was," Lysis agreed, leaning against the wall crossing his arms. Kiku's frown only deepened as she moved forward and ran her hands along the horse's face and pressed her face into her neck. "You've got to remember Princess, when you do reckless things; others can be hurt by your actions."

She didn't move but started to sniffle into the horses neck. He relented and put a light hand on her shoulder and leaned down into her ear.

"She'll be fine, Hime-sama," he told her. "She just needs a couple of days rest. Just like you."

Kiku turned and looked up at him. Two tracks of tears were running down her face. Lysis snorted softly and ran his hand along her cheek.

"You took care of her?" Kiku asked. He shrugged. She dropped her eyes and her face colored. "Thank you."

Lysis's heart raced as he looked into her face. Gods, she was beautiful. Insane, reckless, took more chances than anyone in their right mind ought to. But that was what made her who she was. Her beauty was enough for the Exalted Leader to stake his outrageous claim, but it was more that drew the general to her. She was caring and good. All of the things his tired race longed for and needed. Everything that he needed. He leaned forward and kissed her softly. She didn't pull away from him this time, but rather teased and nibbled his lips. The general started to heat his response, but she pulled her lips away and put a hand on his chest.

"No," she whispered. He looked at her with confusion. Kiku touched his lips with her fingers and shook her head. "I— No."

"What is it?" Lysis asked. The princess regarded him with her dark blue eyes for a long moment and licked her lips with a nod.

"If I accept you," her voice broke, "Ouji-sama will kill you."

Lysis tightened his jaw. He couldn't very well tell her that wasn't true. Dessalen would likely snap his neck himself. Lysis knew how possessive the Exalted Leader could be. Hell, he'd had to put up with that for himself for more years than he cared to count. But these days with Dessalen's single-minded pursuit of the princess that wasn't so much an issue anymore. It was just Lysis's misfortune that he fell in love with the same woman.

"It's my risk," he said. Lysis took her fingers and drew them up to his lips.

"I don't think the others truly understand." Kiku cast a glance back over her shoulder. "Tello-kun and Captain Sangra. They believe because my guardian has ordered it, they're protected. But you know. You know how Ouji is. He—"

"I know." Lysis leaned his forehead against hers. "But I don't care, Kiku. Don't you understand?"

She closed her eyes and leaned against him pushing her face into his chest.

"I don't like you much," Kiku whispered. Lysis smiled looking over the top of her head. "I hate the way you do things. I don't agree with what you do for Ouji-sama."

He nodded. Little surprise there. For all that the gift of war sang in her blood, the princess avoided actual killing when she could. Some would see her soft-heartedness as weakness. He was sure the Exalted Leader didn't view it that way, and he had to agree with Dessalen. Killing was often the easier path, but it wasn't the one that the High Princess would take given a choice.

Kiku leaned away from him and touched his face.

"Like you said," she said. "I can't be reckless when others can get hurt."

"Kiku," he shook his head. "This is different."

"I don't think so, L-chan." A soft smile crossed her features. He ran a hand along her slender hip with a grin. She hadn't called him that since she'd been drugged and he'd rescued her. The memory of her lips seeking his made his stomach curl in hot anticipation.

"L-chan?" He raised an eyebrow and leaned forward to kiss her again. Kiku grinned playfully and pushed him away.

"Mm." She nodded. Then she looked back at the house. "I need to get back before Marlon-sensei catches me out. I'll come back to see Dolly later."

He let her go and watched her walk stiffly back out of the barn with a with a loving pat on the horses nose. General Lysis sighed and leaned against the stall crossing his arms.

"That'll get you killed." He heard a voice out of the darkness. He flicked his eyes and noted Kiku's captain coming out of the shadows. General Lysis wasn't surprised. If the young officer had any sense at all, and Lysis knew he did, the man would have watchers on the princess all the time.

"By you?" Lysis stood up and went back to change the compress on the horses knee. Captain Jace shook his head.

"I don't guard the princess's bed," he said, leaning on the wall to watch.

"Good of you," Lysis grunted pulling off the cooled wrap. He ran his hand along the horse's knee, and she flicked an ear.

"But Leader Dessalen will kill you," the captain said. Lysis nodded.

"I'm aware of the risk, Captain." Lysis stood up and turned.

"It'll make her sad if he does." Captain Jace frowned.

"Your mission is to keep her alive, Captain, not happy." General Lysis smiled and started to walk out of the barn.

"Hime-sama is more than a mission," Captain Jace said as he fell into step with the general.

"A damned dangerous mission." Lysis smirked walking along. The young captain snorted softly next to him. "Did you talk her out of the American operation yet?"

"No," the captain answered. "She's determined."

"Marlon's restricted her from duty for a few days I'm sure," Lysis said. "I'll try again with Catensen."

Captain Jace nodded and headed back towards the barracks that housed his men. General Lysis smiled as he turned his feet back towards the house. He'd get a shower and a clean uniform. Then it would be time to talk to Catensen again.

L-chan, he thought to himself with a grin.

Coming Soon

Made in the USA
Lexington, KY
09 May 2017